I Will Fly to Woodstock

Sally Cissna

*Welcome back to Woodstock
Sally Cissna*

Oshkosh, Wisconsin
2021

Copyright 2021 by Sara L. Cissna
All rights reserved. No part of this publication may be reproduced, distributed, or transmitted in any form or by any means, such as photocopying, recording, or other electronic or mechanical methods without prior written permission of the publisher. For permission requests, write to the Publisher at the address below. Published in the United States by SuLu Press.

SuLu Press
3145D White Tail Lane
Oshkosh, Wisconsin 54904

Publisher's Cataloging-in-Publication Data
I Will Fly to Woodstock/Sally Cissna
Paperback ISBN   978-0-578-25376-3
1. HIS054000 HISTORY/Social History 2. FIC008000 FICTION/Sagas/Family Sagas 3. SOC026000 SOCIAL SCIENCE/Sociology/Women/Religion.
I. Cissna, Sally. II. I Will Fly to Woodstock.

The stories herein are not factual accounts of activities, but rather flow from the author's imagination. However, the general history of the families, the newspaper articles, and the era have been as accurately represented as possible. These accounts are not meant to characterize or disrespect any person or group, past or present. While some words may challenge the twenty-first century sensitivities, including the author's, these terms are true to the times and necessary to the story.

Cover design: Cover picture is a family picture of Ida Wienke and her friend and sister-in-law Lena Wienke relaxing in conversation. On the back is the Spring House on the Woodstock Square which still furnishes a refreshing elixir to all passers-by.

Printed in the USA by Lighting Source/IngramSpark Publishing

First Edition

Dedicated to...

The eight Wienke brothers who changed Woodstock in innumerable ways from the time their father and mother, Carl and Sophia, bought a little farm just west of the cemetery on Kishwaukee Valley Road around 1876 until their deaths.

William J. Wienke b. 1863 – City Trimmer, City Engineer
August (Ed) Wienke b. 1864 – Oliver Typewriter
Charles Martin Wienke b. 1869 – Blacksmith (Beloit, WI)
John Francis Wienke b. 1870 – Grocery Owner, Insurance Agent, City Council Member, Bakery Owner, Founding Member of Grace Lutheran Congregation
Frankov Joseph Wienke b. 1874 – Oliver Typewriter Fire Chief, Founding Member of Grace Lutheran Congregation
Albert Wilhelm Wienke b. 1876 – Prestigious Painter of many buildings in Woodstock, Saloon Owner
Robert Wienke b. 1877 –Co-Owner Saloon, Gambler, Oliver Typewriter Worker
Emil J. Wienke b. 1881 – Emerson Typewriter Worker

Thanks

To Rebecca, my spouse, partner, and most supportive and most challenging critic/proofreader.

To Dixie, my editor and coach who watches the arcs and beats and other dos and don'ts.

To Debi, my hometown editor who makes sure the books stay in their genre and that Woodstock is authentically represented.

To Liz, my cultural editor who helps me decide what to avoid and what to keep of the early 20th Century culture in these sensitive times.

To The Caramel Crisp Writers' Group
- Patrick for always wanting more – more emotion, more action, more drama.
- Joyce for keeping the history, science, and punctuation accurate.
- Sandra for her sense of humor and solid critiques.
- Connor for his friendly smile and ability to help me see the whole picture.
- Michael for helping me with the German language and historical perspective on Germans in America.
- To all of you, thank you for making time each week to support our novel expressions.

And to readers, like you, who love history.

Wienke Family Tree in 1911

Carl (Charles) Wienke and Sophia Sund Children and Their Families

William J. Wienke '63
W: Elizabeth Schuett
C: Frank M. Wienke
Raymond M. Wienke

August (Ed) Wienke '64
W: Katherine Schuett
C: Leah C. Wienke
Alice F. Wienke
Ethel Wienke
Clinton M. Wienke
Edwin R. Wienke

Charles M. Wienke '69
W: Wilhelmine Klingberg
C: Royal C. Wienke

John F. Wienke '70
W: Ida H. L. Doering
C: Helen F. Wienke
Marion E. Wienke
Dorothea E. Wienke

Frank J. Wienke '74
W: Anna C. Wegner
C: Ethel B. Wienke
Bessie K. Wienke
Clayton F. Wienke

Albert W. Wienke '76
W: Lena J. Steinke
C: Evelyn T. Wienke
Arthur R. Wienke
Lucile G. Wienke

Robert Wienke '77
W: Lillian L. Schwamb
C: Linette S. Wienke

Emil J. Wienke '81
W: Ethelyn B. Bean
C: Harvey W. Wienke

Doering Family Tree in 1911

Heinrich (Henry) Döring and Louisa E. Ardelt Children and Their Families

Emma L. A. Doering '70
H: Floyd F. Fisher
C: I. W. Fay Fisher
L. E. Amy Fisher
H. L. Elsie Fisher
Marion H. Fisher
Howard Fisher

R. C. Herman Doering '72
W: Elizabeth M. Leahy
C: L. Elizabeth Doering
Grace J. Doering
William H. Doering

Ida H. L. Doering '74
H: John F. Wienke
C: Helen F. Wienke
Marion E. Wienke
Dorothea E. Wienke

Clara Doering '83
H: Pearle F. Dye

Don't Spill the Beans (1908)

John and Ida Wienke lay spooned in bed in the early morning on New Year's Day. The sky was still dark and would be until nearly eight o'clock. John had already grabbed his robe and slippers and made the trek to the basement to stoke the furnace. Upon his return to the kitchen, he added wood to the cook stove. They had enjoyed the 'leisure' time together under the warm quilt waiting for the house to gain temperature. Satisfied with each other and the world, they snuggled like newlyweds.

"We've accomplished a lot in five years, haven't we?" John pushed Ida's hair away from her face.

"Like what?" asked Ida. She knew the answer to that question before she asked it, but she loved to hear him reminisce.

"Well, let's see…we got married—"

"Eventually."

John chuckled and agreed, "Eventually. And then we built a house and had Helen."

"Yes, but not in that order."

"You are right. Helen came while we were living with Ma and a month early."

Ida snorted. "If that's what you want to believe."

John squeezed her. "And then, opportunity came knocking on the door at five in the morning—"

"Yes, Herman and Bessie—"

"Your brother with a proposal for a store." John's eyes lost focus as he remembered that early morning surprise.

"That was quite a year, wasn't it? The store, my pregnancy, Mamie coming all in a rush, and she was so tiny—"

"Don't forget living in the stable."

"How could I. You sold our house right out from under us, and we found no room in the inn for our child to be born. So, we, like Mary and Joseph, were forced to birth our child in a manger," Ida tapped John playfully on the upper arm.

"I hadn't thought about it like that," John hedged.

"Oh, don't lie. You thought of it too. I was so relieved when Mamie had all her fingers and toes."

"I was so relieved that both of you had your fingers and toes. And then we spent that frosty winter bundled up in the stable while we watched this house go up. Four in a bed and you managed to cook on that potbelly stove."

"Lena and Al were our salvation. Giving us a place to live, feeding us, caring for me in my time of imprisonment—"

"You mean while you were laying in." John's index finger traced down her cheek. "It's true we couldn't have made it without them, but remember, I provided the food from the store. They made out alright."

"What good friends." Ida's eyes misted.

"Yes, what a good friend and brother they have been."

"And now they're gone." Ida's voice caught just a bit. She was still not resigned to the day-to-day loss caused by Lena and Al's move to Beloit.

John gave her another little squeeze. "Don't worry. We'll see them often. They didn't go to the desert to homestead. Just a couple hours away—"

"To homestead?" Ida snickered. "They are still living with Lena's parents. I'm not sure how they are all managing in that little house, four adults and three children."

"Ah, togetherness is next to Godliness," suggested John.

Ida swatted his shoulder. "That's not how it goes. 'Cleanliness is next to Godliness'."

John considered, "I like the first one better. I love being together with you like this."

"But wait, we didn't finish our story. So, then my handsome husband built the perfect house for us on beautiful Lincoln Avenue, and we lived happily ever after."

"Careful, don't tempt fate." They both reached out from under the covers and touched the wooden headboard.

"And then a few years later, along comes Dodi." John smoothed Ida's hair back from her face.

"Dorothea." Ida let the name roll around in her mouth. "A beautiful name."

"Dorothea came at such an awful time though, didn't she?"

"Yes, that was a frightening and sad time, and then Dorothea and Linette were born just two weeks apart, cousins to make us smile again."

"But we lost Bob. He never met his only child." The house ticked as the timbers warmed.

"Yes, the fever took a favorite brother. Your mother is still wearing black. And then a heart attack took Papa Stoffel. I don't think Mama will ever be the same." The house creaked.

"It was a sad time."

Ida forced a happier tone. "But it wasn't all bad news. Think of the progress your store has made. From partnership to sole ownership in barely two years. Woodstock has been kind to us. Herman's Dry Goods store is doing well also."

"Yes, your brother gave us a real foot up. And your sister Clara has become quite a...a...what would you call it?"

"Clara has quite the flare with a pen...she's an investigator of mysteries." Ida chuckled. "She'd love that designation."

John kissed the back of Ida's head. "Is that it? Five years, three children, four domiciles, and my own business."

"I guess so. Doesn't seem as lively when you put it in a list."

"So, what do you want this new year to bring us?" asked John.

"Hm. I can't think of a thing. Happiness, I suppose. Contentedness." Ida avoided the concrete wishes.

John held her tight. "A happy husband."

Ida returned the embrace, "And a happy wife. What about you? What are your hopes for this year?"

"To be successful, I suppose. To have enough to put meat on the table, bread in the cupboard, and pay the taxes."

"Are they coming up soon?"

"Yes. For the new year, I wish prosperity on all of Woodstock so that my customers will all pay up their accounts. Then I'll have no problem with the taxes."

"And if they don't?" Ida sounded worried.

He snuggled in her hair and kissed the back of her neck. "Nothing to worry about, my sweetheart."

She turned and kissed him, and he kissed back. A thump came from upstairs and then the sound of small feet running in the upper hallway could be heard. Helen called down the stairs, her words were muffled by the closed door. Ida disengaged and threw back the quilts.

Ida looked back at John's disappointed face as she pulled on her housecoat. "Dodi must be awake. She's just about big enough to start climbing out over the rail. I don't want Helen trying to lift her out or catch her if she tries to jump for it."

John's eyes took on an even more soulful look.

"Oh stop! Once is enough for a morning."

"I'm still hoping for a boy." He smiled.

Ida leaned down and kissed him, lingering just a bit. "Duty calls. Why don't you go put the coffee on? Can you do that?"

"I don't see why not. I'm a grocer after all. We sell the best coffee in the county, and I've got the ads to prove it."

Ida pulled open the door and there stood their three munchkins, Helen, Mamie, and Dodi, lined up by height, smiles creasing their happy faces. Dodi's chubby legs gave out and she sat down on a squishy diaper.

"Mama! Is it a new year yet?" Helen's eyes glittered in the low morning light.

"Papa! Tell 'bout da bears?" Mamie sat down abruptly, took off a slipper, and emptied it on the floor. She examined the tiny speck of sand. "It was jus' right."

"Mamama. Num." Dodi crawled over to Ida, grabbed her mama's night gown and stood, reaching up.

Ida looked at Helen. "Yes, sweetheart, the new year is here."

***

COOK COUNTY MEN
TO OFFER NEW BILL

The Cook County Republican central committee will endeavor to write a brand-new primary bill for the legislature. It will not bear any resemblance to the Oglesby bill.

A subcommittee of three members of the central body has been quietly named to prepare an outline of the kind of bill they believe the Republican leaders might be inclined to support.

The utmost secrecy has been observed not only as to the purpose of the leaders but as to the personnel of the subcommittee. It now develops that the committee was practically agreed upon ten days ago at about the time that Mr. Pease called his precinct captains together and endorsed the governor. In the same resolutions endorsing the present government was a crack for the Oglesby bill.

The decision of the chieftains to aid the legislature in getting back to earth on primary legislation was reached after it was presented to them that Gov. Deneen would sign almost any kind of bill they would agree upon if it could be put through the legislature.

Woodstock Sentinel, January 2, 1908.

***

"Well, finally a hopeful sign." John folded the Sentinel and laid it next to his breakfast plate. He had had an unhurried breakfast with his family. Following a practice that was becoming more popular among the merchants, John kept the store closed on January first. Today his cashier opened the grocery store, extending his break from the beck and call of customers. He would go in at eight o'clock in case a customer called in an order for meat that must be filled for the ten o'clock delivery run. Even an extra hour at home was nice.

"What is a hopeful sign?" Ida asked. She had cleared the breakfast dishes except coffee cups and was pouring hot water from the kettle into the wash sink. She aimed the stream for the soap to get some hot suds going that would extend all the way through the wash to include the skillet. John could hear the little girls playing in the parlor, their voices rising and falling. No squabbles had broken out yet this morning.

"Looks like Cook County Republicans are going to finally jump into the fray over this direct primary bill, you know people voting for candidates directly without caucuses."

"Mm…" Ida paid little attention to state politics, but she enjoyed listening to John talk about political affairs because he was so enthusiastic and verbal when it came to those subjects.

"The Oglesby Bill," John enunciated.

"Oh. What will it do?" she asked, not turning around, as she continued the twice a day chore of cleaning up the kitchen after a meal. She filled the rinse basin with hot water from the well on the stove and began to rinse the just-washed dishes by dipping them into the basin. The water was hot, too hot to immerse her hands in, but she had heard somewhere that hot water and soap kills germs, so she did it in haste and suffered no more than dry red hands afterward. A little cold cream rubbed in twice a day, and all was well.

"For one thing, it will probably put me out of my town committee job."

"Indeed?" Now she was interested.

"If it passes as it stands, it will mean no more caucuses and no more conventions to select candidates. The primary will be one man, one vote. Whoever has the higher count at the end is the candidate from that party."

"So," Ida considered her words not wanting to sound stupid, "then you won't have to call for the caucuses and oversee them if this bill passes? How will they do a primary? Isn't the idea that the Democrats vote for the Democrat candidates in the primary and the Republicans do the same? How will they tell them apart?"

"I'm not sure."

"So the power then goes to the people rather than the politicians?"

John looked at Ida.

After a bit of silence, she turned around with soapy hands, "What? Did I say something wrong?" Soapy water dripped onto the floor. Ida turned back to the sink. "Would this mean your days as a town chairman are numbered?"

John continued to look at her back for a moment longer before answering. "I thought you didn't care about the politics because you 'can't vote anyway'."

Ida glanced over her shoulder. John saw her small smile. "I read the paper. I care about it for you, and your position on the town committee is a part of the you I love." She turned fully and placed a kiss on the top of his head, dripped water on his pant leg, and then went back to the sink. "And you never know, someday I may be able to vote."

"Although a primary may seem to be more democratic, actually it isn't. The political machine in Chicago will select who will run in the primary instead of a name moving up from town to county to state. So then, the one man would have less say. See what I mean?"

Ida nodded. She tried to listen with care but was still leaning toward a one-man-one-vote primary.

John stood, preparing to leave.

Ida turned and wiped her hands on a flour sack towel. She gave him a big hug around the neck and a proper kiss on the mouth. "Hurry back. I love talking to you."

John smiled and planted another kiss on her forehead. "I'll be back before you can say Jack Robinson."

No caucuses? What would John do if he lost his appointment? He loved the pomp and circumstance of caucus nights so much. What would he do with his time if he's no longer on the town committee? Another thing to worry about.

Mamie came into the kitchen, "Mama?"

"Yes, what is it?"

"Helen go to schoowo?" Mamie asked.

"No, not yet. But I think she'll start going with Papa two days a week next week."

"Aw day?"

"Well, let's see. He will take her with him in the morning, and we will pick her up in the afternoon. So not all day, but she'll be gone for a good while."

"Gut!" Mamie turned on her heel and returned to the parlor.

What in the world was that about? They hadn't been fussing. Ida shrugged. Helen could be bossy with her little sisters. She was precocious, and she knew it.

John and Ida's plan was simply to give Helen a head start on first grade, which, if all went well, she would start in the fall. She would go with John to the store and learn commerce, and she would spend time with Ida in the kitchen learning to cook. Both required numbers and reading. Then in the fall, she would start first grade when she was five and a few months

I Will Fly to Woodstock

old. Ida hoped that these "classes" would put some structure to her day so she could easily slide into first grade in September.

Ida smiled. Helen was going to be something special.

***

Local News and Personal Items

The young people enjoyed a coasting party on the long hill back of Mr. Wheeler's woods Christmas day. A slight accident occurred but no bones were broken.

The Royal Neighbors will hold their next regular Saturday evening, January 10th at Woodman Hall. A good attendance is desired.

An ugly dog belonging to Henry Garben attacked Mrs. John Sahula on the street one day last week, inflicting a slight wound on the wrist. The wound was cauterized and thus far is healing nicely.

Woodstock Sentinel, January 8, 1908.

***

Sewage Purification Works

Woodstock, Ill.

Sealed proposals will be received by the board of local improvements of the City of Woodstock, Ill. until 8 o'clock p.m. on the 24th day of January, AD. 1908, for constructing a system of sanitary sewers and a sewage purification plant including the following list of materials.

> 4470 feet of 21-inch tile pipe sewer.
> 1250 feet of 20-inch tile pipe sewer.
> 1700 feet of 18-inch tile pipe sewer.
> 2870 feet of 15-inch tile pipe sewer.
> 3910 feet of 12-inch tile pipe sewer.
> 10700 feet of 10-inch tile pipe sewer.
> 36500 feet of 8-inch tile pipe sewer.

> 4150 feet of 6-inch tile pipe sewer.
> 280 Manholes.
> 20 Flush Tanks.
> 1 Concrete settling and dosing chamber.
> 8 Sand filter beds 50 x 55 feet.
>
> In the above are to be included all equipment, appurtenances, etc. as shown and specified and required by ordinance.
>
> All bids should be submitted upon the blank forms furnished by the Board and be accompanied by a certified check for the amount not less than 10 percent of the total amount of the enclosed bid.
>
> Payment for all work materials to be made in special assessment bonds bearing 5 percent interest and issued under the laws of the State of Illinois. Said bonds to be taken at par value by the contractors.
>
> *Woodstock Sentinel*, January 8, 1908.

***

William Wienke rolled up the newspaper and brought it down in the palm of his hand. John's oldest brother still felt the sting of his departure from public service every time he read an article about city planning, although it had been months. After twenty years of working for the city culminating in the city engineer position, the city council had pushed him out last fall in favor of a younger, more educated man. The debacle with the city's well had been the final straw. Under Will's watch, a new well had been dug, but not deep enough. He hadn't anticipated the new industry needs in Woodstock. Oliver Typewriter Company and Borden's Milk's condensing plant drained the well each day. The council had dropped the fault at his feet.

Now, the city council had decided to drill a new well and add sewers and a sewage treatment plant. The engineering and planning for the sewer system and the oversight of the project... ach, who was he kidding...he missed it. His new job at the Spedenuter factory making large metal tanks for city water towers, water and sewer systems or stock yards was fine, but the work was heavy, and he didn't feel he could do it for very many years before he would be spent. He was earning more per hour than he had with the city, but he missed the day-to-day responsibility and prestige that came with being the city engineer.

He was glad he had built a big house when he was able. With Lizzie renting out several rooms to Typewriter factory workers and electrical work at John's store, they made it through the lean times after he and the city parted ways. He had put his name in at THE factory, but they seemed to think he was 'overqualified' and had the wrong skills for making the small pieces of a typewriter. He slapped the paper on the arm of his chair. Being home on Saturday afternoons and Sundays was nice. He looked around. What to do? He was not one to have hobbies.

Lizzie asked from the kitchen, "What do you have planned for the rest of the day?"

"Nothing much," he replied. "Maybe I'll clean the stable."

"Okay. Tomorrow we are invited to your mother's after church."

Good. He looked forward to seeing the family. He hadn't told his brothers much about his new job.

"That'll be good," he called to Lizzie.

Will clapped his hands on his thighs, rose, and went to the mudroom. He slipped on his rubber boots and donned his heavy jacket and a cap with ear flaps. "I'll be back in soon," he said back into the kitchen.

"I'll make some fresh coffee to warm you up when you come in, and we'll have some Kuchen."

"Sounds wonderful." William smiled at his wife of so many years and then turned to go out to brave the elements. The sky

I Will Fly to Woodstock

was overcast, and a light snow was falling. He trudged the twenty yards to the stable.

The air was quite a bit warmer in the stable than outside and smelled of sweet hay and dung. He went to the two pens and, talking softly to each horse, haltered them, and tethered them at either end of the short central alley. He gave each a leaf of clover hay so they wouldn't get bored. He forked out each stall into a wheelbarrow and wheeled it to the dung heap behind the barn. Concentrate on the job and let the rest go.

The heap was frozen solid and would have to be loaded and spread in the spring when the weather turned warm. One of the outlying farmers would come and take it to their fields before planting. They were glad to get the fertilizer. But now the freezing weather kept the smell down, and stockpiling made the job easier than hauling the muck out to the country through the snow filled yard and streets each week.

Back inside the barn, Will threw down two bales of straw from the loft and a bale of hay. He filled each stall knee-high with the sweet-smelling, golden stems of straw. He would add to this lush bed daily until the next cleaning a week hence. The rich alfalfa hay went in the manger. One of the horses gave a gentle nicker, ready for a good roll in the fresh straw.

"Just hold your horses." William rubbed the horse's forelock. He emptied water buckets of the last drops left from the night before as he went out to the outside pump to fill them with fresh water. It took a good deal of pumping before the water climbed to the spigot and began running clear and clean into the buckets.

Will retraced his steps to the barn and placed a bucket by each manger. He would have to do that again before bed, because the horses tended to paw at the buckets, maybe in play, spilling the contents rather than saving it for later. He wondered if he should buy a trough to run between the stalls to serve both horses with a pump on it. His company made a few, and maybe he could get a deal on one. He'd have to investigate. On the other hand, a trough would require a lot more water and how long would he have these horses? More and more automobiles could be seen around town. Was a trough worth the expense?

Thinking about the alternatives, Will broke the bale of hay and divvied out half to each manger. He added a scoop of molasses-sweetened grain to the top of each mound and then turned to the horses. They were stomping their feet and murmuring low, demanding heaven before it was served. He led each to his freshened stall and watched as they drank and gobbled down the grain. The big roan, Jake, lay down and took a good roll in the straw then stood, shook, and whinnied at the top of his voice. Will smiled at the histrionics. The smaller paint, Indian Joe, stood crunching on the hay as if to get every last ort of the molasses treat. William smiled and bid them ado, shutting the outside door and tightly latching it.

Will returned to the house, shed his stable clothes in the mudroom, and entered what now seemed to him to be an overheated kitchen. Lizzie was true to her word.

"Sit down and rest awhile." She scraped out a chair for him.

"I rest too much." The correct German retort. He sat.

Her hands encircled his neck from behind for a hug. The tang of barn smell hung in his hair, what was left of it, and on his skin adding an earthiness to the warm, sweet air. She kissed his bald spot. He reached up and took her hands in his for a moment of peace. He was doing 'nothing much.'

They squeezed each other's hands, and Lizzie turned to the stove and furnished him with a steaming cup of black coffee and a slice of sponge cake. She brought her own cup and plate to the table. 'Nothing much' except this.

They smiled at each other and began the ritual of the mid-morning Kuchen and Koffee break, an old German tradition.

"How are you feeling this morning?" Lizzie liked to chat over coffee.

"Okay." Will considered his situation further. "At loose ends, I guess. Weekends are the worst."

"I suppose. Maybe we should get more involved at church."

William shot her a glance. "We got enough religion, don't cha think?"

Lizzie held her counsel.

"Frank was saying that the electrician at Oliver is getting on in years. Can't remember the chap's name."

"Electrician would be an easier job than lifting tanks."

Will nodded. "I wish John would take me on as his butcher. He seems to be floundering a bit. With my experience in Belvidere…for God's sake I had my own butcher shop. I give him hints about the business, but I also need to have a livelihood. To actually help him, I need to get paid."

"And he can't pay you?"

"He says not right now. I think he over-extended by adding the meat counter, but he won't admit it. Stubborn Kraut!"

"Go talk to him again and remember that you are the older brother, not the father."

"Maybe." William's gravelly voice held no high hopes either as brother or father.

"It would be sweet if John and you were in business together." Lizzie's voice rose in a happy lilt.

"Ja, ja! Maybe."

"Now eat your Kuchen before the icing melts. It was still a little warm when I added the frosting."

Will picked up his fork and looked at the yellow cake with the frosting dripping down over the edges. Maybe.

***

Try THE STAR Grocery and Market

Van Camp's Tomatoes, 13c, 2 for..25c
Van Camp's Pork and Beans,10c,..15c
Winkley Sweet Corn, 10c. 3 for...25c
Echo Brand Sweet Co n, 13c, 2 for.25c
Echo Brand Sifted E rlyJunePeas.15c
Lima Beans, canned 10c
Yellow Wax Beans, canned 10c
Large Package Mince Meat:......10c

Meat Department

Porterhouse Steak.................18c
Sirloin Steak.................... ....15c
Round Steak............ ....12½c
Pork Chops......................12½c
Pork Steak ......,..... ... .12½c
Pork Roast..... ....12½c
Salt Pork........................12½c
Beef Pot Roast....................10c
Beef Rib Roast 12½c
Corned Beef......................8c

J. F. WIENKE

NESTER BLOCK   PHONE 501

***

S. &IH. Green Trading Stamp Co.

OWING to the increased demand and growing popularity of the valuable and well-known S. & H. Green Stamps we have finally decided to give them on all purchases. S. & H. Green Stamps are the acknowledged standard of trading stamp values the world over. They are universal trading stamps, operating in almost every large city of the United States, and in many small ones too   :   :   :
The name S. & H. and Quality are synonymous terms. One always suggests the other. Having been before the public for twelve years they have been tried and found not wanting. S. & H. Green Stamps are the most valuable and the only stamps to be found in homes where sensible and thrifty people dominate   :   :   :

***

Ida browsed in Wright's Drug Store on the south side of the downtown square. Mamie and Dodi had fallen asleep in the pram, and Helen was at the store with John. This gave Ida a chance to do a bit of window shopping.

The display of picture postcards in Wright's window had pulled her into the store. She looked at the post card in her hands. The back of the card, she assumed, was for the address and a very brief message. She turned it over. The picture on the front was the north side of the Woodstock Square taken from Benton Street shooting west. The Pleasure Club was front and center taking up the second floor of the first building. Ida squinted at the picture and then accepted the offer of a magnifying glass from the clerk. Way up at the other end of the street should be John's store. But no, the Nester Block was not there.

This picture had been taken before Peter Nester built John's building in 1903. In its place in the picture was the old wooden Donnelly house, now replaced with the modern brick building mid-block. Next to the house was an empty lot with a tree growing in the space where her husband's store now stood. John had made his mark on Woodstock, but one would never know it by these photographs.

On the other hand, the idea of postcards was nice. She could send a brief message and a photo at once when one didn't have time for a full letter.

"I'll take these three." Ida handed the cards to the clerk.

"Nice for a quick note, don't cha think?" The clerk smiled.

"To say you're acomin' or thanks for havin' me."

"Yes, or for Happy New Year to friends in Wisconsin."

"That, too. It'll be three cents."

Dodi raised her head with sleepy eyes, "We get candy?"

"Not today. We have lemon drops at home." Ida smiled at the sleepy girl.

Mamie's eyes were open also, but she lay with arms embracing her smaller sister. With two years and some between them, the size difference wasn't so great, but Mamie, at four, was thin as a rail, while Dodi, at two, still had the rounded curves of baby fat.

The clerk took the proffered nickel and gave Ida two Indian Head pennies in change.

"Pweese, Mama." Dodi's blue eyes were large and pleading. "Pweese."

Ida looked at the pennies in her hand. "OK, we'll have two sticks of licorice also." She handed one of the pennies back to the clerk, who rang up the sale on the huge brass cash register and held out the canister for the girls to get a stick.

"Ah, licorice is good for 'em." The clerk replaced the tight seal on the jar. "T'won't spoil your lunch, will it?"

The girls, lips already turning gray from the sticks, shook their heads in unison.

***

The front door jingled at the J. F. Wienke grocery. With the pram parked next to the bench outside, Dodi led the parade into the shop, her face and hands giving away the black treat just consumed. Helen sat with the clerk behind the counter, pencil in hand. Her somber face and upside down smile said she was not glad to see them.

Mamie looked around. "Where is Papa?"

Dodi squealed, "Papa!"

Helen pointed to the back room.

Mamie ran toward the back room, outdistancing Dodi. She called out, "Papa!!" as she burst into the room, as if she hadn't just seen him a few hours ago.

"Well, look who's here!!" exclaimed John, also as if he hadn't just seen her a few hours ago. Dodi toddled in on Mamie's heels joining in the chorus of greetings.

"Where's your Mama? Did she just drop you here and go off shopping?"

"Mama is in the store." Mamie pointed back the way they had come and smiled because she knew the answer.

"Tore!" Dodi also pointed.

John scooped up Dodi and spun her around once, much to her giggling delight. "Mamie, can you take me to Mama?"

Of course she could, thought Mamie, but this room with its box piles and crates and barrels looked particularly good for climbing. She wanted to stay here and play. She went over and crawled up onto one of the crates, stood up, and stepped up on a barrel.

"Oh no you don't. The storeroom is too dangerous for jungle gyms." John watched Mamie's face fall. She didn't want to go back to the shop. She wanted to climb. She took another step up onto a higher pile and turned toward another even higher crate.

"Mamie." John's voice had changed a little. She turned to look at him and sat down on the higher crate, eye to eye with him.

"I want to pway here for a wittle while." Mamie's arms crossed hugging her chest, a frown very apparent on her little face.

By this time, Dodi was squirming and whining to get down. John tightened his grip on her and turned her up over his shoulder.

"No, you can't play on these crates. First, they might fall on you, and second, you are going to get splinters."

Mamie looked at her hands and then held them out for him to see, "No spwinters." She pushed herself into a stand on top of the crate.

Dodi was pushing back against him, saying, "Down. Down. Down."

John struggled to hang on. "Be still, Dodi." He held out his hand to Mamie. "Come on, Mamie." A bit of iron in his voice.

Mamie smiled her most mischievous smile and stepped up to the next level.

"Down. Down! Down! Want go Mamie!" Dodi cried out loudly and squirmed and pushed and threw herself toward the floor.

"Mama! I need you," called out John.

Mamie squealed with delight, "Mama! Come see."

John shook his head. "Yes, Mama, come see!"

"I'm here, I'm here." Ida came bustling into the room. She stopped and looked around. "What are you doing way up there?"

"Climbing," Mamie squealed.

"Very good but come down now before you fall." Ida looked at John for help.

"I won't faw," the little mountain climber insisted as she looked for her next perch.

Helen came into the back room, "Look Mama, see how I keep the books." She held out an accountants' sheet where she had entered numbers in various crooked columns. She looked up, and in her authoritarian store voice said, "What are you doing? Come down this instant!"

Mamie laughed.

John handed Dodi to Ida.

"Mama, down, peas. Climb!" Dodi threw herself to the side trying to escape her mother's clutches.

John went over to the pile of crates and reached up and caught Mamie under the arms and lifted her down into his arms.

"You are our little mountain goat, aren't you?" John hugged her close. He turned serious, looking right into her face. "But…you must do what Papa and Mama tell you because we don't want you to get hurt. These boxes and crates are very unsteady. Look at them." He reached out and shook the pile, and it moved with ease. "What if you got to the top and they started to fall?"

Mamie stretched out her arms as wide as she could. "Then, I will fly to Woodstock!"

***

That evening at home, Ida took out of her package the two Swastika cards she would send to Lena and Clara. The cards were symbolic of good luck at the new year and well-being throughout the year. The one she liked best had a large golden emblem placed in the center on a nice cream card stock. The saying was a poem:

> In ancient days, the Swastika possessed a magic charm.
> And shielded its possessor, from danger and from harm.
> To you it brings good wishes.
> And if I had the power,
> T'would bring you all that life holds dear
> This very day and hour.

That would be for Lena. The other one was more esoteric, and she thought Clara would like it. Many images of luck were displayed besides five swastikas. A horseshoe, a diamond, a sunrise for light, two hearts with an arrow through both for love, and a globe for travel rounded out the charms – a good card for Clara. She tucked the picture postcard with "almost John's store" into her writing desk.

She turned Lena's card over and examined the writing space. My, she WAS going to have to be a woman of few words.

I Will Fly to Woodstock

> *Dear Lena,   January 29, 1908*
> *I thought about you today and wanted*
> *to say "hello" and send you a bit of*
> *luck for the new year. We are well and*
> *hope you are also. Out of space until*
> *next time.*
> *   Your friend, Ida.*

She must, Ida thought, learn to write smaller so I can say more. She turned over the other card.

> *Dear Clara,   January 29, 1908*
> *This card is to bring you all the luck*
> *of the new year – light, love, and life.*
> *I hope you find them all very soon.*
> *We are well and hope you and Mama*
> *are also. Write and let me know how*
> *you are and when we might see you.*
> *   Your sister, Ida*

Ida addressed each card and put on a one cent stamp. Quite simple, thought Ida. Then again, would Lena and Clara think that she was shortchanging them by sending them these brief messages? Would the picture make up for the lack of news? Maybe she shouldn't send them. She went to the left margin of both cards, and in tiny script, wrote:

> *How do you like this new method of*
> *keeping in touch? Let me know.*

She hoped they would be able to read it. On a whim, in the other margin, she wrote:

> *Penny for your thoughts!*

She was pleased with this last line since the postage was a penny. What will they come up with next?

***

SOCIETY NOTES.

On last Saturday evening a very cordial company of friends gathered at the home of Louis Kirchman in this city, the occasion being the celebration of Mr. Kirchman's 50th birthday. The evening was spent very enjoyably in various forms of amusement and music, Otto Schumann presiding at the piano. The following were present: Mrs. Emil Fink of Elgin, Mr. and Mrs. Charles Kirchman and family, Mr. and Mrs. Fred Schuett and family, Mr. and Mrs. Fred Sahs, Mr. and Mrs. Edward Wienke and family, Mr. and Mrs. William Wienke, Mr. and Mrs. August Kindt, Mr. and Mrs. Otto Schumann, Mesdames Mrs. William Kindt, Mrs. Ernest Bachhaus, Mrs. Chris Anderson, and Mrs.Fred Jooretz.

Woodstock Sentinel, January 30, 1908.

English Lutheran Services.

There will be services at the English Lutheran church on Washington Street next Sunday afternoon at 2:30. Sunday school at 1:30 p.m.

H. J. Behrens, pastor.
Woodstock Sentinel, January 30, 1908.

***

"John, have you thought about what position you will take in the church?" Frank and John were sitting at each end of their mother Sophia's sofa as the women, Sophia, Ida, and Anna, worked their magic making Sunday supper. They had all gone to church to hear the Good News from the pulpit that afternoon.

"Position?"

"Yes, we have two positions on the board to fill, and I know you have been...unhappy with Pastor Behrens, so far."

"I'm not so much unhappy as I am uneasy. I don't think he intends to stay with us past his ordination."

"Why do you say that?"

"I guess I mostly have a feeling, but I don't get the idea that his wife is happy with Woodstock, nor that this was his idea of mission work."

"Mm. Even better to have a say in things that come up."

"I'm hard pressed to get away from the store in the evening just now." John sighed. "I don't want to pay extra for keeping a cashier in the evenings when the trade is low."

"Everything alright?" Frank felt John might be hinting at troubles.

"Yes. I'm tired tonight. I'll think about it. I hope they call us for supper soon, so—"

Three little girls ran into the room, giggling. They stopped and stood in a line from tallest to shortest, looked at each other and the two oldest called out in perfect togetherness,

"Come and get it!" Dodi called, as an echo, "Tum det it!" Then they fell on the floor in a pile of giggles at their deed.

"Oh, you rapscallions!" John said as he rose and pulled Mamie from the pile and headed for the dining room.

Frank was right on his heels. "Yes, think about it, John. It would only be once a month." They dodged Helen, Dodi, and Frank's Clayton who were running circles around the table calling out "Come and get it" over and over.

"I will," John said loudly over the din. He wasn't interested in signing up for any more monthly or weekly meetings, but he felt like something was going on with the pastor that he didn't like. Ida urged him to be patient; that John Behrens was young and would grow into the job. And being on the church council would keep his thumb on the scale. He might even volunteer to be corresponding secretary. He smiled at the thought. Maybe he would agree to join. After all, he was one

I Will Fly to Woodstock

of the founding fathers of Grace Evangelical Lutheran Church.

***

"It doesn't seem like very many women are vying for the gold watch you are offering at the store," Ida said as John slid into bed. He looked dog-tired. He had opened this morning at seven o'clock and hadn't closed until nine o'clock that night. After he had a quick sandwich of cold meatloaf, they opted for going directly to bed.

"Nope, but still, any advertising is good."

"Yes, much better than 'this space belongs to John Wienke.'" She couldn't resist the tease.

"Will you ever let me live that down?"

"Never!"

He shook his head and rolled over, his back to her without a kiss. She snuggled up and gave him a kiss on the neck. When the night was cold and windy like this one, the furnace was stoked high to last until the morning when the inside temperature would be dipping low. When Ida's feet hit the cold wood of the floor before first light, she would don her slippers and hustle to the kitchen to feed the cook stove which most often made it through the night, coals still glowing red in the early darkness, and then go to the basement to throw three or four logs into the furnace. But now the heat being generated made the quilt too much. Ida threw it aside and snuggled closer. "You know, if you'd have an extra gold watch just laying around, I might be able to find good use for it," she whispered in his ear.

Standing of the
Ladies' Gold Watch Contest
At **WIENKE'S**
up to Wednesday noon.

Nellie Begley............12
Agnes Wachtler.......... 7
Maud Hobbs 8
Nettie Burger 10
Mrs. H. Dermont 10

Everybody help the Girls

At the **THE STAR Grocery and Market**
NESTER BLOCK   PHONE 501

He rolled back over to face her, "You could, could you?"

"Yes," she purred, slipping her cool hands along his torso. "And I'd be very appreciative."

"You are such a little flirt." And then John found he wasn't all that tired after all.

***

"Happy Valentine's Day!" John announced before he sat down at the breakfast table. A chorus of female voices answered him with the same. He parceled out the small packages in his hands. Each girl got a Valentine card with cupids wishing them a happy day and a few bits of chocolate tied up in a small square of cloth and a ribbon. "Thank you, Papa," they chorused. "Mama, can we eat it now?" asked Helen.

Ida smiled. "After you eat your breakfast, you may have one piece and then we'll save the rest for dessert after supper."

The little faces fell, but they didn't argue.

Ida looked down. Her bundle was just a bit bigger than those the girls had gotten. She reached atop the ice box and retrieved a flat box and card and presented it to John.

John smiled. "Well, it looks like Papa hasn't been forgotten after all." The card was signed "From your girls."

"Open it, open it," the girls chanted. He read the card aloud. "Be Our Valentine." The "My" in the original greeting had been turned into "Our" very artistically. Three little cupids held forward a bouquet of forget-me-nots in the shape of a heart.

"We found the only one with three cupids." Helen pointed at the card. "You know, like three girls."

"I see that." John turned to the box. He opened it and found a fine blue and gray silk tie. "Oh my, did you girls pick this out?"

"Yes!" they shouted.

I Will Fly to Woodstock

"How handsome a tie! I must wear it today." He reached up and stripped off his three-for-a-dime tie and placed the new one around his neck and began to tie it. The girls watched enthralled with the process of crossing, wrapping and pulling through. "There! How do I look?"

"Handsome," Helen declared, always the willing spokesperson for the group.

"Thank you very much my little cupids, and you too Mama."

"Now, Mama open." Mamie went around to stand by Ida's side.

Ida read her card aloud, as well, "If you'll be my sweetheart, I will be your beau." A boy was down on one knee offering the girl his heart. "Love's greeting to my Sweetheart." She smiled across the table at John, and he winked.

"Open it, open it!" The chant began again.

Ida untied the ribbon holding the drawn-up cloth. She expected sweets of some kind, so when her eyes beheld the sparkle of gold, she gasped. Tears welled in her eyes, and she reached in and held up a lady's gold lapel watch.

The children looked at it with curiosity. "What is it?" Helen asked. "A broach?"

"Well, yes, a broach, but also a watch, see?" Ida pulled open the gold cover to reveal the clock face. The children began clamoring to touch it, to hold it, to listen to it. But Ida's tear-filled eyes locked on John's amused and loving eyes across the table. He winked.

After each child had gotten to hold it and listen to its ticking, John rose and came around the table and pinned it to the front of Ida's frock. "So, you'll always know what time your Valentine is coming home." And he kissed her on the lips...in front of the children...who squealed with delight.

***

GRACE LUTHERAN ELECTS OFFICERS

The members of the Grace Evangelical Lutheran church held their annual business meeting last week Tuesday evening at which time reports were heard from various officers who had served during the organization of the society and the first six months of its existence.

Rev. A. C. Anda of Chicago presided at the meeting and congratulated the members for the splendid progress which had been made during so short a time.

A formal call was issued to Rev. H. J. Behrens as pastor of the new society and the following members were elected as church council: C. C. Harting, Frank J. Wienke, Fred Readel, C. J. Peterson, Frank Foote and John Wienke.

Probably next Sunday or the Sunday following these gentlemen will be installed into their offices, after which they will elect church officers for the ensuing year.

Woodstock Sentinel, February 20, 1908.

***

Wanted
500 Men and Women
BY MARCH FIRST 1908
J. F. WIENKE
Nestrb Block   Phone 501

"Vat does dat mean?" Sophia stared at the paper. Why would John want 500 men and women? Curious. She headed for the phone.

"Wienke's Grocery," John's business voice came across the line.

"John, dis ist your Ma!" Sophia stood on tiptoe to speak directly into the mouthpiece of the wall-mounted phone.

"Ma." Warmth returned to his voice. "What can I do for you?"

"Du come lunch today."

"Ah...I'm working, Ma."

"Put dat boy in charge and come for beef and kraut sandwich."

"Let me see what I can do."

"No! Du not see; du come." And she hung up the phone.

John looked down at the earpiece, now soundless in his hand. Well, he better arrange lunch with Ma today. He replaced the earpiece. What in the world was this about? "Dat boy" was no longer with them, laid off at the end of last month because deliveries were down. Eunice, the cashier, could carry on for an hour or so to cover for him as she did when he went out to deliver orders. If an emergency arose, he was just ten minutes away. Ma sounded urgent like something was wrong. So, as she said, he would go.

John sat at his mother's table with a large, corned beef and sauerkraut sandwich before him. The room smelled wonderful with the bite of sauerkraut filling the air and looked even better with the red of the beef overlapping the fresh white bread on all sides. Rounding out the meal was hot coffee and a scoop of homemade curds and whey, what were they calling them now? Ah yes, "cottage cheese." Ma's curds and whey was the best cottage cheese in the city. He should get her recipe for the store. She came to the table with her plate and put the paper down in front of him folded open to his ad.

"Vas ist das?" she asked.

John was glad that he had just taken a big bite of the sandwich, because it gave him time to think before answering. "What do you mean, what is this?" He managed the words even with his mouth full of the savory combination of juicy beef, sauerkraut, and doughy bread.

"Vhy du look for da men and vimen?" Ma elaborated.

"Well, it's this way." John wiped his mouth with the yellow-checkered cloth napkin that had been provided at his place. "I need customers."

"Du haff no customers?"

"Well, yes, I do, but I can always use more. That's what advertising is for."

"Ach, I know dat. Somethink ist fischtig."

"Not with this great sandwich. Nothing fishy here." John took another large bite.

"Da store ist not so vell doink?" Sophia dodged the change of subject.

John hesitated, chewing, swallowing, taking a drink of the coffee, considering. "Not so well."

"Knew dat! Dis," she pointed at the paper, "say so loud unt clear."

John looked at the ad. He had placed it hoping it would intrigue people to come in and ask what's going on. He'd give away something small as a token, and with any luck, they would stay and buy goods or pay for the ones they had already purchased on credit. His cash flow had dwindled to a small trickle. The meat was spoiling before he could sell it. He often didn't have the cut the customer wanted. He had a cold locker, but that only worked for a day or two before he had to discount. AND he did not have the cash for the taxes due in March. He had hoped that this ad would bring in at least

I Will Fly to Woodstock

enough to pay the taxes. If not, the store, as his mother would say, was kaput!

John's eyes went back to examining his sandwich. He took another sip of coffee, and Sophia rose to gather the pot for a refill.

He said to her back, "Yes, the store is having a bit of a slump. Putting in the meat counter has not paid for itself yet. As a matter of fact, my family eats more of the meat than do my customers." Sophia turned and poured the coffee and then resumed her seat.

"Right now, in the winter, I can freeze some of it, but then the meat is frozen when the customer wants it and not fresh. So, I freeze it or take it home or sell it at a large discount. I've also started smoking and salting some of it, but I'm one man, and it takes time. Ida has pickled some and dried some, and we share the rest. We are getting fat, but the business is not." John stopped. He had told no one, not even Ida, about this, and it felt good to be sharing the burden. "Do you need some good rump roasts?"

"Vat dost Ida say?" Sophia did not let the question distract her.

John laid his half-eaten sandwich on his plate. "She doesn't know most of it. She thinks that we are just well stocked with meat. I've cut back on how much I order, but then I don't have what the customers want, and they go elsewhere. Where I thought the meat business would increase sales, it has actually pushed customers away to the bigger stores that can offer more variety." He shook his head. "Or maybe the downturn in the economy has had an effect. Some are saying that we are having a business depression all over the country just like John D. Rockefeller predicted a year ago."

The fine grocer picked up his sandwich. "Even as prosperous as Woodstock has been, a downturn doesn't bode well for a small store like mine. Just this morning, I heard that

I Will Fly to Woodstock

Austin's is doubling the size of their store and adding cold counters."

"Vas ist das?"

"An insulated case with ice in the bottom and the product above on the ice with sliding glass doors to keep the cold in. Expensive, but great to keep meat and fish fresh and on display. Some, I hear, even run on electricity, although I'm not sure how that makes them cold."

"Du vant to buy one of these kalt counters?" Sophia's voice was kind.

"No. I'll be fine if 500 men and women come into my store by March first," answered the ever-hopeful John.

"Du need loan?"

"No Ma, I won't take your money. I would not put your savings in jeopardy. My brothers would never forgive me."

"Not their money," declared Sophia. "Vat vill happens?"

"Well, if the ad works, we'll see. I have just about used up the money from the split up with Herman, he took more of the merchandise and paid me the difference. When that's gone, if I'm not doing better than breaking even, I'll have to do something."

"Vat vill du vork at?"

"I could have lots of jobs in Woodstock. The typewriter factory is always hiring." He hesitated to consider how much to say.

"Vat else?" Sophia's concern was palpable.

"I was approached last week by our insurance company man. Ida wanted insurance for the house a couple years ago, and we added the store to that so if it would burn down, we'd not lose everything."

"I member vhen du get dat surance."

John smiled at his mother. "This Prudential man wanted to know if I'd ever thought about selling insurance. I hadn't, of course, but he painted a very pretty picture of the money I could make doing so. Company insurance like Prudential replaces the insurance through churches and other societies like the Royal Arcanum at lower cost."

"Hm."

"So, anyway." John studied his sandwich. "Many opportunities are presenting themselves with shorter hours and more income. If I'm smart, I will pursue one or several to see what they have to offer before I even consider shutting the doors for good. I've had a good run, but the store is demanding work and long hours. I must be a jack of all trades: proprietor, repairman, salesman, delivery boy, boss, clean-up man, buyer, and I'm no spring chicken." He took a large bite to avoid continuing.

"Pish!" Sophia waved the comment away. "Du jus' ein Junge - a boy."

He chewed and swallowed. "If the store would bring in more money, I could hire people to do some of those jobs, but I'm down to Eunice and me,"

John took another small bite, one he hoped he could talk around.

"Who at dat store? Didst du close doors to come eat?" Sophia sounded like she felt guilty.

John wiped his mouth and swallowed. "Eunice can handle it for a bit. She'll call here if she runs into trouble."

"Vell, eat den. Da Kuchen's coming. I'm glad du come, and if du need money, jus ast me. Du always dare for me for many years, unt I proud of du and dat store. Hope du hast viel gluck – much luck with your men and vimen."

"Me, too. What kind of Kuchen?" This time the change of subject worked.

"Deutsche Schokolade!"

Mmmm...German Chocolate sounded so good on a chilly day. "Did anyone ever tell you that you are a great cook, Ma?"

"Nein, nur Durchschnitt. Just average." But Sophia's face glowed with pride, something that German Lutherans were not supposed to have.

D Stands for
Doering & Dry Goods.

A full and complete line of Spring goods now in, including Dress goods, wash goods, suits, skirts, waists, Rugs, Carpets, Linolium, etc.

Call and see our line.

***

English Lutheran Services

There will be services at the English Lutheran church on Washington street next Sunday afternoon at 2:30. The Lord's supper will be administered. The Rev. G. H. Gerberdling, D. D., professor of theology at the Chicago Lutheran seminary will preach. Sunday school will be held at 1:30 p.m. Strangers are cordially invited to attend.

Woodstock Sentinel, March 18, 1908.

***

April 20, 1908
365 Lincoln Ave.
Woodstock, Ill

Dear Mama and Clara,
 I so much apologize for not having written for almost a month. We are all fine in case you were worried. Mamie was

down with another bout of tonsillitis but seems to be back to her little old self now. It is frustrating because we cannot do much besides wait it out and feed her tea and honey. Doctor says if she doesn't outgrow them, he'll take them out. I'm not at all in favor of surgery. Seems like more people die from it than are saved, but we'll see. If she's down for a week every two months that's not too bad now, but when she starts school, I know; a long way off, and she's fine and happy now.

Helen still loves her lessons. She seems to be learning fast and comes home from the store with all kinds of stories. Dodi is healthy and full of spirit. Mamie and she seem to get along better than Helen does with either, but then Helen's older and already out in the world. She knows best about most things. Even more than her parents sometimes.

The Wienke family has two new baby boys born in Beloit. Can you imagine... Charles and Winnie had a baby boy, Royal Charles. They are 40 years old! They will be 55 when Royal is 15. On the other hand, newlyweds Emil and Etta Wienke are getting started on a family with a boy named Harvey. I haven't heard much from Lena except through Al who seems to spend more time in Woodstock than in Beloit. He is selling off his property here, however. I think he will buy a saloon in Beloit. Less likely to be closed by the "drys" up there.

We had a chance the other day to spend time with Herman's little Elizabeth. Grace got invited to a birthday party (can you believe it at one year old) and big sisters and brothers were not invited. So, Elizabeth came over and the girls had a grand tea party. Mama you would have loved it seeing your grandchildren playing together so nicely. They dressed up and Helen sat at the head of the table while the others spread around. I made tea and we served it in the little white tea set you sent last Christmas. We put little almond Kekse on the plates and they gossiped about their friends. Elizabeth had a lot of gossip about sister Grace, and did we know that her mama is going to have a baby? Do you know about this? I doubt Elizabeth would know such a thing, but out of the mouths of

I Will Fly to Woodstock 35

babes. *I teased Bessie and Herman about it when they picked her up. They were tight lipped but made no denial.*

I guess that's all the news and "gossip" I have today. I hope both of you are healthy and looking forward to Spring. It seems a little slow this year, don't you think? Let me know when you might come down...Memorial Day perhaps. Clara, will you have some time off? Write and let me know all the news about Racine.

All our love, Ida

***

English Lutheran Services

There will be no preaching services at the English Lutheran church this coming Sunday as Rev. H. J. Behrens will be in attendance at the baccalaureate address given at the Wicker Park Evangelical church, Chicago in connection with the graduation of students at the Lutheran Theological Seminary.

Woodstock Sentinel, April 23, 1908.

***

Rev. Behrens Graduates

Last Sunday, Rev. H. J. Behrens, pastor of the English Lutheran church in our city, was in attendance at the graduation exercises of the class of students of the Evangelical Lutheran theological seminary at Chicago, in which school Mr. Behrens was a student and one of the graduates.

The exercises took place at the Wicker Park Lutheran church. Dr. Ramsey, professor of historical theology at the seminary, delivered the baccalaureate address.

On Wednesday evening the regular commencement exercises were held for the graduating class.

The ordination service for the young preachers will take place at South Bend, Ind. preceded by an examination by a board of examiners of the Chicago synod.

It has taken a great deal of perseverance and hard work on the part of Rev. Behrens to carry on his studies in Chicago, and at the same time attend to the pastoral work of a new and growing charge in this city, and Mr. Behrens is to be congratulated upon his success, both here and at the seminary. He will from now on devote his entire time to his work here and will doubtless accomplish a great deal of good.

Woodstock Sentinel, April 30, 1908.

***

"I carest not. Er ist weg - gone." Sophia punched the dough with her fist, beating out her frustration on it rather than on her former tenant.

"Ma, what did he say?" John was concerned that Pastor Behrens had been rude in the leave-taking from his mother's house.

"Vhat da Bible say? Urteile nicht—"

"That ye be not judged. I know, but—"

"No buts. He ist gone." The heel of her hand pummeled the lump of dough.

"Did he pay for the last month?" John could feel his face getting red.

No answer.

"Ma?"

"John!" Sophia stopped kneading the dough and made eye contact. "He is pastor. Pastors tink no need to pay. Tink should have…how he say…hospitality. I bad person if make pay."

"Ma, for heaven's sake. We pay him so he can pay you."

Sophia harrumphed and slapped the dough.

"Did he tell you where he was moving?"

"To bigger flat at Bocher house."

"Okay, don't you worry about it. I'll take care of it. How much did he owe?"

Sophia stopped what she was doing and turned toward her middle son, arms crossed at her chest, flour-laden hands leaving white splotches on the forearms of her dress.

"John," she said softly, falling into German. "Er ist weg. Ich will keine Hilfe, damit er zählt. Betrachten Sie es als meine Spende an die Kirche. Kommen wir zu etwas anderem."

John didn't understand most of what she said, but he heard 'donate to the church' and 'move on.'

"So, you are giving the money to the church? I don't understand."

Sophia uncrossed her arms and made a gesture flicking her hand in his direction as if to say, 'away with you.'

"My givink to da religious." She pounded the dough a few more times and then broke it into loaf sized portions and put the rolled dough into well-greased loaf pans.

John's mouth watered. He loved his mother's bread. "Did you make only white today?"

Sophia looked up from filling the pans with a questioning look.

"Das Brot. Only white?"

"Ach das Brot. Make vier Roggenbrot," she held up four fingers, "and vier Weißbrot. Da rye comes out soon. Du vant taste?"

"I'd love a slice." John was glad to feel the tension of the room easing.

"Wid Rindfleisch and Kase?"

John laughed. "With beef and cheese? That would be wonderful, I missed lunch. Just a half a sandwich. I'll be having supper soon. Ida doesn't like it when I don't eat on the nights when I get home to actually sit down with the family. Soon I will be fat."

"Ich mag dich auch zu essen. Like du eat, too." Sophia looked him up and down. He was dapper in his gray wool vested suit and blue tie. His bowler sat on the table awaiting his departure. "Du look like guter Geschäftsmann…fine businessman. Proud of du."

John blushed and looked down. When he looked back up, Sophia had assumed the duty of feeding her son.

***

Local Intelligence

Ernst Selter has moved into the rooms in the Wienke house on Washington street, recently vacated by Rev. H. J. Behrens. Mr. Behrens has moved to the Bocher house on the same street.

Woodstock Sentinel, May 7, 1908.

***

Ida picked a large bunch of lilac branches from the bush at the back of their property and added them to the water bucket. The fragrant lilacs joined peonies and iris already cut. She looked over her donation. It seemed adequate. Many others would be bringing buckets just like this to city hall this morning. It was Memorial Day and the flowers would be made into grave trimmings for the soldiers' graves at the cemeteries west of town.

It was early. She had been up with the sun so that John could carry the bucket to city hall on his way to work, saving her the extra trip down to the Square. At around 2:30, she and the girls would walk out to the cemetery, put flowers on Carl Wienke and Bob Wienke's graves and then stand with flags in hand as the long sad parade to the cemeteries arrived. If all went well, they would lend a hand as flowers were placed on all the graves of those fallen in battle. She would have liked to have gone to the speeches, but that was too much to ask from a three-year-old and a five-year-old.

Ida finished up her work and carried the bucket into the house where she added water until about half full and set the offering by the front door where John couldn't miss it. She could hear John getting ready in the bathroom and the commode flushed upstairs. The house was coming alive.

She set the table for breakfast and pulled out the large cast-iron skillet. Bacon, eggs, and potatoes were the fare of the hour. Helen peeped around into the kitchen from the stairwell.

I Will Fly to Woodstock

"Good morning, Merry Sunshine," said Ida.

Helen made a face. "Are we supposed to get dressed?"

"Yes, can you help your sisters while I make breakfast?"

"I suppose I can." Helen disappeared up the stairs.

John came out of the bathroom. He gave her a peck on the cheek. "You were up and out early this morning. My hand looked for you, but you were gone."

"Sorry, darling. Flowers to pick; breakfast to make; children to dress…." She trailed off. She always had plenty to do.

"Ah yes. Memorial Day. Helen has asked if she can come to the Square with me so that we can attend the celebrations there."

"I suppose that would be fine if you can keep track of her."

"We'll go together. I'll be closing the shop from two to five o'clock."

"And then the two of you can meet the three of us up at the cemetery?" Ida placed eight strips of bacon into the hot skillet. The sizzling began immediately.

"Yes, we can do that. Will you take flowers to Pa and Bob?"

"I had planned to. The bouquets may be a bit smaller without Helen's help, but we'll manage."

"Okay then we have a plan."

The children came down the stairs, dressed too warmly for this day which had broken with full sun and a southerly breeze. Ida smiled at them. She would worry about that later.

After the patriotic music was played and the memorial service was read by Chaplain L. D. Fillmore, the main speaker of the day, Mrs. Flo Jamison Miller, matron of the soldiers' Widows Home at Wilmington, Illinois, was introduced.

"What's a matron?" Helen whispered.

"The lady in charge," John whispered back.

They had come at exactly two when almost all the seats were taken but had managed two together near the doors at the back. "So, we can escape quickly," John said. Helen giggled. The next week the paper would say,

> The presence of a lady as chief speaker on such an occasion was somewhat unusual, but if any prejudice existed it was quickly dispelled by the masterly and eloquent manner in which the speaker magnetized the audience and carried them with her throughout the address.

John and Helen were mesmerized if not magnetized like all the rest. Mrs. Miller began:

> Members of the Grand Army, the Women's Relief Corps and Citizens of Woodstock: A few weeks ago, I was present at a memorial celebration of ex-Confederate soldiers at Richmond Va. The chief speaker was a lady. Her opening remarks were: "I, who believe that slavery was right and emancipation was wrong, arise to address you."
> And so, this fine afternoon, I, who believe slavery was wrong, and emancipation was right, arise to address you.
> Today, while 'Universal peace lies like a shaft of light across the land, and like a lane of beams athwart the sea' – every garden has grown a flower for our soldiers' graves. The sweet emblems of peace and love, celebrate the sacrifices and heroisms of war, of war from which at last righteousness and peace have kissed each other.
> Four hundred years ago after months of patient toil and never-ceasing perseverance, Columbus gave to the world a new nation

> pledged to the cause of freedom. Nearly half a century ago the Union army of the North saved this nation from disunion and ruin and presented it to the gate of the civilized world purified and cleansed by fire.

Mrs. Miller moved around the stage with ease, leaning in to look the audience straight in the eye and gesturing as a fine elocution lesson would have taught. John looked at Helen. Her eyes were shining and her hands were following the movement of this fine lady speaker, twitching to be free to copy her every motion.

> The onward march of time brings to us the sweet May-time, when a nation gathers at the graves of her dead in commemoration of their deeds of valor. The day when once more they will mingle with the living spirits of departed heroes. In the sublime sense, in a greatly patriotic sense, the earth and the sea shall give up their dead.

Helen's eyes were wide when she heard this line. She swallowed and she slipped one of her hands into John's.

> Memorial Day is a day of wondrous meanings and hallowed memories. Soiled and fading photographs and old-fashioned daguerreotypes are held in the trembling hands by fathers and mothers who are growing old, by widows whose temples are white and from whose cheeks the roses have vanished, the men and women whose eyes will light up with holy pride of a father's patriotism and self-sacrifice, and by little prattling children who will learn

for the first time to lisp the name of a soldier grandsire and the name of the battlefield on which he fell.

"Like me," Helen whispered. "Like Opa Wienke. Except I don't lisp."

John squeezed Helen's little hand and smiled. Oh, little one. Your grandfather did not fall on the field of battle. He came to America to avoid the battlefield. Someday, you'll have to be told, but not today.

The walk to the cemetery went quickly. John thought about the last time he made this walk behind Bob's coffin and there was an unexpected pang of sorrow that took his breath. It didn't matter if the lost loved one was a hero or a scoundrel, the hurt was the same. The saddest thing was that Bob had just started to show his nobility as a husband and father when he was snatched away. But then, maybe that was true of the boys lost in the wars. Having their young lives snuffed out before they could even begin.

"There you are," Ida's voice broke into his reverie. Helen pulled her hand from his and ran with Mamie and Dodi across the beautiful grass of the cemetery. "Everything okay?"

"Oh, I was just thinking about the last time I climbed that hill on foot."

"Yes, I thought about it also as we came up earlier. I guess this is a day we are supposed to be a little sad."

"Yes." John took out his handkerchief and blew his ample nose. "Helen loved the woman speaker. Now she wants to do that when she grows up."

"Really. Well, good luck making a living wage doing that. I think the only ones who make a living speaking are ministers and politicians."

"Well, you never know."

"Why John, are you saying a woman could be a successful minister or a politician?"

I Will Fly to Woodstock

"Moment of weakness." John smiled and put his hand on Ida's back to guide her toward the festivities. "I have to watch the time. Must be back at the store by five."

"Okay." Ida quickened her pace. "Let's go decorate some graves."

***

Local News and Personal Items.

Mrs. Sophia Wienke and Mrs. Lillian Wienke are visiting Albert Wienke and family at Beloit this week.

Woodstock Sentinel, June 11, 1908.

ENGLISH LUTHERAN.

There will be no preaching service on account of the absence of the pastor, who is attending synod.

The Sunday school will meet as usual at 12 a. m.

GERMAN LUTHERAN.

German service, 10:30 a. m.

English service, 7:30 p. m.

Meeting of Ladies society Sunday afternoon at 3 o'clock.

Rev. John Bertram, pastor.
Woodstock Sentinel, June 11, 1908.

***

Local Intelligence.

Rev. H. J. Behrens, pastor of the English Lutheran church, went to Chicago Monday, and from there to South Bend, Ind., to be in attendance at the ordination service of the 1908 class of theological students who graduated from the Evangelical Lutheran seminary in Chicago. Rev.

Behrens is one of the graduating class. He expects to be home next Monday.

Woodstock Sentinel, June 18, 1908.

***

June 19, 1908
Racine, Wisconsin

Dear Ida,

I only have time for a quick note because I'm waiting to be picked up. Oh Ida, I've found him! Yes, it has finally actually happened. Your good luck card worked. I haven't told Mama yet, but I've found my beloved. His name nor his ways are common. He is a trained electrician, and he is from Akron, Ohio...isn't that exotic? And his name is Pearle F. Dye. Isn't that a wonderfully unique name!?

Do you believe in love at first sight? I do now. All my other beaus pale in comparison. We met at the laundry if you can believe it. He was in need of some repairs on a suit coat, and I was the blushing seamstress. Oh, he is so handsome, my heart practically stopped first time I saw him. Before we finished our business, he had asked me out, and I cannot tell you how quickly I accepted.

I suppose I must tell Mama since we plan to be married very soon. Neither of us can wait, but also, he has a job lined up in Iowa starting July 6th. I must go with him, I must! Iowa, I've heard, is a flat place, but I don't care. Just so Pearley and I can be together and start a family. Oh please, please, please be happy for me.

He is so sweet and kind and loves me so much. When he picks me up today, we will go down to get a marriage license and make an appointment with the justice of the peace. Then we will come back here and talk to Mama. I know this is truly a short time to figure out what Mama wants to do. I will push for her to move either to Emma or to you. Think about it, please.

I will close this now and mail it on the way to the courthouse. Please be happy for me, my sweet sister. I will write to Emma after Mama has decided or maybe call.
I am so happy!
Clara

***

Ida stood, dumbfounded with the letter in hand. How could Clara do this? She hadn't given a wedding date, but....

"Mama, what's bad?" Mamie coughed again. Without thinking, Ida reached down and put her hand against Mamie's forehead. Hot.

"Come on, Mamie." Ida took the little girl by the hand and led her to the kitchen. "Let's have a cool drink."

"Okay," Mamie climbed up to the table and accepted a glass of cold lemonade. She took a quick gulp. "Owa." Mamie clutched at her throat and began to cry. Her crying broke through Ida's reverie.

"Oh baby!" Ida picked up the little girl and took her to the rocking chair. "Your throat hurts bad, doesn't it?" She held Mamie close, her head on Ida's bosom, and rocked. The tears subsided. Ida could feel the fever through her clothes. A cool bath was in order.

"Tick, tock," croaked Mamie.

"What?"

"Tick, tock, clock says."

Ida realized that Mamie's ear was pressing on the gold watch pendant she'd gotten for Valentine's Day, and she was hearing it tick. Ida smiled, rocking, back and forth, back and forth.

"Oh, oh." Mamie pulled back. "No tick, tock."

Ida reached down and unpinned the watch and put it to her own ear. Mamie was right, it had stopped. Ida opened the front and saw that opening had relieved the pressure of the front pressing on the inner workings, and the minute hand began to move again. "Oh my." She showed Mamie. "It must be such soft gold that it stopped because you pressed your ear to it. We'll have to be careful after this not to press on it."

"Okay." A sob escaped from her with the word.

"How about a cool bath instead of a cool drink?" Ida suggested.

"Okay, den nap?"

"Yes, are you tired?" It wasn't time for the afternoon nap.

"Sleepy."

"How about some honey, instead of lemonade? I'm sorry the drink hurt you. I wasn't thinking."

"Mama, think!"

"Honey will feel good." The doctor had said that it would also fight the infection.

"Honey." Mamie nodded.

Ida felt her head again. Yes, another fever. She laid the watch on the side table and stood with Mamie still in her arms and headed for the bathroom. She drew five inches of lukewarm water into the tub and removed Mamie's clothes. She put Mamie in the water and retrieved a cup and the honey from the kitchen. A dose of honey, which made Mamie smile, and she began pouring the water over her arms and back and even her head. Mamie didn't resist the bath and seemed to be in a daze, as she felt the water trickle down her hot skin. They kept this up until Mamie began to relax, and then Ida was holding a sleeping child in the water. Ida stayed that way for a long time, holding Mamie above the water with one hand, while ladling the cool water over her with the other. She felt the forehead again. It seemed to be cooler than before they started. Good, she thought. She reached for a towel and lifted the sleeping child into it. She loosely swaddled Mamie in the towel and carried her to her nap pallet on the floor in the master bedroom.

When Mamie was sick, she often spent the night in their room so that Ida could easily check on her. This bout seemed to be worse than usual. She should call the doctor, although she knew he couldn't do much more than she could, unless she would agree to the leeches. Ida shuddered. Cool baths to ease the fever or swaddled tight to try to get the fever to break. Honey or lemon for the throat and Vicks Vapo-Rub for healing. She removed the towel and reached for the blue jar taking a dollop onto her fingertips. She rubbed the salve onto Mamie's chest and back and neck. She reached up and grabbed a flat rectangle of flannel and wrapped it around Mamie's neck securing it with a tiny gold safety pin. She put Mamie into a flannel nightshirt and covered her with several light blankets. Maybe this time the fever would break and not come back.

"Fight, my precious girl, fight," she whispered.

Ida rose and pulled the door to, but not tight. She would hear if the little girl called out.

As she returned to the kitchen, she caught sight of the letter laying there on the table where she had dropped it. "Clara!" She remembered the drama unfolding in Racine.

She checked the date on the letter. Day before yesterday. They could be married already. And then the phone rang.

Ida snatched up the vile object so that it wouldn't wake Mamie. She hated not knowing who was awaiting her on the other end of the line with unwelcome news.

"Hello?" Tentative as always.

"Ida, sein sie das?" Louisa's familiar voice.

"Ja, Mama, it's me," she replied and then listened to a rant in German, picking up enough to know that Mama was not pleased with Clara's plans, no she wasn't, not even ein bisschen (a little)! She let her mother hold forth until she wound down to a silence. "Bist du da?"

"Yes, I'm still here, Mama. Are they yet in Racine?"

"Ja, sie sind hier." Yes.

"And they aren't married yet?"

"Nein, sein sind nicht." No.

"When are they getting married?"

"Morgen."

"Tomorrow morning!!" Ida yelled at the phone, but then quieted her voice listening for cries. "Sorry, I didn't mean to yell. I can't come tomorrow. I have a sick child and—"

"Mamie ist wieder krank?"

"Yes, she is sick again." Is she ever not sick? Ida felt herself tearing up. "Oh Mama, Ich kann mir im Moment keine Sorgen um Clara machen." She started to cry, sobbing into the phone. I can't worry about Clara, right now.

Her mother was silent. Two mothers, concerned for their daughters. "Ida, es tut mir Leid. So sorry."

Ida controlled her tears, "Who is this man?"

"Not know…von Ohio. Nimmt Clara nach Iowa. Pearle Dye. Ich habe ihn einmal getroffen."

"Only once? You've met him only once? Oh Mama, I'm so sorry. I can't come right now. Can Emma?"

"Emma kommet morgan."

"OK. Gut. She'll come in the morning. That will help. Es tut mir leid. Let me know what happens. We should hang up. Zu teuer. Too expensive."

"Ja, Ich werde Ihnen Bescheid geben.

"Yes. Yes. Please let me know. Ich liebe dich. I love you."

Ida hung up the earphone and slumped onto the steps in the kitchen. She listened for Dodi. Her sweet little voice was jabbering away in the parlor as she readied her dollies for a nap. Ida rose and went to check on Mamie. Sound asleep.

Clara! 'Be happy for me,' she had written. Love is something we should not thwart. If this is the one, who am I to try to stop her, thought Ida.

"Mama?" Dodi's voice floated up from below her.

"Hi, Baby. Are your dollies ready for their nap?" Ida reached down and took the two-year-old in her arms.

"Mamie?"

"She is asleep. How about you and I lie down in Mama's bed."

Dodi's face brightened into a smile - the most beautiful thing Ida had seen all day.

***

ATTEND SESSION OF LUTHERAN SYNOD

Rev. H. J. Behrens and Mr. Charles Kirchman attended the convention of the Chicago synod of the Evangelical Lutheran church held in South Bend, Ind. The Chicago synod is connected with the General Council of the Evangelical Lutheran Church of America, which is the second largest Lutheran general body in America, having a communicant membership of nearly three quarters of a million and a baptized membership of over one million.

Grace Evangelical church of Woodstock is connected with the Chicago synod. The synod is composed of the pastors of the congregations and the lay delegates from each congregation. Mr. Charles Kirchman was the lay representative of the English Lutheran church of Woodstock.

The sessions of this convention were very interesting and showed progress in all branches of the church's activities. The parochial report showed that the communicant membership of the synod has increased one tenth. The synod co-operates in the support of a Lutheran mission in Porto Rico, and the missions at Rajahmundry, India. The synod is, however, exerting itself more especially in home missions by which is meant the ingathering of the unattached Lutherans and others from our own country, of which there are millions. All of the

I Will Fly to Woodstock 50

immigrants from Norway, Sweden, Denmark and Finland and most of them from Germany are Lutheran. It is a great task of the Lutheran church of America to furnish those people a church home and make out of them good citizens for our land.

At this convention of the Chicago synod, June 17-21, the Rev. H. J. Behrens was ordained to the holy ministry Sunday morning in Holy Trinity English Lutheran church of South Bend, Ind. by the president of the Chicago synod, the Rev. H. B. Reed.

Rev. Behrens received his classical training and two years of theology at Capitol university, Columbus, O., and spent two years at the Theological Seminary of the Evangelical Lutheran church in Chicago. His training has been in both English and German, and he is able to preach in the German language.

Grace English Lutheran church of Woodstock is his first parish and was organized by him last summer, while a student at Chicago. The congregation has grown rapidly and has prospects of continued growth and large influence.

Woodstock Sentinel, June 25, 1908.

***

"Mama! Mama! Mama!" came the cries from upstairs. Ka-Boom! Lightning flashes washed the walls and ceiling. Ka-Boom!

Ida rose and grabbed up her housecoat and nudged John as she left the room, "We need you, Papa!"

Flash, Ka-Boom! The lightning and thunder were almost simultaneous.

John rolled over and sat up. The storm must be right over the house. He grabbed up his robe and tried to shake off the sleep. He could hear crying coming louder as the children

I Will Fly to Woodstock

came down the stairs. He tied his robe and went to the bottom of the stairs in the kitchen to receive Helen and Mamie into his arms. Distraught, Dodi hid tight against her mother's bosom and screamed with each boom of thunder.

They went into the parlor and sat together on the davenport.

"There, there, don't be afraid," Ida cooed and rocked Dodi. "Papa and Mama are here, and we are all..." Ka-boom! Followed by a frantic scream from Dodi.

Ida looked at John with fear in her eyes also, "That was very close, Papa."

"It didn't hit us. We would have felt the shudder and smelled it."

Dodi sobbed. "W-w-what hit?" John held Ida's eyes and shrugged. Sorry.

Ida decided it was time for a story. "We were just wondering if the ice wagon hit our house."

"Da ice wagon?" Mamie never heard of the ice wagon hitting the house.

"Yes." Ida continued. "In the early, early morning before we are all awake, the iceman harnesses up his wagon and starts off out to the icehouse to get the chunks of ice to deliver. But sometimes when the rain is hard, the horse gets crazy and starts running fast through the slippery streets." By this time, she had all three girls and John hooked. They looked at her with interest. "The driver most often is thrown off the wagon or jumps off as the wagon careens through the streets." Ida gestured with her hands bouncing off the furniture.

"C-c-creams," sobbed Dodi.

"Yes, and the horse with the wagon going hither and thither behind it races through the streets." Ida motioned a circuitous route and worked a clap of thunder, much further away now, into her demonstration. "And, as it runs the wagon hits things like trees and houses and street light poles and makes a terrible noise."

Dodi hiccupped and looked skeptical. Ida hugged the little girl in her arms.

"The wagon is strong, and so are the houses and poles, but it sure makes a lot of noise with its high wheels and all the loose ice blocks slamming around. Eventually, the horses get tired and stop running, and then the driver gathers the reins and gets back up on the wagon and goes on his way. I think tonight is one of those nights." Ida finished, and Dodi nodded.

John, still looking at Ida with a slight smile, shifted in his seat. "I think the wagon has moved on to McHenry, so we can go back to sleep. What do you think?"

As they got up, John motioned that he was going to look around outside. Ida nodded.

"Can we have milk now, since the milkman might not make it in da morning?" asked Mamie.

"I think that is a great idea, Mamie! Milk will help us sleep." Ida herded the little ones into the kitchen. "Time for Midnight Milk."

"Midnight Milk." Helen, who had been stalwart throughout the experience, snickered.

"Midnight Milk!" Mamie and Dodi repeated in unison.

John went out on the front porch to look over the neighborhood. All was quiet on Lincoln Avenue in the light rain. But then he could hear some excitement up the hill toward Dane Street where Frank lived. In the now still night air, voices called out and hoofbeats of running horses sounded, but John saw no orange glow. He better phone just to make sure. He went back in and picked up the telephone earpiece and clicked the ear stanchion for the operator, but the girl did not respond. Dead. He hung up.

"I'm going to get some clothes on and go up to Frank's," he told Ida. She looked up with concern. "No glow, no smoke, just noise."

"No smoke?" Fear widened Dodi's eyes.

"Yes, go. We'll be fine, won't we, girls?"

"Papa?" Dodi's eyes brimmed with tears. The dam on the right eye burst and a single huge tear made its way down her ruddy cheek disappearing into her high-necked nightgown.

He knelt so he could look right into her bright blue eyes. "Now don't you worry about a thing. I'm just going to go check to make sure the horse and wagon didn't hit Uncle Frank's house, okay? You stay here and take care of your sisters and Mama. I'll be right back."

"O-tay." Another tear, on the left this time, slipped down Dodi's cheek. John wiped it away and headed for the bedroom.

John slipped under the covers.

"Everything alright?" asked Ida.

"Yeah. One of Frank's big trees got hit and fell across the street, but it missed all the houses. Had the whole neighborhood up. The tree took down some lines, so the city workers are there now."

"That was quite a storm." Ida ducked under John's arm. "Now that we are parents, we can't be afraid of storms anymore, can we?"

"We can be afraid, but we dasn't show it to the little ones."

"Good, because I was afraid. I'm glad it happened at night, so you were here with us." Ida cuddled into his arms. And they went back to sleep, comforted from the fierce reality of nature.

***

"Yoo-hoo! Anyone home?" Clara's voice drifted in through John and Ida's front porch screen door.

Helen called out, "Mama! It's An Clara!"

Ida stopped destringing green beans, took a deep breath, stood, and removed her apron. She could hear the girls enthusiastically greeting their aunt. Without hurry, Ida walked around to the foyer and looked out on the porch. Clara sat in

# I Will Fly to Woodstock

one of the wicker chairs with the girls in front of her. A slim man stood at the bottom of the steps, hat in hand. He was handsome, Ida had to admit.

"How good to see you girls. Look how you've grown," a radiant Clara held court. She glanced up, "Oh, Ida, there you are." Clara stood.

Ida came out onto the porch and greeted her sister, "Clara." They gave each other a quick peck on the cheek and stepped back. Clara motioned to Pearle. He came up onto the porch two steps at a time. He had plenty of wavy medium brown hair held in a very contemporary style with Macassar oil. With deep brown eyes, almost black, his darker complexion complemented Clara's lighter one. They made a striking couple. A city man, he dressed in the dapper fashion of the day complete with spats to keep his shoes clean while walking the dirty streets of their village.

"Ida, I would like you to meet my husband, Pearle Dye. Pearley, this is my sister Ida Wienke and my nieces, Helen, Mamie, and Dodi."

Pearle did a courtly bow. "How do you do?"

Ida curtsied and put out her hand. "I am fine, how are you?"

Pearle took it and squeezed slightly and then released her hand. "I am just great!"

They stood looking at each other for a long moment.

Pearle recovered his aplomb. "It is so good to meet you, Ida. Clara has told me so much about you and your home is beautiful and—"

"How do you do?" Mamie's small voice came from below.

Pearle turned to the girls. "Hello, Helen and Mamie." He bowed and clicked his heels. Mamie giggled.

"How do you do?" Helen curtsied, and Mamie followed suit.

He turned to Dodi. "Hello, Dodi." He bowed and again clicked his heels.

Dodi attempted a curtsy but lost her balance and fell to the deck. She quickly stood and tried again, with a bit more success. "Howdy do."

Ida had not taken her eyes from him as he interacted with her daughters. Now she said, "Girls, can you go in and pick up your toys? We'll be right in, and I want the parlor to look wonderful for our guests."

"Fine, Mama." Helen went over and held the screen door open.

"Okay." Mamie took Dodi by the hand and led her into the house.

"Ida," Clara began. "I—"

"No." Ida put up her hand and looked away. "Let me have my say before the girls get too curious." She brought her gaze back to take in both of them, "I, first, want to congratulate you on your marriage. I hope you'll be incredibly happy with each other for a very long time."

Clara smiled at Pearle, moved over to his side, and slipped her hand through his arm.

"But I am very disappointed with you, especially you, Clara!" Now she looked directly into Clara's eyes. "How could you do this to Mama? No engagement!" She looked at Pearle, "No asking for your girl's hand!" She looked back to Clara. "You didn't introduce him to Mama until the day of the wedding. What were you thinking?"

Clara glared at her and dropped Pearle's arm. "We weren't THINKING about anything, Ida. We are in love. Nothing Mama could have said, no amount of thinking, would have changed that."

Ida stared at her for a long minute. "Well...you hurt her mightily, and you will have to make amends. And now you move off to Missouri—"

"Iowa." Pearle corrected.

Ida shot him a look. "To do what?"

"I have a job with the electric company as a lineman waiting for me there, Ma'am, starting on July sixth."

Ida looked down at the floor and shook her head. "So that was the rush?"

"Yes," Clara and Pearle replied in unison.

"Nothing else?" Ida looked at them again, gauging their truthfulness.

"Oh no! You thought…no…we've only known each other for a month."

"A month."

"A month," Pearle agreed.

"Okay." Ida tried on a brief disingenuous smile. "You'll have the upstairs front bedroom. Helen will move in with Mamie. Clara, you know which one. Why don't you take your valises up and get settled in? Clara, when you are ready, I can use help in the kitchen fixing lunch. I am happy you have stopped on your way west."

Clara rushed to her sister and took her into a firm hug which Ida returned. Clara whispered into her ear, "Thank you."

Ida pushed back and looked at this girl who now was a woman and gave her as honest a smile as she could muster. "You're welcome."

***

John pushed back from the table. "Shall we adjourn to the porch for a cigar, Mr. Dye?"

Pearle followed suit. "Don't mind if I do, Mr. Wienke."

Clara wrapped her arm in his, unwilling to let him 'adjourn.' "Can I come too?" Her voice cooed. "I do love a good cigar."

Pearle looked at her quickly, seemed to discern that she was joking, and joined in. "I think not, young lady. You have duties in the kitchen. No cigar for you."

Clara pouted out her bottom lip. "Is that all you think of me? A scullery maid? I am going to have to re-educate you, kind sir."

"I'm looking forward to it."

"Whoze little ducky is zoo?" Clara's finger traced down Pearle's cheek.

"I'z your little ducky, my darling." And they kissed, which sent the little girls into a bout of giggling and lolling over on their chairs.

Ida's authoritative voice broke in. "Very well, then. To the porch with you both. We will go get lobster hands in the dishwater. Girls to the parlor. Time to put the dollies to bed."

Pearle smiled and slipped his arm out of Clara's grasp.

John had watched the exchange with some amusement, but now sobered and led the way through the parlor and out onto the porch. The summer sun was yet to set, and the evening was warm and lovely.

John offered a cigar and Pearle accepted. Both men bit off the end and spit it over the porch rail into the yard. John took out his match safe and struck a match. He held the light out to Pearle who puffed until the tip was glowing red. John shook out the match and dropped it over the rail. He struck a new match and lit his own cigar. They stood at the rail for a few minutes, puffing on the stogies to make sure they were well started, and then John turned and motioned Pearle to a seat.

"So, you are going to climb poles in Ohio?" John began.

"No, Iowa. I'm from Akron, but we are going to Denison, Iowa."

"Oh, sorry. I always get those two confused."

Pearle chuckled. "Four letters and all."

"Yes. I suppose. What do you know about Denison?"

"Mm," Pearle said as he drew in and blew out a smoke cloud toward the sky. "Not much, but the job seems legit. Putting up wires for the county. My training is in electrical current, and I'm a member of the IBEW. "

"Mm," John sucked and blew a plume. "I'm not familiar with that."

"International Brotherhood of Electrical Workers."

"Ah, a union."

"Yes. Are you anti-union?"

"No, not at all." John hoped he sounded genuine. "When they are needed. I've heard that pole work is dangerous."

"Only if you don't know what you are doing. It's all about knowing where you are and where the electricity is."

"My brother, William, is an electrician. He was our city engineer for many years. Worst that's happened to him was he lost his footing on his own basement stairs and broke his leg."

"Easy to do, but not something a pole climber wants to happen…losing one's footing, that is."

"No," John tapped the top of his cigar with his middle finger causing a large ash to drop from the tip. He nursed it until it was glowing red again.

They drew and blew for a few minutes.

Pearle broke the silence. "How is business in Woodstock?"

"Good. Woodstock has remained prosperous throughout the downturn."

"That's great. How was that accomplished?" Pearle seemed genuinely interested.

"We have one benefactor, the Oliver Typewriter Company. Oliver and now Emerson Typewriter have kept the town as close to one hundred percent employed as is possible in today's economy. In addition, we have had a building boom, and early investors in land in and around Woodstock have made money hand over fist. Anyone who wants to can live very well hereabouts without unions."

"And you are one of the lucky ones who has opened a store and is making a living at it?"

"Some would say."

"I would love to see your store. Maybe tomorrow?"

"Sure. I leave at about six in the morning. Can you handle that."

"Well....I...."

John laughed and then drew on his cigar.

Pearle collected himself. "Maybe Clara could bring me down later in the day?"

"Of course. Or Helen would love to bring you down. She is our most efficient worker right now."

"Helen?"

"Yes. She is ready to go to school, but too young so we are 'educating' her on our own. My part is taking her to work with me and teaching enterprise. Ida teaches her homemaking."

"Clever." He sucked in and blew out toward the street, and then looked at the cigar. "This is a very good cigar."

"Thank you. I purchase them at the ice cream parlor on the east side of the Square if you want to stock up tomorrow."

Pearle guffawed. "At the ice cream parlor?"

"Yes. Why? Isn't that where they sell cigars in Akron?"

"Not really." Pearle drew on his cigar and made a smoke ring. "I purchase my own at the Pickle Palace. I just have to be careful which I smoke: the green ones or the brown."

John chuckled. He liked this man - clever, sincere, seemingly a hard worker. Clara could have done much worse.

***

I Will Fly to Woodstock

July 2, 1908
365 Lincoln Avenue
Woodstock, Illinois

Dear Mama and Emma,

    Well, Clara and Pearle have come and gone. They stayed but only one night since they had to be in Iowa by the 6th. They showed up here yesterday at lunchtime and we put them back on the train for Iowa today at 1:00. If all goes well, they will be in Davenport by evening and will switch to a sleeper, arriving in Dennison early morning July 4th. I told them they were cutting it a little close with Pearle starting on the line on the 6th, but they only had eyes for each other.

    To see Clara so happy was heartening. She has been so depressed about not having a beau and now, quick as a wink, she has a husband. They were a bit much with their cooing especially the "Whoze litto ducky is zoo?" and "Iz zoo little ducky." The girls genuinely loved the visit and will be repeating those phrases for the next month. Mr. Dye was very polite and very handsome. Except for absconding with Clara off to the west, he seemed a perfect gentleman, and they seem well matched. Time will tell.

    I hope all is going well with you all there. I was glad to hear that Mama has come to stay with you on the farm for now. I want Mama to come down for a month in the fall or sooner if we can arrange it. I am certainly willing to split her staying between Mount Pleasant and Woodstock. We will need to talk it over.

    I suppose the house should be sold, as you said Emma. Has Mama agreed with that decision? She certainly cannot handle the house alone. Have you moved all the furnishings to the farm or are you going to sell them, too? If the latter, do not sell Mama's writing desk. I've always loved that little drop leaf front and the various drawers and cubby holes. Of course, the fact that it came to America with us will eventually make it an heirloom that I can pass on to one of the girls. Also, that little drop leaf table that I got her one Christmas a few years ago, don't sell it either. And of course, pictures. Don't throw out any

I Will Fly to Woodstock

pictures. *We can come and help with this process (or at least the girls and I can come) if you just set the date. I doubt Herman will want anything, but I suppose we should ask.*

That's all the report I have, and I want to send this with John at noon, so it makes the afternoon train to Racine.

Let me know what I can do.

Love to all,
Ida

***

"Ida! Bitte! Ich werde in Racine bleibe!" Louisa was emphatic.

Ida and Louisa sat across from each other at Ida's kitchen table. Ida had just broached the subject of Louisa moving to Woodstock to live with John and her, but Louisa was having none of it. She was going to stay in Racine. She was not going to move in with either of her daughters' families.

"Oh Mama, ich verstehen. I know; I understand. But with Mr. Stoffel gone now almost three years and with Clara gone to Iowa, what is in Racine for you?"

"Mr. Stoffel." Louisa sighed. "Ich vermisse ihn immer noch so sehr."

"I know. We all miss him. I'm sure that it has been hard to make ends meet without an inheritance."

"Ich habe ein Geheimnis," admitted Louisa.

"A secret?"

"Herr Stoffel hat mich etwas unter der Matratze gelassen. Ich bin nicht reich, aber mir geht es gut."

"He left you a little under the mattress? How much? Are you rich?"

"Keine Sorge. Ich habe meinem Kopf, meine Kirche, meine Freunde, meine Kunden, meine Leben in Racine."

"I do worry. Your customers? I understand your church, your friends and even your life, but your customers? Your hands are not up to doing sewing. Is that what you mean? Either Emma, Herman or I can give you a roof over your head. We can bring you back to visit your church and friends. I don't want you to feel that you must go back to sewing. How much did he put under the mattress?"

"You neva mind. Es ist nicht Ihr Geschäft."

"But Mama, your wellbeing is my business."

"Nein ist es nicht." No, it is not!

Ida looked down and closed her eyes. She could feel her heartbeat surging in her ears. Her blood pressure was high again, she supposed. She continued without looking up, "And how far will it get you?" Be calm. Think. She looked directly at her mother. "How long can you survive without income?"

Louisa looked away and responded quietly, "Weit genug. Ich bin alt. Ich werde bald sterben. De Einsparungen bleiben bis dahin bestehen Wenn nicht, kann ich einen Roomer wie Mr. Stoffel haben. Vielleicht einen neuen Ehemann finden." Far enough. I am old. I will die soon. The savings will last until then. If not, I can have a roomer like Mr. Stoffel. Maybe find a new husband.

"Don't say that!!! You aren't going to die soon." Ida put her face in her hands. Dropping them, she tried a calmer voice. "Getting a roomer isn't a bad idea, but it will be a lot of work, cooking and cleaning. And what if something goes wrong? What if you fall or are sick?"

"Ich melde mich!" Louisa raised her left hand to ear and with her right hand she circled as if she were contacting the hello-girl for a call.

"You'll call me." Ida paused, out of steam. "I don't want to fight. If that is what you want, so be it. You call me anytime, or Emma is even closer, and we'll be there sobald wir konnen - as soon as we can."

Louisa smiled and patted Ida's hand, "Youse gut girl."

I'm not so sure about that, Ida thought. 'As soon as we can' might be a whole day or even longer. If Louisa was laying on the floor with a stroke.... Ida felt her eyes well up. She took a deep breath. Better not to dwell on it. Louisa was an adult and should be able to make her own decisions, at least for now. If she started to go crazy as many of the elderly did, they would be forced to step in.

"Ich liebe dich, Ida." Louisa smiled.

"I love you, too, Mama."

***

July 11, 1908
The Prairie Hotel
Main Street
Denison, Iowa

Dear Ida, John and the little ones,
Here we are in Denison, a pretty little town with a town square much like Woodstock's, now that I think of it, except the courthouse is in the middle of the Square. Someone told me that the town was planned out and then people were invited to come. Isn't that what John said was true of Woodstock?
Denison has everything a person could want including two banks, three grocery shops, six mercantiles, a hardware store, a shoe shop, three drug stores, a bookstore, a library, and a music store! And about 3,000 people. The streets are wide, and the homes are all new, well, not all of them, but all are well-kept. We are staying at this hotel...one of five in Denison...until we can find rooms or a small house to rent. Denison is nice enough, I guess, but what happens when we run out of clothing which will happen any day find one.
Businesses here make most of what we need to live so I'm thinking that the need for importing much will be small, and what we do need will be brought in by train. Denison sits on two rivers and so this area is a bit hillier than the plains we traveled across from Chicago. We are surrounded by miles and miles...unending miles... of farmland on all sides. Pigs and cows seem to be most prevalent and wheat the major crop.

As for culture, the German influence is strong. The opera house is called the Germania Opera House and is owned by the Germania Society which I have already joined. It will allow me to keep up my German.

I'm not sure if Pearley has a liking for the shows at the Opera House, but I will take him anyway and to church. The church is a German Lutheran, of course, but some others are the Baptist, Methodist, Episcopal, Presbyterian, and Catholic. I will try the Lutheran and the Episcopal to see which is more to my liking. Pearle says he doesn't care which.

Oh Ida, we are so happy. Pearley's job is out in the open air, which he loves, and he is getting to know the county already. All the little towns are being electrified and so his crew puts up the lines to hook up one and then goes on to the next. Another crew comes in and hooks up the individual houses. When he gets home at night, right around dark, we go down and have supper in the dining hall, and then we cuddle and coo until we are asleep. As the days grow shorter and we get our own lodging, we will do more than eat and sleep, but it has been a very nice 'honeymoon' at the Prairie Hotel. Pearle said we would start looking for permanent lodging tomorrow since it is Sunday.

This letter is getting long, and I'll have to pay more to send it if I'm not careful, but I have so much to tell you. I will write again soon and let you know what else I have discovered about Denison.

What have you heard from Mama? I haven't had a letter yet, although I have written. Will she come live with you or with Emma? Herman? Wouldn't that be something? Mama and Bessie sharing a household. Ha!

Love to all of you,
Clara and Pearle

***

"Ida, hurry up. We'll miss the ride." John called in through the screen door from the front porch.

"You and the girls start walking. I'll catch up. If I don't, hold the rack for me," Ida called back.

"Fine. Come on, chickens." Dodi and Mamie giggled.

"Papa, we aren't chickens." Helen was adamant.

"Well, what are you then?" John's voice was full of teasing.

The voices faded as the four started down Lincoln Avenue. Ida packed the fried chicken in the picnic hamper and added tin plates to cover Ma's recipe German potato salad and Lena's recipe bean salad, then finished by tucking in a jar of Mamie's favorite bread and butter pickles. John was carrying another basket with two jars of lemonade, a fresh raspberry Kuchen, tin cups and cutlery. All the food was to share with the other families at the picnic. Ida loved potluck dinners, a time to taste and test new food on the children. She always came away with two or three new recipes for her box.

Ida closed the double lid and hefted the hamper. Not too bad. She could manage it. As she passed through the parlor, she gathered the red plaid woven picnic robe from a chair and put it in the basket. It would be exactly right for the five of them to sit on while they ate. Ida stood thinking for a moment about what she might have forgotten and then plucked up her bonnet letting the screen door slam behind her. Ida bustled down the steps and onto the wooden walkway which ran along Lincoln Avenue. Her high button black and white boots with an inch heel clicked on the wood in a very satisfactory way as she fast walked after her family.

As she turned the corner from Lincoln onto Throop Street, she could see John and the girls turning onto Washington a block away. She hurried after them and arrived in front of the church on Washington Street just as John lifted Dodi up onto a hayrack, a flatbed wagon with a four-foot-tall gate along its backside. A large hand-painted sign spanned the back: "Grace Lutheran Sunday School Picnic."

"John." Ida came up behind him.

"Oh good! Let me have that." He put the hamper up onto the bed of the wagon, next to the one he had carried, and turned back to her, put his hands on her waist, and easily lifted her up so she was seated on the side. As daintily as possible, she curled up her legs into a kneeling position and then stood up. Mamie and Dodi were seated on a mound of hay near the back gate. She went to join them pulling the baskets in close to make room for other people. "Where's Helen?"

Mamie made an exaggerated shrug, shoulders to her ears, palms to the heavens. Dodi looked innocently at her mother and said, "All gone."

Ida looked at them. What were they hiding? "What do you mean, all gone?"

Mamie cocked her thumb at the second hayrack as if to say, "She went thataway!" The second wagon was full of people sitting in the hay and cross-legged on the bed, and many legs dangled over the three open sides. Several men stood with their backs leaning on the back gate. A good deal of chatter emanated from that direction.

Ida stood and called out to John, who was standing nearby talking to Frank.

"John? Can you go check on Helen? Mamie thinks she's on the other rack."

John looked over at the top-heavy wagon. He and Frank walked over and scanned the crowd.

"I don't see her, do you?" he asked Frank.

"No."

"Helen?" John added his voice to the cacophony.

No answer emerged.

They walked up the row of vehicles, all horse drawn and saw nothing. They retraced their steps scanning the church and grounds.

A horse snorted and whinnied.

"Let's get this show on the road," someone called out, and a cheer went up.

John turned toward the hay wagons and took a deep breath, swallowing down anger and maybe a little fear.

"Helen? Helen Wienke?" John's voice was loud enough for the whole congregation to hear.

The crowd quieted. A clutch of little girls on the second rack pulled back, and Helen stood up. Ida had laid out a yellow gingham knee-length frock that morning to go with the yellow handmade bonnet with crocheted daisies over the right ear. Ida couldn't see Helen well from her vantage point, but she could imagine her serious little face under the brim of the bonnet.

"Yes, Papa? Helen's blue eyes looked directly at him with no apparent shame at being called to center stage.

"Come here."

Helen looked around at the sea of faces including her friends, but she didn't move.

"Helen, come here...please." John restated.

Helen stood her ground.

"I need to talk to you for a moment." John tried a gentler tone.

"I want to ride with my friends."

A horse and buggy went past the church, hoofs clapping, harness jangling.

John frowned. He looked at the ground and then back at Helen.

"Okay. That will be fine." He looked at the adults, most of whom were smiling knowingly. "Will someone take responsibility for my willful daughter?"

Mrs. Kirchman elbowed her husband. Mr. Kirchman stood. "We'll keep track of 'er."

"Thank you, Mr. Kirchman." John's eyes went back to Helen for a moment. "We will talk about this later."

Her eyes could no longer hold his, and she looked away.

John moved away as conversation resumed.

Ida had heard every word from her seat on the first hayrack. She smiled. At that moment, she loved her husband so much. He had become a fine father.

***

The processional lurched into motion. The horses strained at their bits. Ida settled her back against the gate with Mamie on one side and Dodi on the other. All three had bonnets that matched Helen's in style, but not in color. Mamie's bonnet was a light pink with a crocheted wild pink rose on the right. Mamie would have preferred red, but she had so much in red, and pink was a good color this time of year in her mother's opinion. Ida's bonnet was light green with an orange daylily – a ubiquitous flower, but one of Ida's favorites. Dodi's bonnet was light blue with a blue chrysanthemum over the ear. Ida had thought that the mum would be an easy addition, but it had turned out to be the most difficult of flowers to crochet.

The trip to Hannaford's Grove was bumpy, especially after the wagons turned onto the lane taking them from the graveled road to the picnic spot. Holding on to the gate as it jolted from side to side was challenging. Ida had centered herself so she and the girls would be less likely to be thrown off and her ploy worked. On the other hayrack, several young men lost their footing, falling to the thick growth of hay on either side of the wagon as it passed down the track. They leapt up laughing and ran alongside the rest of the way into the grove of oak trees.

Ida wondered where John was riding as he had not come to join them. She screwed her body around to look back. Ida could see several other conveyances turning into the dirt track behind them: A fat black pony pulled a red cart with wooden wheels with three children on board; a fancy pink hard-topped carriage pulled by two white horses straight from Cinderella; an old-fashioned Irish jaunting car with ladies' seats on each side facing outward while the driver faced forward on the front bench; and last was the fire wagon from Oliver Typewriter pulled by two spotted horses. At the reins was Frank Wienke, and she recognized her dear husband who was acting as the brakeman.

As the parade rolled to a stop, Ida saw plank tables set up on sawhorses waiting for the potluck lunch to be laid out. She hoped John would come to collect her since she was quite sure she would not be able to carry both baskets. She made her way to the edge of the wagon bed as others bounded off and up the knoll to the clearing. She looked down. The hay field was waist deep with lush foliage. She looked at the girls. They were going to disappear when lifted to the ground. She looked around. Where was John? Ida sat down on the edge trying to keep her skirt from riding up her calves. She slipped down over the side and felt her ankle give way with a sharp pain in the heel that brought tears to her eyes. She fell sideways into the grass disappearing from the view of the children.

Mamie rushed to the side in a panic, "Mama!"

Behind Mamie, Dodi took a great gasp of breath, tears filled her blue eyes. "Mama!" she screamed; the word caught in a sob. The scream brought a hush over the activities for a moment.

"I'm alright," she called up to the girls working for a cheerful lilt to her voice. Still sitting in the tall grass, a grimacing Ida separated it so she could see the terrified faces looking at her over the edge. "It's okay. Don't worry. I just turned my ankle." At that moment she felt strong hands grasp her under her arms and pull her to her feet.

"Are you alright? I saw you fall."

"Oh John, there you are. I turned my ankle when I slid off into the grass. It'll be fine."

"Okay. Don't cry, Dodi. Mama's fine. Come here." Dodi came to the edge and walked off into John's arms. "I'll be right back." He grabbed up the heavier basket and hurried off.

Ida turned her foot to assess the damage. A sharp pain made her breath catch. She continued to circle it until the pain eased a little. Not too bad. She'd walk it off. John came back and took Mamie in one arm. He reached up and brought down the food basket. "Can you manage?"

"Yes," answered Ida quickly with a smile.

He led the way up the hill toward the tables. Ida took a step. Her ankle, bound as it was in her high boot, held, but the pain was intense. She gathered her skirt in one hand and took another step. Better. She limped slowly out of the weeds and up the rise to the closest table.

"Mrs. Wienke," Mrs. Kirchman called out to her. "Are you hurt? Here, sit down on this stool."

"No, no. I just turned my ankle getting off the hayrack." But she sat.

"Oh, my goodness. We'll find a way to send you home." Mrs. Readel turned in a circle to look for help.

"No need." Ida stopped her. "I'll restrain myself from the afternoon races and all will be well."

Mrs. Readel chuckled. "Which are your baskets?"

"Those two right there. Mrs. Kirchman, thank you for helping with Helen's plight."

"I think she learnt her lesson, don't you Mrs. Readel?" Mrs. Kirchman replied.

"Yes, I'm sure she will be sayin' sorry at prayers tonight."

"The thing is," Ida leaned forward, "we would have agreed that she ride with her friends. The problem was that she disappeared without permission, and she must not do that."

"I thought as much," said Mrs. Readel. "Are ya feeling well enough to help unpack your baskets?"

"Of course." Ida stood on one foot, lifted the food basket to table, and began the task of laying out the fare. She pulled out the two boxes of fried chicken and placed them with the sandwiches that most women had brought. The chicken was still warm, and the odor wafted to the other helpers.

"Mm. Smells so good." Mrs. Readel sniffed the air and smiled at Ida. "Good to have a butcher's wife in our midst."

Ida smiled and pulled out the two salads and the pickles and limped along the table to where the 'dishes to pass' were spread out. She added the bowls with the impressive display of various potato salads, slaw, pickles, cold beans and kraut. Limping back to the baskets, she lifted the second basket to the tabletop and removed the Kuchen. Moving gingerly to the dessert table, she dropped off the cake. And then leaned gently on the side of the table, careful not to upset the apple cart.

Her foot and ankle throbbed, and she felt a little nauseated. She was sure that the tight shoe was holding in the swelling. She needed to keep it moving so that the pain didn't get worse or, alternatively, get off it for the duration. Once she sat, she'd probably be down until the party was over. She removed the blanket from the basket and looked across the side of the knoll for a place where they could sit and eat. She picked a spot close-by the tables, near the trunk of an oak tree, peg-legged over to it, and spread the blanket. She went back to the tables and gathered the nearly empty baskets and carried them back to where the picnic robe was spread.

"Mrs. Readel," Ida called over to the woman busily arranging platters and bowls. Mrs. Readel looked up. She limped a few steps toward the woman. "Do you have some work I can do while standing still or maybe sitting?"

"Oh, Mrs. Wienke, you don't have to do anything. You go sit down. If'n I can find something ya can do while a-sittin', I will bring it to you."

"Oh, Mrs. Readel, thank you so much. I'm sorry to be so clumsy. I slid off the rack and next thing I knew I was on the ground."

"You go rest. We have ice for the ice cream. I'm sure we can spare a little."

"That would be wonderful. But please, bring me a task so I don't feel completely useless."

Mrs. Readel smiled warmly and nodded.

Ida cautiously slid down onto the picnic robe. She tucked her feet back under her and closed her eyes, willing the pain away.

"Here ya go." Mrs. Readel stood over her, her face wreathed in sunlight. In one of her hands was a large butcher knife and in the other were twos cloth bag. "Rolls. Kin ya cut the rolls?"

"I can do that!" Ida reached for the knife and bags.

"T'other bag's the ice."

"Wonderful! Thank you so much." Ida took the ice and put it against her boot. It would make the ankle a little cooler maybe, but she wasn't going to take off the boot until she got hom. Ida wondering distractedly what had happened to John. She would need him or several strong men to help her get up after the festivities. No doubt he would find her when the food was served.

In the meantime, John had taken the girls to the playing field. Some men and older children played a game of 100 in the open field. All but the pitcher and batter became outfielders. A caught fly ball counted twenty points and a successfully grounded ball counted ten points. First one to one hundred got to be the batter. John stopped to watch for a few minutes, but then Dodi pulled on his pant leg.

"Weddy, set, go!!" she called out and ran away from him. John took off after her, quickly scooping her up with much squealing and giggling. The two girls and John made their way to the other side of the clearing. Races would be held after lunch with prizes, and several men were pacing off fifty yards. They ended up approximately at the same place, turned, shook hands, and planted a flag at the finish line. They reversed their course taking twenty-five paces and planted a second flag at the halfway point. John's little girls were not old enough for the formal races to be held later. Girls had to be six years old to participate.

I Will Fly to Woodstock

"Shall we do a race?" John suggested.

"Yes, yes, yes!" The girls jumped up and down and danced around.

"Let's go round up your friends." They made their way back to where families had begun to spread out their picnic blankets. John smiled and waved at Ida. She waved back. Then as loud as he could muster, John called out, "Any little ones who would like to do a twenty-five-yard dash come with us." A hush fell over the crowd and then a squealing cheer rose in intensity as the little folk began endorsing the idea.

He turned, and holding his girls by the hands, he acted as Pied Piper going back down to the field. Once there, he knelt and looked Dodi in the eye. "Do you think you can start them off?"

"Yes, Papa. Weddy, set, go!" she replied, a skill she had learned from Mamie.

By that time, the tiny throng had caught up with them accompanied by a few parents. He sent one mom and one dad down to the finish line, halfway down the course, to act as judges, and then turned to those gathered. He looked over the participants.

"Okay. Let's start with the older children so the younger ones can see how it's done. How many of you are five years old?"

Two boys and three girls raised their hands.

"Here we go then. Line up at the start line and our starter, Dodi will say—"

"Weddy, set, go!" Dodi blurted out.

"Not yet!" The experienced Mamie corrected. "When Papa tells you."

Dodi looked chagrined. "Okay."

John smiled. "When you hear 'go' you run down the field to where Mr. Foote and Mrs. Friedberg are standing. First one there wins." The participants nodded and got ready to run.

John nodded to Dodi.

"Weddyyy. Setttt. Go!" drawing out the first two words dramatically.

They took off down the field with a blond-haired boy crossing the finish line first. The small crowd of small people went wild.

"Well done!" called out Frank Foote. "Give him an extra piece of cake!"

John laughed and called, "Four-year-olds." A boy, four girls, and Mamie went to the line.

"Weddysetgo!" Dodi fell over laughing as the six dashed down the field. Mamie held her own for the first half of the race, but then fell behind. This time a red-headed girl won.

"Another piece of cake!!" Mr. Foote called out.

"Three-year-olds."

Three little girls were coaxed to the line.

"Me too!" Dodi insisted.

"You are only two," Mamie reminded her sister.

Dodi's eyes welled up. Mamie shook her head and looked away.

John looked around. "Any two-year-olds want to run?" No one answered.

"Okay, Dodi, you run in this race, and I'll start it!"

The four little ones took their places.

"Ready!" John called out. "On your mark! Get set!"

Dodi turned to him, hands on hips, "Papa! You do it wight."

"Oh sorry. Okay. Get on your mark. Get yourself ready. Get set—"

The four took off.

"Go," John called after them.

They ran together with Dodi almost in the lead, but then she collapsed just before the finish line and the other little girls followed suit. They fell into a giggling pile.

"Pieces of cake for all!!" shouted Mr. Foote. The crowd of little ones cheered the mere idea of cake.

Mamie stuck her hands out to her sides and called out, "Let's fly!" She ran up and down the slope, and soon a dozen 'aeroplanes' flew in joyful circles in Hannaford's Grove.

A dinner bell rang out. Helen stood up the hill near the tables with a large triangle dangling from her left hand while her right hand moved the striker around side to side to side. The sound was very pleasant, and it set John's stomach to growling.

"Come on! I'll race you up the hill." He ran, but the children quickly outpaced him, and he reached the top out of breath.

Helen, still ringing the bell, stood near the area staked out by Ida for their picnic.

"Goodness, John," Ida greeted him. "Aren't you too old for running up hills?"

He leaned with one outstretched arm against the tree and slowed his breathing. "The slope was steeper than it seemed."

Ida smiled. The ringing stopped. Pastor Behrens stepped forward and said grace. John noticed that Ida did not rise for grace. After the Amen, he came over and crouched down beside her. "Your foot?"

"Yes. Can you make me a plate? I'm afraid I will be staying right here the rest of the afternoon. The ladies gave me some ice."

"Do you want me to take you home?"

"Heaven's no! How embarrassing that would be."

"Do you want me to take off your shoe?"

"I'm afraid I'd never get it back on and—"

"Mama?" Mamie stood looking down at her mother. "What if I have to go potty?"

"I'll take her." John jumped in. "We'll be right back."

***

The whole group watched and participated in the afternoon races, except Ida. She instead took several turns cranking the ice cream paddles.

The results of the contests were posted in *The Sentinel* the following week (August 6, 1908).

> Prizes were awarded as follows:
> Boys over 10 years, 50 yards – Emery Kirchman.
> Boys between 6 and 10 years, 50 yards – Frank Bachhaus.
> Boys under 6, 50 yards – Russel Friedberg, Clarence Readel.
> Girls over 10 years, 50 yards – Alta Kirchman.
> Girls between 6 and 10 years, 50 yards – Grace Kirchman.
> Fat ladies' race, 25 yards – Mrs. Charles Bachhaus.
> Lean ladies' race, 50 yards – Mrs. Frank Foote.
> Medium ladies' race, 50 yards – Emma Handel
> Booby prize – Mrs. H. J. Behrens.

The booby prize was a wooden spoon with the phrase 'Last in the race, but first in our hearts' burned along its length. It was given to one of the last place runners. A red-faced Mrs. Behrens accepted it and held it up for all to see. Ida noticed when the cheering stopped, Mrs. Behrens' smile quickly fell from her full face as she looked down at the utilitarian tool. What was she thinking? One of the ladies walked by and congratulated her, and a flash of what might have been anger crossed her plump young face before a smile lit it. Maybe no one had explained what an honor it was to get the booby prize. It was all in playful fun. Ida tried to put herself in Mrs. Behrens' place. It was difficult. The butcher's wife was supposed to be fat. Maybe the minister's wife wasn't?

Helen ran and lost in the six-and-above-girls race even though she was only five. The field had left her behind in a

I Will Fly to Woodstock 77

hurry, but she had run through to the end and celebrated her friend Grace's first-place victory with enthusiasm.

When everyone came back up the hill, they had a choice of vanilla, chocolate, or strawberry ice cream. Dodi chose chocolate, and Mamie chose strawberry. Helen and Grace Kirchman sat by a big oak tree and shared a bowl with all three flavors. Ida brought a spoonful of the dessert to her mouth. The cream of the frozen liquid was sweet and cold. A piece of fresh strawberry melted from the rest and Ida was taken back to the wild strawberries gathered in the spring. Such a treat on a summer day.

Her ankle throbbed. She wondered if she would be able to stand on it. She would put it in a pan of icy water and Epsom salts when she got home.

John sat near-by playing twenty questions with a group of little girls. They certainly seemed to flock to him. Maybe routinely dealing with three made entertaining six just that much easier. Ida caught his eye and smiled. He smiled and tipped his bowler hat in her direction.

After they had lapped up the last of the ice cream, the whole entourage packed up, climbed back aboard the carts, onto the hayracks and into the carriages, and headed back to Woodstock. John arranged that he, Ida, and the children, yes, Helen also, would ride back in the pink princess carriage and be dropped off at 365 Lincoln Avenue to save Ida's injured limb. He had ceremoniously picked her up and carried her to the carriage through a cheering crowd and then doffed his hat with a deep bow, much to everyone's delight. By the time the coach pulled up to drop them off, Dodi was asleep in Ida's arms, and Mamie was dozing against John's shoulder.

John woke Mamie who yawned and then stretched. "Did we fly away to Woodstock?"

John smiled. "Yes, we did, my girl. Yes, we did."

John stepped out and took Dodi from Ida's arms.

"Helen, Mamie, help your mother down and make sure she doesn't fall."

On cue, the driver, Frank Foote, swung down from the seat and offered Ida his hand. She stepped out on her good foot, but then winced as she stepped on the damaged one. Frank quickly grabbed her arm and supported her as she stepped up onto the boardwalk and walked up to the porch steps.

"Thank you, Mr. Foote."

He tipped his hat, "Mrs. Wienke. I wish you good night."

Helen and Mamie dragged the baskets up the walk as John emerged from the house. "Well done my little chickens!"

"Papa." A listless Helen. "We aren't chickens."

John scooped up Ida, carried her up the steps, across the porch, deposited her in the parlor on the davenport. Then he rushed back out, grabbed up a basket in each hand and ushered the girls up the steps and into the house. Setting down the baskets, John turned and firmly shut the outer door. The whole house seemed to give a sigh of relief.

***

Inside, Helen went directly upstairs without a word. John looked up after her. He said to Ida. "Dodi is asleep on our bed. I will go talk to Helen for a moment, and then I must go down to the store for a while. Take off your shoe, and we'll see what the damage is when I come back down."

"Oh my, I had forgotten about the store."

John looked aghast. "Forgotten about the store? Ida, how could you?" He laid the back of his hand against his forehead as if to faint from the shock. And then they both chuckled. "I'll be right back."

"John." Ida's voice stopped his momentum just for a moment. "Be kind to her."

John nodded.

Ida unbuttoned the high shoe and slipped it off with a good deal of difficulty. The ankle was swollen and coloring ominously. She sighed. This was going to make things difficult for a few days. She put a sofa pillow on the coffee table and put her foot up on the pillow.

Mamie climbed up beside Ida and leaned on her shoulder. "Mama, does your foot hurt awfully?"

Ida looked at the pale, dusty, exhausted girl. "No sweetie, it just hurts a little. But how do you feel?"

"Tired. Can I just sleep here?"

Ida put her arm around her middle daughter, "For a little while."

"Okay. Just for a little while." Mamie's eyes closed.

***

Ida looked down at her ankle. "Well, this is a fine kettle of fish."

Two days after the accident, the foot was swollen and black and blue, and it still throbbed near the heel. She was sitting at the kitchen table with her foot up on a chair. John had made his own breakfast, a Braunschweiger sandwich, before leaving for the store.

The day before, John had taken Helen and Mamie to church, while Ida had stayed home like an invalid with Dodi. Dodi had been such a good girl. They do seem to know when something is wrong, Ida mused. What am I to do?

The phone rang. She went to stand and slowly limped to the phone. It stopped ringing. She sunk down onto the stairs below it. John had been so clever to put stairs up from both the front foyer and from the kitchen. They met at the middle and then made a ninety degree turn to continue to the upper floor together.

The phone began ringing. She stood on one foot and clasped the earphone to her ear. She could listen sitting down, but she'd have to stand to talk. "Hello?"

"Ida?" John's voice was in her ear.

"Who else would it be?"

"You didn't answer the first time. I was concerned."

"My giddyap is a little slow this morning."

"Yes. That's what I wanted to talk to you about."

"Ok, talk away."

John paused. "Are you okay?"

"John." Ida rubbed her forehead. "I'm standing on the steps, on one foot with no idea how I'm going to feed my children. Please don't ask if I'm okay."

"Okay, but are you—"

"JOHN! Tell me what you want to tell me so I can go sit down."

"Okay, sorry. I want to get you some help for the next week or so. Any ideas?"

Ida looked at the earpiece, shook her head and sighed.

"Ida?" Ida heard the tiny John voice coming out of the speaker. She put the piece back to her ear.

"Well, I suppose, first, you should call Dr. Windmueller and have him drop by to see if my ankle is broken. If so, we will have to regroup. If not, maybe he can at least wrap it or something. Can you do that?"

"Yes, I should have thought of that."

Ida rolled her eyes. "While you are doing that, I'll try to think of someone who would be willing to come and help for a few days, and don't you dare suggest, Bessie."

"No, why not?"

"Just because. I'm thinking maybe one of your sisters-in-law. They have been able to spare a bit of time in the past."

"Ok, I'll get right on it. Helen should be able to help with breakfast."

"We'll just do oatmeal. Easy, and she has made it before. But tonight—"

"Don't worry I'll bring home food from the diner for tonight."

"Great. Now I must go put my throbbing foot up. Tell Dr. Windmueller to just come in. The girls will greet him. I'll be in the parlor with my foot on the coffee table."

"OK. We've got a plan." John sounded pleased.

***

She hobbled back to the table and put her foot up on the chair. Mamie poked her head around from upstairs.

"Mama? Is your uncle all better?"

"No, sweetie. My *ankle* is worse, I think. Can you do something for me?" Ida emphasized 'ankle' but smiled at the child's mistake.

"Yes."

"Go see if Helen is awake, and if she is, ask her nicely to come downstairs. I need her help, or we'll all starve."

Mamie's eyes got big, and she backed away and ran up the stairs calling out "Helen! Helen!"

"Nicely!" Ida called after her.

In a few minutes all three girls were in the kitchen, each with a job. Helen was taking care of the cooking, while Mamie put bowls and accoutrements on the table with Dodi's help. Mamie poured brown sugar into a bowl and onto the painted-wood countertop. Dodi carried cups, bowls and silverware to the table one at a time. Ida stood on one foot to reach the things that were too high for the little girls, but it seemed to be going well so far. Dodi dropped a spoon, and it skittered across the linoleum and under the cupboard.

"Oh, oh." Mamie stooped to look under the cabinet. "You can reach it, Dodi."

Dodi's reluctant hand slid under and came out triumphant.

"Hoorah!" Ida clapped. Dodi jumped up and started clapping also and dropped the spoon again. It slid away again under the cupboard.

"Oh, no!" Ida's hand went to her forehead.

"I get it." Dodi leaned down low and in one swoop snatched it up and held it as high as her little arm could stretch.

"Just put that one in the sink, okay?" Ida suggested.

Helen stood at the stove stirring the oatmeal. She stood on tiptoe to peer over the edge into the mushy contents. "It's getting thick, Mama."

"Good."

"It's sticking to the spoon bad," Helen added.

"It must be ready. Stop stirring and bring the pot to the table. Put it here on this potholder. Okay. Can you get the bottle of milk from the icebox, Helen?"

Helen came back with the quart glass bottle half full of milk. Ida stirred the oatmeal a few times and then split it into four bowls. To each portion she added two tablespoons of brown sugar and a splash of milk.

"I want more milk," said Helen.

"I wan milk," said Dodi.

"Please?" Ida suggested.

"Please, may I have more milk?" Helen complied.

"Peas, milk?" Dodi followed suit.

Good training. Ida doled out the bowls and the four of them settled down to fill their tummies.

After a few minutes of silence, Helen spoke up, "Will I have to make lunch and supper, too?"

"Papa is bringing home supper, and we'll make sandwiches for lunch."

"Papa gets supper?" asked Dodi.

"Yes. From the diner."

"Oh, Mama, can I walk down and help him? He will need help carrying it." Helen always tried to be a grown-up.

"Me too!" said Dodi.

"No, I think not. You girls are too little to be going alone."

"Dodi's little, but I'm not," Helen pouted.

"Dodi's not little," said little Dodi.

Mamie was sitting staring at her bowl, holding her spoon over the surface of the milk pond.

"Mamie, what's wrong?" Ida asked.

As if she had been awakened from a stupor, Mamie looked up, blinking. Her eyes had that glassy look they got when she had a fever.

"Are you feeling okay, sweetie?"

Mamie shook her head. Helen hopped off her chair and put her wrist against Mamie's forehead the way she had seen her mother do.

"She's hot."

"Come here, Mamie." Ida held out her hands.

Mamie got down and came around to Ida and climbed up in her lap. Ida felt her head. Helen was right.

Helen settled herself on her chair and took another bite of her porridge. She made a face and reached over and added brown sugar. "Mama, when can we go school shopping? You know the first day of school is coming up fast now that the summer is almost over."

"School shopping?"

"Remember. You said that you and I could go buy some clothes and other things, so I'd be ready when school started. School starts exactly twenty-five days from today. Do you know what we must get? I would like at least three new frocks and new shoes and...."

Ida let Helen go on while she tried to decide what to do. Mamie needed to be cooled down and her foot needed cold also. Maybe a tub of cold water with ice in it for both of them. Dr. Windmueller was coming today so he could look at both the foot and the fever, so that was good.

"...and so, we must go, soon, Mama. Mama, are you listening?"

"Yes, Helen. We will go soon. Thank you for reminding me. But first Mamie and I have to go take a cool bath. Would you like that, Mamie?"

"Mama, I don't like dis oatum that Helen make," said Dodi. "Be s'cused?"

"You may be excused, but first you need to take your bowl and spoon over and put them in the sink. That's right. Thank you. Now you can go play."

"In my jammies?" asked Dodi.

"Yes, it will be fine for today."

"Yippee!" Dodi ran from the room and turned toward the parlor and her toys.

"Do I have to do the dishes?" asked Helen.

"No, we'll leave those for your father."

Helen giggled.

"Can you go get your book and sit in the parlor with Dodi while Mamie and—"

"Oh, Mama, I hate doing that!"

"Just this once, under these special circumstances. You did a great job with breakfast. For a little while, I may need to count on you to help like that."

"Okay." But Helen didn't sound okay.

"Thank you, Helen."

Helen climbed the stairs to get a book.

"And now for us."

"Mama, how long is twenty-five days?" asked Mamie.

"Don't you worry about that now. Let's just get you cooled down. Are you afraid you'll miss Helen?"

"No. I'm not afraid. It will be quieter then."

"Yes, it will be."

***

Dr. Windmueller arrived in midafternoon during nap time. Ida answered his soft knock with "Come in," which was easily heard through the screen door, but didn't rise to greet him. She was seated on the couch with her foot up on the coffee table.

The doctor removed his hat. "What happened here?"

"Before we talk about that, can you go to the back bedroom and see Mamie? She and Dodi are napping on our bed. She's hot again and seems a little lethargic. If she wakes up, she'll probably just go back to sleep. If you need me, I'll come."

"No, no. I can find her." He disappeared for a few moments and then returned to sit in John's chair.

"Yes, she is infected again. But her fever doesn't seem that bad. You must be giving the Bayer powder."

"Yes, that and letting her sleep as much as she wants."

Now, he manipulated her foot, feeling the joint with his fingers, watching for a flinch from Ida. Then he went to the heel area and pressed into the back of the ankle. Ida drew in her breath quickly, and her foot jumped trying to escape.

"Hang on. I need to feel the damage." He gently began to probe again.

"Yes, that hurts. What's back there?"

The doctor didn't answer but put her foot back on the pillow on the coffee table and rose to retrieve a chair from the dining room.

"Here, let me help you up." Dr. Windmueller took her hands and pulled her up on her good foot. "Can you kneel on this chair?"

Ida knelt.

Through her dress, the doctor squeezed her calf and her foot flexed.

"Ouch!" Ida's head snapped to him. "That hurt!"

"Yes, I'm sorry, but it tells me a lot. The tendon that runs from your sole to your calf feels like you have torn it. But this test proves that you didn't sever it. Did you hear a pop when you fell?"

"No. No pop. Will I be able to walk again?"

"Can you walk now?" He helped her back to the davenport and put her foot back up.

"Barely. Okay, yes, I can, but it hurts…a lot." Ida did not look at him. She adjusted the pillow.

"You will be able to walk. Have you been doing the stairs?"

"No. That hurts too much."

"That's because you have to push off with your toes to go up the stairs. It will be a while before stairs or standing on tiptoe stop hurting, but they will."

Ida looked up with tear-filled eyes. "I can't carry my baby. I can't stand to make a meal. I can barely walk between the couch, table, and bed. What am I going to do?" Ida pulled her ubiquitous handkerchief out of her sleeve and dabbed at her eyes. "How can I run a household with this lame foot?"

"You are going to keep on doing what you can and that will gradually increase." He patted her hand. "The ankle isn't broken, but sprained, but most of the pain seems to be coming from the torn tendon. I will wrap the whole ankle to stabilize it for a week and prescribe laudanum to sleep. You can also take the Bayer powder along with Mamie for some pain relief during the day. You'll get twice as much powder as compared to her."

Ida nodded.

"So where to start?" Dr. Windmueller reached for his bag and began unpacking rolls of wrapping.

"So, I'll be able to climb the stairs?"

"Not at first, I'm afraid. It will take several weeks, maybe even a month or more to heal, and I don't want you to aggravate it by doing too much right at the beginning. No stairs, no tiptoes, slow walking, no running."

Ida nodded and wiped her eyes again.

"With just a little extra help over this next week or two, you should improve slowly. You'll have a limp for a time and using a cane when you go out would be smart, so you don't fall again."

"Thank you, doctor." Ida quickly wiped her eyes and blew her nose.

"That is quite alright." The doctor smiled. "Now let's make you feel better."

***

ENGLISH LUTHERAN
There will be services at the English Lutheran church next Sunday evening at 7:30 p.m. Sunday school will be held at 12 a.m. Everybody is welcome.
Woodstock Sentinel, July 30, 1908.

GERMAN LUTHERAN
Confessional service, 10 a.m. Regular morning service and communion, 10:30 a.m.
Woodstock Sentinel, July 30, 1908.

***

"What the heck!" John couldn't believe what he was seeing.

"Papa, the children's ears!" Ida rose and limped to the sink beginning to prepare the wash water for evening dishes. She could just about make it through the process now without stopping to rest.

"Yes, our little ears." Helen put her hands over her ears. Mamie did the same. Dodi was a little slow on the uptake, not knowing why she was covering her ears, but she followed her big sisters' lead.

"Sorry." John smiled at his three monkeys all avoiding evil. Then he turned his attention to Ida. "Why can the German Lutheran church hold services in the morning, and we cannot? I am so tired of not knowing when the service will be or even if we'll have a service. Looks like the good pastor is in town this week unlike the past few. How can we grow a church when the pastor is missing half the time and we don't meet at the same time two weeks in a row?"

"Indeed."

"I'll go call Frank." He looked at his children, still hear no evil, hear no evil, hear no evil. "It might be good to just keep your ears covered."

"John!" Ida scolded him again, and the girls collapsed in giggles.

***

"Are you joshing me?" asked John.

"Nope." Frank sounded exhausted. "He said we don't keep him busy enough, nor do we pay enough, so he is doing pulpit supply while Pastor Jacobson is taking the waters in Missouri for his health, and therefore, our service must be in the evening."

"For how long is Pastor Jacobson taking the waters? How long must we stay with the evening service instead of moving to Sunday morning?"

"I'm not sure, but what can we do? He is filling our position and doing what we asked him to do."

"Well, I for one, don't like it. I will look forward to our next board meeting when I will say so. Split loyalties. Is he our minister or are we to go back to being the ugly stepchildren of another church?"

"Okay, we'll talk about it at the board meeting. Try to calm down. The parishioners like him."

"Do they or are they only glad to have someone to fill the pulpit? I'm not convinced."

"Okay, go get some sleep. We'll figure it out."

"Fine, but—"

"No buts, nothing we can do tonight." Frank hung up.

***

English Lutheran
There will be services at the English Lutheran church next Sunday evening at 7:30. Sunday school will be held at 12 noon.

Strangers are welcome at all services.

Woodstock Sentinel, August 13, 1908.

***

September 5, 1908
532 Chestnut Street
Denison, Iowa

Dear Ida and John and little ones,

It looks like we are into the autumn on the great plains already. All the green has disappeared, and the sunflowers are all eaten up. Geese and other birds have been flying over, headed south or west. One thing that I can't get over here is how big the sky is. Since the land is flat, once one leaves the rivers and climbs to the prairie, one can see from horizon to horizon. It makes me feel small and helpless, but then my wonderful Pearley dear, comes home and we have such a wonderful time together. He says the job is A-OK and we are saving a lot of money for our future family. Nothing to report yet, but it has only been a few months.

How are all of you? In good health, I hope. How is your foot, Ida? Seems to me, the damage must have been more than just a strain. Whatever is a tendon? Do I have one? I've turned an ankle several times, but never found it much of an impediment. A couple days' rest, and I was up and at it again. I'm glad you got some help so that John didn't starve. Mama wrote that Mamie is still not completely over her cold of the summer. That seems like a long time. What does the doctor say?

We have rented a small house with two bedrooms – for when you visit, ha! – a kitchen and dining room combined and a parlor. Biggest problem is that it doesn't have indoor plumbing so I'm back to emptying the commode or going out in the dark night. And boy Charlie, does it get dark here. In our area of

I Will Fly to Woodstock

town, we have a few streetlights, but not many. But, oh Ida, you should see the sky at night. A million stars, stable and shooting. So beautiful.

    I can't believe that only a year ago I was writing about the boys of Racine destroying streetlights. Here I write for the paper about nothing because there isn't much to write about. I spend most of my time....hm...how do I spend most of my time, ha! Mostly I wait for my attentive husband to return. Oh yes, I do cook and clean, and I have been going to the German Lutheran Church. The congregation only has about 30 members, but we sure can sing. The people are nice people and have accepted us as if we were here from the old country. Fine people. Pearley doesn't go much, or at all, because of work and because he doesn't know German. Oh well, I will believe for the both of us.

    That's about it from here. Do write and let me know all the antics of the little ones. I must prepare for my own.

Love,
Clara

***

Wright's Aeroplane

    The Wright aeroplane, which is to be tested by the United States government at Fort Myer during the present month has recently made a record of successful performance in France which entitles it in serious consideration in this country. It seemed to be necessary for the Wright brothers, who are natives of Ohio, to win triumphs abroad before their own countrymen would give them the credit now seen to be their due. The recent exhibitions at the Le Mans racetrack, near Paris, have convinced the Frenchmen that the Wright brothers are no bluffers. While the aeroplane which Wilbur Wright operated there broke no records during its first flights abroad nor even equaled its performances on this side of the water, it did enough to convince the foreigners who watched its ascents that its inventors had progressed further than any of their rivals in the solution of the problem of flying with a machine heavier than air. Foreign students of the science of navigating in the air have generously complimented the American inventors on their achievements. The latter have already demonstrated the practicability of their aircraft, whatever the outcome of the tests to be passed at Fort Myer. These tests, of course, are designed to determine the value of the Wright aeroplane to the United States government. The government does not take many chances on things of this kind. It does not embark in experiments until shown that practical results can be attained.

Orville Wright is in charge of the aeroplane operations at Fort Myer, and they are conducted before a board of army officers. The machine for use by the signal corps of our army and now under test at Fort Myer is forty feet from tip to tip of the wings and is made of ash and of "silk spruce."

Expressed in more detail, it may be said that the government tests require that the aeroplane, if accepted, must carry two persons having a combined weight of 370 pounds and sufficient fuel for a flight of 125 miles. It must have a speed of forty miles an hour in still air.... In addition to this the machine must make an endurance flight of at least an hour and sustain itself in air continuously, returning to the starting point and landing without injury. It must be capable of being steered in all directions, of being under perfect control and of ascending in any country likely to be encountered in field service. Its simplicity of construction must be such that any reasonably intelligent man may become proficient in its operation, and it must have a device permitting safe descent in case of accident to the machinery. The specifications of the test provide for three trials for speed and three for endurance, both to be completed within thirty days of the date of delivery.

If the Wrights deliver a machine to the government capable of making forty miles an hour and passing other tests, they are to receive $25,000. If greater speed is attained their pay will be increased in proportion.

Orville Wright's own description of how the machine flies appears in an article by him in the Century Magazine.

"The machine is placed upon a single rail track facing the wind and is securely fastened with a cable. The engine is put in motion and the propellers in the rear whir. You take your seat at the center of the machine beside the operator. He slips the cable, and you shoot forward. An assistant who has been holding the machine in balance on the rail starts forward with you, but before you have gone fifty feet the speed is too great for him and he lets go. Before reaching the end of the track, the operator moves the front rudder and the machine lifts from the rail like a kite, supported by the pressure of the air underneath it.

"The ground under you is at first a perfect blur, but as you rise the objects become clearer. At a height of a hundred feet, you feel hardly any motion at all, except for the wind which strikes your face. The machine coasts down at an oblique angle to the ground and after sliding fifty or hundred feet comes to rest. Although the machine often lands while traveling at a speed of a mile a minute, you feel no shock whatsoever and cannot, in fact, tell the exact moment at which it first touched the ground."

Woodstock Sentinel, September 24, 1908.

***

I Will Fly to Woodstock

John finished reading the description of flight aloud to Mamie as she sat mesmerized by the vision of a man flying through the sky. They were sitting together in his big chair down in the basement workshop.

"Is Mr. Wright sitting up or lying down?" was her first question. She had seen a picture in the paper one time of a man lying down on an aeroplane.

"I think he is sitting up and another man is sitting next to him…the mechanic who fixes something that breaks on the plane."

Mamie flinched a little. "Breaks in the air?"

"I would hope not, but maybe."

"How would he fix it up in the air?"

"I don't know," John admitted.

Mamie sighed. She and Ida were slowly getting better. She liked these times when just she and her Papa could have discussions.

"Papa, are you going to fly in an aeroplane?"

"Maybe, but probably not."

"Why not?"

"It's going to take a while before commoners like you and I will be allowed to be passengers. Right now, the seating seems to be limited to just the inventors."

"I would like to be an inventor."

"You would? Well, I guess there are women inventors. I don't see why you couldn't be. I've always wanted to be an inventor, too"

Mamie smiled at this gentle man. "I know. Mama said."

"She did, did she?"

"You want to be a politician, an inventor, and a baker."

"Well, I guess you've got my number." John reached over and tickled the flat little belly lightly.

Mamie giggled. "I want to be a mama and an inventor and a flier and a farmer."

"A farmer?"

"Yes, I like growing things like tomatoes and beans and peas."

"If an aeroplane comes to Chicago, do you want to go see it?"

"Oh yes, Papa. That would be very fun."

"Okay. Let's watch the paper for it. I'm sure it won't be long before it happens."

Mamie gave John a big hug. She couldn't wait until the aeroplanes came to Chicago.

***

"Oh, Mama! School is so splendid!" Helen flew in on a gust of warm air midafternoon. Ida, Mamie and Dodi looked up from their tasks and stared at her wide-eyed. Helen tore off her coat and hung it on the peg opposite the door and skipped into the parlor. Ida sat with her leg extended, foot upon a pillow on the coffee table. Her Achilles tendon was nearly healed, but the doctor said to elevate it each time she rested so that her recuperation could be complete.

Ida had spent much of the last month preparing Helen for the big event - the first day at the Clay Street school. Using a cane and the pram to prop her up, she had taken Helen shopping for shoes and frocks, foregoing the handmade variety in deference to her heel on the treadle of the sewing machine. She needed a slate and chalk, paper and pencils, a ruler, and Crayolas. One day last week, she had walked the six blocks with Helen to the school to set up her desk, meet her teacher, and get her books. Today, on this special 'first day' morning, John had walked her and two other children on Lincoln Avenue to school, and Ida arranged that Helen would walk home with another mother on the block.

Now she twirled around, her school frock tangling around her knees. "Mamie, Dodi, you are going to love school!"

"Slow down, little miss. Come here and sit and tell us all about it." Ida motioned to the davenport beside her.

"Oh Mama, I can't sit down. They make us sit almost all day, which is fine because what we are doing is so much fun! We got to listen to real books that the teacher read out loud and to do numbers on the slates, and I have a poem I must memorize for Friday and a workbook to do for tomorrow, and at recess, we played Red Rover, and I almost won. And...," she finally took a pause, breathless. She fell sideways and sprawled on the hassock with a giggle. "I LOVE it!"

Ida smiled. It seemed Helen had found her forte.

***

Lose Pastor to Nova Scotia

Rev. H. J. Behrens, who has held the pastorate of the English Lutheran church in this city for the past eighteen months, has decided to accept a call to Rose Bay, Nova Scotia. His resignation will take effect Nov. 1. Rev. Behrens' successor has not yet been named. Rev. Behrens has been highly appreciated here and his many friends regret his departure.

Woodstock Sentinel, October 5, 1908.

***

"Highly appreciated? The scoundrel!" John was incensed.

"John!" Ida's tone was decidedly harsh. "Stop it! Be glad your nemesis is leaving."

"Ida, I told you he would not stay, that he had better things on his mind."

"Yes, you did, but what would you have had us do and better yet, what will we do now?"

"And is he leaving the other church up in the air also?" John glared at the tabletop.

I Will Fly to Woodstock

Ida shook her head. "No, I think their pastor is back from Arkansas."

"Of course, he is. Wouldn't want to leave the Germans in the lurch! We didn't have to say HIGHLY appreciated. When I think of all the times that he was unavailable for services or the way he treated Ma, I—"

"John! Being a good Christian and saying that he has been highly appreciated and will be missed seemed to be the right way to publish this news to the rest of the city.

He looked up. Ida stood with arms crossed a wooden spoon in one hand as if she was about to administer corporal punishment. He sighed.

"We cannot afford to be seen as punitive or we will lose parishioners. Aina?"

Ida was right. They must save their reputation. Say goodbye, shake his hand, and wish him well.

"Yes, yes, of course. It's just that…." John took another cleansing breath. "I guess we'll discuss this at the next board meeting. Where will we find another minister at our level of pay and no parsonage?"

Ida also didn't know what they would do now. She would try to go with John to the board meeting. They would probably need a correspondent to ask the district for help. Some small churches looked for ministers for a long time. I hope we are not one of those, she thought. I also hope that we will not have to eat crow and join forces with another Lutheran church, finding one minister for both groups. On the other hand, maybe a yoke like that might work.

"I'm going to bed." Ida wiped her hands and removed her apron.

John's worried continence looked up, "OK. I'll be right along."

She turned at the door to the dining room and looked at her loyal husband. He was back to staring at the tabletop. He seemed to be very angry lately, blowing up at small things. She wished he'd talk to her about it, but she knew that he first had to figure it out and then they'd talk. "Don't be too long, okay?"

"I won't. See, I'm coming right now." He stood and smiled a tiny smile at her. "I'll be right there."

***

Local News and Personal Items

The Ostend Sunday school will hold a chicken pie social at the home of H. N. Thompson Friday evening of this week. Supper 25 cents each.

Woodstock Sentinel, October 29, 1908.

Mrs. Charles E. Hughes.

Mrs. Hughes, wife of Charles E Hughes of the state of New York, is not quite big enough to be statuesque, yet she cannot be called petite. She is well proportioned, moves with gentleness and dignity, her features almost classical in repose. A kindly light beams from great brown eyes, which gleam from a face suggesting ivory, and she grows vivacious and enthusiastic when a favorite topic becomes a subject of conversation. A mass of brown hair is in perfect harmony with her face and figure.

She is a woman whose culture enables her to be of much aid to her distinguished husband.

Woodstock Sentinel, October 29, 1908.

***

Ida folded the paper. The girls were asleep, Helen was at school, and she was enjoying a cup of reheated breakfast coffee and the paper, but this article had brought her up short, coming as it did just after John and she had seen "A Woman's Way" at the Opera House. The play was a melodrama and had some very suspenseful and realistic scenes of a New York "dive" where a woman goes to find her wayward husband. The paper had said that the play "tells the story of a wife's faithfulness through all things." Ida wondered if she would be a faithful wife like that if John strayed. Was she an aid to her distinguished husband?

She knew that John had been noticeably quiet of late and didn't really want to talk about the store or finances. She had not been asked to scrimp, so she assumed, rightly or wrongly, that money was coming in. He still brought home the best meat from the store for them, and she made a lot of their clothes, and the garden harvest carried them through the winter. But something was wrong, she just felt it. It felt like...like...like he was giving up. But if he wouldn't talk it over with her then she would just have to wait and see what happened and hope that she was as much of a helpmate as Mrs. Charles E. Hughes.

Ida rose from her musing and checked the icebox. Nice and cold. Good, and the laundry was out on the line. She had time to lie down for a while until the girls woke up. Then she'd have energy for the rest of the day. Too much thinking wears a person out. Yes, she'd take a little catnap, and all would be well when she awoke.

***

Local Intelligence

Rev. H. J. Behrens and family left the first part of the week for their new home in Nova Scotia.
Woodstock Sentinel, November 5, 1908.

***

CUBS ARE SUPREME IN THE BASEBALL WORLD

Chicago will hold its world's baseball championship title for at least another year. The Cubs by shutting out the Tigers at Detroit Wednesday, 2 to 0, established themselves as the monarchs of the diamond. They eliminated the Tigers in four out of five games and won their glory in the most clean-cut and decisive manner. In their long struggle for another title of world-beaters the Cubs overcame every obstacle in a thorny patch, and now stand out above all their rivals in a class by themselves. In driving the final spike through the pennant and into the masthead the Cubs gave the Tigers their worst trouncing of the entire series.

To wind up the bobbins of the American League champions the Cubs went at them with the best they had at their disposal and fought an aggressive battle from the very onset.

The confidence of the National Leaguers was marked. They knew as well as they knew their names that they were the masters of the Tigers, and every catch, every throw and every move by the Cubs bespoke their superior skill as mechanics and their absolute confidence in each other and the team as a whole. In justice to Manager Jennings and the Tigers they must be awarded much credit for the game stand they made. While it was a foregone conclusion that the Cubs would capture the big share of the glory, the Tigers put up as valiant a stand in the last ditch as ever a beaten band of athletes did.

While the integrity of the national game needs no defense, it brought great satisfaction to the Cubs to be able to say they put the Tigers out of business in four out of five games. Last year they did it in four straight.

Wisconsin Gleaner, October 15, 1908.

***

Emil finished reading aloud the *Wisconsin Gleaner* article he had saved for this occasion and looked up to face his six older brothers who sat relaxed around the saloon table. He raised his bottle, "All hail the Cubs."

"All hail!" The men saluted the team together, and they all took long draws on the heavy, homemade dark German beer in the dusty brown bottles.

The Wienke family had come to Beloit to have Thanksgiving dinner together. John had closed the store Thursday and Friday for a "family emergency," so they could spend time with Al and Lena and the children. After a huge and sumptuous meal and much expressing of thanks, the women and children had settled for afternoon naps or handiwork and the men had come to see Al's new saloon.

The establishment was quiet. The brothers sat at the only occupied table. The men looked around. Dust motes circulated in the afternoon sunlight coming through the front windows which were dirty and streaked. Their steps coming in the front door had disturbed the long-accumulated dust on the floor leaving footprints.

"No one can say we haven't been here." Ed used his bottle to note the path from the door. The others smiled and sipped from their bottles which had made distinct rings in the dust on the table.

John had furnished a kerchief before they sat down to wipe off the chairs, so the men wouldn't be embarrassed by taking the dust with them out into the world on the seats of their pants.

Their eyes followed the curve of the carved wooden bar displayed against the back wall. The wood looked dried up and old. Cobwebs draping the back mirror and a few empty bottles lay scattered along the back bar.

"At least the mirror is in one piece." Frank looked at the bar mirror "You don't want to start the whole business with bad luck." All seven reached and touched the wooden tabletop.

The tables and chairs, other than the ones they used, were shoved in a pile in one corner. Spindles were missing from many. The place smelled like beer, cigar smoke, old wood with a muskiness of mouse droppings. The chandeliers were tin and had not come on when Al turned the electric switch. William spent a few minutes futzing with the switch and tracing wires. "Problem is," he finally declared, "the building has no service." The others nodded.

Luckily, they had been blessed with a sunny late fall day in Beloit, Wisconsin, so the light filtering in was adequate.

Al carried in a crate filled with bottles, brewed in his own basement, and it wasn't half bad.

"Nice place, Al." Will faked a cough into his hand.

The others laughed. Al's "new" saloon was certainly nothing to write home about, but John had no doubt that it would be stunning once Al's artistic hand came to rest on it.

Al, good naturedly, raised his bottle, "Here's to Will, our patriarch!"

"Will!" sang out the others taking a sip from the bottles.

"And to Bob, who would be beside himself that our Cubs won the championship two years in a row." Emil was the first to invoke their dead brother's name. Heads nodded around the table.

"To Bob!" They raised their bottles toward the ceiling before sipping again.

"Can you just imagine the scene he'd be making?" Charles' eyes didn't leave his bottle.

John looked around the circle of faces, his brothers, older now, but still in the prime of life. God had been good to them, all married and all with children now.

"Gee, how did you afford this place?" asked Frank.

The others fell into great chuffs of laughter.

"Go ahead and laugh, but I got it for a pittance and in this part of town close to the mills. You are just a few weeks early to see it in its glory. You come back in spring, and we'll see who's laughing. I'm going to be a rich man!"

"Here's to getting rich!" Frank raised his bottle. "To getting rich!"

They drained their bottles.

"More beer, more beer," Charles started the chant knocking his bottle bottom on the table. A large cloud of dust raised toward the ceiling causing several to sneeze or cough.

Al looked around and the overblown hacking. "Kätzchen." He looked down at the box, a smile playing at the corners of his mouth. "You're all a bunch of kittens." He produced seven more bottles. Emil traded up and flipped the lever wire up releasing the bail holding the cork in the bottle neck. The cork sprung from the bottle with a 'pop' and the beer fizzed up the neck and down the side of the bottle wetting the dusty tabletop. Emil smiled and took a slug from the bottle. "Fresh!"

"What will you do if the antis make a move in Wisconsin to impose prohibition?" asked Ed, looking from the bottle in his hand to Al.

The men were quiet awaiting Al's answer. Al, also looking at the bottle in his hand, finally broke the silence. "It would make a nice bakery, don't cha think?"

Another guffaw from the group, but John looked around and thought, yes, it would! The group fell to talk of business, politics, and religion. John was somewhat quiet throughout, thinking his own thoughts for the most part. Finally, Al noticed. "And John, lettuce consider the life of the grocer? Do you carr-ot-all about the trends or do you just want to squash the competition with your clever meat cleaver?"

John and the rest chuckled at the clever plays on words, "Well Al, the business isn't what it used to be. The trends are toward self-service shopping and grand inventories. Hard for the small grocer to keep up. I'm thinking of switching trades,

I Will Fly to Woodstock

so if prohibition closes your saloon, maybe I'll come to be your baker."

The others laughed, possibly not sure how to take the comment. "Really?" Al responded. "If not a baker, what would be your next choice of career?"

"Insurance." John was truthful in the admission. "Prudential has come to Woodstock and the owner of the agency has been pursuing me. Just this week they sweetened the pot again with an eventual partial interest in the agency and a particularly good salary with commissions. Shorter hours. Weekends off. Hard to turn down."

"And why, pray tell, would they want an old bald-headed guy to sell door-to-door?" Ed rubbed his own bald head.

John feigned a hurt look, "Old! I'm not old, oh wait, you were looking in the mirror, right?"

The others sniggered at the old joke. John addressed the question. "He thinks that I am politically well-connected and well-known in the community. Good combination for trusting a salesman."

"Sounds about right." Will sipped from his bottle.

"Wow, weekends and evenings off?" Charles was somewhat glassy eyed at the idea. "You better get on your horse and go accept that offer."

"Not yet. I haven't talked to Ida about switching yet, so please don't spill the beans. I want to see what Christmas brings, and then we'll decide what to do. But yes! Weekends, evenings AND holidays off. Hardly seems possible. Might be worth it just for that."

Frank shook his head. "I wondered what was up, but I didn't know that you had that card up your sleeve. I thought the grocery was just in trouble."

"Well, while the negotiation has been drawn out, I'm pretty sure now that I'm going to be an Insurance Agent."

"Here's to closing doors and opening doors." Al toasted his brother.

"Here, here!"

"And here's to not spilling the beans." Emil held up the last of the second bottle.

"Here, here!"

***

***

GERMAN LUTHERAN

Regular services next Sunday at 10:30 a.m. The celebration of Christmas will be as usual. Children's service on the evening of Dec. 24; regular Christmas service on the morning of Christmas day at 10:30.

Rev. John Bertram, pastor.
Woodstock Sentinel, December 17, 1908.

ENGLISH LUTHERAN

There will be services next Sunday evening at 7:30 o'clock.

Sunday school at 12 noon. Everybody welcome.

The Christmas exercises at the English Lutheran church will take place next Wednesday evening at 7:30 o'clock. Everyone invited.

REV. W. E. BUCHOLTZ,
Pastor.
Woodstock Sentinel, December 17, 1908.

***

Grace Lutheran.

The Grace Lutheran Sunday school enjoyed a Christmas tree with appropriate exercises and festivities at the church on Washington street on Wednesday evening.

Woodstock Sentinel, December 24, 1908.

Danish Lutheran.

The Danish Lutheran society will have Christmas services with appropriate exercises at the church on Washington street on Saturday afternoon at 2 o'clock. A Christmas tree will be prepared for the children loaded with good things for all and a program rendered to interest both young and old.

Woodstock Sentinel, December 24, 1908.

***

Ida luxuriated under John's arm as they sat on the davenport awaiting the new year. This time they had not made a big deal of the evening, and all three girls had retired early. Dodi's birthday in the middle of December had dominated the month. Mamie and Helen had gone all out decorating with Happy Birthday banners on butcher block paper, and Ida had made a grand three-layer cake.

The Doerings had come to the party. Bessie was great with child. The prospective sisters Elizabeth and Grace, who were now three and one, were extremely excited about the baby; Elizabeth claimed the baby would be a new sister.

Then, just yesterday, they had received word that Herman and Bessie had been blessed with a boy, William.

Louisa had come on the train from Racine with Emma and her five children – fourteen-year-old Fay, twelve-year-old Amy, ten-year-old Elsie, seven-year-old Marion, and six-year-old Howard. They had celebrated Dodi's birthday on the thirteenth and then had an early Doering Christmas a week later before they headed back to the farm in Pleasant Prairie, Wisconsin where Floyd was the manager. Helen had been in her heyday as mistress of ceremonies for both the birthday and the Christmas celebrations.

"Helen is quite a little lady already, isn't she?" Ida tried not to sound prideful.

"Yes she is," John agreed.

"Are you sad that we didn't have a boy?"

"Of course not. Besides, we are still trying occasionally, aren't we?" He leaned down and kissed her tenderly on the lips and extended the kiss to breathlessness before pulling back.

"John, the children—"

"Are in bed. Are you sure you need to see the New Year roll in?" he asked, his voice husky.

"Hm, let me see." She put her finger to her temple as if thinking. "I've been waiting for it for three hundred sixty-four days, twenty-four hours and forty-five minutes…can't you wait fifteen more minutes?"

"Nope!" And with that he stood them both up and drew her by the hand toward their bedroom. "A boy!" he exclaimed loudly.

"Hush, you'll wake—" Before she could say more, he turned toward her, stopping her protests with his mouth while his hands made her swoon.

"A boy," she whispered. "Let's try for a boy."

Die Bückelhering (1909)

DR. E. WINDMUELLER

PHYSICIAN & SURGEON, Sentinel Block Day and Night. Special attention given to obstetrical practice. Telephone: Office, 312; Residence, 534. Hours: 2-4 & 7-9 p.m.

Woodstock Sentinel, January 7, 1909.

***

The walk from 365 Lincoln Avenue to the Square was a cold one this January afternoon. As they walked, Mamie quietly held her mama's right hand while Dodi skipped ahead, running back when there was important news..

"Mama?"

"Yes, Dodi."

"I named Merry like Merry Christmas? She has rose cheeks and smile lips and blond hair so looks like Merry."

"I think that would be fine."

'I like her lots. She can play wid Mamie's dolly an' read wid Helen an' sleep with Papa."

"Oh, really. She will sleep with Papa. What about poor Mama?"

Dodi looked up at her for a moment. "You can sleep with her, too. Oh look, a dog." She dropped Ida's hand and began trotting down the walk toward the German Shepherd. She turned as she ran and called back, "Does it have a home? We should take it home. It's hungry and tired and—" She tripped on one of the boards and fell.

As Dodi scrambled to her feet, no worse the wear, Ida caught up and grabbed her arm. "No, I don't think we can take it home. It probably belongs to the Chamberlain's. Come here, let's go across the street." Ida checked both ways. No traffic.

"Nooooo." Dodi planted her feet. "I wanna kiss it." She lunged toward the large black dog that guarded Chamberlain's gate.

Ida let go of Mamie, caught Dodi up in her arms, and stepped off the boardwalk and into the street. She reached back and helped Mamie down, and they crossed to the other side.

"No. No. NO!" screamed Dodi.

On the far sidewalk, Ida set Dodi down and looked into her eyes. "Stop it right now! We don't have time for such hysterics. We must get to the doctor's office for your sister." Dodi calmed to a whimper. Ida took both girls by the hands and continued toward the Square with Dodi still struggling a bit.

"Oh," said Dodi.

Now what? Ida looked down at Dodi. Her little round face was crunched up with concern.

"What's wrong?" Ida asked.

"Mitten gone." Dodi looked at her bare hand.

"When did that happen?" Ida looked back up the walk to where they had crossed the street. "You two hold hands and don't move. Stay RIGHT HERE."

"Yes, Mama," both said.

Ida moved back up the block scanning the ground until she found the little blue mitten just off the walk where they had crossed. She stepped off, felt a twinge in her heel, but it held. She retrieved the mitten and looked back to where she had left the girls. They stood quietly on the walk still holding hands.

As she made her way back to them, Ida thought about how quiet Mamie was being. It was out of character for her. She would usually be the one talking non-stop and skipping before them down the sidewalk.

They turned onto Cass Street and Ida said, "Wave to Papa." She and the girls paused in front of the store.

"Papa," Dodi squealed and ran up to the window banging her hands on it. John noticed the uproar and came to the window to wave back. Mamie raised her free hand in a half wave and leaned against Ida's leg. Ida reached down and picked her up. So light for a four-year-old. Dodi weighed more than Mamie now. Mamie buried her face in the fur around Ida's collar, and they walked on, Dodi managing to look in at every window they passed.

It was chilly in the doctor's office. Ida and Mamie shed their coats in the waiting room, but she left Dodi's coat on, removing only her hat and mittens.

A few minutes later, Dr. Windmueller looked into Mamie's mouth. "Say ahhhhhh," he instructed.

Mamie said, "Ahhhhhhhhh."

"Well," said Dr. Windmueller. "I see inflammation in her tonsils. They are very swollen and red with white pustules. How long has she been running a fever?"

Ida hadn't realized she was running a fever. She hedged a bit, "A couple days."

"Only a couple days?" he asked.

"Oh doctor, I don't really know. If I feel that she is too hot, I put her in a cool bath and try to bring it down. She hasn't been hot like that for several months. And now that it's cold out, well," she paused, wondering if she should tell him. "Well, I take her outside and we sit in chairs to try to get cold enough to make her heat subside. I don't really see the difference between that or an ice bath. But she hasn't needed that for a while. I did notice that she is awfully quiet today and not playful like usual, but...."

The doctor put his ear to Mamie's chest and heard the typical thump-a-thump of a child's heart. No murmur, he thought, that's good. He felt Mamie's neck under her chin and felt her wince when he reached an area under her jaw near her ears. His expert fingers could feel the swollen lymph nodes on both sides. He patted Mamie's shoulder and turned to Ida.

"She has what is called 'quinsy throat.'"

"Quinsy?" Ida hadn't heard of that.

"Yes, quinsy. Basically, she has a bad tonsil infection. You know what tonsils are, right?"

"I think so."

"Two skin pads on either side of her throat at the back of the tongue. The tonsil on the right is very infected and is encroaching on her airway."

"Encroaching?"

"Yes, closing off her airway."

"What! How will she breathe?" Ida knew she was being too loud and just a bit hysterical. She closed her eyes and took a calming breath.

"It hasn't closed off yet, but that tonsil is full of pus and we need to drain it, so it doesn't."

"Oh," Ida looked at her hands which had begun to shake.

A tiny hoarse voice from the table said, "Will it hurt much?"

The doctor turned back to Mamie. "A little, but not much. It will taste bad."

"Oh," said Mamie.

"Here, Mrs. Wienke, sit down here." He gestured toward the chair.

Ida sat down and took Dodi on her lap.

He turned back to Mamie. He tied a white cloth around Mamie's neck covering the front of her smock like a bib and then laid her down on the wooden table. A blanket had been folded just the size of the table and a white cotton sheet covered it.

The doctor's office had an interesting number of appliances and bins and bottles to choose from. Dr. Windmueller took down one labeled 'Iodine' and a cloth-wrapped bundle which he unrolled to display fine instruments: three scalpels, several probes, and a pair of scissors.

He went to the door of his apartment, opened it and said, "Martha can you come help me for a few minutes?"

"Sure." Martha came into the room and closed the door behind her.

"Mrs. Wienke, this is my girl, Martha. She answers the phone, makes appointments and helps out on occasions like this."

"How do you do?" said Ida, lowering her eyes in greeting.

"Martha, this is Mamie. She has a very sore throat, and we are going to try to get the bad stuff out so it can start to heal."

"Hi Mamie." Martha touched the little girl on the shoulder. "Don't be afraid, your mother and I are right here."

Mamie tried to smile but failed.

Martha got another sheet and covered Mamie completely up under her chin. "I'm going to cover your eyes, too, so you can't see anything to make you scared, okay?"

Mamie nodded.

The drape went behind her ears and around and up over her nose and eyes so that just her mouth was showing. Martha peeked under the cloth. "Are you okay in there?"

"Yes." Mamie's voice sounded scared and far away.

The doctor picked up the scalpel and turned to Ida, "You and Dodi might want to look away just so you don't gasp and scare Mamie who is being so brave."

Ida nodded and she buried her face in Dodi's hair looking at the floor.

Martha prepared several clamps with a hunk of cotton in each to use as swabs.

"Okay, Mamie, open your mouth as wide as you can."

Mamie complied, and he slipped a wooden peg between her upper and lower teeth to keep it open. She squirmed. Martha held her shoulders to the table. Very quickly the scalpel went into her mouth and sliced open the abscess. Yellow-white pus exploded out of the tonsil. Martha quickly provided swabs, and the doctor cleaned up the liquid as Mamie gagged several times. In a flowing motion, the doctor removed the sheet from around Mamie's head, took the wooden peg from her mouth, sat her up, and gave her a metal bowl. "Spit all the icky stuff out into this bowl, Mamie."

Mamie retched and spat. Spat and retched. And spat and spat. The flow of putrid discharge slowed. The tears flowing down Mamie's face did not, but she kept on spitting.

"What they do to Mamie?" Dodi's voice came as she looked on in horror.

Ida turned Dodi's face back toward her chest. "It's okay, sweetie. They are making her all better." Ida also tried not to look up at the child on the table.

"Do you feel like you can let me see now, Mamie?" the doctor asked.

She nodded but looked miserable. She opened her mouth, and he took a quick look.

"Well, that looks a lot better. Can you breathe better? Does it hurt less."

Again, Mamie nodded.

"Good. Now we have only one more thing to do."

Martha had poured a portion of iodine into a dish and held a new clamp holding a cotton clump to the doctor. He dipped the cotton in the iodine and said, "Mamie, open as wide as you can and say ah."

Mamie's tears continued, but she did her best to comply. Her 'ah' was raspy and soft. The doctor swabbed the back of her throat and her tongue and gums with the red liquid. Mamie gagged hard and started to actively cry, her shoulders shaking.

"Okay, Mama, Mamie needs you."

Ida stood and put Dodi on the chair, went to her second-born, and took her into her arms. "You are so brave, my darling" she cooed as Mamie sobbed.

"The iodine tastes terrible, but the taste will wear off as she eats and drinks," said the doctor. Martha gathered the instruments and bowls and swabs and took them from the room.

As Mamie's sobs subsided, the doctor said, "We'll continue routine use of the Bayer Powder…three times a day with meals. That's for the long-term starting now. I also want you to use honey regularly by the spoonful to ease the soreness of her throat and Vicks on a cloth pinned around her neck to add warmth and vapors. Understand?"

Ida stepped back from the table in case he wanted to take another look. "But doctor, I've been doing those things each night for a few weeks and she's only gotten worse." Ida's hands shook. She clasped them at her waist to stop the spectacle.

"Increase the honey to every two hours and keep the cloth on all day and night. Add Vicks salve two or three times during the day and then the Bayer powder one teaspoon with each meal."

Ida took a large breath. "Okay," she managed. "How serious is this?"

"Very serious. Right now, she has infected tonsils. The ultimate solution is to take them out, but we can't do that until they are infection free or at least a lot less infected. So, let's start now to try to accomplish that. Eventually, we will probably have to bleed her a bit—"

Ida blanched and the doctor noticed.

"Or maybe not. Let's let the honey and the Bayer do their work. Make sure she has lots of liquids; tea, warm lemonade or orange juice, and lots of water. Try to stay away from milk for the next little while. It's okay on cereal, but not to drink.

Mamie is a very sick little girl. You will need to watch her carefully. If she starts to have trouble breathing or you can't wake her up or her temperature goes way up, and the Bayer isn't working then we will need to put her in the hospital so she can have intensive care."

"Okay." Ida felt a bit faint.

"Keep her quiet and warm with lots of chicken soup," he smiled at Mamie and tousled her hair a bit. "After she is all better, we'll schedule to have the tonsils taken out. Maybe in the fall, if she can stay fever free."

"Thank you doctor," Ida managed before he disappeared into another room where a child was coughing.

Ida put Mamie's coat back on. "Can you walk?" she asked the little girl.

Mamie nodded.

"We will go to the grocery and Papa will find a way to get us home, okay?"

"Okay," she croaked.

Ida lifted Mamie off the table and let her legs get under her before asking her to stand on her own.

She lifted Dodi down and the three of them left the room together.

***

Personal Interest

Mr. and Mrs. John Wienke's daughter Mamie Wienke has been down with a severe case of tonsillitis. Miss Wienke is being lovingly attended to by her mother and grandmother, Mrs. Louisa Stoffel, visiting from Racine.

Woodstock Sentinel, January 14, 1909.

***

ENGLISH LUTHERAN

There will be services next Sunday afternoon at 2:30 o'clock at which Rev. H. R. Reed, president of the Chicago Synod of the Evangelical Lutheran church will preach. Communion service will follow the preaching.

The annual meeting of the society was held Sunday Jan 10. The following officers will serve the society during the coming years:

    Financial Secretary – Charles Kirchman
    Recording Secretary – Frank Foote.
    Treasurer – Frank J. Wienke
    Trustees – C. C. Harting, F. C. Readel, Charles Backus.

W. E. Bucholtz, Pastor.
Woodstock Sentinel, January 21, 1909.

***

Personals

Herman Doering of Woodstock, Ill., spent Sunday with his mother, on Huron Street.
Racine Journal-Times, February 11, 1909.

ENGLISH LUTHERAN

There will be services next Sunday evening at 7 o'clock. Rev. Bartholomen of Chicago will preach.

Sunday school at 12 o'clock noon. Everybody invited.

Woodstock Sentinel, February 11, 1909.

***

February 26, 1909
Denison, Iowa

Dear Ida, John and little ones,

Thanks for the long letter explaining the situation with Mamie. I am heart-sick that she is going through this again. It sounds like Oma's attentive care worked, along with the leeches. Maybe there is some good in those awful, slimy leeches, after all they are God's creatures too. Ha! Mama stayed for a month? How did you stand it? Did she go to church with you? Or did you go with her to the German Lutheran? I bet you went with her, right? It was very brotherly for Herman to escort Mama back to Racine. I wonder what he was up to. Ha!

Things are about the same here. Pearley works all day, long hours, but we have our evenings and nights and most weekends unless there is a storm to take down the lines. He is such a good man and I am so lucky to be his wife.

I am a bit at wits end since Christmas is over. I did some volunteer work with the needy at church over the holidays, but I guess they aren't so needy now that the new year has come as the church isn't sponsoring any more drives now. You asked how I used up the hours of every day? I clean, I cook, I wash, I sew. I've been taking in a little sewing for others to make some pin money. I don't hate it as much as I used to in Racine. And I read. I know, it doesn't sound like much, but we're happy. That's what counts.

Did I tell you there is a Normal college here in Denison? When the weather breaks, I'm going to go see if I can be of some use to the students. I don't know what, but I want to be with young people. The church people are all nice, but old or older and I don't have many real friends among them. We will see what comes of it.

I'm also going to talk to the newspaper and see if they need a reporter. It's only a weekly and doesn't have much distribution, but maybe. As long as the reporting is during the day, it shouldn't affect my night life and wifely duties at home.

Well, time to get supper. Pearley will be here in about an hour and I don't want him to see what a sloth I have become. No baby yet but we wait impatiently.

*Love to all,
Clara and Pearle*

***

THRONGS AT CAPITAL WITNESS INAUGURAL
Taft and Sherman Sworn in as Heads of the Nation's Official Life

In the presence of scores of thousands assembled from all parts of the earth, and surrounded by the highest dignitaries of the government, William Howard Taft assumed the burdens and responsibilities, the duties and the honors of the office of President of the United States. On the stage erected on the east portico of the national capitol, the place hallowed by the memories of Lincoln and Grant and Garfield and McKinley, the oath of office was administered to President Taft, and he delivered to the listening throngs the address in which he accepted the office conferred on him by a majority of his countrymen. Shortly before this event his colleague, Vice President James Schoolcraft Sherman, was inducted into office. In accordance with historic custom, the latter took the oath in the chamber of the United States senate, over whose deliberations he will preside for four years.

Principal among the features of inauguration day were the taking of the oath of office by President Taft, the great inaugural parade and the splendid inaugural ball. Other features of the day of scarcely minor interest to the thousands who filled Washington as it was never before filled were the drive of the retiring president and the president-elect from the White House to the capitol, the taking of the oath of office by the new vice president, the return to the White House by President Taft after the inauguration and the fireworks display back of the White House in the evening. In each case there were thousands to see and hear and applaud the inauguration ceremonies, which it is generally agreed, were the greatest and most magnificent in the history of the United States.

Woodstock Sentinel, March 18, 1909.

ENGLISH LUTHERAN

There will be services next Sunday at 2:30 o'clock. Rev. Bartholomeow of Chicago will preach.

Sunday school at 12 o'clock. Everybody welcome.

Woodstock Sentinel, March 18, 1909.

HART'S GROCERY TO DACY BLOCK

S. L. Hart has made a lease for the large storeroom and basement in the Dacy block formerly occupied by M. N. Wien. He has placed carpenters at work in the new quarters, who are busily engaged fixing up the shelving and otherwise re-arranging the furniture.

The present Hart quarters in the Furer block have been leased to Wagner & Cowlin, who will occupy them with a hardware store as soon as they are vacated by Mr. Hart.

Woodstock Sentinel, March 18, 1909.

Republican Township Caucus

The Republican voters of the town of Dorr are requested to meet at the courthouse in the city of

Woodstock on Saturday, March 20th, 1909, at 2 o'clock p. m. sharp, for the purpose of placing in nomination candidates for the office of supervisor, town clerk, assessor, collector, one commissioner of highways, (3rd district), three justices of the peace, three constables and one trustee of schools, to be voted for at the coming township election.

Also, the selection of a town committee and the transaction of such other business as may properly be brought before the caucus.

ROBT. Mc LEAN,
J. F. WIENKE,
Town Committee
Woodstock Sentinel, March 18, 1909.

***

John laid down the paper. He would have loved to have been there in Washington for the inauguration. What a spectacle it must have been. Maybe next time, he thought. His wished-for political career had come to nothing as had his grocery business. It was time to talk things over with Ida. He had held off with Mamie being sick. It had been hard on Ida to have the other children staying with their Aunt Elizabeth and Uncle Herman, and Mamie making only slow progress. But they were now all back together again, and Mamie seemed to be getting back to her lively self. The doctor was still worried, but the new regimen and the leeches seemed to have solved the fever problem. Maybe they could even avoid the surgery in the fall.

They were sitting and enjoying the quiet on this Sunday evening. The girls were asleep or at least in their own bedrooms, and Ida was on the davenport crocheting...what was it...must be a quilt in pretty blue four inch by four inch squares.

"That quilt is going to look very nice when you are done," he ventured to open the conversation.

Ida looked up. "Well, thank you, John. Maybe it will have to go on our bed if you like it."

"That would be nice," he said. "Ida, there is something that I've been meaning to talk to you about."

Ida's hand went to her chest. She lay down her square and turned her full attention to him, "Yes, John?"

"I had an offer to buy my stock and equipment at the store and took it."

Ida's face paled. "Okay, but why, who? What happened?"

"Hart's Grocery is expanding into the space that Wien's just moved out of on Benton Street."

"Yes, I read that."

"When I heard about it, I approached him and asked if he'd be interested in incorporating my stock into his larger space. And after some dickering, he said, 'yes.' Except for the meat. I'll find another butcher to take that. And—"

"But, why, John. Why do you want to close the store?" Ida asked in a calm, even meek voice.

"Because...," John cleared his throat and then plunged ahead. "Because we have been barely breaking even every month since I put in the meat counter. And because, I've had a better offer." Pretty smart, he thought, putting those two ideas together.

"Oh, John!" Ida threw up her hands, closed her eyes, and turned her face away. "I just knew it! I knew that the meat business was an over-reach for a small store. I have to tell you, I'm very hurt that you didn't confide in me from the very beginning. What's the 'better offer'?"

"Prudential Insurance."

"What? What do you mean 'insurance'? Do you mean they will pay for our loss?"

"No, no, not that. Prudential needs agents with connections, and they have asked me to work for them."

"An insurance agent? Is there security in that? It seems a very unstable business just by its nature," Ida said with creased brow.

"No, not at all. It is a growing business," he put the emphasis on the word 'growing.' "And they're just getting started here in Woodstock. I'll be getting in while the business is still young with no investment – unless I want to – and the pay is good, and the hours are great just 8 o'clock to 6 o'clock and no Sundays or holidays...," he trailed off. Talking too much, he thought, she'll think I'm uncertain.

"Insurance agent. I don't know. It sounds shifty." Ida's hand that had been clutching the front of her jumper lowered to her lap and caressed the yarn.

"You can think about it, but it won't change anything. The deal is done with Hart, and I start with Prudential on April first. I'll have about two months of training, and then they will give me an area of the northern Illinois district to work which will probably be here in town and include the Square. They like that I know everyone. They've been after me for over a year." Shut up, he again told himself.

Now he could tell she was getting angry because her face reddened. "Over a year? You've known about this for over a year and not one word to me? Well, then you don't need my opinion at this late date, do you? Just do as you please and tell me after you're finished." Ida wrapped up and put away her handiwork.

"Ida, I—"

"Don't 'Ida' me just now. I thought we were in this together, but I guess not. You could have at least dropped a hint at what was going on...or better yet, talk to me about the offer and your plans," she emphasized the word 'your' to stress how he had not included her and the children in his decision.

"Yes, I know, but I didn't want to bother you with it...you know...with Mamie—"

"Oh no you don't. Don't blame Mamie or my weakness as a woman or anything else. This one is on you, John! I'm going to bed. You don't have to follow right away!" And with that she got up and went through the dining room into the bedroom and sharply closed the door.

John sighed, leaned forward and put his head in his hands. She had every right to be mad, he supposed, but still, he had just withheld to protect her, and if he was honest, because he was embarrassed. This new job would be so much better for all of them with more time and more money. He picked up the newspaper again, unenthusiastically, and looked at it unseeingly. Big change was in the wind. Ida would be fine. She just had to make a point, but she'll see how good this change will be. "I hope," he whispered.

***

Hart's Grocery Moves

S. L. Hart, the grocer, has been moving his stock of goods for several days and is now located in his new quarters, formerly occupied by M. N. Wien, corner of Benton and Lumber streets. The room he is now in is much larger, affords more room, and better light than that in which he was formerly located, and the store altogether presents a very handsome appearance.

Woodstock Sentinel, April 1, 1909.

***

Ida placed the meat platter and mashed potatoes in the middle of the dining table. Her family was arrayed around the linen-covered table: John at the head, Helen to one side and Mamie and Dodi on the other. She removed her apron and sat.

I Will Fly to Woodstock

"Whose turn?" John reached for Helen and Mamie's hands.

"Mine." Mamie smiled at him.

After the circle was complete, they bowed their heads, and Mamie said, "Dear Father, we give thee thanks for this our daily food. Amen."

John added, "And bless the cook." He looked up at Ida, but she wouldn't meet his eyes. The circle broke and Ida reached to put potatoes on Dodi's plate and then her own. She passed the bowl counterclockwise to Helen.

John cleared his throat. "I made my first sale today."

Helen said, "That's good, Papa. What did you sell?"

"A life insurance policy, if you can believe it." John looked at Ida with a smile that quickly faded as she was buttering a slice of bread and did not seem to be listening.

"To whom." Helen was getting to be a good conversationalist.

"Who other than Judge Donnelly."

"Really, Papa. You are so smart." Helen again.

Mamie piped up, "We went to the Square today."

"You did?" John had been at the Square all day, making the rounds of the businesses, trying to sell policies.

"Yes, and we saw Aunt Bessie and Willy."

"You did? What were they doing at the Square?"

"Mm...I think they went to visit Uncle Herman." Mamie opined.

"Where were Elizabeth and Grace?"

"At home with the nanny," said Helen.

Dodi looked at Ida, "Can we get a nanny, Mama?"

Helen jumped in, "Dodi, you don't even know what a nanny is."

"Is it like a dog?" Dodi guessed.

"No. It's like...um...like staying with Oma."

"Oh—"

"Okay." Ida corralled them. "Everyone put their minds to eating or we'll be here all night."

John laughed. "Can you girls imagine sitting here eating all night?"

The girls giggled.

Ida shot him a disconcerting look. It said, 'you too mister!'

John lowered his head and cut his meat and added a bit of mashed potato to each bite. How long was this going to go on? It had been two weeks since Ida had retired alone, and still he had seen no break in the wall of silence.

"This is good, Ida," he said, but no answer came from the other end of the table.

***

English Lutheran

Last Sunday afternoon eight young persons were confirmed in Grace English Ev. Lutheran church. The attendance at this service was evidenced by almost every seat being occupied. The service was impressive and edifying. The church was decorated with ferns and flowers.

The Easter service will be at 11 a.m. Rev. H. J. G. Bartholomew of Chicago will officiate. The Lord's supper will be administered. An opportunity will be given for a special free will offering for the benefit of the congregation.

"Let us hold fast the profession of our faith without wavering, for he is faithful that promised; and let us consider one another to provoke unto love and to good works, not forsaking the assembling of ourselves together, as the manner of some is." -- St. Paul.

The Woodstock Sentinel, April 8, 1909.

***

"Good," thought Ida as she examined her handiwork in the newspaper. "That ought to pull them into the service."

If they could keep people coming on Sundays, they had a chance at survival even though Rev. Bartholomew, the paper had finally spelled his name right, was lackluster on his best day.

Like last Sunday, Palm Sunday, which he dedicated to doubting Thomas, even though Thomas doubted after the Lord was risen on Easter. That aside he basically just told the same story she'd been hearing since she was a child and then said, "Don't be like Thomas." And that was it. She was sure he was bound for administration, not the pulpit. But to give him credit, he had shown up for every service coming out from Maywood by train. He was young. Who knew - maybe they would grow up together, and he would become beloved. He still had another year at the seminary, surely there would be growth in his skills. She could forgive him his shortcomings.

"Mama," Mamie interrupted her thoughts.

"Yes, Mamie. What can I do for you?"

Mamie giggled. "You sound like you're at the store."

"I'm practicing my politeness." Ida sat up more primly in her chair.

"Oh. How do you do?" asked Mamie.

"I am very fine. How are you?"

Mamie giggled again. "I am just fine!" she said emphatically.

"Well, I am so glad. Now what can I do for you?"

"Mama, are you still mad at Papa?"

Ida was surprised by the question. "Come here." She took Mamie up into her lap. "Why would you ask such a question?" she asked the little girl.

"You and Papa seem sad. Is it because we can't go to his store anymore?" Mamie seemed to be trying to figure this all out.

"Well, you are too young to understand completely, but I was very surprised when Papa sold the store. Now we need to get used to this new job and hours. Things are just so different."

"I'm not sure Papa likes his new job," Mamie opined.

"Why do you say that?"

"He isn't jolly when he gets home. I don't hear you laugh with him." Ida thought about her musings about Pastor Bartholomew. Maybe it was time to forgive John also, after all, Easter was a time for rebirth.

"Well, we will just have to jolly him up when he gets here tonight, okay?"

"Yes!" Mamie clapped her hands with enthusiasm. "What shall we do?"

"We don't have a lot of time. Let's see. How about we make a sign that says, 'Welcome Home, Papa!'" suggested Ida.

Mamie thought about it for a moment. "How?"

Ida put Mamie down and crossed the kitchen and reached to the back of one of the lower cupboards. "I have just the thing!" She removed a half-used roll of butcher block paper.

They retreated to the dining room and Ida rolled out the paper onto the table. Now what could they make the letters out of. She could draw them on and then have the children shade them in. No, she decided that they wouldn't stick with it long enough and she'd end up with endless shading herself. What else?

"I know!" she said and started for the stairs.

"What? What do you know?" Mamie called after her.

"Stay there, I'll be right back."

She returned momentarily with an armload of used wrapping paper, salvaged from packages over the years, of all different patterns and designs. "Okay, I'm going to draw the letters on the paper and you are going to cut them out. When Dodi wakes up from her nap, the two of you can paste them onto the long sign. I will stir up some paste before then."

I Will Fly to Woodstock

Mamie clapped her hands and climbed up to the table. "May I sit on the table?" she said using her polite voice.

Ida smiled. "Yes, just this once." And she lifted Mamie up on the table, found a pair of scissors from her sewing kit and they set to work. By the time she heard Dodi waking up, they had most of the letters cut out. Mamie had started out clumsy with the scissors but had improved with each letter. It didn't matter if they weren't perfect. "Papa won't care," she told the child.

She left Mamie to her work, retrieved Dodi from her bed and sat her down with a cookie and milk at the kitchen table while she made paste from flour and water in a bowl. She mixed the concoction until it was smooth and liquid enough to brush on. Two paint brushes from the basement, and she moved the entire process to the kitchen floor. She placed the letters in order and then cut off the rest of the roll of paper. She split the paste into two bowls and set the girls to working from the middle outward. They worked diligently with Mamie finishing first and moving to help Dodi brush and place the letters at the other end.

The back door burst open, and Helen rushed in with a burst of cool air. It felt good in the hot kitchen. She stopped abruptly, looking down at the two girls making the sign.

"That's spelled wrong," she said with her authoritative voice.

Ida looked over her shoulder. 'Welcome hoem P' the sign read.

Mamie looked up, "No it's not!"

"Yes, it is!"

"Hello, Helen." Ida turned the girl to her and leaned down to hug her. "How was school?" Then quietly in her ear she whispered, "It's okay if it's spelled wrong. Little girls sometimes spell things wrong."

Helen shrugged. "Okay. School was fine. We are studying plants now."

"Well, it's a good time to study plants in the spring. Why don't you run up and change into play clothes and then you can help the girls hang the sign if you would like."

Dinner! thought Ida. She quickly put a pan of water on to boil. She had taken out a bottom rump in the morning which she was marinating in the icebox. Sauerbraten was one of John's favorites. Three days ago, she had combined water, cider vinegar, red wine vinegar, onion, carrot, salt and pepper, bay leaves, cloves, juniper berries and mustard seeds in a hot saucepan to simmer and then cool. The beef was rubbed with grease saved from other cooking, on all sides, placed in a hot skillet, and browned. Then the round was put in a wooden bowl and covered with the marinade and a towel and put in the icebox, turning it each day to make sure all the meat was covered. Today, it was ready to cook, so earlier she removed it to a roasting pan, added sugar to the mix, and put it in a somewhat warm oven for the day. The smell of it had been permeating the atmosphere for hours.

Now she quickly sifted together flour, baking powder, and salt. She added just enough milk and mixed to just the right texture. She took teaspoon sized portions and dropped them into the boiling water and covered the pot. She looked at the time. He'd be there in 20 minutes. It was nice knowing exactly when they would hear the knob turn.

The girls had finished pasting on the letters and were washing up in the bathroom while the sign dried. 'Welcome Hoem Papa.' Ida smiled. Perfect.

"Where shall we put it?" asked Mamie.

"Put it?" echoed Dodi.

Ida got some string, and they made 4 ties at the top and took it around to the foyer. "How about right here from the stair rail. Then he'll see it before he even removes his hat," she suggested.

"Yes, yes!!" The girls were jumping up and down with glee. Helen came down the stairs. "I can tie them," she said. Ida left them to it.

"Call me if you need help. And then come help me set the table, okay? Mama still has work in the kitchen. He'll be here very soon."

In the kitchen, Ida removed the roasting pan from the oven and removed the meat to a platter. She strained the solids out of the marinade and put the pan on the hot stove. From the cupboard she grabbed a tin of gingersnaps and broke them into the mix, stirring as the liquid thickened. She removed it from the heat, stirred in raisins, covered the pan, and checked on the dumplings. Ready. Draining them, she added butter to keep them from sticking together, but left them in the warm covered pan for now. In the meantime, the girls had returned to the kitchen and were busily setting the table.

And there was the door. The girls dropped what they were doing and raced for the foyer, "Papa, Papa, Papa!" Ida wiped her hands on a dish towel, took off her apron, and went around to the foyer. The girls surrounded him, taking his coat and hat to be hung up. John stood looking steadily at the sign.

"Welcome ho-em, Papa!" she said as she leaned up to kiss him on the cheek. The girls squealed and led him to the dining room with the almost-set table. "You wash up. Dinner is ready," said Ida.

***

John said nothing, but his eyes betrayed his pleasure at such a homecoming. The 'women' went back to work as he retreated to the bathroom, where he felt such a sense of relief that he had to sit on the edge of the tub for a moment afraid his legs wouldn't hold him. They had weathered the storm...again. They would not have been able to do such a party if he still had the store. This new arrangement was going to be good for them all, he just knew it. "Thank you, Lord," he murmured as he rose to wash his hands.

***

Local News and Personal Items

Ed Wienke, living on Washington street, has installed a new Kimball piano in his home.

The men from J. P. Miller Well Co. of Chicago who have been here more than a year, having completed their work, left Tuesday morning. While here they lowered one well and bore a new one for the city and one for the Oliver Typewriter company, which was just completed last week. The Oliver well is 1200 feet deep and is said to be a very fine one.

Plantation songs by the colored Jubilee Singers at the Opera House, April 16.

Do you want a man for mayor, even if he be otherwise satisfactory, who wears the Barnes-Olsen brand? Do you want the word to go out throughout McHenry County and the Eighth Senatorial district that A. J. Olson and C. P. Barnes control the government of the city of Woodstock? If you do not, vote the People's ticket.

On August 10th, two days after the August primary at which time A. J. Olson was nominated for senator, on motion of his candidate for mayor, and seconded by himself, the coal contract for the city of Woodstock was let to the Western Coal & Dock Company, which was represented by Olson's Lake County campaign manager who is also a close personal friend of C. P. Barnes. Our home man, A. F. Field did not get a look in against Olson's campaign manager.

A gasoline engine of a fairly docile type is a big improvement over the average windmill in that it is not put out of business by a windstorm and will jog along satisfactorily whether the wind is blowing or not. Besides this, when properly mounted it can be taken where the owner wills to saw wood, shred fodder, grind corn or do other useful tasks.

Louis Gibson has sold out his interest in the store and expects soon to be a traveling salesman for a firm in Chicago.

During the heavy winds storm of last week Wednesday the windmill on Richard Reed's farm was blown down.

The Woodstock Sentinel, April 15, 1909.

***

Churchmen Withdraw Objections

Announcement has been made of the withdrawal of the objections made by some of the Catholics and Lutherans of the state to a bill codifying the Illinois school laws, which has already passed the senate and is awaiting action in the house. The point was raised that the section making it a misdemeanor to prevent by threats, menace or intimidation any child from attending public school might be construed as a blow at parochial schools.

The legislative committee of the German Catholic societies and some of the Lutheran leaders were convinced that the section refers to racial and not to religious conditions and have withdrawn their objections.

The Woodstock Sentinel, April 22, 1909.

***

ENGLISH LUTHERAN

There will be services next Sunday at 2:30 o'clock. Sunday school at 12 noon. Everybody welcome. Rev. Bartholome of Chicago will preach.

Woodstock Sentinel, May 1, 1909.

***

Ham Peddlers Arrested
Denison

Recently two strangers came to Denison to sell hams to eager housewives. While one of them argued with the mayor as to the amount of the license, the other did a thriving business selling hams which he claimed were of his own curing and raising. Just how many ladies paid 16 cents a pound for packing house picnic hams which they can get at any of our stores for 11 cents, it is hard to tell. When officers got onto the fact of what the men were selling, and also, that they had skipped out, they were arrested at Vail, brought back to Denison, and forced to part with their profits and then some before they got out of town. The 'home-grown' hams were received by peddlers by freight that morning from a Des Moines packing house.

Crawford County Courier, May 11, 1909.

***

Political News
From Denison

Ninety-three women voted at the special election held here on the proposition to spend $4,000 for additional grounds for school purposes. The women gave a majority of fifty-one for the tax while the 281 men only gave the tax a majority of three. It was the afternoon for the meeting of the Penelope club, and many women voters came to the polls in society gowns. The school board plans in time to erect a gymnasium and manual training building on the newly acquired property.

Crawford County Courier, May 21, 1909.

***

Denison, Iowa
May 30, 1909

Dear Ida, John and little ones,

How are all my wonderful nieces? Helen, are you all through with fifth grade, yet? You are such a smart little girl. Keep up the good work! Mamie, how are you feeling, sweetie? I was so glad to hear that you are back to your giggly self. I hope you have a great summer! And Dodi, what a big girl you are getting to be. What do you want to be when you grow up? You should write and tell me so I can make plans! Aunt Clara loves you little dumplings.

And how are Ida and John? I hope you are well as we are. Hasn't the spring been wonderful! I bet your garden is glorious right now, Ida. Flowers, flowers everywhere. We have mostly sunflowers here. Large platters with small gold leaves around the edge and a brown seedy middle. Although they bloom in the fall. Otherwise, we only have flowers that people plant, mostly petunias and poppies and peonies. Ha.

Well, I did it. After months of trying to get something in the almost-dead Denison Report, I took my wares further afield and found an outlet in Marshalltown, the Crawford County Courier. They will take short Denison stories and pay 5 cents a word. I can call them in or mail them. Enclosed is my first story for them. $4.10. They don't count numbers or 'a'. It isn't much but is a little pin-money to buy cloth and ribbons, and sundries when I want them. It will also get me around town more and besides it's fun, although I must admit that the stories are harder to find in quiet little Denison than they were in loud, large Racine. For one thing, they have no lake and so no lake storms. Who knows, maybe we'll have a cyclone that I can ride. Ha!

It was quite a sight to see the ladies in their gowns lined up to vote. I think it's about time we all have the right to vote in any election, don't you? Have you had speeches and rallies in Woodstock? John, are you a supporter of equal rights for

I Will Fly to Woodstock

women? Pearley says that he is in favor of equal rights for me, but he's not so sure about the other women. Isn't that sweet?

Being a lineman is such hard work, Pearley comes home every night just exhausted. He must climb the poles and put heavy wire onto glass insulators...I think I have that right. There isn't electricity going through the wire when he is putting it up. But if some wires blow down then they must be very careful that the power has been turned off before they touch it. One of his buddies got shocked and fell right off the pole and killed himself twice over. Pearley promised me that he'd always wear his safety belt, so if he gets shocked, he'll hang up there and not break his neck falling. I worry about him every day. But he makes a good wage and seems to still like the work, so who am I to complain?

I went up to the Normal to see if they needed help with the youngsters and found out that it's an exceedingly small school. They said that I had to have two years of education beyond high school to teach classes in sewing. Can you believe that? What is that going to teach me about sewing? So, I told them no thanks. They did have a position for a cook, but I'll be jiggered if I try to earn money from something I dislike so much. I told them I'd think about it, but I'm not.

Other than that, life goes on. Our snow wasn't half bad this winter and so we had an early spring by the accounts of the farmers around Denison. It was certainly long enough for me, but no longer than Wisconsin winters. Now I'm writing about the weather, how boring. Will write again when I have more to say.

Love to all of you,
Aunt Clara and Uncle Pearle

***

Insane Over Religion

Wausau, Wis., April 23. – John Gustin of Doering, WI, brought through this city on his way to the Northern Hospital for the insane, chewed flesh from his fingers and tore his clothing into shreds. A few weeks ago, officers brought a man and his wife through here on their way to Oshkosh, both insane. A new religious cult has been formed at Doering, similar to the Holy Jumpers and Holy Rollers. It is alleged that the man and his wife, as well as Gustin, went insane as the result of their worship.

Inter Urban, May 31, 1909.

***

"So, now what are we supposed to do?" John was frustrated. The synod had reassigned Pastor Bartholomew to an office job.

Frank and John were relaxing with a cigar in the parlor while the ladies cleaned up after a fine dinner made by Anna and enjoyed by all. The children were playing around the kitchen table.

"Well," said Frank. "I'm not sure. I know the congregation is getting tired of waiting, but then we don't want to just jump into another call without being sure. We decided that Bartholomew was not the one and so he has been reassigned."

"Will the district give us someone else?"

"Maybe. They are looking, but we are going into the summer and all the students have been placed."

"So, who will preach until then?"

"We will," said Frank.

"What?"

"Yup, we have smart people who have a good understanding of scripture. We'll also get some visiting ministers from here or there. It will be a challenge, but we can do it."

"Count me out. I know nothing about anything. I'm not getting up there to preach."

"I thought you would have jumped at the chance, John. How would you ever have been a politician without giving a speech?"

"Giving a speech is different from preaching."

"Not that much. We shouldn't have to do it for that long. A new crop of students will be ready in the fall."

"Well, good luck." John was unconvinced. "I'm afraid this is going to shake the faith of many people in our goal of a separate church. I will do what I can from the pews."

"Great! And you will be on what's called a 'call committee'."

"What is that?"

"It's the group who will interview and preview a minister before we call him. Sort out the Bartholomews and the Behrens if you know what I mean."

"I guess I could do that. When will you announce all this?"

"Next Sunday; you'll be there, right?"

"Of course. I can't say I'm sad to see the good pastor Bartholomew go. I might even be able to do sermons as well as he did." John chuckled.

Frank looked pleased. "So, you are volunteering?"

"Oh, no, no, no. Let's just pray we can do better next time."

"Amen!" said Frank.

***

LOCAL NEWS

The project of stamping all letters with weather forecasts for the day when received at their destinations is under consideration by the post office department. The government makes a daily forecast of the weather which is supplied to all post offices. By stamping the letters with the forecasts, the people would receive their information directly, and rural route persons especially would be greatly benefited.

If your property is not covered by adequate fire, lightning and tornado protection against loss, call at the Prudential insurance office and ask for John Wienke to remedy the defect.

Out of 2,590 boys recently examined in the schools of Kansas only six cigarette smokers were found to be what would be generally called "bright." Ten of the remainder were average students, while all the rest of the 2,500 were found to be poor at their studies or worthless.

There are four things that a farmer of good health is justified in going into debt for – namely, tilling the wet acres on his farm, a manure spreader, fences that will enable him to keep sheep and a soft water cistern for the good housewife.

Woodstock Sentinel, June 10, 1909.

CHURCH NOTES
PRESBYTERIAN

The Friends in Council met at Presbyterian church Wednesday afternoon to tie a comforter and will be next Wednesday at the home of Mrs. Herman Doering to continue their work.

Woodstock Sentinel, June 10, 1909.

ENGLISH LUTHERAN

There will be services next Sunday evening at 7:30 o'clock. Sunday school at 12 noon. Everybody welcome.

Woodstock Sentinel, June 10, 1909.

***

COMMONER ASSERTS HE WILL NOT BE DEMOCRATIC CANDIDATE FOR PRESIDENT
TALKS TO ENORMOUS CROWD

Fifteen hundred people, embracing the culture and intelligence of Racine's population, crowded into Lakeside Auditorium on Saturday evening, and heard William Jennings Bryan, three times Democratic candidate for president of the United States, deliver a lecture upon the subject, "The Price of a Soul."

The Commoner looks well and hearty and expressed himself as feeling unusually well. Being questioned along the line of politics he said that not again would he be a candidate for the presidency, that he was not a candidate for United States senator from his state. He did not say what he would do, however, if his people insisted that he be a candidate for the high honor.

That Mr. Bryan was pleased with the immense throng of citizens and ladies present was evident from the expression on his face.

Racine Journal-Times, June 21, 1909.

***

PERSONAL ITEMS

Frank Wienke is in charge of the Pig Racing at the Typewriter Factory summer picnic at Fox River Grove at Cary on July 24.

Woodstock Sentinel, June 24, 1909.

ENGLISH LUTHERAN

There will be services next Sunday afternoon at 2:30 o'clock.

Rev. A. C. Anda, Western District Superintendent English Home Missions, will preach. A good attendance is desired. Rev. Anda will meet with the call committee as they begin to examine candidates for their ministry.

Woodstock Sentinel, June 24, 1909.

***

Personals

Mrs. H. C. Doering of Woodstock, Ill. is visiting the home of Mrs. A. J. Leahy of Washington Avenue.

Racine Journal-Times, June 30, 1909.

***

ENGLISH LUTHERAN

There will be services next Sunday at 11 o'clock. Sunday school at 12 o'clock.

Woodstock Sentinel, July 1, 1909.

***

"Hurry, Mama!" called Helen in through the front door. "Oma and Papa just pulled up."

"Yippee," called out Mamie as she brushed by Helen, who was holding the door open. Dodi was right behind her. Last out was Ida with a large picnic basket with lunch and a cloth bag with sweaters and sundries for a day at the Square. It was the 4th of July and with all the children healthy, they were ready to make a day of it. John had asked Sophia to come with them which necessitated taking the surrey, but they were early, and it would be easy to find a horse tie close by the Square. Jake, the horse, had on a jaunty straw had to protect him from the rain which was threatening or the sun if it decided to show its face. The six of them had just enough room if Mamie and

Dodi stood in front of Ida and Sophia. Helen, dignified, in a hat and flowered dress would sit on the bench like an adult. After all, she would be seven in only a few days.

The few-block ride to the Square took some time. The streets streamed with people headed down to the festivities. Most people walked, but a few drove loud horseless carriages. They crawled along as slow as the horse-drawn carts but spewed their stinky exhaust into the crowd escorting them. The carriages of both kinds made their way carefully. John tried to warn people as they approached, but at times, just fell in line behind the people in the street. Jake plodded along keeping his eyes open for trouble.

"It voud be besser to valk," said Sophia.

John agreed but said nothing. His mother was still able to walk a few blocks, but he felt better having the carriage at hand if some emergency happened.

"We'll get there," said Ida. "There's no hurry."

"But Mama," said Helen. "There is a hurry. Did you know they have cotton candy? We must hurry before it's all gone."

"They will make more," said Ida. "Everyone just hold on. Mamie, are you holding on tight?"

From the front, she heard Mamie's voice all but drowned out by the noise of the throng, "Yes, Mama. Oma is holding on to me tight."

"Good. Stand still for Oma," she called back. She wrapped her arms tighter around Dodi who was big-eyed and still as a mouse in front of her. Dodi relaxed a bit in her supporting arms and turned around to face her.

"Too lout," she said, covering her ears. "Home?"

"No, we are almost there. Just close your eyes and don't be scared."

"Otay," said Dodi and she snuggled up to her mother's breast and closed her eyes.

The carriage lurched over a curb and John was able to get the horse turned onto one of the side streets. They found a horse ring under a tree, good for Jake, and dismounted the carriage. It would still be a block and a half walk, but the horse would stand ready should he be needed.

Mamie was concerned. "Will Jake be okay?" she asked. The draining of the tonsil abscess had been a huge success, and she was back to her lively self. She had been without fever for several weeks, which the doctor took as a particularly good sign.

"Jake will be fine," John assured her. "He'll just take a nap and converse with the other horses. I'll come back and check on him now and again."

"I'll come with you," said Mamie.

And with that, they all made their way onto the sidewalk. As they turned the corner onto Cass Street, they walked right by John's empty store. John looked at the store as they passed. His name was still emblazoned on the front window, but a sign there said CLOSED.

Dodi pointed at the storefront, "Papa's 'tore."

John smiled at her. "Yes. Yes, it was." Ida said nothing and kept her gaze out toward the Square.

Their eyes and ears and noses were treated to incredible delights. The stores, courthouse and Opera House were all decked out in red, white, and blue bunting. Even the jail had streamers attached to the bars on the outside windows. American flags flew from every pole, even some that weren't meant for flags. When they had progressed into the Square itself, they could see that the four entries to the central park had been decorated with arches that the revelers would go under to reach the bandstand and other amusements. Red, white and blue were certainly the colors of the day.

John could see that the doors of most of the stores around the Square stood open on this Monday morning. Visitors from all over the county would take this opportunity to find sale merchandise and refreshment in these establishments. He had done the same for the last five Fourth of Julys, sacrificing time to enjoy the day with his family, in order to earn vital midsummer money. Last Fourth, he had offered ham sandwiches and other picnic food, and had done well with sales on the day. Many people brought their own picnic supplies as they had today...ham sandwiches, German potato salad, a fruit salad made fresh that morning and lemonade. The heft of the basket was not great, but they could supplement from the vendors if necessary.

Rata-tat-tat! Firecrackers were heard in several directions as they passed under the arch on the west side of the park. They would find a little grass to spread their blanket to use as a home base for adventures out into the crowd. Rata-tat-tat! Dodi clung to Ida face buried. Ida ended up carrying her the last block. Ida understood how frightening a crush of people could be for a little one. She had handed the cloth bag off to Sophia and had scooped Dodi up as they dodged around clusters of people.

"Over here," John's voice came to them on the wind. Perfect, he had found a sliver of ground by a tree no less. They unburdened themselves and settled Sophia on a blanket against the tree and Dodi in her lap. The wind had come up a bit.

"It's going to rain," said Ida.

John looked at the sky. Gray clouds hurried their way from west to east. "Just a sprinkle."

"Oh no." Mamie's eyes were wide. "What about Jake?"

John looked at his sensitive daughter. "He's been rained on before. Besides, he has his straw hat for protection."

Mamie's face said that she was unconvinced.

"We'll try to stay here if it just rains lightly. If it gets harder, we'll have to scurry to shelter," said Ida.

The sprinkle tried in earnest for a few minutes and then died away.

"Look over there." Helen pointed across the park. "A merry-go-round! Can we go, Papa?"

"Sure, come on chickens...ah...I mean children." John held out his hands.

"Oh Papa. You are so silly." Mamie laughed as she took one, and Helen took the other.

"Dodi?" John said.

"No!" said Dodi, and she buried her face in her grandmother's bosom.

"She vants to stay mit Oma," said Sophia.

"Okay then! Let's go." Off they went toward the merry-go-round.

Ida smiled. Those girls loved their Papa so much. And so do I. Ida rose.

Dodi raised her head. "Mama?"

"I'll be right back, Dodi. You stay with Oma. Are you okay with that, Ma?"

"Ja. Ja. Ve be fine," came the answer.

"Ver goink?" Dodi sounded very much like her grandmother.

"Just to look around."

"Otay," said Dodi. "Canggy?"

"I'll see what I can find," promised Ida.

But before she could go in search of candy, she stopped and turned in a circle, "Oh no, I smell smoke." As she turned toward the south, she saw it. The fire whistle had begun to blow and soon they could hear the clanging of the fire wagon as it rounded the corner, coming around the Square on Jefferson and then Calhoun and turning up Dean to the Square. Smart men, Ida thought since Jackson and Benton were blocked by the carnival rides. As the wagon turned on to Van Buren, she saw that it was the Oliver wagon with Frank at the reins.

The horses pulled to a stop. Five firemen in full protective dress jumped from the wagon, pulled down the hose. Two fighters grabbed the seesaw handles of the pump and began pumping with much gusto to start the water flowing. It poured out through the hose onto the large bonfire set at the corner its only purpose being to be put out. Just as the water began to stream, the city Fire Department wagon pulled out of their station a block away and galloped up the short length of Johnson Street. The delay had been, she supposed, gathering the fire fighters from their homes and holiday before they could make a charge toward the fire.

The fire was now out, and a call went out faintly over a blow horn, "The winner of the $15 prize is the Oliver Fire Brigade!" The crowd cheered, and the town fire boys helped clean up the water-soaked mess, piling it onto a buckboard pulled up from near-by.

Ida turned and waved to Dodi and Ma and made her way out of the park through the Main Street entrance and continued up Main to Blecher Brothers Model Bargain store.

"Well, well. Mrs. Wienke how are you today," Jim Blecher came around the counter to greet her. His gray hair was done up in a pompadour and he had a red, white and blue top hat perched on top. He removed the hat and bowed deeply.

Ida bobbed a small curtsy. "Just fine, Mr. Blecher."

"And your little ones?"

"Off with their father riding the merry-go-round," she replied. "Well, two of them are, the third would like some candy, and I saw by the paper that on Saturday, you had your vacuum-sealed hard candy on sale for 10 cents a pound."

"That I did!"

"Well, as today is a holiday, does that price still stand?"

"For you it does, Mrs. Wienke, for you it does. It's just so nice to have you stopping by to look around our store."

"Well, thank you, Mr. Blecher. You have done a very nice job with it. Now about the vacuum seals, can you show me how that is done?" she said as she eyed two large glass jars and their metal top seals. This was the newest thing in candy, moving from the large tins with metal covers to glass with the seals to keep the candy fresh and not sticky in the humidity of the summer.

After buying a pound of various candies, peppermints, cinnamon, lemon drops, licorice, and of course, chocolates, she exited the store through the back, coming out onto Benton Street. The Square she noted had become even more crowded. People lined the streets as if to watch a parade. The Auto Parade! She looked at her broach clock and hurried up the half block up to the Square.

She crossed the street and had just enough time to bring the candy to Dodi and Ma, who declined an offer to watch the parade from the street and return to a place near the east gate to await the motor cars. As she focused on the first car just coming around the corner from Cass onto Johnson, a gravelly voice behind her made her jump.

"Hello miss. Are you here all alone?"

It took her a moment to still her racing heart and then she turned to her very sneaky husband and said, "Why sir, why do you ask?"

They continued the playful banter as they watched the cars slowly slide down Johnson, turned onto Van Buren and then Dean and away from the Square. The cars were not as exotic to the eye as they had been even a few years ago, but the owners had decked them out with ribbons from the roof line and bunting on the doors. The cars that were topless had beautiful ladies riding in the back waving and throwing candy to the crowd. Eventually, John placed his hand on her hip and pulled her closer. She leaned back into him, and they stood very still. And the cars rolled by.

After a full and tiring day, John gave Sophia, Helen, and then Ida a hand up into the wagon. Then he lifted a sleepy Dodi up to Ida and Mamie up with their grandmother before he climbed in and took the reins.

I Will Fly to Woodstock

"Back," he called out to Jake and pulled back on the reins. Jake obediently backed a few steps so they were out on the street. "G'yap." John snapped the reins so they slapped on Jake's hind quarters. And they began moving west on Jackson. John thought about the frantic run down Jackson Street he had accomplished on that New Year's Eve just eight years ago; from home to the Opera House in the deep snow just to dance with Ida, and now look. He glanced around at his tired, but happy, family.

"Well, what did you chickens like best?" asked John as he made the right turn onto Tryon Street. They would take Ma home first, and of course, she would invite them in for Kuchen and coffee, something he was sure Ida would not be in favor of, but maybe.

"Papa," Helen said in an exasperated voice. "We're children, not chickens."

"Oh yes, sorry," apologized John for the ump-teenth time that day. "What did you children like best?"

"I liked the merry-go-round and the train the best." Helen was, as always, the first to answer.

"I liked...um...the greased pig and the races," said Mamie.

"Which races?" Helen wanted specifics.

"The bag race and the potato race." Mamie turned to her mother. "Can we try that when we get home, Mama?"

"Sure." Ida readily agreed. "But probably not today."

"Just those two?" asked Helen.

"Um...I can't really think of...." Mamie's voice trailed off.

"What about you Dodi?" Helen had taken over the role of inquisitor.

"Canggy," mumbled Dodi.

"Mama?" Helen again.

"Hmmm....I guess I liked...the parade of cars."

John smiled. "Me, too!"

"Oma?"

"I like da picnic. Dat vas gut potatoes, Ida."

"Thank you, Ma. Your recipe."

"I knost."

They continued on to Oma's house and begged off the Kuchen as they needed to get tired children and a horse to bed. Just as they rounded the corner at the top of the hill onto Lincoln Avenue, the sky burst with color.

"Oh!" Mamie sat up straighter.

A soft boom was heard delayed by the distance. Then another flower in the sky.

"Fireworks." Miss Helen verified.

John pulled Jake to a stop, and they watched through the trees over the Square to the fairgrounds as reds and whites and blues rained down on their beloved city. Dodi had fallen asleep on Ida's lap, so they just stayed for a while and watched, enjoying the company and the show. At one point a large American eagle appeared after an explosion. It swooped toward the ground and back up slightly before fizzling. Belatedly, they heard the scream of the bomb that made it.

"Oh my!" said Ida.

"And the eagle screamed," said John.

"What?" Ida asked.

"Oh, just something Bob and I talked about one time. Remember he was on the fireworks committee for the city the year he died? He was so excited and asked me what would make a good firework, and I suggested a screaming eagle, but I was thinking on the ground. Looks like they got the eagle flight-worthy this year."

"The eagle flew to Woodstock." Mamie smiled at John.

"Yes, I believe it did."

The paper would say four days later, "At 8:00 p. m. began the fireworks which were witnessed by large crowds of visitors. These fireworks continued until a very late hour and were much enjoyed by all."

But up on quiet Lincoln Avenue a very small crowd oohed and aahed for only about a half hour and then made their way down to number 365. The brand-new, shiny numbers glowed silver from the front porch post in the coach light. John turned Jake up the lane beside the house and stopped him just short of the stable. He dismounted and took Dodi from Ida's arms and balanced her on his shoulder with one hand as he reached up to guide Ida's descent. As he passed the sleeping child back to her, their eyes met, and he kissed her properly on the lips, lingering just a bit.

"Best day I ever had," called out Mamie, already on the back stone porch. "Papa, mama, this was the best day ever."

***

THESE VISITED THE OLD HOME
List of Those Who Registered at Racine for Record Breaking Festival of July 5th and 6th

Among them: H. C. Doering and wife, of Woodstock, Ill.

Racine Journal, July 10, 1909.

***

ENGLISH LUTHERAN.

The Ladies' Aid society of the English Lutheran church will give an ice cream social on John Wienke's lawn on Lincoln Avenue, west of the Catholic church, on Tuesday evening, July 20. You are invited to come. Ice cream and cake, 15 cents.

Woodstock Sentinel, July 10, 1909.

***

MISS LORIMER HAS NARROW ESCAPE

Senator William Lorimer's daughter had a narrow escape from injury at McHenry last Friday.

Miss Lorimer was automobiling with Miss Fitzgerald on Main Street when the steering wheel suddenly broke and Miss Lorimer was unable to guide the machine.

Before she could stop it, the auto dashed against a tree, and Miss Fitzgerald was thrown out, but Miss Lorimer escaped by clinging to the steering wheel. Neither of the ladies sustained serious injuries.

Woodstock Sentinel, July 15, 1909.

***

The Prudential
A Leader in Public Usefulness.
7,731,739 Policies in Force
THE PRUDENTIAL HAS THE STRENGTH OF GIBRALTAR
Insuring $1,434,551,347

Total Number of Claims Paid Since Organization
Over $1,180,000.

Paid Policyholders During 1908, over
19 Million Dollars.

Total Payments to Policyholders Since Organization, Plus Amount Held at Interest to Their Credit,
Over 313 Million Dollars.

THE PRUDENTIAL INSURANCE CO. OF AMERICA
JOHN F. DRYDEN, President   HOME OFFICE, NEWARK, N. J.
Agents Wanted to write Industrial and Ordinary Life Insurance
Good Income—Promotion—Best Opportunities—Swl

Branch Office in Woodstock

Geo. L. Ridgeway, Agency Organizer.   J. F. WIENKE, G. C. PETER, Agents.
Queen Ann & Second Streets

The Woodstock Sentinel, June 17, 1909.

***

CITY MAIL DELIVERY TO BEGIN OCT. 15
Put up House Numbers.

Residents and businessmen are requested to promptly put up their house numbers, if they have not already done so. No mail will be delivered at houses where the numbers are not properly displayed as required by the city ordinances.

Residents are also urged to procure private boxes or drops for the receipt of mail, the use of which is advantageous both to carriers and the public, as they facilitate speedy delivery.

Woodstock Sentinel, July 22, 1909.

***

"Ida! Ida! I think we found someone!" called out John bursting in the back door. He had stayed on after the afternoon Sunday service to talk to the rest of the call committee about a new candidate who two had gone to hear preach in Aurora that morning.

Ida rushed from the bedroom in her petticoat. "Hush, John. We are sleeping."

"Well, wake up! We need you to write a letter. We've found a minister!"

"We?" She glanced around John's tall frame at the three men who had come in off the porch behind him.

"Oh my," she giggled. "I must put some clothes on." And she turned and ran back to the bedroom as quickly as possible leaving the men red faced.

John followed her into the bedroom. "Shhhh." She put her finger to her lips and nodded toward the three sleeping children on the bed. "Go find refreshments for your friends," she whispered.

John retreated to the kitchen and had gotten the men seated each with a glass of water when Ida bustled in. "I'll make coffee," she said.

"Ida—" started Frank.

"Oh, don't worry about it." Ida broke him off. "At least I had my Sunday petticoat on."

The men laughed self-consciously. And then it was forgotten.

Coffee started, Ida gathered pen and paper. "Tell me." Ida seated herself at the table.

"Rev. Reed...," began Frank.

"You remember the President of the synod who was here in January?" John filled in.

Frank shot him a look. "Rev. Reed called me two weeks ago and said that they had someone who was interested in a parish that he could grow: Rev. Roger Kauffman. Rev. Kauffman had been doing an interim position in Aurora and their call committee called him, but he wanted a smaller congregation...more of a challenge. So, Clayt and I went to Aurora to church this morning and then met with Rev. Kauffman to see if he would like to consider Woodstock. And he would!"

John could contain himself no longer, "So we want you to write a letter inviting him to come next Sunday to preach."

Silence fell. Frank looked steadily at John.

"Sorry." John looked at the floor but was still smiling.

"Yes, Ida," Frank shifted his gaze back to her. "We need a letter to do that."

***

GRACE LUTHERANS HAVE A NEW PASTOR

Grace Evangelical Lutheran church (English), which has been without a pastor for nine months, since the former pastor, Rev. Behrens, left for Nova Scotia, rejoices in the fact it again has a regular pastor on the field, Rev. Roger C. Kauffman from Aurora, Ill.

Rev. Kauffman comes from an old Pennsylvania family. His early life was spent near the city of Reading, about fifty-eight miles north of

Philadelphia. He received his earlier education in Oley academy, one of the many advanced private schools which offered such good opportunities to the young men of that state. He taught school for one year and in the fall of 1899 entered the Freshman class of Michlenberg College, which is the best Lutheran college on the Eastern slope of the Alleghenies.

He graduated from that institution in the spring of 1903, and in the fall of that year entered the Philadelphia Lutheran Theological seminary. Here he studied under men like Prof. Clay from the University of Pennsylvania, who is considered one of the greatest Assyriologists of the present time, and Dr. Jacobs, who is called the farthest advance scholar in dogmatic theology of the Lutheran church in this country.

Rev. Kauffman was ordained in Philadelphia, June 13, 1906, by the officers of the ministerium of Pennsylvania. He asked for a letter of honorable dismissal directly after ordination and came West and was received into the Chicago synod June 15, 1906.

He took charge of the then disorganized mission of Aurora, Ill., and there he has labored until the present time. The progress of the congregation was remarkable. Worship was held in the third story hall, which was very inconvenient, when he came there, they now have changed their place of worship to a beautiful chapel. The congregation owns property worth $15,000. The Sunday school is one of the best organized schools in the synod.

Grace Lutheran church now looks forward to a brighter future and greater progress. Rev. Kauffman will preach on Sunday afternoon in the German Presbyterian church on Washington street. He will put forth every effort to interest all

who may come to hear him, and all are invited. In the evening, he will preach at Queen Anne.
Woodstock Sentinel, August 5, 1909.

Local News and Personal Items

Rev. Roger C. Kauffman, the new pastor of Grace Lutheran Church, arrived here Monday from Aurora to take charge of his new pastorate. Mr. Kauffman is making his home with Mr. and Mrs. J. F. Wienke.

Mr. and Mrs. Emil Wienke and child, from Beloit, were down over Sunday for a visit with relatives.

Aurora [Illinois] is believed to have broken all records in these United States as to the number of cases of appendicitis developing there in proportion to population. The peculiar part is that the doctors at Aurora list most of the cases as sympathetic appendicitis. It is alleged that many persons who visit one ill with the affliction have been stricken shortly after sympathizing. An Elgin businessman recently visited an Aurora person who was afflicted and within two weeks he was suffering from a pain where the appendix is located. – McHenry Plaindealer. What Next?

William H. O'Brien left today for Richmond to take possession of the drug store which he recently purchased in that village. Young Frank Wienke accompanied Mr. O'Brien to Richmond and will assist him there for a time.

New cent pieces bearing the head of Abraham Lincoln, instead of the Indian which has previously been the distinguishing mark of that coin have been turned out by the government. Distribution of which began Aug. 2. It is estimated that there are now $16,000,000 in cent pieces in circulation in this country. Through the kindness of Marshal L. T.

Hoy, a limited supply was brought to Woodstock and distributed by him.

Woodstock Sentinel, August 5, 1909.

***

INVESTIGATE THE TUBERCULIN TEST

Just before the final adjournment of the recent session of the Illinois general assembly a joint committee was appointed from both the house and the senate to investigate the tuberculin test and the pasteurization of milk and its products.

The resolution providing for this committee was passed at the suggestion of Speaker E.D. Shurleff, who has been making an active fight to protect and advance the interests of the dairymen throughout this district.

Since the completion of its organization, the members of the committee are engaging in getting together the laws and conditions in other states. It is not probable that they will begin making evidence before the month of September.

They are also watching the contest in the city council of Chicago over the pasteurization ordinance. In the Chicago council an attempt is being made to repeal the law authorizing pasteurization, but the men who want to repeal the law are in favor of the tuberculin test, so that the result of the controversy does not interest the farmer much.

Woodstock Sentinel, August 6, 1909.

***

ENGLISH LUTHERAN

English Lutheran services next Sunday afternoon at 2:30 o'clock.

Sunday school at 12 noon; also, services at Queen Anne's church Sunday evening at 7:30. Everybody invited to attend these services.
Rev. R. C. Kauffman, pastor.
Woodstock Sentinel, August 19, 1909.

***

THE WOODSTOCK PUBLIC LIBRARY

On the 10th of August, President E. E. Richards, of the board of directors, prepared the annual report to the mayor and city council for the year ending June 1 last. The President reports: Number of books purchased, 219; periodicals purchased, 16; received by gift, 2; visitors during the year, 20,263; books loaned, 11,578; books of fiction purchased, 200, history, biography, etc., 19; books rebound, 100; books in the library, of which 800 are historical, about 4,500.
Woodstock Sentinel, August 26, 1909.

Local News and Personal Items

Mrs. Hofstetter and Miss Hofstetter of Aurora, Ill., visited Rev. Kauffman here Sunday.
Woodstock Sentinel, August 26, 1909.

***

Ida considered breaking in on her brother's long-winded promotional speech about the new Ten Thousand Club and their plans. Seems he and just about every other business owner in Woodstock had joined forces to promote Woodstock.

"As a matter of fact," said Herman, "now that we have officers and are organized, we will be inviting every citizen regardless of occupation to become a member. The idea came from out west. Montana, I believe. And it won't be all work, but we'll sponsor evening activities and entertainments to keep

I Will Fly to Woodstock

the people coming down to the Square. Weekly band concerts, for example."

Roger, the new Pastor at Grace Lutheran, had let the upstairs front room in John and Ida's home until he could rent a house, a commodity which was still hard to come by in Woodstock. He was engaged to a young lady from Aurora, Blanche Hoestetter. They were in the midst of planning their wedding, but, according to Roger, they would stay with the Wienkes "until you kick us out." A man of charm and wit, he had quickly become one of the family. Tonight, Ida had invited Herman and Bessie Doering for supper to meet Rev. Kauffman and things were going well.

Of course, Herman's ambition was on display as always. "The Fourth of July day was such a success this year, it got everyone worked up on how we can keep that excitement year around. And we have a committee encouraging new factories to move here, like a new typewriter company called Emerson that is looking for a place to call home. New factories, more employment, more houses, growth!" He seemed to have finally run out of steam.

"Including the pastors?" asked Roger Kauffman.

"Of course," said Herman. "We'd love to have you join."

"And when you say citizen, do you mean women citizens, too?" asked Ida.

"Well, no, I don't think so," Herman hedged. "You wouldn't want to be a part of that, would you, Ida? Bessie? Don't you have enough to handle with the children and the house? And it's a rowdy bunch of men when we get together. Having women in the room would stunt the...um...vitality of the conversations."

"Improve your language I think you are saying, right?" Bessie chimed in. "So how is this different from any other way you men have found to get away from your wives and children? Aren't you worried about the invited pastors objecting?"

"Well, it's not...I mean...it's not to get away from our wives and children. It is to...um... promote our good city and bring more people to Woodstock to spend money and...." Herman did his best to pull back his comments.

"And the spoils will go to our wives and children," broke in John.

"Et tu, John." Bessie was laughing.

John chuckled, "Yes, me too. I'm glad the new club has been opened to all citizens since I am no longer a grocer, and therefore, would be forced to sit blandly at home with my wife and children while the other men of the city make decisions and smoke cigars. I think it's a great idea, Herman."

"You would, eh?" said Ida, a little pink in her cheeks now. "Another excuse to leave us to our own devices. Maybe we need a women's On Woodstock! group to promote...um... domestic endeavors. To show to the world," her voice was rising in oratory style, "that the women of Woodstock make the best pies," she gestured to the right, "the best bratwurst," she gestured to the left, "the best Spanfarkel!!" She had risen from her seat with her arm outstretched, hand in a fist. "Have the cleanest clothes, the smartest kids...."

Roger was laughing hard now, a great impressive belly laugh.

"Yes! Yes!" agreed Bessie. "A great idea. We, the women of Woodstock, would show the world," she too rose and raised a fist to the sky, "that nothing holds back women with a cause. And while we are away 'making arrangements,' the men would have responsibility for the children. Only seems fair, right Ida?"

"You are so right, Bessie! And what could the children bring to the table, do you think?"

"Why parks and playgrounds, of course!"

The two men were also laughing loudly now at the women's antics, the ruckus enough that Helen, Mamie and little

Elizabeth Doering came and stood in the archway between the parlor and the dining room, wondering what was going on.

"Yay!" said Elizabeth, jumping around a little. "We like parks!!" Which brought another round of hilarity from the adults.

Helen shook her head and said, "Grownups." She turned back to the parlor herding the other girls before her. "You just never know what they are about."

As the laughter subsided, Herman held up his hands in surrender. "Some of your ideas have merit," he said once he'd gained their attention.

"Well said," opined Roger.

"Thank you. Let me talk to some others and see about women joining us. I hold no position, so it's not my decision, but let me see what I can do."

Ida smiled with satisfaction. Men just needed to be guided to the right decision. She knew that Bessie wasn't interested in joining, but she was. Guess we'll have to wait and see if Herman could act as advocate...or not.

***

CARRIE NATION AT ELGIN CHAUTAUQUA

Mrs. Carrie Nation appeared on the Chautauqua program at Elgin last week, and it is said that the smasher of saloons was in a fighting humor. She had expected to find Elgin a clean, moral city, she declared, but after discovering that Elgin could boast of but one hotel without a bar attachment, the watch city lost favor in Mrs. Nation's eyes.

After a strenuous search Mrs. Nation found the bar-less hotel, the Town Block hotel by name, and going up to the clerk of the establishment, she half scared him out of his senses by her sudden declaration of, "I am Carrie Nation. Do you know why I am here?"

He evidently didn't and was too overcome perhaps to inquire, but she enlightened him in the next breath by informing him that she had come there because there was no saloon in connection with the hotel.

That same afternoon she sought the mayor at his store, and accosted him thus: "Is this the mayor? I see you smoke in your store?"

And then they proceeded to exchange ideas on the tobacco and liquor questions.

"Do you favor the saloon?" she asked Mayor Fehrman.

"Licensed and well regulated, yes," he replied.

"Would you license thieves and murderers in your city?"

"No, but that's different."

"Not a bit. It's worse. You're a Republican, I suppose?"

But she had another guess coming here. Mayor Fehrman is a Democrat.

"Well, you're not as bad as a Republican," she told him. "Democrats might be as bad as Republicans if they had a chance, but they haven't got it. I detest the Republican party because I've got it with the goods on."

"Mr. Mayor," she asked, "if you could cast a deciding vote, -- if your vote would wipe every saloon off the face of the map, how would you vote? Would you vote to keep them?"

"I believe so," the mayor frankly replied. "If I didn't, I would be a hypocrite. I have said I favor the licensed saloon, carefully regulated."

"So would the devil," was her startling rejoinder. "Hell is filled with hypocrites and sinners."

Woodstock Sentinel, September 2, 1909.

***

'Well, I better be off to the office. I have seven appointments today to talk with folks about their insurance needs." John stood from the breakfast table.

"I'm certainly happy the Lord hasn't required my services this early on a Friday morning," said Roger Kauffman. The time was seven a.m. "I will linger on for a while with this excellent coffee."

John and Ida chuckled. They had grown to love Roger's presence in the house, and the girls adored him. The whole family was hopeful that he and Blanche would stay on after the wedding. The church continued to look for a suitable parsonage, but so far had no luck.

John gave Ida a kiss on the cheek, grabbed up his hat from the peg, and headed out the back door.

Ida retrieved the coffee pot and warmed both their cups before sitting down again. She especially appreciated the adult company and discussions that Roger provided.

"Roger, what do you think about Carrie Nation? She was in the paper again yesterday."

"Carrie Nation. Well, I don't know much about her. She's a Methodist, I believe. She had a vision from God, I'm told, that told her to smash saloons until the liquor stops running."

"I thought the prohibitionists just sang hymns until the bars close."

"I believe they do that also, but I've heard that if she can gain entrance to the establishment, she smashes all the bottles…with a hatchet."

"With a hatchet?"

"Yep, that's what I hear."

"Well, she surely is dedicated to the cause. Why don't they arrest her?"

"God's work, I suppose. I heard that one bar down south put up a sign that said, 'All Nations are welcome except Carrie."

Ida chuckled. "Paper says she was in Elgin last week bothering the mayor, but I didn't hear about any smashed-up saloons. I hope she doesn't come to Woodstock."

"Mm. Might not be so bad. She might wake some up to the vile results of over-drinking."

"That doesn't sound like a German response."

He chuckled. "I never turned down a dark beer or a fine cigar."

"So, all nations are welcome, even Carrie?"

"For sure! Alle Nationen sind willkommen."

***

Local Intelligence
Albert Wienke of Beloit was a visitor at the fair Thursday.

Woodstock Sentinel, September 16, 1909.

***

September 20, 1909
365 Lincoln Avenue
Woodstock, Illinois

Dear Clara and Pearle,

I hope this letter finds you well and in good spirits. Thank you, Clara, for your letter sharing all the news from Dennison.

I very much enjoyed the articles you send with your letters. They were both moving and a bit humorous. You are doing a wonderful job with keeping the world aware of Dennison, Iowa. Please send more!

Pearle, we were pleased to hear that you made foreman in such a short time. Does that mean you don't have to climb the poles as much? Does it mean you get more pay? John continues to talk with Oliver to try to convince them to insure their employees as well as their building and machinery. If we had an outbreak of influenza or the fever, many employees would not be able to work. The doctor bills would pile up for them and the company would lose money from low productivity. If they had insurance on each one, they could help with the bills and get them back on the line more quickly. Happier employees are more productive. John says, the company could even insure itself against an epidemic. Isn't that something? So far, they haven't been swayed, but John can be persuasive when he wants to be.

I assume, no baby news yet. Don't worry, it will happen when you are ready, God willing. I pray for you about this every night.

The children are doing well. Mamie has been healthy all summer and the doctor is now pushing for us to get the tonsils cut out so she doesn't have to take the Bayer powder all the time. I suppose this is a suitable time for it since she is not in school yet. By the way, she absolutely loved the moccasins you sent for her birthday. She wears them constantly. I will have her write a thank you to come with this letter.

Helen is the toast of the second grade. She is very smart, they tell me, and her confidence is great, but I hope she isn't headed for a Humpty Dumpty fall. Her class has been writing patriotic speeches. One will be chosen from each grade and then the grand prize winner will give their speech at the dedication of the new monument being put up in the middle of the Square on Veteran's Day, I believe. No doubt one of the older students will win the contest, but Helen is working hard on her submission. I will keep you posted.

Dodi is a chubby, mostly happy, child. She seems a bit afraid of crowds and loud noises and we keep explaining the noise (thunder, firecrackers, hammers) away, but it doesn't seem to help. I'm hoping her ears become less sensitive as time goes on. She talks more and more, but also is a girl with a temper when she doesn't get her way. Right now, she can't understand "too little." I assume you can relate to that. But then she is so frightened when she is included that all she wants to do is sit on my lap, bury her face and cover her ears. I think most of this will disappear when she is older and can keep up with her sisters.

That is about all the news for good old Woodstock. I hope fall is beautiful in Iowa.

Love to you both, Ida and all

***

DIED IN SQUALOR
Owner of 200 Acre Farm Lived Miser's Life

Mahala Snellbaker, a maiden lady who has been a resident of Denison for twenty years, died Tuesday. Altho the owner of 200 acres of fine land, three miles south of Denison, she died in wretched surroundings, having been miserly in her habits of life.

Crawford County Courier, September 10, 1909.

***

EVERYBODY HAD A RIDE
Auto Day Proved Great Success at Denison.

Acting on the suggestion of the Denison Review, businessmen of Denison made a great success of their "auto day." One thousand persons, living outside the city limits and whose trading place is Denison, came to town and had a free ride in the best autos the citizens owned. From 10 in the forenoon to 5 in the evening autos were driving around the streets and country roads filled with farmers and their families, many having their first ride of this kind. It was a great day for the merchants and the stores were crowded. It gave parents a chance to give their children an auto ride and thus made the day one which will be a notable event in their lives.

Crawford County Courier, September 13, 1909.

***

Robber Gets $85

John Krauth, a Denison young man, was held up the other night while walking in the Denison Park with his best girl. A burly fellow with a handkerchief over his face shoved a gun against John's stomach and compelled him to give up a pocketbook containing $85. The girl was too badly frightened to scream until the robber had made his getaway.

Crawford County Courier, September 16, 1909.

***

DANISH BATTLE TUBERCULOSIS

Danish dairymen seek to head off an infection of their calves by tuberculosis by removing them from their dams at once if the latter are found to be tuberculous. This malady is one that is not inherited at birth but contracted by drinking germ laden milk. Thus, removal and giving the calves pure milk insure their healthy development.

A lot has been written and considerably done of late along the line of eradicating tuberculosis from dairy herds for the sake of these animals and the hogs that may follow them. It is about time the babies in town and country homes who are compelled to subsist largely on milk from tubercular cows had a word said in their behalf. It

may be that dollars don't talk so loud for them as for the animals in the pen or feedlot, but common decency and humanity should.
Woodstock Sentinel, September 23, 1909.

***

ENGLISH LUTHERAN

English Lutheran services on next Sunday evening at 7:30. At this service the Rev. R. C. Kauffman will be installed as the regular pastor of Grace English Lutheran church by the Rev. A. H. Arbaught of Chicago. A good attendance is desired. Services at Queen Anne in the afternoon at 3 o'clock.

Sunday school at 12 o'clock noon.

Rev. R. C. Kauffman, pastor.
Woodstock Sentinel, September 30, 1909.

***

"Mama?"

Ida looked up from cutting vegetables for Hühnerfrikassee or what Americans called chicken fricassee. Chicken and mushrooms were already in the frying pan having been fried in butter without browning. She had sprinkled flour into the pan, added water, brought it to a boil, and then moved the pan to a cooler part of the stove where it would simmer until thickened slightly. The aroma was beginning to smell like Oma's kitchen.

Frikassee was just a 'leftover' meal to use up vegetables at the end of the week before they spoiled. Ida thought about how some foods bring back memories of one's childhood, especially when these memories are the pleasant ones like playing dolls under the kitchen table with Emma while Louisa cooked in the kitchen, at a time when they were too small to do much more than stay out of the way.

"Mama?" Mamie said again. "Is something wrong? You look funny."

Ida laughed. "No, my darling girl, nothing is wrong. I was just remembering playing with dolls with your Aunt Emma under the kitchen table while Oma cooked."

"That would be fun."

"It was. The good smells of the kitchen swirling around, the chilly air coming under the table each time she went out on the porch to get something from the outside icebox. We each had a doll. Mine had dark hair, and I named her Gertrude or Gerty—"

"Like Unca Frank's horse?"

"Yes! Exactly. And Emma's doll had brown hair and was named…let's see, what was her name…Ach, how can I forget such a thing? Her name was something funny. Maybe Scamp or Scout, no wait, Silly Sally, I think it was."

Mamie giggled, "What a funny name."

"Oma had made some clothes for the dolls from leftover scraps of our own frocks, so we matched our dolls. We had tea under the table—"

"Instead of on top of the table."

"Yes, and the chair legs were the rooms. The bedroom for Gerty was under one chair and for Sally was under another chair."

Mamie squatted to look under the kitchen table.

"We had such fun," remembered Ida.

"Can I play under the table?"

Ida bent and looked under the table. "I suppose so, but—"

"Goody. I'll go get Dodi."

Ida watched the little girl skip out of the kitchen and disappear into the parlor. Her heart jumped with love for the thin, pale, but happy five-year-old. She had been fever-free for a month. If this continued, she would have her tonsils out after Thanksgiving. And next year she would be going to school.

Soon the girls were installed below the table with the chairs pushed partially in, chattering away about their dolls. Dodi's doll was Dolly in an aqua-blue dress with a lace collar, and Mamie's was Peggy in a red dress with tiny white polka dots.

Ida turned back to the fricassee. She checked the pot. The chicken was almost ready for deboning. After she had removed the bones and pulled apart the chicken, she mixed in small whole carrots, fresh peas, a handful of shallots, along with a half a cup of cream and a slosh more and added a bit more water and replaced the heavy lid. She looked at the clock. 4:15 o'clock. The mixture would be almost ready at quarter to five when she'd add the white asparagus and by five o'clock when John walked through the door, supper would be ready.

From under the table came the sweet voices. "When Papa comes home, Dolly, we must have dinner ready," said Peggy.

"Otay," said Dolly. "I will make the ice cream."

"Good," said Peggy. "I will make the cake."

"Otay," said Dolly. "How much time do we have?"

"Plenty of time for a story before he comes," said Peggy. "I will tell it."

"Otay," said Dolly.

"Once upon a time," said Peggy, "There was a little girl who had a doll named Gerty, like the horse."

***

ALL THINGS DENISON
by Clara Daring
ACCIDENT ON THE LINE

Harry Wilson, a traveling sign painter, came near being killed at Arion by being struck by the Illinois Central flyer, while crossing the track. He was badly bruised but not seriously injured. The lines of the Northwestern, Milwaukee and Illinois Central cross at Arion and travelers at night cannot tell from which way the train is coming. Many accidents have occurred there.

The town who owns the roadway has suggested that a trainman be posted who could lower gates depending on the track being used. The railroad has suggested that the town build a viaduct over the tracks to eliminate the problem altogether. So, a stalemate has come about with human life hanging in the balance.

Crawford County Courier, October 8, 1909.

***

October 8, 1909
Dennison, Iowa

Dear Ida and all,

Glory Be! I'm famous, well maybe not famous, but known to Iowa! Dennison had a German Day and the editor of the Crawford County Courier liked so much what I'd been doing that he sent me out to "get the story." He also liked that I could understand German. So, I did. I went and took notes on everything that happened and then wrote a story on the day and sent it to him and he was so impressed he sent it out to all the other newspapers in the state. AND Des Moines picked it up and published it with very little editing. My name wasn't on it, just the newspaper's, but it was my work!! I've enclosed a copy from the Register, and also a couple more that I did for the Courier. Also, an article about the influenza John should take to heart.

I am so happy that my reporting is being accepted and appreciated. It was a great German day. I felt so proud to be German and the speeches were inspiring. Maybe some of that came through in the writing.

Otherwise, we are fine. Pearley dear is loving his new position. He still must go up the poles on occasion, but not nearly as much as before so I am happy about that.

Thanks for all the news of the kiddies. Just thought I'd share the good news. No baby yet.

Love,

Clara

***

German Day at Denison
Iowans Celebrate Landing of First German Immigrants

Denison, Ia., Oct. 7. – SPECIAL REPORT of the *Crawford County Courier* – German day was appropriately celebrated yesterday at Denison by the Germans of this vicinity. There was a large attendance at the Brotherhood Park. Prof. J. F. Harthun, the editor of the Zeitung, presided. He delivered an appropriate introductory speech in German. Mayor W. C. Rollings spoke in English and delivered an address of welcome on behalf of the city of Denison. Rev. Mr. Hansen of Schleswig, delivered an able and scholarly address in German, giving a historic account of the first German settlements, which was full of information and sound advice.

Carl F. Kuehnle of Denison delivered an address in English. He gave an account of the landing of the first German immigrants at Germantown, Oct. 6, 1683. These German settlers came for religious and civil liberty, to escape the persecutions of petty tyrants in the Fatherland and to better the condition of themselves and families. Mr. Kuehnle mentioned the fact that these settlers were the first colonists to protest against human slavery. In 1688 they prepared and signed a protest and sent it to the monthly meeting at Richard Worells' denouncing slavery, which is the first recorded protest in America against this inhuman traffic.

Mr. Kuehnle said by the last census there were over three million German-born Americans in the United States, and over ten million German parents and that at least one-third of the entire population had German blood in their veins. The celebration of German day does not mean that our German-Americans love Germany more than they do America, nor that they owe allegiance to the tri-color of Germany. Though they love the Fatherland and its flag, like a faithful wife who leaves the parental home and clings to her husband, the German loves the land of his adoption above all else.

Mr. Kuehnle spoke of the sterling qualities of the Germans. Their devotion to principle and duty, love of country and home, their industry, integrity and respect for law and their cheerful view of life and realism. He also spoke of the great opportunities of American citizenship and urged the parents to give their children a liberal education and, if possible, a college training.

Mr. Kuehnle's address was frequently interrupted by applause and was full of sound Americanism.

Des Moines Register, October 8, 1909.

MUCH INFLUENZA IN LONDON
Turned-Up Trousers Blamed by Physicians for Epidemic

LONDON, Oct. 7. – Americans who are suffering from "colds" at this season will sympathize with their "cousins" in the British capital, for influenza has already made its appearance in London in the guise of a catarrhal affection of the nose and throat of an unusually tenacious and severe variety.

A physician connected with one of the great London hospitals has suggested as one of the causes of the outbreak the habit of turning up the trousers. This fashion, he says, is responsible for many autumn coughs and colds contracted before the system has had time to become accustomed to the constant foot dampness which for every Londoner is a winter portion. The turned-up edges of the trousers become soaked through, and then act as wet bandages around the ankles.

Des Moines Register, October 8, 1909.

***

SOCIAL EVENTS

A happy company of children gathered at the home of Mr. and Mrs. G. W. Lemmers on Saturday to help their little daughter, Mary, celebrate her fourth birthday. The afternoon was passed in playing, as only children can, and a 5 o'clock luncheon was served in the dining room, the little guests being seated around the table which was gay with its pretty decorations of colored lanterns, while on the center of the table was the birthday cake with its four candles, brightly shining, and at each plate were prettily dressed dolls and little pumpkin pies that served as souvenirs of the occasion. At 6 o'clock much to the delight of the children, the baby carriage of the sweet little hostess was drawn up to the front door and the merry company were conveyed to their homes in the neighborhood. The children present were: Elizabeth Doering, Gladys Kline, Helen Johnson, Grace Doering, Norma Bodenschatz, Helen Lemmers, Hebron.

Woodstock Sentinel, October 21, 1909.

REV. R. C. KAUFFMAN WEDS IN AURORA

Rev. Roger C. Kauffman of Woodstock was united in marriage on Wednesday evening, Oct. 20, at 8 o'clock, at the home of the bride's brother at Aurora.

The bride was attended by her sister, Miss Margaret Hoestetter. Rev. Gold of Madison who was to have been best man was unable to be present because of the serious illness of a relative. Rev. Anda of Chicago performed the marriage ceremony.

Rev. Kauffman is pastor of the Grace Lutheran church in this city, in which capacity he has served since August. During his brief pastorate in Woodstock, he has made many friends, with whom The Sentinel joins in extending hearty congratulations.

Rev. and Mrs. Kauffman will reside in Woodstock, where Rev. Kauffman will continue to serve as pastor of Grace Lutheran church.

Woodstock Sentinel, October 21, 1909.

***

Roger carried Blanche over the threshold with a flourish and sat her nimbly on her feet in the foyer of 365 Lincoln Avenue. John, Ida and the children clapped and cheered their entrance with Mamie and Dodi jumping around with joy.

"Well, there you have it!" bellowed Roger. His face was ruddy with excitement. "You are home!"

Blanche demurred slightly, reaching out to hug Ida and kiss her on each cheek.

"You are home," said Ida.

John broke in by taking Blanche's hand to his lips. "Welcome."

"Welcome. Welcome," sang the girls. Then all three of them curtsied.

"What a homecoming." Blanche seemed nearly overwhelmed with the excitement of the moment.

"John, can you help me get the luggage?" Roger reached for the door.

"Certainly." The two men went out to retrieve the five cases stacked there, brought them in, and took them up the stairs.

"Mrs. Kauffman," said Helen. "May I escort you upstairs to see your rooms?"

"Why certainly." Blanche smiled at the polite girl and allowed her to take her arm. Walking side by side didn't work very well after the turn was made for the final flight, so Helen took the lead.

Ida looked at the little girls and decided that they should not go up with the others. "Come on, girls. Let's go make some refreshments."

Supper had already been eaten and cleaned up, but there was always Kuchen to be found in Ida's cupboard.

Ida put a pot of coffee to boil and then took the cake from the pantry and cut two by two inch pieces and put them on a plate. She handed the plate to Mamie. "Please, put this on the dining table."

Mamie took the plate, juggled it a bit, requiring Ida to steady it until Mamie had it under control.

Ida got dessert plates and forks. The plates went to Mamie and the forks to Dodi. "Spread them around the table. The fork goes on the right."

Mamie held up her right hand. "This right, Mama?"

Ida smiled. "Yes, that's right."

Ida took three small glasses and poured milk into them and into a creamer. These she placed on a tray along with four cups and carried them to the table herself.

The entourage came down the stairs.

"Oh Ida, it's beautiful," exclaimed Blanche. "The lace curtains are exquisite. Did you make them?"

"Not the lace, but I did sew some hems," was Ida's modest reply.

"And the afghans. One for each of us, right?"

"Yes, for the cold nights when the furnace can't keep up. You'll have to decide who gets which color, purple or pink."

"Purple," said both Kauffmans in unison trying to beat each other to the punch. They laughed.

"Oh my, maybe I'll have to get busy on a third one."

"No need, we'll share, right Roger?" Blanche sidled up to him and took his arm.

"Right." Roger looked a bit disconcerted and then said, "I guess it's time—"

"For cake!" said Mamie.

"Cake?" Roger winked at Mamie. "Did you bake a cake for us?"

"Nooooo." Mamie blushed a little. "Mama did. It's chocolate."

"Well, no one can pass up Ida's Schokoladenkuchen."

Now, Ida blushed.

John smiled. "Come to the dining room. There's just enough time for Kuchen and coffee before bedtime."

As they retired to the dining room, Blanche linked arms with Ida. "You know," she said in a hushed tone, "I could use some pointers on Kuchen and other cooking. Will you mind having an apprentice?"

"Not at all. It will be fun." Ida said, coming to her place at the table. "Reverend Kauffman, would you bless this gathering and this cake?"

"Of course," he said, just a little too loudly. They bowed their heads.

"Heavenly Father, we ask a blessing tonight on the Wienke family who has rescued us from the dark streets of Woodstock and welcomed us into their embrace as we start our life together. We also ask that you bless this fine cake and each of us to thy service. Amen."

***

GRACE LUTHERAN HAS NEW HOME

The Grace Lutheran society has purchased the German Presbyterian church property on Washington street. The German Presbyterians decided to discontinue the church society and authorized the trustees to sell the property. The trustees did so, and it was purchased by the Grace Lutheran society, who had no building of their own in which to hold services.

Woodstock Sentinel, October 21, 1909.

UNIVERSALISTS TO DISTRIBUTE FUNDS AND DISBAND

The Universalist society this week distributed funds among Woodstock organizations as follows:

Seven hundred dollars were given to the public schools toward enlarging the school library as a memorial to Miss Alice Blakeslee. Miss Blakeslee was during her lifetime a staunch Universalist, and it is especially appropriate that this memorial should be in the Woodstock schools where Miss Blakeslee taught for several years.

To the Woman's Relief corps was given $500 toward the monument fund.

Four hundred dollars were donated to the public library.

The fourth donation was the amount of $1178.89 to the Ladies Cemetery association to be used in erecting a chapel.

The Universalist society deserves much credit for the generosity and public spirit which it has displayed in distributing these funds. Every dollar has been placed where it will forward a good cause, and the society's act has been much appreciated by Woodstock people. It is such generosity as this, such interest displayed in the advancement of loyal schools and organizations, which insure the progress of our home city and its institutions.

Woodstock Sentinel, October 21, 1909.

***

ALL THINGS DENISON
by Clara Daring
RESULT OF QUOITS CONTEST
Three Sets of Games Going Five Hours
W. H. Case Wins Medal

The Crawford County horseshoe pitching contest closed late yesterday afternoon. There were seventeen contestants for the gold medal offered by Dr. Philbrook, of this city. The contest took place in front of the courthouse and attracted a large number of people. Three sets of games were in progress continuously for five hours. W. H. Case, of Deloit, the next station north of Denison, won twelve out of thirteen games; H. Koenekamp, of Denison, won nine, lost two; Perry Huckstep, of Deloit, won eight and lost four. These three leaders had a final contest, as the rules of the contest provided for this. Huckstep lost to Koenekamp and he to Case, who was declared the county champion. The pegs were forty-five feet apart and twenty-one counts for a game. Such a contest will now be an annual affair for this county.

This reporter must admit that this is a harder game than she first realized. Given a chance to sling the horseshoe, the effort resulted in a pop fly which landed only five feet closer to the far peg. A second try, while not as sky-worthy, still covered only half

I Will Fly to Woodstock

the distance. The strength and accuracy of these men should be admired.

Crawford County Courier, October 22, 1909.

***

"Okay, Papa, you sit right here."

Helen had moved the coffee table to the side in the parlor and placed two dining room chairs where it had been. Ida sat in one of the chairs and John took the other. Mamie and Dodi were on either end of the davenport behind the wooden chairs.

"Okay, now you pretend that you are in the front row of seats at the Square, and I am up on the stage."

"Okay, we're ready," said Mamie.

"And Mamie and Dodi, you be quiet like you would have to do if you were in church."

"Okay." Dodi shouted and threw her hands up in the air.

"Don't do that." Helen instructed.

"Okay." Dodi said even louder and threw her hands up again.

"Mama," Helen whined.

Ida turned to face the two little girls. "Like you were in church."

"Yes, Mama." The little girls smiled at each other.

"Okay." Helen went out of the parlor to the foyer. In a loud voice she said, "And now we have Helen Wienke."

The crowd applauded.

Helen came out of the foyer and bowed.

"Helen," interrupted Ida. "You should probably curtsy instead of bowing."

"Okay." Helen went back to the foyer. "And now we have Helen Wienke, winner of the speech writing contest at the Woodstock schools."

Helen emerged and did a fine curtsy center stage. She walked forward a few steps and began:

"Today we honor both our hometown heroes and heroes from around the world who have kept our country whole and safe for children to grow healthy and strong. Our Woodstock Rifles didn't think about themselves fifty years ago during the battle of Pea Ridge. They were thinking about their parents, their brothers and sisters, their friends, their hometown and their country when they faced down the Rebs on that hill, because their top priority was saving and reuniting America. Even when they were outnumbered, they did not give up. They faced head-on an enemy that was determined to destroy our United States of America. They fought on and on and were finally victorious over Johnny Reb!"

Helen paused a little and the audience applauded.

"Helen," said Ida. "Could you act out what you are talking about more? You know, maybe hold an invisible rifle over your shoulder or make a mean face as you talk about them facing the enemy?"

"I can probably do that. But won't I look silly?"

John jumped in. "Remember last year when we went to that Memorial Day speech. Remember how the speaker used her hands and face and actions to illustrate what she was saying."

"Yes. I guess she didn't look silly," agreed Helen. "Okay."

Helen shouldered an invisible rifle and she crouched in an attack stance as she 'faced the enemy.'

"During the battle of Pea Ridge, our hero, Captain Merritt Joslyn, led the Woodstock battalion in a brilliant charge that scattered the rebels like chaff before the wind." Here Helen made an elegant gesture with her right hand up and away as the wind might blow. Then she got a worried look on her face, eyebrows wrinkled inward in an expression of concern.

"But as the Woodstock Rifles approached the rebel stronghold, sharp shooters on a hill began to shoot them one at a time. Many died."

The audience moaned.

Helen pointed up toward the top of the hill. "Our brave soldiers rushed up the hill, trying to ignore their friends who were falling around them." She gestured to the ground to the right and the left. "But they found the way blocked."

An audible gasp broke the silence.

I Will Fly to Woodstock

Helen paused looking at the ground as if all was lost. But then her face came up, eyes squinted, a bit of a smile. "That was when our oh so sneaky Captain Joslyn ordered the soldiers into the woods." Helen bent at the waist and walked stealthily across the room. "On they went from tree to tree, the forest hid them from the crack of rebel rifles." She scurried from tree to tree, peeking out at the top of the hill. "They kept creeping forward through the woods until they had surrounded and captured Johnny Reb and his flag."

The audience broke into applause.

"And when those below," Helen pointed downward, "saw the stars and stripes unfurl," she pulled a small flag out of her jumper and held it up, "on the mountaintop, they knew that the Union had been victorious. And everyone knew that Captain Joslyn and the Woodstock Rifles had saved the day."

Hoorays sounded from the davenport.

"Because the Woodstock Rifles gave their lives, and men just like them all across the Grand Army of the Republic gave theirs, our United States was saved and our freedom is forever. So today, we say God Bless our soldiers, our sailors and our Woodstock Rifles who keep our children safe. I am glad to be one of our children. God Bless America!"

The audience again sounded a great appreciation and rose to their feet.

And Helen's face turned red, but she managed another curtsy before escaping to the foyer.

***

Work Has Begun

Work has begun on Tuesday on the foundations for the new Emerson typewriter factory and is being rushed rapidly forward. Charles Giertz and Son, the Elgin firm which has done so much work there in the past, has the contract and will put a large gang of men on the building operations. The building will be in the shape of an I., 225 feet south and 360 feet facing on East Street.

A sidetrack has been staked out from the railroad at the Clay Street crossing. From there it will run east on Church Street through the south part of the Blakeslee property to the location of the factory. It is said that the track will be laid in a few days, so that the building materials can be unloaded from the cars directly on the grounds.

Woodstock Sentinel, October 28, 1909.

***

ALL THINGS DENISON
by Clara Daring
QUEER BUSINESS.

A lot of supposedly honest and respectable people in some sections seem to consider a neighboring orchard as semi-public property and raid it without compunction whenever the fit takes them. These people may not realize that it costs the owner just as much to prune and spray his trees and till the ground as it does his neighbor to care for a corn, potato or small grain crop. Yet these same folks would consider it mighty queer business – stealing – if the orchard owner should go into their fields, husk and make off with a sack of corn or dig and appropriate a bushel of potatoes. The proposition is just as broad as it is long, and the ethics involved make no distinction between a crop that grows on trees and that produced on stalks or vines.

After a number of thefts of this kind, the Denison police will be fining anyone found stealing fruit or vegetables from a neighboring field during this harvest time. Be forewarned.

Crawford County Courier, October 28, 1909.

***

Local News and Personal Items.
The ladies of Grace Evangelical church tendered a reception to Rev. Kauffman and wife on Tuesday evening of last week at the pretty home of Mr. and Mrs. John Wienke, on Lincoln Avenue. A large number of friends were present to greet their beloved pastor and welcome his charming bride. A substantial gift of money was presented to the happy pair with the best of wishes of the friends present.

Woodstock Sentinel, November 4, 1909.

***

> School children
> should eat
>
> **Quaker Oats**
>
> at least
> twice a day
>
> Assorted china in the Family Size Package

***

Ida hurried down the wooden walkway to the corner where it turned into cement and then down onto the Square. She pushed a pram with Dodi inside, bundled against the wind and led Mamie by the hand. Mamie was dressed in her best Sunday coat with the fur around the hood and down the front. She had a cute little dress that Ida had made in rusty red and yellow fabric with crocheted leggings under it. She looked like a little pixie in her finery. Dodi was happy to be "inside" the hooded pram where she could peek out, but not be the center of anyone's attention.

Today was Veterans Day, the day when the city honored all who served as members of the Grand Army of the Republic (G.A.R.) during the wartime. In past years, the city gathered flowers and walked them en masse to the Chicago and Northwestern depot where they were loaded into a special train and sent to Chicago to decorate the graves of the fallen soldiers and veterans. The crowd then walked the two blocks to the Square for a simple ceremony honoring those who were from Woodstock.

The ladies of the Women's Relief Corps (W.R.C.) in Woodstock had worked tirelessly over many years to raise funds for a monument to members of the G.A.R. and specifically to the "Woodstock Rifles" who had fought with the Union. During her years in Woodstock, Ida had read about and donated to their efforts and appeals for funds. But that wasn't why she was hurrying to get to the celebration today. Today, Helen was to recite the speech she had written for the dedication of the monument.

The crowd was thick in the Square, even though she and the girls were a bit early for the two o'clock start. People crammed the park cheek to jowl. She made her way to a spot right in front of the Court House where she could see the bandstand where the presenters would be speaking. She heard the fife and drum coming onto the Square from the east followed by the ladies of the W. R. C. and the men of the G. A. R. marching in formation around the Square. They entered on the west side right in front of where they were standing.

The bandstand sat near the center of the park but Ida was hard pressed to get any closer. The cobblestone street made it hard to push the pram and even if they were to cross the street, they would have not been able to get into the park nor see the stage better than here. Better to stay perched on this bit of a rise.

As the dignitaries found seats on the dais, the Oliver Band swung into Stars and Stripes Forever, one of Ida's favorites. Mamie marched around their small space in time to the music. Ida smiled. It was so good to see her second child finally enjoying life. Next month the doctor would remove her tonsils and that would be that.

Rev. Hay from the Presbyterian Church stepped to the podium. Ida strained her ears; she could just barely make out that a man was speaking even though he used a megaphone. Everyone bowed their heads. She reached down and stopped Mamie's wandering and whispered, "Pray." Mamie folded her hands and looked at the ground.

"Mama," Dodi said into the silence. "Mama, I'm hungry." A few in the crowd snickered a bit. Ida bent to the pram and whispered, "You'll have to wait a bit. We have to wait for Helen's speech. Here, I brought these biscuits. Would one of these do?"

"Okay," said Dodi in what seemed a shout. How long was this prayer? Ida unwrapped a biscuit and handed it to her, rose up and reestablished the penitent position, hands clasped and head bowed.

A rustle in the crowd indicated that the prayer had ended. Ida removed a picnic blanket from the pram and spread it on the ground so she and Mamie could sit and be somewhat comfortable. It wasn't November-cold today, that they could be thankful for, but it was chilly. Down in the crowd, the wind was blocked, and they settled in to listen to the speeches.

Alfred Stills got to his feet on the stage. His voice was robust and audible even at this distance although often it was drowned out by laughter or applause from the crowd. At the end of his remarks, he announced the grammar school chorus and about 300 youngsters, including Helen, filed into position before the dais. They sang with gusto a song called, *America the Beautiful*, a song that Ida had never heard.

> "Oh, beautiful for spacious skies,
> For amber waves of grain,
> For purple mountain's majesty,
> Above the fruited plain!
> America! America!
> God shed his grace on thee,
> And crown thy good with brotherhood,
> From sea to shining sea!

Ida's eyes filled with tears. Such a beautiful song and such a happy chorus. Yes, please God, shed your grace on my country.

> O beautiful for heroes proved,
> In liberating strife.
> Who more than self their country loved
> And mercy more than life!
> America! America!
> God shed His grace on thee
> Till selfish gain no longer stain,
> The banner of the free!
> America! America!
> God shed his grace on thee,
> And crown thy good with brotherhood,
> From sea to shining sea!

The whole crowd responded with thundering applause. Ida found her hanky and wiped at her eyes. And then there she was. Her little girl walked confidently onto the stage. A woman in a red, white, and blue ensemble followed her out and held a megaphone so Helen could use her rhetorical style without encumbrance and still be heard.

Afterwards, she would tell Helen that she had heard every word of the speech and that it was marvelous. Truth is, probably only one in ten in the park could hear every word of the wee voice telling them of the sacrifice and the bravery of the soldiers of the Woodstock Rifles and their advance to victory.

She took a moment to smile at the crowd and then curtsied. She stepped forward to look into their eyes. "Today we honor...and safe for children to grow.... The Woodstock Rifles didn't...themselves, but they did...faced down the odds...fifty years ago...they were outnumbered by those ...destroying our United States...Johnny Reb!" During this portion of the speech, Helen shouldered her invisible rifle which came down in front as she faced the gray army.

"...battle of Pea Ridge, our captain Merritt Joslyn...brilliant charge...chaff before the wind." Helen watched the chaff blowing away for just a moment, then returned to her task with an excited voice.

"As the Woodstock...rebel stronghold, sharp shooters .... Many died." Helen pointed to the top of city hall, and many in the crowd looked up at the cupola. "Our brave soldiers rushed up...sneaky Captain Joslyn ordered the soldiers into the woods." Helen bent at the waist and walked stealthily across the stage. The megaphone lady crouched and crept along at her side. The crowd had fallen silent, caught up in the telling. "...from tree to tree, the forest keeping... crack of rebel rifles....slipped....forest...surround Johnny Reb." Helen made a large arc on the stage to come back to face the audience. "...those below saw...stars and stripes unfurl...knew...victorious." Helen held up a small flag on a stick and let it wave it in the breeze. "...Woodstock Rifles...saved the day." The crowd cheered.

"Because...gave their lives...like....the Grand Army of... was saved. Today...say God Bless our soldiers... sail...Rifles...keep...children safe." While she was saying this, Helen walked to the edge of the stage and reached down. She motioned the megaphone away, picked up a six foot long flagpole with a three foot flag, almost too big for the little girl, and turned to face the crowd. She raised the flag, kept the end of the pole on the ground, and let it unfurl. A wave of applause began and grew as she shouted in her loudest voice "God Bless America and the Woodstock Rifles!" as she waved the flag back and forth. Most of the people were on their feet hooting and hollering above the applause.

Even the people gathered around Ida, Mamie and Dodi who had not heard all the words, stood and clapped vigorously. Helen took a curtsy and then waved to the crowd as she walked across the stage and exited.

"Harrah for Helen!" called out Mamie.

Indeed, thought Ida, Harrah for Helen!

Lena Seiler stepped forward and explained how the W.R.C. raised the money for the monument at teas and socials, but then in the last year the merchants and town dignitaries had made large contributions so the whole town could celebrate on this day. Then followed the formal presentation of the monument to the city by the W.R.C. and in acceptance of the monument on behalf of the city by Mayor Donovan.

Six grandchildren of veterans of the war came on stage and were led over to a rope tied to the tarp covering the statue. They pulled but the tarp would not budge. In the end, two men came to the rescue. They had to pull hard on the rope and untangle the tarp, and finally they unveiled the beautiful statue. As the tarp fell to the ground, the crowd gasped at the monument's majesty and broke into cheers of approval. Somewhere a cannon boomed, and the dedication was marked with a twenty-one-gun salute from a regimen dressed in Union uniforms.

In front of and above them was a life-size union soldier standing atop a graduated pedestal which began with a nine-by-nine-foot base in dark Quincy marble. The second and third giant stone cubes held the inscription "Erected To The

Soldiers 1861-65." Above that a slightly smaller cube displayed symbols on each side – an anchor, crossed rifles, crossed sabers and a cannon – representing the Navy, the Infantry, the Calvary, and the Artillery branches of the Army with cannonballs at each top corner. Atop this block was a round column capped with a Corinthian capital upon which the Barre-marble Union sentinel soldier stood at parade rest with one knee flexed forward slightly wearing his Zouave or light infantry uniform and 1858 style kepi or cap. He held his best friend, his musket, in front of him, stock on the ground and barrel encircled by both hands.

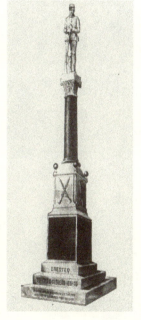

The high school boys chorus sang the *Battle Hymn of the Republic*, and then someone named Fish, Ida was sure that's what she heard, read Lincoln's speech at Gettysburg, always a crowd pleaser. There were short speeches by dignitaries...too many in Ida's mind.

"Mama," said Mamie. "When can we go? I'm cold."

"I think it's just about done," Ida said to the child. "Let's stand up and get ready so we can make a dash for it." As they did so, Ida realized everyone else was also rising from their seats and removing their hats. She heard the first strains of *America* by the Oliver Typewriter band. She stood a little straighter and sang the National Anthem.

> My country, 'tis of thee,
> Sweet land of liberty,
> Of thee I sing;
> Land where my fathers died,

Land of the pilgrims' pride,
From every mountainside
Let freedom ring!

Our fathers' God to Thee,
Author of liberty,
To Thee we sing.
Long may our land be bright,
With freedom's holy light,
Protect us by Thy might,
Great God our King.

***

DOERING'S
Thanksgiving
Linen and China
Sale

Many Articles at ½ price.
Sale Begining
Saturday, Nov. 14th

***

Homecoming at Corliss

The village of Corliss, Wisconsin held a homecoming on Friday. An epidemic of scarlet fever in the village impaired the success of the affair.

Inter Urban, November 6, 1909.

***

ALL THINGS DENISON
by Clara Daring
ALL DOORS SWING INWARD
Judge Church Orders Change in New Court House at Denison

Judge Z. A. Church of Jefferson arrived in Denison yesterday noon and opened the November term of the district court. His first official act as judge was to order County Auditor M.J. Collins as custodian of the Crawford County courthouse, to have all outer doors to the building swing outward. This order means considerable outlay of money as the doors are very large ones, of solid oak. The courthouse is a new one and why the doors were not made to swing outward originally is a mystery. State Architect Berlinghof of Nebraska was the architect.

Crawford County Courier, November 18, 1909.

***

THE BOOSTERS WORK
Commercial Club Will Do
Great Business Soon

Denison Commercial club held a "guest night" at Hotel Denison on Tuesday evening, at which time there were ninety plates laid.

The "booster" spirit has taken a strong hold upon the club members and there will be something doing in Denison from now on. Not satisfied with having secured a Carnegie library, a $150,000 courthouse, a $55,000 hotel, a $20,000 hospital, a $75,000 cold storage plant and a $50,000 college, the businessmen are going better.

> After the supper Carl F. Kuehnle, president of the club, called upon the different committees recently appointed for reports. George Naeve, of the financial committee, reported enough funds with a little boosting to insure a $30,000 Opera House; Mr. Gulick, as chairman of the committee on the Opera House site reported progress and without doubt a most desirable location will be secured. Mayor Rollins reported for the paving committee, that he had looked up prices, etc., and the subject will be taken up among interested property owners.
> Judge Z. A. Church of Jefferson was present and was called upon to talk and in the course of his remarks said what he has often said elsewhere.
> *Des Moines Register*, December 4, 1909.

***

Ida reread the final sentence of the article Clara had sent her. Odd, she thought. Maybe Clara had gone on and on about his remarks and there wasn't room in the paper for the whole column. It was her second Denison report in the Register in as many months. She had to admit, her little sister had a flair to make a boring story interesting and sometimes funny. But then that's the kind of gal Clara was. She looked over at her sleeping child.

Mamie lay in the hospital bed sound asleep. That's good, thought Ida. Sleep is the best cure. The surgery had gone well and was short, less than a half hour. The tonsils were gone, and the doctor had said they were an awful mess. Years of infection had left them swollen and pock marked. The danger now was that taking them out might have released that infection into her body, and so she would stay here in the hospital for a few days until they were sure going home was safe.

I Will Fly to Woodstock

Ida leaned back and closed her eyes. She had been at bedside for just about 24 hours. She had slept in fits and starts last night but now was ready for a nap. She dozed off. She found herself in the Opera House and a minstrel show was on the stage. She saw strong man John over to the side waiting his turn to perform. The audience was laughing, but it wasn't at a person in black face, but rather a harlequin, a jester of bygone days, called Joey in England and 'pickle herring' (Bückelhering) by Grandma Doering. He appeared to be taking the part of the interlocutor but without speaking. His colorful but mismatched apparel with one sleeve purple and the other green with the colors reversed on the pant legs, was joyful, and his face was stretched into a wide comical grin. A bejeweled yellow collar hugged his neck, and his hat had three stuffed horns with tinkling bells at the end of each, two purple and one yellow. The audience laughed again, but then went suddenly silent. Ida looked over her shoulder and found that she was alone in the large auditorium. When her eyes swung back to the stage, she realized that her seat had been moved onto the stage. Was she now part of the performance?

The expressive white face of Joey had a slightly ruddy, bulbous nose, but it was his own. He cavorted around a bit, as a harlequin should, tumbling and miming joy at being noticed by her, asking her with his hands to 'watch this!' He ended the act with a deep sweeping bow which threw him off balance. As he fell, he tucked into a somersault and ended up cross-legged on the stage floor. Ida clapped her appreciation for his agility. Then she felt the kind eyes look deep into her soul. The wide smile changed to a portentous frown. Profound worry lines etched across his forehead. His hands traced pantomimed tears down his cheeks. Why was he crying? Had someone been hurt? She looked around and saw no one.

Pickle herring began to play a lilting tune on a squeezebox. Ida covered her ears. The music was too loud, echoing off the walls in the confines of the stage. Was he trying to wake the dead? The fellow stood and danced a little jig down a hall, and Ida followed with her hands over her ears. She tried to ask him to stop playing, but words wouldn't come out of her mouth. She put up her hand, palm toward him. Stop! He immediately did. His right hand pointed to the left. She followed his gesture and saw a door. He moved on and the loud music began again. So loud. She tried to go toward the door, but her feet wouldn't move. She fell to the floor with little or no grace and tried to crawl toward the door but to no avail. She closed her eyes.

When Ida opened her eyes again, she was sitting in her chair in the hospital room, but the very loud music was still coming from a squeezebox playing harlequin. She wanted to pinch herself, but she couldn't move. Why couldn't she move? Why couldn't she talk? Why wouldn't he stop playing?

Joey stopped playing and pointed slowly toward the bed. The sad look on his face with an enormous upside-down smile made Ida's stomach lurch. The music began again, but quieter and more dirge-like now. He sadly shook his head. Ida quickly looked at her daughter and then back to the clown. The man and his music were gone.

Now Ida could move. She got up and went to the bedside. Mamie was very white almost blue. "Nurse," Ida called out in a panic, "Nurse, come quickly!"

A woman in white bustled in. "What's wrong?" she asked.

"Didn't you hear the music?"

"What?"

"Is she blue?" Ida pointed to Mamie.

"Music?"

"LOOK AT HER!" Ida screamed.

The nurse looked down at Mamie, sucked in breath, and ran to the doorway of the hall. "Call the doctor," she shouted to the desk nurse. She went to Mamie and sat the little girl up and shook her gently, saying, "Mamie, Mamie, look at me. Open your eyes. Mamie."

"Mamie," said Ida, rather sharply, "Wake up!"

The nurse said, "She's breathing, but not well."
The doctor rushed in.
"That was quick," said the nurse.
"I was just coming in to check on her. What happened?"
"Mom discovered that she was turning blue. She's pinked up a bit by being sat up, but there has been no eye fluttering or consciousness. She doesn't seem to be getting enough air in."
The doctor marched to the window and flung it open. A cold breeze rushed into the room. "Here," he said, "roll the bed over here and get some extra blankets."
As Ida stood there shivering, she was amazed at how quickly Mamie's color improved when she was put in the frigid blast. Blankets were piled on to the bed over her inert form, even covering her head with one as a cape would.
The cold also served to wake Mamie up. She moaned, hand struggling to get free of the blankets.
"There, there," cooed Ida. "You're fine. Do not try to talk. Remember you had your tonsils out."
Mamie whimpered and whispered, "Hurts."
"Your throat?" Ida asked.
"Effrewhere," Mamie whispered.
"Everywhere?" the doctor echoed. He took one of the blankets and put it around his shoulders and handed one to the nurse and then to Ida. "What do you mean, Mamie, everywhere?" he asked.
"Here and here and here," she whispered, moving her hand under the mountain of blankets.
"Wait, wait. Let me peek under and see where you are pointing."
Mamie pointed to her arm and her stomach and her leg and her chest and her throat and...everywhere.
"Okay. Let me try to move your legs. Try to just relax and let me do the moving," he said as he reached under and moved her right leg and bent it at the knee.

Mamie moaned and began to cry, tears running down her cheeks and being absorbed by the head blanket.

"It hurts bad, huh?" the doctor said.

Mamie nodded her head slightly and winced again at the motion.

The doctor tucked Mamie back under the covers and said, "Mrs. Wienke, can I talk to you for a moment? Nurse, please check the patient's temperature."

"Yes, doctor," said the woman in white.

They stepped into the hall. "I should call John," Ida said.

"I think Mamie has rheumatic fever," said the doctor.

"What! No, no. You must have it wrong. She is just a little girl who had a tonsillectomy." Visions of Bob Wienke's funeral flooded her mind. The wailing, the flowers, the pregnant widow, the walk to the cemetery, the sound of the dirt hitting the wooden coffin—

"If her temperature is high, we will be ninety percent sure."

"But...," Ida's head was swimming. The doctor led her to chairs that were in the hallway and sat down with her.

"Take some deep breaths, Mrs. Wienke."

Ida did as she was told and felt better.

"Rheumatic fever occurs after a person has another infection. Remember when Mamie had that bad bout last winter? I said we are going to have to watch her closely because this can lead to other worse conditions?"

"Yes, I remember. And there I was dragging her out in the cold instead of calling you to come to the house."

"There is no way you could know. This was a different kind of infection. She has spent most of her life with fevers and chills. And the chilly air might have been good for her. The infectious germ is called a staphylococcus, and it can lead to rheumatic fever. If it does, there isn't any way to stop it from doing so. It's up to the patient to fight it off."

Ida knew that he was talking so that she could pull herself together and listen.

I Will Fly to Woodstock

He continued, "So now we must let this run its course while keeping her under tight observation. You go call John, and I'll talk to you both about what this might bring."

Ida blindly made her way to the nurse's desk and asked to use the telephone, but once she held the earpiece, she couldn't remember John's number. She stood there in a daze and finally told the hello-girl Sophia's number who was sitting with Dodi.

"Ma, Mamie is very sick. Can you call John and have him come to the hospital? I can't for the life of me remember his number," she said, and then burst into tears.

"I vill call now!" Sophia hung up.

Ida clicked the earphone hook down and tried to clear her mind. John would probably not be in the office but rather off on appointments. He could be halfway across town or God only knows where. Who else could she call? Then she called her own home number, hoping he'd pick up. He did.

***

Rev. Roger Kauffman strode onto the floor and went directly to Ida and gave her a big hug.

Ida clung to him and said, "Thank God, you picked up the phone. I can't get a hold of John."

Then he backed off slightly and asked, "What are they saying?"

"They say," Ida sniffed, "that she has rheumatic fever. She almost stopped breathing and might have had Bückelhering not told me to look."

"Bückelhering? Pickle herring, the clown?"

Ida realized belatedly how crazy that statement sounded. "Yes, in a dream," she said.

"Oh. You had a dream and in it Bückelhering told you to check on Mamie?"

"After I woke up, he told me."

"Really. Well, it was nice of God to send someone familiar."

Ida considered this a bit. She supposed Bückelhering was better than the Almighty himself. They say that a person can't look away from the face of God.

"What's happening in there now. Is she awake?" he nodded in the direction of Mamie's room.

"I don't know if she's awake. They are trying to freeze her with fresh air."

Rev. Kauffman looked confused. But he let it go as he had the Bückelhering visitation.

"The doctor wants to talk to both John and I," she buried her face in her hands and mumbled through her fingers, "I'm afraid he is going to tell us that she is going to die."

"Let's not get ahead of ourselves." The good reverend placed a consoling hand on hers. "How about we pray that she will be fine and that John gets here soon?"

"Okay," Ida said as she bowed her head.

Roger began, "Merciful Lord, God of all those who suffer, hear our prayer...."

***

Real Estate Transfer

John Stafford and w. to Herman C. Doering, pt lts 5 and 6 blk 1 Woodstock $2000.

Woodstock Sentinel, December 9, 1909.

ENGLISH LUTHERAN

Morning services at 10:30 a. m.
Sunday school at 12 n.
Services at Queen Anne at 2:30 p.m.
Ladies' Aid on Thursday, Dec. 16 at the home of Mrs. Joe Fierke.

R. C. Kauffman, pastor.
Woodstock Sentinel, December 9, 1909.

***

CITY IS DIVIDED INTO FOUR WARDS

By the courtesy of City Clerk Lynn Richard, The Sentinel publishes this week a map of the city of Woodstock showing the exact boundaries of the four new wards into which the city has recently been subdivided by an ordinance of the city council.

This map is published by the Sentinel notwithstanding the strenuous efforts made by its competitor, the "official" city newspaper, to prevent it. Editor Lemmers, by calling to his aid the mayor pro tem, succeeded in preventing The Sentinel from using the plate which was made at the payers' expense for such purposes and thus compelling this paper to go to the expense of having a plate all its own made, or defer publishing the map until said time as it might please these gentlemen.

In this instance "official" merely means a chance to sit next to the grab bag, while the taxpayer holds the bag.

The Sentinel believes in good sharp competition, if fair and honest, but striking below the belt is not in our line of business. Neither are such methods appreciated by the public which believe in a fair fight and a square deal. The plate in question is public property and was made with the taxpayers' money in order that through its publication the voters of this city should have abundant opportunity to learn what the new ward lines are.

Woodstock Sentinel, December 16, 1909.

Eight Aldermen Hereafter
Under the new arrangement Woodstock will have eight aldermen after next spring's election, instead of six, as at present. Each ward will be represented by two aldermen instead of three, and as the term of each alderman will remain two years as before, one alderman will hereafter be elected from each ward each year.
Woodstock Sentinel, December 16, 1909.

***

Mamie lay on the daybed in the parlor watching her sisters playing with their just opened toys. She was too tired to join in. She had come home from the hospital a few days ago, not because she was better but because it was her Christmas wish, and the doctor believed that her mother could watch her as well as the nurses could.

"She'll have to rest and drink a lot of water," the doctor had said. "She should eat as much as she can and build her strength back up. Let her go at her own pace. Children want to be up and about. She'll know when it's time."

"Is her heart okay?" asked John. It was Bob's heart that had given out when he died of the rheumatism.

"Her heart sounds just fine," the doctor had said, maybe too robustly. "But we need to build her up so that she can fight off the next bout of the fever."

"The next bout," Ida sat down heavily in a hospital hallway chair. John put his hand on Ida's shoulder.

"Yes, the next bout," predicted the doctor. "Rheumatic fever seems to be hard for people to kick once they have it. Hopefully, this will be the only bout she has, but more likely, she will have several more before it's over. That's why it's so important to build her body up. She needs to gain back the weight she's lost and then some. I don't mean get her chubby, but she needs to have some…what shall I call it…surplus to fight with."

Ida nodded, "She's always been a light eater. I'll do what I can."

"Maybe feed her six smaller meals a day, if need be. If she complains of aching or pains in her joints or pain in her chest, call me at once, night or day. Those would be the first signs of a return. Do you have a porch?"

"Yes," said John, glad he could finally add something.

"Is it enclosed?"

"No."

"Bundle her up and get her out in the fresh air every day. Have her walk up and down the porch. It can be slow, but we need to build up her legs, and the fresh air will be good for her breathing. If it seems to be too much for her, if she gets out of breath, let her rest. If she has chest pains, call me."

Ida reached up and rested her hand on John's. "Oh doctor, there is so much to remember, I don't know if I—"

"You'll do fine, Ida. Don't worry about doing it all. Just watch her with a goal of getting her up and around on those wobbly legs. Okay? Okay." He shook hands with John and hurried off down to another room where they could hear the sounds of childbirth. Strange, thought Ida, why would a woman come to a hospital just to have a baby? Is that what they would have been required to do five years ago if the hospital had been here?

Suddenly, Ida was taken back to that time. The fear that the baby, that Mamie, would die before she was born or be impaired once she was born. A feeling of dread crept up Ida's spine. She stood up and rushed into Mamie's room.

"Ida?" said John, following her. "What's wrong? Is she alright?"

They stood at the bedside looking at their sleeping child, concern etching their faces with deep lines. Ida turned to John. Tears streamed down her face. "Oh Papa, this is all my fault.

The eclampsia. She was born weak and now can't fight off the rheumatism. It's all my fault." She fell into his arms and buried her face in his lapel. John embraced her as he had so often done in times of trial.

"It isn't your fault. Getting eclampsia wasn't your fault. There was absolutely nothing you could have done to stop it, but remember you did lots to make sure you didn't lose the little one." John looked down at 'the little one,' and she looked back at him. "Well, hi there Mamie."

"Papa, can we go home now?"

"You bet. Come on, mama, let's get some clothes on this little one so she doesn't freeze her toes outside. We are going home."

***

ALL THINGS DENISON
by Clara Daring
Denison Buried

An old-fashioned snowstorm starting Monday night with Denison and vicinity completely covered with from twelve to eighteen inches of snow and zero temperatures is predicted. The east and west roads are badly drifted, and the rural carriers have difficulty in making their trips.

Coming from Illinois, this reporter is amazed at the height and breadth of some of the drifts that have been built around town. Some shovelers have actually cut a tunnel through so that a shopper can access the grocery or laundry. Denison is truly a wonder to behold, no matter the season.

Crawford County Courier, December 22, 1909.

***

GRACE LUTHERAN
Christmas festival on Friday evening at 7:30.
Church services Sunday morning 10:30
Sunday school service at 12 noon.
Services at Queen Anne in the afternoon at 2:30.
R. C. Kauffman, pastor
Woodstock Sentinel, December 23, 1909.

Christmas in the Country
The Olmsted Sunday school will have Christmas exercises Christmas eve at the schoolhouse. Everybody having presents, bring them, and you will be more than welcome. The weather has been bad, and but little preparations have been made, but come out and help us. We wish your presence.

On account of bad weather our Sunday school has not been very well attended. The sheds are full of snow and there is no place to hitch horses, until the neighbors turn out and do some shoveling.
Woodstock Sentinel, December 23, 1909.

Sweeping Out the Old Year
On New Year's Eve in Yorkshire and some other parts of England people with blackened faces, decked with ribbons and paper flowers, etc., each carrying a broom, go the round of the houses and offer to sweep out the old year for the occupants. They are generally rewarded with crescent shaped New Year's cakes or butter and eggs.
Woodstock Sentinel, December 23, 1909.

Waiting for the Children
An old woman hobbled up to the conductor of the train and said excitedly: "Vondt you to pleece holdt on yet, Meester Gonduckitor, vile my two grandtkinder comes by the drain? I runs off

midouit dem undt dey is goming so vast dey can, yes."

The conductor looked impatiently at his watch, then at the woman's pathetic face. Then he consented to wait a little, as the train was on time.

Five minutes later two blue eyed, chubby cheeked children came on the run, rushed up to their grandmother, kissed her, helped her on to the train with her birdcage and basket and then hurried away.

What the conductor thought is none of a refined person's business – Chicago News.

Woodstock Sentinel, December 23, 1909.

***

Ida laughed out loud at the grandma holding up the train just to see her grandchildren. It seemed like something either of their own mothers, Sophia or Louisa, might do.

She was reading last week's paper which she was forced to skip at the time with Mamie coming home. Helen and Dodi had participated in the children's program at Grace Lutheran, as they were finally calling the congregation rather than the English Lutheran. In the major scene of the evening, Helen had been the angel who cried out the good tidings, and Dodi had been a chubby little lamb on all fours in a costume Ida had made for her with cotton balls all over it. Dodi took the part very seriously and interrupted with drawn-out 'baas' multiple times during the play until the angel had to tell the sheep to be quiet now so the glad tidings could be heard. The play was sweet and funny. Mamie had gone with them, sitting between John and her in the front pew so she could see everything. She had giggled when the angel reprimanded the sheep, as had the entire congregation. So, between getting ready for the play and coaching the children on their parts, making cookies and other sweets for the holiday, and keeping up with Mamie's regimen, the month had been a busy one.

I Will Fly to Woodstock

"What's funny," asked John. He was working on this week's paper.

"Oh, just this story from last week's paper about the grandmother who held up the train," answered Ida.

"Held up the train?" John tried to remember the story. "I don't remember that story. How much did she get?"

Ida giggled, "The ill will of the conductor." She egged him on.

"I don't remember it." He looked back to his own sheet.

"That's okay. I think it is just meant as a joke."

"Okay." Already distracted.

Helen and Dodi were playing nicely beneath the pretty Christmas tree, laden with tinsel and strands of popcorn and cranberries. The star at the top had a candle in a reflector and so it shone brightly. Mamie lay on the davenport with her head against Ida's thigh. She dozed in and out as she watched her sisters in play and listened to the low murmurings of her parents' voices. Nearly bedtime, thought Ida, but she wanted to finish the paper and give the girls a few more moments under the tree; they seemed so content. She wasn't sure if Helen was going to demand to stay up until midnight to bring in the new year, but they would take that up privately.

A sharp rap at the front door brought Roger Kauffman quickly down the stairs as if he had been expecting a caller. His smiling wife was quick behind him. In his robust and jovial way, he threw open the door. Ida and John had risen but stayed glued to their spots in the parlor. From the porch came words of good cheer, "Happy New Year, father!!"

Roger's laughter was loud and friendly. "Happy New Year to you, my good man! However, I am not the man of the house. John?"

Tentatively, John came forward. He addressed the lead fellow, "Yes, I'm the man of the house." The man's grin was white against his black face. He doffed his stove pipe hat and said, "How d'ya do?"

"Just fine, thank you. How can I help you?"

"Well, my friend, it's not what you can do for us, but rather what we can do for you. We be chimney sweeps, and we have hear-ed you had a wee bi' o' bad luck this year." John knew that the accent was put on, but it was still charming. Ida, Helen and Dodi had all come to see the spectacle and stood slightly behind the man of the house.

John nodded, "Our little girl, Mamie, has been sick." Ida nodded.

"Oh, that's so sad." His mouth turned dramatically down at the corners. "May we come in so we won't be a wasting this good warm air that you have paid dearly for?"

John looked at Roger, who nodded enthusiastically.

The six of them stepped back and allowed the three men to enter. They all were in black with soot covered faces and all of them carried quaint brooms that looked handmade.

Ida bustled back to the parlor and grabbed up the paper and found again the article about sweeping out the Old Year. Cookies, butter and eggs. She went directly to the kitchen.

"Good sir," the lead sweep bowed to John. "We bring you salt," he handed John salt in cloth tied with yarn, "that your new year will see good fortune. We bring you bread," he handed John a loaf of fresh bread, "that you will have an abundance of food."

John accepted the bread in his other hand and said, "Thank you."

"And finally, we bring coal," he held out a lumpy bag with a twine draw string. John looked at his two full hands. Roger stepped forward and accepted the coal. "We bring you coal for an abundance of warmth this winter and next."

"Thank you," said John.

"And now with your permission, we will sweep the old year from your home and be on our way."

Again, Roger nodded.

"Okay." John welcomed them in with a broad wave of a hand and a slight bow.

The little girls peeked out from behind their father, but now, Helen stepped forward, "I'll show you upstairs."

"Well, thank you, young miss." She took his hand and, accompanied by Roger, mounted the stairs.

"We'll do the downstairs and basement," said the second sweep. Ida appeared in the doorway and said, "Come with me. John will take one of you to the basement."

John still looked a little befuddled but beckoned the third sweep to the basement door.

"I go with Papa," said Dodi slipping her hand in his.

Ida led the way to the back porch, kitchen, bathroom, bedroom, dining room, keeping the parlor for last. The sweep swept the corners of each room with his broom but stopped short when he saw Mamie on the davenport. "Hello, young miss," he said.

"Hello," said Mamie.

"We hear you aren't feeling very well," he asked.

"Not very good," she answered politely. "Are you here to make me better?"

"I hope so. We are sweeping out the old year tonight. Do you want to get rid of the old year?"

"Yes, that would be very fine," said Mamie in her most grown-up voice. She looked at her mother, "Then I'll be all better!"

"Yes," said Ida. "I hope so."

The sweep began to sweep around the room, sweeping the corners and the davenport, without touching Mamie. He swept the ceiling and the floor and the walls and the windows and then with a flair swept everything out to the entry hall. Turning toward Mamie, he said, "Can you feel the old year leaving?"

"Yes," said Mamie. "All gone." She held up her empty hands.

Ida hustled back to the kitchen and brought out the cookies, eggs and butter, each wrapped in cloth and tied with string. As the sweeps and their escorts gathered back in the entry hall, the head man flamboyantly threw open the door and with a flourish they swept the old year out onto the porch, and then following it out, they swept it out into the yard and the cold north wind of the night.

They turned back, removed their hats and bowed. John took the packages from Ida and went out into the cold. He thanked the sweeps for their efforts.

He improvised, "I give you ...."

"Cookies," Ida whispered from behind him.

"...cookies to make your life sweet. And...'

"Butter," Ida whispered.

John looked bewildered, but began, "And butter to—"

"To make your life tasty," Ida broke in.

"And—" John looked at the lumpy bag in his hands and then at Ida.

"And eggs to make your lives...um—," Ida tried to fill in.

"...fertile." Roger snickered, but then urged John on. John finished with a bow and handed the goods one to each sweep.

"Thank ye kindly." The sweeps bowed again, replaced their hats, winked at those watching, and made their way down Lincoln Avenue singing. The party, gathered on the porch, joined in.

> "Should auld acquaintance be forgot,
> and never brought to mind?
> Should auld acquaintance be forgot
> and days of auld lang syne?"

> "For auld lang syne, my jo,
> for auld lang syne,
> we'll tak' a cup o' kindness yet,
> for auld lang syne."

Die Dicke Muss Schlafen Gehen (1910)

Snow had fallen all night. Ida looked out at the piles and wondered how many inches had accumulated so far. She could barely make out the house across the street, the white blanket was so thick and steady. Looking past the house and into the distance was impossible. In general, Ida liked snow, and certainly, the children loved it. But too much snow would end travel on foot with the children for a while unless John was with her to carry one of the little ones.

Ida could already hear sleigh bells coming and going on Lincoln Avenue. John had left a half hour before, trudging east toward the Square, his wool coat over a warm scarf up around his ears, his head covered with a smart Homburg wool felt hat with an upturned brim to keep the snow away from his face, his galoshes clipped all the way to the top so he could plunge through the drifts without getting snow in his shoes.

The hat the girls had picked out for their Papa for Christmas was a warm one, but not stylish. Leather outside with fur inside, it would be the warmest hat John had ever owned, Ida was sure, and today would have been a perfect day to test its value. But he had opted for fashion instead of warmth. She had watched him this morning from the east side window until he disappeared into the swirl of snow.

"Mama?" Helen had sneaked up behind her, and she giggled as Ida jumped at her voice.

"Lord have mercy, Helen, you scared me."

"I know." Helen was still snickering.

"What do you need, young lady?" Ida smiled.

"Is this frock okay for school today?" She indicated her gray wool smock and blue leggings.

"You look very fashionable," said Ida. "That outfit is good and warm for a snowy day."

"That's what I thought, too." Helen looked down at herself. "Mamie says that she wants leggings just like mine, only red."

"Oh, is Mamie awake?" Ida started for the stairs. "I should go up and check on her."

"She's fine. I checked on her," said Helen. "Come help me with my hair."

Ida listened at the stairs. All was quiet. "Mamie?" she called up.

"She's fine," said Helen. "She probably went back to sleep."

"I'll be right back, and we'll find a pretty ribbon for your hair," Ida said as she mounted the first five stairs to the landing.

"Mama!" Helen switched into her store voice. "I need my hair done NOW!"

Ida looked back. Helen stood between the kitchen table and the sink with arms akimbo. Her brow was furrowed, and the corners of her mouth turned down into an amazing frown.

"Now, please!" Helen repeated, a bit softer.

"But we have plenty of time to do it before you must leave for school." Ida found her tone pleading. "I have to—"

"No, you don't." Helen stomped her foot. "She's fine. I need you now." The emphasized 'I' indicated that Mamie did not need Ida now.

Ida dismounted the steps and took Helen into her arms, "Honey, what's wrong? Don't worry. I'll be right back."

"No, you won't. You'll go up there and sit beside her and rock her and talk to her. You never do that with me anymore.

Or Dodi. Everything is Mamie, Mamie, Mamie! You need to pay attention to me this morning...." A sob escaped. "Please."

"But, Helen, you are a big girl and can dress yourself and take care of yourself. You don't need me to dress you or rock you. You are healthy and smart, and I'm so proud of you."

Helen relaxed against her mother's frame and put arms around her waist. And then suddenly, she was crying. Ida stood, two arms around her oldest, most independent child. She put her arm around her, led her to the parlor, sat and piled the six and a half-year-old onto her lap in the green rocking chair with the padded wooden arms. They rocked, and Helen's tears became only a sniffle.

"Now," said Ida. "What has happened? Is everything at school alright?"

Helen let out a shuddering sigh. "I think so. Don't you have to come talk to my teacher anymore?"

Ida considered this question. She had last talked to Helen's teacher at the beginning of the school year. Sometimes, if there were problems, a teacher would ask to see the parents, but usually the first meeting was all that was required. "She hasn't asked to see us, has she?" Ida said, uncertainly. She needed to check on Mamie. She strained to hold her anxiousness at bay.

"No," said Helen miserably.

What in the world was this about? "Would you like me to make some cookies and bring them one day for all the children? And then I can talk to your teacher."

Helen's head came up, now she was smiling through the tears, "Yes, yes, I would!" she said enthusiastically. "Without the others."

Ida was confused, "Others?"

Helen nodded her head emphatically, "Without Mamie and Dodi."

"Oh." A light dawned. "Without your sisters."

"Yes!" said Helen.

"Well, I think we could arrange that. Oma Wienke could surely watch them for a morning. How about next week Monday? We can make the cookies on Sunday afternoon when Papa is home to entertain the little girls."

Helen gave Ida a tight hug, "Oh Mama, that would be so great."

"OK," said Ida. "It's a deal!" and she moved to get up.

Helen cuddled close. "Just a minute longer, okay, Mama?"

Ida put her arms around the little girl. "Yes, a minute longer."

***

Ida was a little nervous as she entered the Clay Street School and walked toward the door of Helen's classroom. She had a large tray of sugar cookies that they had cut out in the shape of hearts. It was a little early for Valentine's cookies, but the heart shape had other meanings besides a valentine. Helen had approved yesterday as she helped with the cookies. She was so excited before going to school this morning, going over and over their plan so Ida would do everything right. It was a pleasure to see her oldest once again enthusiastic about her lot in life.

The plan was for Ida to come at morning recess: "About 10 o'clock," Helen had said. "So, we can eat them right away. And then you stay until lunch, okay, Mama?" Ida had agreed.

But now she felt like she was breaking in on a lesson as she looked at the teacher in front of the class writing on the board. Ida pulled open her coat and looked at her lapel watch. Ten o'clock on the dot. The teacher turned from the board and seemed to be indicating that they were taking a break. Several boys rose from their seats and ran for the door, pushed past Ida, and headed for the bathroom, she suspected. With the door open, there was nothing to do but to go on in.

I Will Fly to Woodstock

The teacher looked up in surprise. "Mrs. Wienke. How nice," she said with a big smile.

"Miss Ives, I brought a little something for your morning recess since the children can't go out in this cold," said Ida.

"Mama!" she heard Helen call out and then a beaming Helen stood at Ida's side. "I'll take them." Helen took the tray and put it on a small table at the side of the room. "Did you bring napkins, Mama?" Helen asked.

Ida reached into her crocheted bag and brought out cloth napkins. Helen skipped across the room and took them from her. "Look what my Mama brought us!" she announced to the children. "Cookies! Now everyone, take a napkin, first. There are enough for everyone to have two. I helped cut them out and bake them yesterday. You'll see how good they are!" Ida smiled. Helen was in her element.

Ida turned back to the teacher and removed her coat and scarf, "Miss Ives, I'm sorry that I haven't come in sooner to talk about how Helen is doing. As you know, my second girl, Mamie, has been ill."

"Yes, I had heard. How is she?"

"Much better. She will join your first grade in September."

"Very good. I will look forward to having her."

They sat down in two chairs at the front of the room, "How is Helen doing? I know she is competing with all these seven-year-olds, and I worry…."

"Nothing to worry about. I doubt that any of the children in the class even know she is only six. She is big for her age and certainly can take charge of the others." Miss Ives waved her hand slightly to indicate how the children had lined up straight as a pin to get the cookies being doled out by Helen. They both smiled.

"That she can. She has always been a bit…um…bossy," said Ida.

"She is smart and doing very well in all her subjects, but seems to like writing and reading the most," said Miss Ives.

"How do you think having both girls in the same room will work? You have first through third here, right?"

"I think they'll be fine. Having siblings in one room happens often. Do you foresee any problems?" Miss Ives deftly reflected the question back to Ida.

"Well, no, I suppose not. Mamie is much quieter than Helen, and she is used to her sister being the leader. I just worry about Mamie…she's not been well, and since this last bout with the rheumatism, she is…I don't know…less active and adventuresome. We'll have to see how she is in fall. I would hate to see her not start with her age group."

"The differing personalities are probably good as they will establish their own circle of friends."

"Yes. They already have done that at Sunday School."

"Good. Well…anything else? I need to get back to the history lesson about George Washington."

"How wonderful. Do you mind if I stay a while? And watch?"

"Not at all. And thank you for the cookies; they made the children's day."

Especially Helen's day, thought Ida. "No problem at all. I should have done it sooner."

Miss Ives smiled and rose and in a loud teacher's voice called out, "OK children, take your cookies back to your desks so we can learn more about our founding father, George Washington. And how about we thank Mrs. Wienke and Helen for bringing this delicious treat in today."

"Thank you, Mrs. Wienke and Helen," the children said in unison.

As the children scurried back to their desks, Ida noticed that Helen's desk was first in her row. Of course, it was. She exchanged big smiles with her daughter. Of course, she is a front-row student.

***

Sheriff Arrests Two Ladies

Sheriff Cummings was called upon to arrest two well-dressed young women who had taken rooms at the Evers Hotel. Word came from Dunlap that they had jumped a board bill of $26 there. They gave the names of May Evans and Maud Sterling.

They claimed that they came to Dunlap by inducements held out to them at Omaha by R. A. Barsbay of Dunlap, that there was work for them there, and he would guarantee their board until they had work. They found nothing and came on up to Denison. Officer John Albert of Dunlap took them back to answer for the charge.

Crawford County Courier, January 15, 1910.

***

Denison, Iowa
January 19, 1910

Dear Ida, John and dearest children,
Remember when Mama used to say that too much progress was not good? Zu Viel Ist Genug! Well, I am writing to you tonight using an old-fashioned kerosene lantern that I had to buy down at the hardware store because we have lost our electricity in Denison. Pearle has worked all day with the others to fix the problem, but I am questioning if there is a fix. It's dark now, and the only light in the house is this lantern. It scares me to death. What if I trip while moving it? What if I set the house ablaze? It gives good light if you sit right up close. I had forgotten how inconvenient it all was before we got electric lights. Phooey!

Not much going on here. It's cold, very cold, and we've had some snow, which just makes me want to stay inside and cozy by the fire...in the dark. The wind was strong from the northwest the last few days, so it even feels colder...in the dark.

Speaking of being in the dark, I've enclosed an article about two women who were enticed out here by a man who claimed he would pay for their room and board until they found 'work'. But then when they got here, he was nowhere to be found, and they ran out of money. So now they are in jail. I would love to go pursue that story, but it's too cold and dark to ride down to Dunlap. Isn't it sad when women are so desperate that they will follow a man anywhere? Ha!

As you can see by the enclosed, I've been doing a few stories for the paper, but I haven't felt much like getting out and about to hunt them down. I'm beginning to hate winter...especially in the dark. So, I need to get myself up and going soon as it is light tomorrow, probably by 8:00 o'clock a.m. What time does it get light in Woodstock? Seems like it's later here. But the days are getting longer. It is light until 5:00 in the evening already. The town and church seem to be just quietly coasting right now...in the dark and the cold. All our effort goes into keeping warm...in the dark.

My eyes hurt from straining at this. My love to the little ones. Stay warm. Did they get a box from Aunt Clara and Uncle Pearle for Christmas? I do hope so, although I didn't send it until just before New Year's. Next year, I'll do better.

Happy New Year, my beloved family. What do you hear from Mama? I think I'll write to her tonight also...in the dark.

Love, in the dark,
Clara and Pearle

P.S. I held this to put in articles and now it's January 31. The lights are back on thanks to my Pearle dear and his army of electricians. He got a little frost bite on his forehead that night I wrote this letter, but he's fine now. I am so proud of him. The temperatures are a bit milder and the wind a bit softer. I am adding an article from just a day ago about a pastor in Denison. I found out he was doing this query from one of my acquaintances at the German Lutheran. She was appalled. I went to see him and got the scoop.

***

Denison Mostly Dark

Owing to an accident at the lower plant, half of the town is without electric light. A cylinder head was knocked out of the larger of the two engines and the smaller one is able to supply light only to the business houses.

Crawford County Courier, January 20, 1910.

***

ALL THINGS DENISON
by Clara Daring

Pastor Propounds Queries
Denison Minister Gathering Data for Series of Special Sermons.

Rev. DePree, the Presbyterian pastor in Denison is gathering up material for a series of sermons for the near future by sending out a string of inquiries to citizens asking their opinions as to church matters. Among his questions are ones such as these: 'Why does a Christian church fail to reach the people?' 'Why do not more men go to church?' 'What is the most serious mistake of the church?' 'In what way do Christians fail?' 'What manner of person do you think a Christian should be?' 'What kind of a preacher do you like?' Good questions for all of us to think about.

Crawford County Courier, January 28, 1910.

***

"John, why does a Christian church fail to reach people?" Ida laid aside Clara's article clipping.

John looked up at Ida. "What?"

"I just got one of Clara's articles." She pointed at the clipping. "There is a minister out there who is going around asking people questions like, 'Why does a Christian church fail to reach the people?'"

"So?"

"So, why does it fail?"

"I didn't know that it did fail."

"OK, better yet," Ida again read from the clipping, "'Why do not more men go to church?'"

John just stared at her, mute.

"Well?"

"I go to church," said John.

"I know you do, but why don't other men?"

"Other men go to church."

"I know they do, but what about the rest?"

"All women don't go to church."

"But the men, John, why don't the men go?"

"Oh, for heaven's sake, Ida, I don't know. Maybe they work on Sundays like I used to. Maybe they don't believe. Maybe they are scoundrels. Maybe they are overly tired from a week's work." He looked back at his unread paper.

"Women are tired from a week's work also."

"True, so why don't women go to church?" John did not look up.

"We do. More women than men go to church and yet all the positions like board members and ministers are men. Why is that?"

"Oh, here we go." John's hands collapsed the paper on his lap and looked at his wife. Ida's eyes were sparkling with enthusiasm, her cheeks rosy. He wouldn't dissuade her now. He might as well listen.

"Women are more involved, kinder, and more compassionate. Look at Ladies Aid always giving back to the community and helping others. Women are freer to be available when help is needed. Women are smart about money as we handle the finances for a home. Women have more stamina. We can work all week, care for children and still be enthusiastic about going to church. So, why are there only men in charge? And why do men not come to church more regularly?"

John shook his head and looked down at his ignored newspaper. "Well, I'm not sure, Ida. Maybe it's because the men do what they can and while they can't be involved in the day-to-day mission, they can come to a meeting once a month."

"Hm."

"Or maybe it's because all the women are in church that the men don't go. You know, they take a vacation once a week."

Ida stared at him for a moment and then burst out laughing.

"You might be right," she admitted.

John smiled.

After she had recovered herself, they spent a moment in silence. John turned back to the paper, then Ida said, "On another topic—"

John collapsed the paper in his lap once again. "Oh Ida, I just want to read the paper."

"I'll be quick. Did that woman they reported in the paper come to your office?"

"What woman?"

"There," she pointed to the front page. "That story right there." John turned to the article.

She Failed in Woodstock.

Aurora, Kankakee, Streator, Ottawa and other cities report visits from a hypnotizing girl perfume saleslady, who has gathered heaps of silver coins by selling small bottles of alcohol as high-priced perfumes. Dressed in good clothes and wearing an alluring smile she approaches her victims in business offices and public places, shows a sample bottle of fine perfume and asks to hold the intended victim's hand while she pours a few drops of the perfumery on its back. This request is almost invariably granted, and she succeeds in exchanging an ounce bottle of alcohol for a round silver half dollar. She even challenges such persons whom she spots as "dead game sports" to shake dice, match coins or even "throw at a crack."

This young lady was in Woodstock where she did her best to ensnare the masculine element with her wiles. But alas, her efforts here were all in vain, her bewitchery was to no avail, and she was forced to depart defeated. All of which goes to show that the sterner sex in our bright, bustling little city are proof against the dazzling smiles of itinerant vendors of fake goods.

Woodstock Sentinel, February 3, 1910.

John remembered well the day that the gypsy had walked into their office, the bell jingling as she opened and closed the door. They rarely got visitors without appointments, but a walk-in, especially a very pretty woman in an elegant and revealing red dress, was always welcome.

She said "Hello" with a contralto voice which spoke volumes of her many strengths.

John's partners Ted and Rudy seemed frozen in their seats, so he stood and stepped forward.

"Good afternoon. How can I help you?"

"Tis I who can help you." Her accent was slightly old world, and John was immediately on guard.

"And how am I in danger?"

"Ah Monsieur, evil surrounds you, but I can ward it off if you are interested."

I Will Fly to Woodstock

John looked at Ted. With his hands he urged John on, 'after you.'

"That may be true, but I'm sure we can also help you. Do you feel that you are in danger?"

"In danger?" The question seemed to knock her a bit off her game.

"Yes, in danger…from wind, fire, flood, injury or death itself." John quickly listed the dangers Prudential insured against.

"I am not in danger of those things. I travel by the wind, cook by the fire, bathe in the flood. Nature is my sister. But do you realize the evil that lurks in every doorway waiting for you to look away at the wrong moment? I have come to give you a talisman of protection," said the lady in red.

John chuckled. "A talisman? Well, I don't have a talisman against evil, but I do have policies that will protect you from loss should your home be washed away while you are bathing."

She warmed to her task. "I have a magic talisman that can protect you from danger and pestilence no matter where you travel." She held up a small bag, about three inches square with a drawstring.

"The talisman is in there?" John was having fun with this sale. "Can I see it?"

"Yes, it is in here. But no, you cannot set your eyes on it or it loses its power." She drew out the word 'yes' in an attempt to sound exotic.

He picked up a sales folder which had graphic illustrations of the protections that Prudential provided. "Here is what we offer." He spread the contents out on the counter between them and began his best sales pitch. "If you will agree, we can protect your home from the three biggest losses due to wind, fire and flood. And for only a pittance we will add a death benefit for the breadwinner. Is that you?"

"Breadwinner?" she laughed. "Yes, you could say I'm a breadwinner. In this pouch is a button from the shroud of

Jesus. It is the most powerful talisman that we have. For you only five dollars."

"Only five dollars? Our protection is a bit more expensive, but for five dollars a month, you could have protection for your house and barn to the tune of $5,000 if a cyclone should carry them away. Does your talisman pay out like Prudential?"

"Five dollars a month?"

"To get $5,000 of protection."

She stood there looking at the brochure, but then held up the packet, "Last chance or I move on down the street. The button of the lord Jesus for only five dollars. Are you very sure you are not interested in getting this charm to protect your wife maybe? It brings good luck in addition to protection."

"I'm very sure that I do not want or need it. Are you very sure you do not want Prudential protection for your family?"

Bested, the woman smiled and withdrew, again jangling the bell over the door. The men looked at each other and then had a good laugh.

After quickly perusing the article, John admitted, "Why yes, she did come in,"

"Did any of you buy her fake goods?" asked Ida.

"Nope. I sold her insurance," said John. Ida burst out in laughter again. "Or at least I tried to. She was pretty, but no match for the likes of me."

"Good! I knew I could trust you."

"Of course, you can!" John wondered what exactly that meant.

"I love you, John Wienke," said Ida.

"And I love you, too" said John, just a bit confused about what had just happened, but was glad it all ended with smiles.

***

Denison Loses Good Man

Denison, Feb. 16. – L.M. Bear, who has been the night watch at Denison for twenty-five years, died Monday. The funeral and interment will take place this afternoon. The fact that Denison has had no great fires and few night depredations, is largely due to the efficiency of Mr. Bear.

Crawford County Courier. February 16, 1910.

***

"Mama," said Helen, as she came down to breakfast. "Have you heard about the comet that is maybe going to hit the earth?"

"What?" Ida turned from the stove where she stirred oatmeal. "Going to hit the earth?"

"Maybe, a bunch of kids saw it, not last night, but the night before when it was getting dark."

"How could you see a comet before dark? Someone is playing a joke on you." Helen always took things so seriously.

"No, they aren't. I think it showed up because of how bright it was. I wish I could have seen it. But the comet is coming back in about two months. Right now, it's going around the sun, but then it will come back at us and might hit us."

"Helen, what ARE you talking about?" Ida forgot momentarily to stir the oatmeal.

"The COMET," Helen said loudly as if Ida were hard of hearing.

"Who told you this?" Ida turned back to the stove.

"Miss Ives. She explained after some of the kids said they saw it. She says we'll all see it when it comes back. Isn't that exciting?"

'Exciting' wasn't the word that Ida would use. If this comet was expected here, why hadn't the paper written about it. Of course, maybe they would. They wouldn't get the paper until later today, but still someone should have said something. She looked at her little girl and marveled at her composure and intelligence.

"OK, you keep me up-to-date about it because the paper only comes out twice a week," said Ida.

"OK," said Helen. "What are you making?"

"Oatmeal."

"Oh. I'll have toast."

"Where are the little girls?" Ida glanced at the stairs.

"I don't know. I think I heard them talking. Shall I get them?

"Would you, please?"

Helen went over to the stairs and mounted just far enough so she could look around the corner and up the stairs to the second floor. In a very loud voice she called out, "Mamie, Dodi, breakfast!"

Ida rolled her eyes. Not exactly what she expected from "go get them," but she could hear them coming down the stairs already. She wondered if they were sitting on the top step listening all the while.

"Helen, put out the ice card, will you please?"

"OK." Helen got down the white 8 X 10 cardboard placard with the word 'ICE' on it in red letters from the kitchen windowsill. The card in the front window would alert the iceman as he passed that they needed an ice block. Upon seeing the sign, he would carry the block up and around to the back porch icebox. He would discard the old nearly used up block out in the yard and replace it with the new one.

"No iceman." Dodi covered her ears.

"Don't worry, Dodi. The iceman will be careful. He won't hit the house," said Mamie. Ida placed a bowl of oatmeal before her and added brown sugar and milk. Mamie smelled it and then began to stir the concoction into a porridge.

Helen returned from the parlor after placing the card in the front window. "Mama, didn't we just get ice two days ago?"

"Two days?" Ida considered. "Are you sure that wasn't last week?"

"Yes, then too," said Helen. Ida had to believe her; she kept track of everything.

"It's really cold outside. Why do we always need new ice?" Helen sat down at the table.

"It's not that the ice is gone, I guess. It's that the ice stinks. I think fish were frozen in the ice before cutting it," said Ida.

"Tinks!" Dodi laughed.

Ida and Helen stood looking out the back door onto the stone porch that was John's pride and joy. The white metal ice box had seen better days. Ida went out on the porch and opened the box. The ice was only a quarter gone, and the strong odor of fish wafted out. She opened the food compartment. Not quite as strong here, but still it smelled fishy. She collected the butter and took it back into the house.

The toast browned on the wire rack on the cook stove, and she removed the cloth covering from the butter and put it on the table. She slid the toast onto a plate and put it next to the butter. Helen pulled the toast over in front of her and began buttering it. The golden-brown home-made bread began to glisten with the melting self-churned butter. She took a big bite.

Helen's face registered disgust. Helen spit her mouthful of bread and butter onto her plate. "Oh! Ick!"

"Helen, manners," said Ida. "What's wrong?"

"I'm not eating that." She dropped the toast on to the plate with a clatter. "It tastes awful!"

Ida brought the butter up to her nose. It smelled like fish. The smell must have permeated the whole box and the food therein.

"I'm sorry." Ida thought quickly. "Have some oatmeal. You like oatmeal." She poised the pot over a bowl ready to fill it.

"No, I don't!" Helen pouted and waved the pot away. "I already have an icky taste in my mouth. Oatmeal would just make it worse."

"OK, I know what." Ida bustled to the cupboard and pulled down a box of shredded wheat.

"Piwows." Dodi threw up her hands in excitement.

"How about a pillow, Helen?"

"OK," said Helen.

"Piwows!" said Dodi.

Ida placed a shredded wheat "pillow" in Helen's and Dodi's bowls, scalded a little milk on the stove and poured warm milk over them. She added two heaping teaspoons of white sugar and placed the sugar bowl on the table between the girls in case the cereal needed more sweetening.

Helen took a tentative first bite, not trusting the milk, perhaps.

"Good?" asked Ida.

"Good," said Helen.

"Gut!" said Dodi.

What should she do about the icebox? Ida went to the parlor and removed the ice card from the window. Might as well not pay for more stinky ice. Maybe the ice wasn't causing the smell, but rather, the box itself. She had heard of boxes absorbing smells over the years, and finally being found unusable. She had had this one since they were married and set up housekeeping with John – eight years. Surely, iceboxes should last longer than eight years.

Ida decided that once Helen left for school, she'd try to reach John and talk it over with him. Maybe if he could see to it immediately, they would have a new icebox from Belcher Brothers delivered by nightfall. I wonder if they have oak ones in stock. One with a better air seal between compartments perhaps. With golden hinges and handles. Ah, wouldn't that be something. Yes! She would call John, and he would take care of everything.

***

Halley's Comet

"Persons who fear a collision between the earth and Halley's comet, which is coming toward us at the speed of several thousand express trains, will be more scared than ever when they learn that the visitor is about 1,000,000 times as big as our own little planet, However there's no reason to fear," says Prof Edwin B. Frost, director of Yerkes observatory, "for old Mother Earth will not be affected by the comet, because it is made only of gaseous materials, and not solids."

When asked if the near approach of the comet to Venus and the earth would affect these planets Prof. Frost said, "It won't affect the orbit of Venus or Earth, but it is likely to affect the comet's orbit. That is one reason why we wanted to get meridian observations, which will show almost exactly these orbital changes."

"There will be an interesting spectacle, by the way, on May 1, when the comet is near Venus. The planet and the comet will be practically the same distance from the earth, and everyone will be able to see their relative size."

"And the comet will, of course, appear much smaller?" The suggestion was made.

"Oh, by no means! The comet's bulk exceeds that of Venus by about 1,000,000 times. It is not solid matter, however. It is gaseous and its mass is comparatively slight. Therefore, its attraction will not affect the planets, while the solid, heavy planets are likely to affect it a good deal. The Earth and

Venus are about the same size, so that the Earth, too, is about one-millionth of the size of the comet. Following the phenomenon of May 1, the Earth will pass through the tail of the comet. This will be on May 18."

Woodstock Sentinel, February 17, 1910.

***

"Whatcha doin', Mama?" Mamie crawled up beside Ida on the davenport.

"I'm looking at this year's seed catalog." Ida held it up. The Burpee's catalog had a bunch of pink sweet peas on the front.

"Those are pretty. Will you grow those?"

"Yes, I love sweet peas and they climb."

"They climb?" In Mamie's experience, plants just stood still.

"Yes, up a trellis. See these little strings right here?" Mama pointed to the runners in the picture. "These are like fingers that grab on and hold tight, so the plant grows up the trellis and doesn't fall off onto the ground."

"Really? I want to see that."

"In summer. We'll look together. What else do you think we should plant? I just put sweet peas on the list. What else?"

"Peas, pick-els, 'matoes, corn and brok-lee!"

"OK! Those are on the list. How about green beans and carrots?"

"Yes, those, too. And radishes. I love radishes!"

"And green onions, cauliflower and Brussels sprouts?"

"OK, but I don't remember what sprouts taste like."

"Um...they taste kinda like cabbage...OH! Cabbage, we must have cabbage!" Ida quickly wrote down cabbage in big letters, a staple of their diet, on the list. "Thanks for reminding me."

"And oranges and apples," said Mamie.

"We can't grow oranges and apples," said Ida as she turned the pages of the catalog.

"Why not? I like 'em. And peaches and pears."

"Well, all of those grow on fruit trees, and we don't have any of those trees."

"Buy 'em from the catalog."

Ida laughed, "Maybe I just will. They will take a long while to bear fruit, but a nice pear tree would be wonderful."

"Yes! And I will climb it and get the sweet ones at da top where da sun shines." Mamie stood up on the davenport and climbed up on the back.

"Hold on there, young lady. You get back down here. This is not a tree to be climbed!"

Mamie let go and fell back to the seat giggling. She seemed to be feeling good today. Maybe the sweeping out of the old year had worked.

"Well, tell you what. You can help me put in the garden this year, since you are so interested. It never hurts to know how to grow your own food. Now let's see, the fun part. What flowers shall we get?"

"Sweet Peas! And dandy-lions!" Mamie jumped just a little on the couch.

"Dandelions. I don't know about that!" said Ida. "I don't think we have to plant dandelions. They just grow all by themselves."

"Like me!" Mamie threw her arms up in a V.

***

The Home Supply of Ice

Much may be added to keeping the quality as well as to the enjoyment of the food supplies for the home if a supply of ice is available during the warmer months of the year. In cities and towns of any size the consumer has his wants in this line met by putting up the "ice" card. With country dwellers the matter is not so simple. For those who wish to lay by a supply of ice for next summer a few suggestions may be helpful. An outbuilding of about the size required for the necessary supply may be utilized. This should be so situated that there will be good drainage from a point below the lowest tier of cakes. A space of a foot or fourteen inches should be left between the body of ice and the walls of the enclosure. The cakes should be packed in regular fashion for economy of room, with enough space between them so as to give free drainage to the bottom. The sawdust or other material used in packing should be poured in between the ice and the walls as the pile increases in height but should not be packed down. When the last tier of ice has been laid a ten-inch layer of packing material should be placed over the whole body of the ice. The air chamber above the ice should be kept well ventilated during warm weather. A supply of ice is often kept by cruder methods than those above outlined, but not with so satisfactory results.

Woodstock Sentinel, February 17, 1910.

Farm, Orchard and Garden
By F. E. TRIGG

Sensible parents will keep the sick cat and dog confined in some place away from the little children who may be in the home. A sick cat often transmits disease, while no one ever knows when a sick dog is going to run amuck.

Thirty inches of snow on a level in most of the north, central and eastern states, accompanied by blockade of railroads, scarcity of fuel and intense cold, suggests the fact that the climate has not changed enough so that we are rid of the "old fashioned winter."

Woodstock Sentinel, February 17, 1910.

Sentinel Protests

The Sentinel wants to protest against the wanton destruction of the street sign boards, which are posted on the street corners about the city, and the disfiguration and destruction of which in several places have been called to our attention. We don't know who the guilty persons are, whether men or boys, but every citizen should protest against these things and help the officers guard our beautiful city and its public property against lawless depredations.

Woodstock Sentinel, February 17, 1910.

***

Ida opened her new ice box. Beautiful and of strong construction, it would last a long, long time. It was oak and finished with thick varnish to protect the surface. The fittings were gold, not real gold she was sure, but shiny gold all the same. The inside was lined with tin to keep odors from soaking into the wood giving the appliance a longer life. The pride she felt in owning it was undeniable. But she quickly reminded herself, 'Pride goeth before the fall.' She must be vigilant for the bad luck this box may engender.

John was able to secure the box in one day to avert catastrophe. Everything in the old box had to be examined and declared edible before stocking the new box. The milk in its sealed glass jar was fine, but most of the other goods had to be replaced. Isn't it funny that they didn't notice the rising stench until it had advanced so far along as to be unbearable?

Ida was making Leberkase, so that she would have meat for lunches for the next week. She put pink curing salt, pepper, nutmeg, coriander, paprika, marjoram, ginger, cardamon, onion and garlic into a big bowl and added ground pork and pork neck meat. She used clean hands to mix the meat and the seasonings well until it looked like pink paste. She moved this into a loaf pan and into a medium oven. The loaf would bake for about an hour. The baking meat made the house smell wonderful. While the meatloaf baked, she carried several buckets of hot water to the washer in the basement and did a load of clothes. She carefully rinsed and wrung as much water from them as possible and then carried the basket of wet clothes upstairs, put on her coat and a scarf and went to the backyard to hang the clothes in the freezing air. The sun was out, so maybe they would dry before they froze on the line. One could always hope.

Returning to the kitchen, she added two buckets of water to the hot water reserve tank on the stove. The loaf looked ready to come from the oven, and so she removed it and set it to cool on the sideboard. While waiting for the loaf to cool and the girls to finish their nap, Ida went to the parlor and sat in the rocking chair and closed her eyes for fifteen minutes.

By some inner clock, she rose, used the bathroom, and then checked the pan – cool to the touch. She cut the loaf into slices about a finger thickness and packaged them in butcher's wrap and put them in the ice box. She could hear chatting upstairs and knew the little girls were up. Helen was due from school at any moment. They would need a small snack to tie them over until dinner. She retrieved the milk from the porch and cut a square of chocolate Kuchen for each of them. Mamie and Dodi came down the stairs, hand in hand, with sleepy but happy faces that brightened even further with the sight of the milk and cake. And Helen burst into the kitchen from the back porch, full of stories about her day at school.

She got the children set up at the kitchen table and retreated to the back porch where she pulled some bratwurst from the ice box. Continuing to the basement, she selected from last summer's canned goods a clear Ball jar with sauerkraut, another with green beans, and a third with strawberry preserves. The effort in the summer made the winter fare so much easier.

Back up in the kitchen, she put the bratwurst into a pan of water and brought it to a boil. She set the pan to the side of the main eye plate so that it would continue to simmer but not boil. She put the kraut in another pan and the beans in another and set them aside. The brats would take 30-40 minutes to cook. She went to the ice box and removed a cheesecake she had prepared the day before using quark she made by warming sour milk. The recipe was an easy one calling only for quark, cream, eggs, vanilla, raisins and sugar. She had not yet tasted the finished product. She ran through the process in her head assuring herself that she hadn't forgotten anything. After baking, she placed the cake in the ice box overnight to firm up. Now, she took the cake out and ran a knife around the edge of the pan and turned it out onto a plate. Beautiful. She opened the strawberry preserves and the smell of sweet fresh strawberries wafted from the jar. She covered the top of the cake with at least a half an inch of sweet preserves. And then set the cake back in the ice box to keep it cold.

The girls had retreated to the parlor to play. Ida cleaned up their dishes and then checked the brats. Almost done and almost 6:00. Perfect. She put the pans with the sauerkraut and the beans on the stove directly on the eyes of the stove and covered them, and then added a log to the coals in the box.

Ida heard the front door open and cries of "Papa, papa, papa." She wiped her hands on her apron and removed it. Going around to the front foyer where John had removed his heavy topcoat, scarf, hat and galoshes as the girls danced around him.

"Good evening, Papa," she said with a quick peck on the cheek.

"Good evening, Mama. Something smells wonderful." He pecked her back. Ida went back to the kitchen, put her apron on and checked the pots.

"Helen, Mamie, please come set the table," she called out. Mamie came immediately followed closely by Helen, while she heard Dodi squealing as Papa scooped her up for a romp. The girls set the dining room table properly, fork to the left, knife 'looking under the plate' to the right with the spoon next to it, and then carried the bowls of food into the table, along with condiments of spicy brown mustard, tomato sauce, bread and sweet bread-and-butter pickles.

"I love it when we have kraut and bratwurst," said Mamie.

"Me, too," said Helen.

John and Dodi were called to the table, and Ida once again removed her apron, draping it over a kitchen chair. She took her place at one end of the table with John at the other, Helen to the right and Mamie and Dodi to the left. The Kauffman's had been invited to another parishioner's home for dinner tonight. Ida felt only a little guilty that she was happy to have only her own family at the table for a change. Having the Kauffman's with them was a joy, but it also made the table conversation much more adult. Seeing her children happily chattering to their father gave Ida extraordinary joy. They all became quiet and folded their hands and bowed their heads.

"Helen?" said John.

"Dear Father, we give you thanks for this our daily food. Amen."

"Amen," chorused the others.

The food tasted good and was filling, but when Ida brought out the cheesecake, everyone clapped their approval. And she couldn't help feeling proud to be a homemaker – as usual, the feeling came with that small trepidation of warning about pridefulness.

After dinner, Ida washed the dishes with hot water drawn from the reserve. She wiped them and put them away, while John and the little girls played in the parlor, and Helen did homework at the kitchen table. At about 8:00, Ida called out "Kiss your Papa goodnight. It's time for bed." Since the girls took baths on Saturday night, tonight they were just powdered and dressed in their flannel nightgowns. Prayers were said, and they were tucked into their beds. Ida sat in the hallway so that everyone could hear and read one chapter of *Alice's Adventures in Wonderland*. John had purchased the book for the girls for Christmas, and it was tiny in comparison to any normal book he might have chosen, only six inches high and four inches wide. Ida was glad that she had her spectacles to help magnify the print. The leather cover over cardboard was a brilliant red with a portrait of Alice in gold leaf centered on the front. Tonight's chapter was 'A Mad Tea Party.' Almost immediately, Dodi snored softly in her bed. The others were allowed to read their own books after Ida finished. But tonight, Mamie was also asleep by the end of the caper. Ida went from bed to bed pulling up the warm quilts. She stopped at Helen's bed last.

"I have to read this book for school tomorrow," said Helen.

Ida looked at the book, *The Story of Washington Carver*. "That sounds like a good book. Do you need my help?" asked Ida.

"I don't think so," said Helen. Helen sat up and leaned forward to hug her mother. "Good night, Mama."

"Good night, Helen. Sleep tight. Don't let the bed bugs bite."

"Ick, Mama," Helen looked furtively around for bed bugs.

Ida laughed, and in Dodi's voice said, "No bugs!" and covered her ears.

Helen laughed and settled down to her reading.

Ida made her way down to the parlor where John sat perusing the paper. She settled on the davenport and found her crocheting and began to hook yarn.

"Everyone alright?" John asked.

"Everyone is fine."

They sat in comfortable silence for a few minutes.

Ida abruptly dropped her hands to her lap and looked at John.

"What's wrong, Ida? Do you not feel well?"

Ida shook her head, her eyes looked off in the distance, and her hands were still. "I left the clothes on the line. And now it's dark. What will the neighbors think?" She sighed, wound up her handiwork, and went to the front hall and pulled on a coat.

John stood and joined her. "I'll help." He pulled on his galoshes over stockinged feet.

"Such a mensch you are." Ida smiled at him. "No rest for the wicked." She tied a scarf babushka style around her head.

He pulled her close, "You, my dear, are anything but wicked."

They enjoyed a brief kiss and snuggled for a moment, and then went to the back door and out into the frosty night air to gather the long underwear off the line.

***

Door Township Caucus

The Republican voters of the town of Dorr are requested to meet at the courthouse in the city of Woodstock, on Saturday, March 19, 1910, at 2 o'clock p. m. sharp, for the purpose of placing in nomination candidates for the office of Town Clerk, Assessor, Collector, one Commissioner of Highways (1st district), one Justice of the Peace (to fill vacancy), one Constable (to fill vacancy) and one Trustee of Schools, to be voted for at the coming town election. Also, the selection of a town committee and the transaction of such other business as may properly be brought before the caucus. ROBERT MCLEAN,
JOHN F. WIENKE,
A. J. MULLEN,
Town Committee.

Woodstock Sentinel, March 10, 1910.

***

Would Push Work of Mid-Iowa Road

The plan suggested in the Times-Republican several days ago, for the building and maintenance of a good road thru central Iowa, east and west to attract automobilists thru the city, has been taken up in earnest by the Commercial Club of Denison, a lively western Iowa town. This club is taking the initiative and has mailed letters to all commercial clubs between and including Clinton and Council Bluffs, with the object of interesting all towns in a river to river dragged road through mid-Iowa, following the Northwestern railroad.

The Denison club has suggested that the journey to this city, or wherever the meeting be held, be made in automobiles. Some city in the eastern part of the state can entertain the automobilists of that division on the evening before the day of meeting, and Denison will care for those of the western division. On the meeting day the two processions will start toward the meeting place.

Des Moines Tribune, April 15, 1910.

***

Emerson Factory Near Complete.

The Emerson Typewriter factory is fast nearing completion and preparations are being made for the grand opening, which promises to be a big event.

The opening is going to take place on Thursday, April 21. At six o'clock a banquet will be served to the stockholders. Beginning at 8:30 a musical entertainment and dance will be given to which everybody is cordially invited without charge. A big time is planned, and the management wants everybody to come to the entertainment and hear the music and participate in the general good time.

After opening the company will begin moving immediately and it is expected that the plant will be in running order by May 15.

Woodstock Sentinel, April 15, 1910.

***

ALL THINGS DENISON
by Clara Daring
Too Swift a Pace

The citizens of Vail, the next station east of Denison, have risen up in indignation over the alleged immoral conduct of a farmer living three miles north. His name is Henry Bohnker, a well-to-do farmer. His wife being dead, the home has been kept by two daughters, both less than 16 years of age. Bohnker has been in the habit of going to Omaha, it is alleged by his family, and there spending large sums of money on lewd women. Recently he induced two women to come from that city to his home and has been living in a manner to cause scandal among his neighbors and humiliation to his married daughters and to those at home.

Thursday the sheriff was called, and he brought Bohnker and the two women to jail with a charge of lewd and lascivious behavior. His lawyer asked that he be declared insane.

On petition of his two sons-in-law, Judge Church of the district court has appointed E. T. Ryan, a leading businessman of Vail, as Bohnker's guardian. The insane commission refused to commit him to the asylum, finding him sane except in the matter of spending his money on fast women.

Citizens of Vail feel that they have made a move in the right direction in this manner, the presence of the two with minor children being the last straw. One of the daughters claimed that one of the women was about to marry Bohnker to account for her being at his home. The women were given a chance to take the first train back to where they came from and did so.

It does seem a pity that a man of marriageable age should be thwarted in his bid for happiness, but in this reporter's mind he must find a better way to court than he has thus far. Hopefully, his guardian will take this matter seriously, so that no harm comes to the young girls in Mr. Bohnker's care.

Crawford County Courier, April 16, 1910.

***

Church News
Congregational Church

Services for Sunday April 24. Morning worship, 10:30. Theme of the sermon. "Patchwork; the new cloth in the old garment." Sunday school, 12, noon. Subject for study, "Warning and Invitation." Y.P.S.C.E., 6:30. Topic "Christ winning the world."

Evening Service, 7:30, with short sermon on "Gideon and his army." Reference will be made to the "Great White Plague," following the suggestion of the National association for the study and prevention of tuberculosis that on April 24 attention should be directed to this subject in the churches of the United States.

Wm. Kilburne, pastor.
Woodstock Sentinel, April 21, 1910.

***

May Day, 1910
365 Lincoln Avenue
Woodstock, IL

Dear Sister and Brother,
 I laughed right out loud at the story about Mr. Bohnker and his trials and tribulations, Clara. What a wonderful tail of nosy neighbors and a man who probably had just found his life mate. Poor fellow.
 Have you two bought a car? It almost sounded like you were personally involved in the scheme by the Denison Commercial Club to build a road across Iowa. Do you think they could really do it? I wonder if I could get the autoists around here to build a hard road from Chicago thru Woodstock and on to Davenport. Then there would be a road between us that we could travel on and see each other occasionally. How many days would it take by auto to get to Denison? Is this not your third article in the city paper?
 The children are doing well. Dodi is finally growing taller. She is still chubby but starting to lose some of her baby fat. Mamie told me to tell you that she is feeling so much better now that summer is coming. She says she will miss the snow but can't wait to help with the garden. We'll see how long that lasts. Helen is doing very well. Looks like she will have no problem going on to the third grade at the end of the month. She is still quite the reader and would rather read than clean her room or help in the kitchen or even play with the other girls. I have continued to encourage her to begin to learn to cook, but she usually has her nose buried in a book while stirring the pot. Ha!
 John is fine. He seems to be doing well at his new career. The company is terribly busy with the new Emerson typewriter factory about to open. It has brought many fresh faces to Woodstock and a few old faces. John's youngest brother, Emil, may be moving back to Woodstock to take a job at the Emerson factory. He and Ethel and little Harvey will be staying with Ma Wienke until they can find their own place...if he gets the job. Anyway, lots of new construction, new houses, new businesses opening.

We just love our new Pastor Kauffman at Grace. He is such a jolly soul but also a good serious bible scholar which really shows in his sermons. He and his new wife lived with us in Helen's front room for about six months while we looked for a parsonage which they finally found down on Dean Street and moved in March first. The house isn't near the new church, and he will have a fine walk through the Square each day going to work. Did I tell you that we bought the German Presbyterian church when it closed? – yes, I think I did. It is getting all fixed up for us with a coat of paint in every room. We truly feel like God has watched over us this year.

Well, I better get my lazy hide moving and start supper. It will be just sandwiches tonight...I've started a new plan – No cooking on Sunday, only leftovers. Hope you are both doing well. Keep those articles coming. I'm still laughing.

Love,
Ida, John and the girls

***

Church News
Grace Lutheran

No services at all on Sunday. The decorators and painters will be occupying the building during the week and it will not be ready for occupancy by Sunday.

Services at Queen Anne at 7:30 P.M.

The choir will meet at the home of Mr. Frank Wienke on Friday evening at eight o'clock.

Rev. R. C. Kauffman, Pastor.
Woodstock Sentinel, May 5, 1910.

Sentinel Sidelights

Blame it on the comet.

Which is the worst, a bribe giver or a bribe taker?

Next in importance to the Easter hat is the graduation gown.

Woodstock Sentinel, May 5, 1910.

***

***

Social Events

Fourteen ladies of the Woodstock Women's Club [among them: Mrs. H. C. Doering] went to Chicago on Tuesday morning to be present at the annual May breakfast, given by the social Economics Club in the Mandel banquet room. At a reception given previous to breakfast, the ladies had the pleasure of meeting the guest of honor, Miss Clara Barton.

Woodstock Sentinel, May 12, 1910.

***

River-to-River Road

The committee of the Denison Commercial Club, which is boosting the river-to-river auto road along the line of the Northwestern railway, has issued a call for the meeting to be held in Boone to formulate plans for completing the western division of the plan, and contemplates a pilgrimage of autoists on the date yet to be fixed, with brief stops and speeches at the towns along the proposed route.

Crawford County Courier, May 6, 1910.

***

Signs for Auto Route
River-to-River Road Promoters Give Instructions to Local Officials
Bad Roads to Be Reported

The Executive Committee of the Iowa section of the official Transcontinental Good Roads route has issued a circular of instructions regarding the marking of the route thru the state with sign boards. These signs and material for proper markings are to be furnished free to the different chairmen in the towns and will be placed by them. The circular of instructions follows:

The official sign will read: "Iowa Official Trans-Continental Route." This sign will be placed on board, size 8 x 24 inches, two-inch black letters on white background with two-inch space at bottom of sign for arrow.

One official sign to be placed at each section corner on post, whitewashed, not less than twelve feet high. Sign to be eight feet from the ground. At every crossroad, not on a section line, one white pole, without sign, will be placed.

At any turn of road, all fence posts or telephone poles on corners are to be whitewashed, and official signs are to be marked with an arrow to indicate the direction of the turn to be taken.

Commencing at Clinton, each town is to place signs to indicate the next town west on the route and the distance to the next town.

Each town may have the privilege of making more than one route to the next town west. Each town is to place signage in or thru their town as they wish. Each town is to furnish speed limit signs and danger signals where needed.

If at any time, sections of the road may be impassable by reason of washouts, repairs on bridges or for any cause, the town chairman on each side of such a section will display from a white pole at or near the post office, a red flag in the daytime and a red light at night. This will be a warning to the automobile tourist to stop and consult the bulletin which will be posted on the white pole, which will give information in regard to the condition of the road and directions as to the best way of continuing the trip.

County vice presidents and town chairmen will at once secure the permission of local telephone companies to use their poles for guide boards, and without delay arrange their route and whitewash posts.

Four hundred official sign boards are being finished for immediate delivery. Sign boards will be sent to each town chairman by M. J. Dannatt, vice president, by freight upon remittance being received covering the amount of cost of signs at 15 cents each.

Sign boards reading, 'Danger, Run Slow' will be furnished at the same price as the official sign.

I Will Fly to Woodstock

One brass stencil arrow will be furnished free to each county vice president for making signs at turns in the road."

The enormity of the job of posting signs for easy and safe travel from the Mississippi river to the Missouri river is unprecedented. Miles of prairie and acres of swamp land separate the two waterways with only a simple one lane path to guide the traveler. The idea that this could become a well-traveled road via horse and automobile baffles the mind as does the idea of the hours and days spent bumping over rock and field on one's derriere. Maybe before the road is built, better and more comfortable seating should be secured for the vehicles involved.

Crawford County Courier, June 2, 1910.

***

Ida sat down at the kitchen table. Lunch sat in the icebox ready, but John must be running late. She expected him ten minutes ago. The girls were spending the day with Elizabeth, Grace and Willy over at Herman and Bessie's, so she could catch up on some housework. While she waited, she picked up the *Woodstock Sentinel* (June 16, 1910). "Let's see what news is news."

Oliver Factory News

Frank J. Wienke has been busy covering his house with a new coat of paint.

Miss Letah Wienke entertained a few of her immediate associates at a theater party Monday night, the occasion being in honor of her birthday.

It's sad, thought Ida, that we learn about our family from the Newspaper. I completely forgot about Letah's birthday, but then Letah has never remembered my birthday, Ida sniffed.

She turned to the "People's Column." Much information could be gleaned from reading the ads there.

>**FOR SALE** – The Sherman Block, good income property, on the Square. M. Sherman & Sons.

Really? A whole business block for sale. That didn't happen often. Maybe the Sherman's are moving. I'll have to ask John.

>**GIRL WANTED** – for general housework. Mrs. Adam Jung, 353 Lincoln Avenue.

Mrs. Jung is getting a housekeeper! Would wonders never cease. Aren't her children grown and out of the house? Ida tried to think. If so, why does she need a housekeeper? Her house is just about the same size as this one. And she's only cooking for the two of them. Strange. Maybe she's unwell. I'll call her later, Ida promised herself.

>**FOR SALE** – Seven room house and barn and four large lots near the new factory. O. Brown, Phone 1152.

I will pass this ad along to Ma for Emil and Etta. Probably just about the right size for them for right now, and of course, little Harvey.

>**Public Notice**
>The public is hereby warned not to trust anybody on my account after this date. EMIL SCHOEPKE.

What did that mean? Strange to see 'Emil' just after she was thinking about Emil Wienke. Wasn't life bizarre sometimes? Think of one Emil and up pops another.

I Will Fly to Woodstock

> **FOR SALE** – Rubber tire buggy, nearly new. New rubber trim harness: light express wagon, sleigh runners included. Call at Peet's wagon shop.

Well, isn't that something? Putting tires on a buggy. Should make for a smoother ride. That might really help old Jake. I'll have to point that out to John. Where is that man? She looked down at her lapel watch. Twenty minutes late. Maybe he got hung up with a client.

> **FOR SALE** -- $400 Shoninger piano only $150. $100 Regina Music Box, only $25. One Graphophone with 18 records, $25. Bookcases, tables, chairs, desk, ice box, Sideboard, etc. All Bargains. M. Sherman & Sons.

Well, there you have it! The Shermans must be moving if they are selling their tables and chairs. Wouldn't it be wonderful to have a Graphophone? I'll have to talk to John.

> **LOST** – A small soft gray kid pocketbook somewhere between Woodstock Dry Goods Store and Mrs. Bernrenter's residence last Saturday morning, containing quite a sum of money. Finder leave at Sentinel office or Post office and receive reward.

Ida tsked. Good luck getting that back. The 'finder' has already received his reward. I think that is how John walks to work. I'll have to have him look along the way when he goes back this afternoon. Some extra pin money would be welcome.

> **WANTED** – I want your order for nursery stock; you want our goods. The Coe Converse & Edwards

Co. always take care of their customers. Please hold your order till I come. M. A. ZABEL., Sharon, Wis., Agent for the Coe Converse & Edwards Nursery Co. at Ft. Atkinson, Wis.

"Ah!" said Ida excitedly. "Coe Convers & Edwards is coming! I'm getting twelve raspberry bushes, twelve blackberry bushes and thirty-six strawberry plants!" she said as if Mr. Zabel sat across the table with his order book in hand. "I wonder when he will be here?" She'd have to watch the paper, but Ida's order was ready. "Let's see what else?" She continued reading aloud.

LOST – Between cor. Grove and Madison streets and 825 Seminary Avenue, a pair of eyeglasses in case. Reward—

The back screen door swung open and in came John. He was breathing rather heavily as if he had run to get home.

"Well, hi there, stranger!" Ida looked up from the paper. "Were you running? Not on my account, I hope."

John chuckled. "Sorry, I'm late." John leaned over and kissed her on the cheek. "I'll wash up and be right here." He removed his hat, placed it on the table, and went to the washroom.

"That's okay," Ida said to his retreating form. She rose and went through the screen door to the porch to gather sandwiches and applesauce from the icebox. She raised her voice. "I am glad you're home. I have a lot to talk to you about."

***

Ida and Dodi pushed through the door of H. C. Doerings Dry Goods Store. She had been in the store a number of times and was always impressed by the high ceilings and bright displays. Herman had a flair for presentation that was difficult to match in other mercantiles in Woodstock. Instead of hiding stock behind counters and in drawers, he displayed the dresses, hats, suits and even undergarments for all to see and touch. She looked down at Dodi who was leaning hands and forehead pressed against a glass display case. Inside was an exhibit of broaches and timepieces.

"Good afternoon. How can I help you today?" a crisp female voice said behind her. Ida briskly pulled Dody away from the case leaving handprints on the glass and turned to the clerk.

"Is Mr. Doering in the store?"

"And who may I say is calling," asked the pretty young woman. She was attired in a burgundy wool traveling suit with skirt above the ankle and what appeared to be a manly tie. Ida reminded herself that styles change, and hemlines were creeping up. Her brother would be the one who would introduce the modern to quaint Woodstock.

"You're new here, aren't you?" Ida removed her glove and extended her hand. "I'm Ida Wienke."

"How do you do? I'm Mary Hurley." Mary's smile did not quite reach her eyes as she took the proffered hand.

"How do you do?" Ida smiled.

Mary turned toward the rear of the store. "I'll let him know you have come to call."

Ida called after her, "Tell him his sister wishes a word."

Mary stopped and looked back. "Yes, Ma'am." She smiled again, this time genuinely.

A far cry from coming in the grocery store door and calling out, "Herman?" Ida looked around. The store was empty of customers as far as she could tell, and Mary was the only obvious clerk in attendance. Ida reminded herself that people were probably engaged in their noon repast rather than shopping.

Ida had come to talk to Herman about the situation with their mother. Emma had written that Mama was failing and that they needed to 'do something.' She had suggested that Mama come to stay with each of them for a few months in rotation. Ida was skeptical that Mama would agree to the idea, but Emma asked Ida to see if Herman was amenable to the suggestion before they broached it with Mama.

A far door flung open with a bang. "Ida! Do come back," called out a male voice. With Dodi in hand, Ida walked toward the back of the store. Herman stood there, wiping his mouth with a napkin.

"Unca Herman!" Dodi called out.

"Well, hi there Mamie...er...Helen!"

Dodi giggled. "You know my name, Unca Herman. I'm Dodi!"

Herman gave her his most engaging smile. "Oh, that's right. Dodi. How are you today?"

Dodi knew the convention. "I'm fine; how are you?"

"I'm fine also. It's good to see you both!" His eyes lifted to Ida.

"I'm sorry. Did we come at a bad time? You are enjoying your lunch."

"No, no. I'll enjoy it more with company. Come in." Herman ushered them into a large ten by fourteen-foot office with cream walls and a thick red and blue Persian rug on the floor. The pictures on the walls were of East Asian design, one with peacocks and one with – well, Ida wasn't sure, but they were striking. Large three-foot high urns stood in two corners and East Indian baskets had been placed here and there, hopefully, none with pythons inside. The effect was both exotic and modern, but most of all, rich.

"You've redone your office," said Ida. "Very nice!"

"I sit down?" said Dodi.

"Yes, you may. Don't touch anything."

Herman chuckled. "Touch anything you want, Dodi. It's all replaceable."

"Who was your decorator?"

"Guess."

"Bessie?"

"Yup, she did a nice job, didn't she?"

"Yes, it is very…elegant."

Herman settled himself behind the walnut desk after beckoning Ida to a leather settee. "What can I do for you?"

Ida sat on the edge of the settee with a straight posture. She removed her left glove and placed the pair in her lap. She looked at Herman but kept Dodi, who was up examining the relics, in the corner of her eye. She tried to relax. Not an easy proposition in this environment.

"Do I need a reason to call on my favorite brother?"

"Of course not." Herman took a modest bite of his sandwich. It did not look like he had brought it from home. He probably sent Mary out to one of the cafes for it.

"I am down on the Square doing a little shopping. Mamie is at Ma Wienke's, learning about using herbs in cooking—"

"How nice."

"Yes, I've tried to get Helen's interest up, but she only has eyes for 'reading and commerce' as she puts it."

"Mama, what is dis?" Dodi held a foot-tall hourglass at arms-length with one hand.

"Oh my, Dodi, be careful with that," said Ida as she stood.

Herman stood also and reached Dodi before Ida could move. "Here let me show you what it does. It can help us tell time."

Dodi's eyes got big. "Like Mama's broke clock."

Herman gave Ida a quizzical look.

"Broach watch." Ida indicated the watch pinned to her chest. She sat back on the couch sliding back into its luxury.

"Yes, well, almost like that." Herman turned the hourglass over so about half the sand was on the upside and set it on an side table. "Let's say that you had a dog named Freckles." Herman looked at Ida. "I always wanted a dog named Freckles." Back to Dodi. "And your Mama says in a half hour you must take Freckles for a walk. How would you know when a half hour has passed?"

Dodi did a perfect shrug with her upside-down hands clearly showing that she didn't know how to tell time.

"What you can do is turn this glass over and let the sand in it slip to the second bulb, like this." He followed his own instructions, turned the artifact over, and set it back on the table. "When all this sand has run to the other bulb about a half an hour will have passed, and it will be time to walk Freckles."

Dodi squealed her delight. She sat down on the floor; her eyes glued to the falling sand. "I will tell you when."

Herman looked at Ida and winked. He returned to his seat and took his final bite of the sandwich.

"How are things in the store?" Ida asked. She didn't often talk business with men except John, but it seemed like the right thing to ask.

Herman wiped his mouth and sat back. "Well, since you ask, things are not going as swimmingly as I would like them to. I've had to let a couple people go and as you can see the crowds are not knocking the front doors down. Finances are fine, but not growing the way a true businessman would like to see them expand. So, I'm weighing my options."

Ida brightened. "Are you thinking about going back to Racine?"

"Oh, heaven's no! Never! George Murphy and I are thinking of merging our stores into what's called a 'department store' here in Woodstock.'"

"Like Wien's?" asked Ida.

"Like Wien's. Only bigger. He would most certainly be a competitor. But we would carry many things he doesn't, like drapes and carpets."

"Mm." Ida had run out of business items to talk about. "I had hoped you might be thinking about going back to Racine because of Mama."

"Mama?"

"Look," said Dodi. "See how full it's getting." Dodi pointed to the bottom lobe.

"Yes, Dodi. That's pretty amazing, isn't it?"

Dodi nodded her head several times and went back to watching fine blue sand rain down.

Herman leaned forward with his elbows on his desk. "Mama?"

"I'm worry," said Ida. "I worry that she is all alone there. That she will fall, and we won't find her until it's too late or that we will find her, and she'll have broken something, and we will be hard-pressed to take care of her. I know she is still doing things on her own, not asking for help, climbing up on a chair to reach the kitchen shelves, carrying things up and down stairs. I've asked her about getting some live-in help or even a roomer or two, but she doesn't want to cook for other people. She seems scattered when I talk to her on the phone.

I Will Fly to Woodstock

Hard to keep a conversation going even in German, and my German is leaving me faster than a stein of beer in a thirsty man's hand."

Herman smiled.

"I just wish I could convince her to move down here where she'd have two children to look in on her or she could live part of the time with each of us—"

"Wait, wait, wait. Let's not get ahead of ourselves. I'm not sure I'm ready to take her in with three little kids and a particular wife. I'm not sure that Bessie and Mama would be a good match living together. So that's a 'no.'"

Ida felt a little heat in her cheeks. "Well, she'd be more than welcome to come live with me after all the years she took care of me."

"I believe I've done a lot for this family. I put my whole savings into that grocery store." He said 'grocery store' with what seemed to be a bit of scorn in his voice. "I bet my entire livelihood on it. I'm not about to put my marriage in the hands of relatives. I've done enough."

Ida felt the numbness of dread settle in her chest. Should she ask or just let old dogs lie? She took a deep calming breath. "Herman, I don't know what happened with the store. Can you tell me?"

Herman looked at the newspaper that had wrapped his sandwich. "I'm sorry that John couldn't survive without my involvement, but that should tell you something."

"What? What should it tell me?" Ida was finding it hard to breathe.

Herman looked at his sister. "I know this is hard to hear, but John is not a businessman. He has the passion, but not the talent. He is not ruthless in his business plans, but rather bends to the customer's desires."

Ida felt her cheeks flush and drew in breath.

Herman continued. "I'm sorry, but I had to pull out. We were buying horseshoes in case someone might need one for above a door while he was vetoing any product with the word 'Woodstock' on it. I have seen how such products sell and support the shopkeeper. He is so…so…old-fashioned."

"You quit him because he was old-fashioned? Do you hear what you are saying?" Ida knew her voice was just a bit too shrill.

Dodi looked at her mother, concern written on her face. Ida smiled. Dodi smiled and went back to the sand.

Herman's hands went to his face, covering it. He massaged his forehead. "Ida."

"Herman. I must admit that I had hoped your partnership would last longer. You said that you and John would go your own ways when each of you was ready for that step."

"If I had waited, we'd both be bankrupt."

Ida glanced at her youngest daughter and tried to keep her tone conversational. "Maybe. Or maybe you would have established the kind of store that you are anticipating with Murphy with John. Have you thought about that?"

Herman closed his eyes for a moment and then said, "I don't believe that would have happened."

"Why?"

Herman shook his head. "This community was not then ready for an unusual way to shop."

"But now it is?"

"We'll see. Ida, listen, I was odd-man-out in that grocery. The people didn't want service. They wanted John to…um…flirt with them. I'm sorry but that's the truth. The old ladies came in and expected him to smile, compliment them, cater to their every...well...not every need...but their every merchandise need."

Ida lowered her voice. "Oh for heaven's sake, Herman. Are you a little boy? John, of course, was simply better known in Woodstock—"

"Of course, he was. I know that some of it was my fault." Ida waited.

"Okay, listen. I had just gotten married and my wife was expecting a certain...lifestyle. And she still does. I must find a way to make the money that will support that lifestyle."

"So, if I follow. You and Bessie wanted to move up socially and being a 'grocer' was not good enough for you?"

"No, you aren't listening—"

"Unca Herman?" Dodi's blue eyes were round and clear as she put on her best begging face.

Herman took a deep breath and smiled. "Yes, Dodi."

"Do you have cangy at this store?"

"I think we do." He reached into a side drawer and pulled out a bag of lemon drops. "Do you like these?"

Two exaggerated nods.

He held out the bag. "You can have three," he looked at Ida, who nodded.

Dodi took four and went back to watching the sand fall.

Herman cleared his throat. "I'm sorry. Ida, I don't want to hurt you or John. I love Bessie and my children and they MUST come first, before John, before you, before Mama. Of course, I want to help, but she cannot come to live with us. Bessie would never...tolerate that."

Ida was unsure what to say. She heard him saying that John was not a 'good' enough businessman, that Bessie was running his life, and that she and the rest of the family were not important anymore.

"Ida?"

"Let's get back to Mama."

"Okay. Has there been some kind of episode that makes you bring this up now?"

"Just a letter from Emma, asking about my plans to visit or have Mama visit this summer and during the holiday season. She seemed a little...um...perturbed at our lack of participation. And wondered if we could share responsibility a little more."

"What do you mean? I see Mama whenever I'm in Racine. What more does Emma want?"

Ida hedged a bit. "She didn't ask you for anything. She asked me to talk to you and see what you thought. I simply felt like Emma was implying either that Mama is slipping away more than you and I know or maybe she is at her wit's end dealing with her and she seemed to be asking for our help. I think Emma has the same worries as I do about Mama being there alone, and Emma sees her a lot more than either of us."

"She's closer!" Herman's voice was a bit too sharp. "What about Clara off in the hinterlands."

Dodi looked at her uncle, but then popped the last lemon drop into her mouth.

"I believe...and you should agree...that Clara truly put in her time with Mama over the last years."

Herman again looked at his desktop and shook his head. "So, what does our elder sister want us to do?"

"I don't know for sure, but maybe each of us take Mama a couple months at a time."

"Look. I am very willing to be Mama's travel mate when she wants to come down. I'll even pay her fare. That duty is probably better done by a man than a woman—"

Ida glared at him. Herman noticed.

"No, no. I mean if Mama should start to fall or stumble, I am stronger and can handle a person of her size better than a woman might."

Ida looked at her hands and glanced at Dodi, who still seemed mesmerized by the sand as she sucked on the hard candy. "I suppose you are right. Okay, well at least that is something. When would you be able to get away from the store?"

"Right now, it would be difficult, but if the merger goes through, it should be easier. I'd have to also check with Bessie."

"So, you'll do it, but not right now." Ida shook her head, and now she took a deep calming breath. "Emma and I might end up sharing custody, so any help you can give us would be welcome."

"It's done! I HAVE TO GO WALK FRECKLES!!" Dodi yelled and headed for the door.

Both Ida and Herman burst out in laughter.

"Oh Dodi." Herman stood and went over to her still chuckling. He knelt down so he looked her in the eye. "Remember I said, 'Let's SAY you had a dog named Freckles.' You don't really have a dog, do you?"

Dodi paused. She stared first at the door and then turned to look at her mother, her eyes filling with tears. The tears started rolling down her cheeks. "I want a dog named Freckles," she sobbed.

Ida put her arms out to her little girl and held her close. "I'm sorry, honey. Maybe someday."

Dodi continued to sob.

"Now look at what you've done." A small smile played at the corners of Ida's mouth. "Now we have to get a dog."

Woodstock Sentinel, June 30, 1910.

Woodstock Sentinel, June 30, 1910.

Business Firms to Consolidate.

Another important change in business firms is contemplated in the near future, which will mean the consolidation of two of our most important mercantile firms under one management.

This change is the announcement just made of the forming of a co-partnership between George L. Murphy, the surviving member of the firm of Murphy & Mullen, and Herman C. Doering, who for several years has been a successful merchant in this city.

The new firm will consolidate the stocks of both institutions, the intention being to vacate the store now occupied by Mr. Doering about September 1. Previous to that time Mr. Doering will reduce his stock, making it possible to find room for it together with the Murphy & Mullen stock, which will also be reduced by special inducements to buyers.

Woodstock Sentinel, June 30, 1910.

***

FACTORY FOREMEN UNITE IN PROTEST

We, the undersigned foremen, assistant foremen and inspectors of the Oliver Typewriter company, desire to publicly express our thanks to the many owners of automobiles in Woodstock who so kindly extended the use of their cars for our annual picnic last Saturday. At the same time, we desire to express our hearty disapproval of the item published in a local newspaper last week and which reads as follows: "The foremen will be entertained by the political bosses of the community at Twin Lakes in a short time." The picnic, as is well understood by everybody, is an annual affair, entirely in charge of the foremen, non-political in every respect and all expenses borne exclusively by us. Any contrary insinuation such as the above we consider nothing less than an insult both to us and to those who so kindly granted us the use of their cars.

Signed by 83 men, including Frank Wienke and Ed Wienke.

Woodstock Sentinel, July 14, 1910.

***

I Will Fly to Woodstock

John pulled out a chair and settled at a table with Frank and Emil. They had agreed to eat Saturday lunch at Dirrenberger's Restaurant, since Ida and the girls were spending the week in Racine with Ida's mother, Louisa.

"John!" said Emil. "Long time no see!"

"Hi, there." John shook hands warmly with his little brother and nodded at his other little brother. "Frank."

"John," said Frank.

John looked at the menu. He liked eating lunch at a restaurant. If one chose well, one would also have supper from the portions. The waitress approached in her starched white apron and hat.

"Gentlemen, what can I get for you today?" Her sultry voice caused all three men to look up at the buxom brunette.

Frank found his voice first. "Good afternoon, Jannette. I'd like the Ruben with extra sauerkraut and bread pudding with cream."

Hm, thought John. That sounded good but wouldn't be enough for two meals. "Do you have liver and onions today, Jannette?" he asked.

"Yes, we do, Mr. Wienke. Is that your choice?"

"What is the vegetable?"

"Carrots and peas." Jannette made vegetables sound like a wonderful delicacy to be eaten after a sexual encounter.

John shifted in his chair a bit, uncomfortable. "Yes. Okay. That's my choice."

Emil continued to look at the menu, a small smile playing across his face, his amusement at his brother's expense. "Let's see. I think I'll have the brisket sandwich with red potatoes and the vegetables."

"Now that's a good choice!" said Jannette, enthusiastically. "My favorite." She drew out "favorite" lowering her voice to a purr; Emil's turn to feel uncomfortable.

He looked up and smiled, "Good!" He closed the menu and handed it to her.

"Coffee all around?" Jannette asked.

"Yes," the three men answered.

"I'll be right back with that," said Jannette as she turned from the table.

"Good night!" Frank said to John in a near whisper. "She has your number!"

"I hope not!" John said with a belly laugh. "I think she is all purr and no scratch."

Emil and Frank laughed. "Just looking for a better tip, I would guess," said Emil.

"I hope so." John considered the lack of intimacy he had with Ida now that the girls were older and less predictable in their wanderings around the house.

"So, did you get the job, brother?" John changed the subject.

"Not yet," said Emil. "I think my interview went fine, but they didn't say 'you're hired,' so I'm not sure. We would like to move to Woodstock. It's still so quaint here, small town compared to the city; good place to bring up children."

"Are you saying you and Etta are expecting again?" asked Frank. "Are congratulations in order?"

"Sadly, no. And it's not from lack of trying." Emil said, blushing a bit.

"Here's to 'trying'!" said John, and with their filled coffee cups which Jannette had discreetly placed on the table as they talked, they clinked a toast.

"What would they have you doing?" asked Frank.

"Same old thing. Die casting. Although starting from the ground up, so a good opportunity for advancement."

"Well, we hope it works out. All of us would be happy to see you move down here!" said John.

"To Woodstock," said Emil.

They raised their cups in salute.

Jannette served their food with a coy smile. "Anything else, fellas?"

Eyes on their food, the men tried not to make eye contact with her or each other.

"Nope," said Frank. "Everything looks good."

Jannette swayed her way behind the counter.

"Makes me wish that Ida was in town," said John, under his breath, smiling.

"How are Ida and the girls? How is Mamie?" Emil asked before digging into his food.

"Good as can be expected, I guess," said John. "She has too little stamina, but the doctor says to keep pushing her a bit to build that up. She will go to first grade in September, and we'll see how she does there. It's hard to tell if she's excited about it or not."

"Does she know other children going into first grade?" asked Frank.

"One or two from Sunday School, so that is good. She seems to be studious if Sunday School is any measure. You should hear her recite Bible verses. Recitation is her strong suit. She's such a little thing, saying all the big words. Makes me proud."

***

And in Racine…

"Emma, what is it you are the most worried about?" asked Ida.

"Mama living alone, of course?" Emma snapped.

"I mean specifically."

Emma took a breath. "Specifically? Well, she doesn't seem to have much to say nowadays, not that she's ever been a big talker, but certainly more than now. I worry that her mind is not as sharp. That she'll forget to do something important like feed the wood stove on a cold day. I don't think she should be alone for another winter."

"Is she still taking care of herself? Eating, bathing, shopping for groceries?"

"Yes. For the most part. One of us drops in on her about once a week just to make sure she has groceries. When it's me, I try to cook something that she'll have for a few days. She talks less and remembers less, but she gets some good zingers in. Just you wait."

Ida mulled over what her sister had said as she finished wiping the last of the luncheon dishes. She and Emma had had only a little time alone to talk about the Mama issues brought up in Emma's letter. Was this the time for action as Emma thought? Should they force Louisa to make such a big change? Would it be right if Louisa was not asking for help?

Ida hung the towel on the rack and went into the front room with all its memories of her courtship. "It's nap time," she announced.

"Aw Mama." Helen looked up from the ubiquitous book.

"You don't have to sleep, but you do have to go lay down, so your sisters will do the same," allowed Ida.

"Die Dicke muss schlafen gehen," said Louisa.

Ida and Emma covered their mouths, so the girls would not see their smiles. "The fatty must go to bed," Mama had said. Little doubt existed but that she referred to Dodi who still took a daily nap. Luckily, the girls spoke little German.

"Jeder muss schlafen gehen," replied Emma. "Everyone needs a good rest."

The girls got up, headed for the stairs, and retreated to their pallets on the floor in their Uncle Herman's old room. Emma sat down on the couch, tucked her stocking feet up under her, and leaned into the couch pillows. "Mama, willst du dich hinlegen? Do you want to go up to your bed?"

"Nein," came the answer. "Ich werde heir auf meine Stuhl bleiben." I will stay here in my chair.

"OK," said Ida as she mounted the stairs. "Mach ein Nickerchen gut, meine süße Mama." Nap well, my sweet Mama.

***

FOR RENT – Store now occupied by H. C. Doering. Vacant Sept. 15. Apply A. J. Zoia, Woodstock.
Woodstock Sentinel, July 21, 1910.

***

Amending a Proverb

There are a lot of silly proverbs knocking about. Take for instance, "If pigs had wings, they would fly." Now, this is absurd. Do you know what sized wings a pig weighing eighty pounds would require in order to fly? They would measure about thirty yards from tip to tip. A nice state of things to keep pigs in an aviary with wings that size! The proverb would run much better:

If pigs could fly
Pork would be high.

-- *London Scraps*
Woodstock Sentinel, August 4, 1910.

***

ALL THINGS DENISON
by Clara Daring
When Roosevelt Comes

President Roosevelt will pass thru Denison Friday Aug. 26, at 11:30 a.m. according to the Northwestern schedule. The distinguished American will make a ten-minute stop and the people of Denison and those in this vicinity mean to make the most of it.

The Commercial Club met and arranged a program and appointed committees for the occasion. It is expected that a large crowd will be on hand. At the time when Hon. L. M. Shaw was in his cabinet, President Roosevelt made Denison a visit, remaining some hours. Would that he do the same this time.

The ladies of Crawford County are planning to come out in force to advocate for the vote, an option to which we hear the former President is sympathetic. They are hopeful that he will address this issue in his brief remarks.

Crawford County Courier, August 22, 1910.

***

Hello Girls on Strike

The force of telephone girls at Denison on the Crawford County exchange have struck. The girls claim that they are obliged to work in close, uncomfortable quarters, the management refusing to open a door to let a draft of fresh air circulate; also, that they must labor ten hours with no relief for dinner, forced to eat their lunch while continuing to work.

The manager claims the girls talked too much with the public and so he shut the door.

Crawford County Courier, August 26, 1910.

***

Helen looked at the clock. "Mama, we are going to be late!!" she called up the stairs.

"Just one moment," her mother called back. "I'm just putting a ribbon in Mamie's hair."

"But we are going to be late! Hurry up!"

Ida chose not to answer this second demand by her smart seven-year-old. She tied the ribbon that pulled back Mamie's hair. The red ribbon was Mamie's favorite color. "Are you excited about school, Mamie?" Ida asked.

"Yes," said Mamie. "I will see Gloria and Ellen there." She paused, "And Helen."

"Yes, you will. And you'll start learning about things you never even thought of before," said Ida.

"What 'bout me?" said Dodi. "Me, too."

"You are too little to go. You're only three," said Mamie.

"Dodi, we will have great fun here at home. Mama needs you to stay home with her to keep her company."

"Mama!" a call from downstairs.

"We better go down before Helen leaves without you." Ida lifted each girl off the bed.

"We're coming now, Helen," Ida called out.

"Mama!" Helen met them at the bottom of the stairs. "We are going to be late!"

Ida looked at her lapel watch, "No, you'll be fine. Anyway, Mamie's all ready for her first day at school." She put Mamie's sweater on and looked Helen over. She had dressed herself and done a superb job. She did have fashion sense.

Ida walked the girls to the door. "Now Helen, you are responsible for helping Mamie if she needs something. I want you to hold hands while crossing the streets and look both ways for horses coming…or autos, heaven forbid. Do not expect them to stop. When you get to the tracks. Stop, even if the others don't. Look both ways and listen before you cross. Will you be okay?"

"Yes, Mama," both girls answered.

"Well, it's only six blocks. Just hold hands the whole way today, okay, Helen?"

Silence. "Helen?"

"OK, but just today then she'll know the way."

I should have said this week, thought Ida. "Well, she might need a little help the rest of this first week too. Okay, off with you. Be careful, and I'll have a snack when you get home this afternoon."

"Bye, Mama," both girls called out as they climbed down the front steps and headed for the wooden sidewalk.

"Come here," Helen said to Mamie, and she took her hand forcefully, and they began the walk.

"You'll be alright," Helen encouraged her.

"I know," Mamie answered in a small voice.

"You know that they are going to call you Marion, not Mamie."

"Why?"

"Because Marion is your name, not Mamie."

Mamie considered this. She didn't hate or love the name Marion. She had a cousin named Marion, but her name had always been Mamie. "I will tell them, I'm Mamie."

"It won't matter. Susie Philips tried that, but they still just call her Susan."

"Oh," said Mamie. She was slightly disheartened, but then thought to put a positive light on it. "Marion will be my grown-up name."

"Okay. Good," Helen agreed. She tightened her grip on Mamie's hand. They had passed their Uncle Frank's house on Dane Street and were approaching the wider and more-traveled Washington Street. "This is a street."

Mamie smiled, "I know."

"We must cross it. What we do is look one way and then the other and then back the first way."

"Why back the first way?" Mamie didn't see the point.

"Well, because while you are looking the second way, a horse might sneak up on you, and then you might step out and get hit."

That made sense. They stopped at the crossing. They looked to the right and then to the left and then back to the right. Helen moved as if to step off the boardwalk, but Mamie didn't move. She looked back to the left. Helen hesitated. "What are you doing, Mamie?"

"I'm looking the other way again for the sneaky horse," she looked back to the right and then to the left. "It could sneak up when we are looking the other way."

Helen stepped into the street and somewhat roughly pulled Mamie off the boardwalk. "You only have to look forth and back three times. That's good enough. Otherwise, you might never make it to school."

Mamie nodded. Helen was right as usual.

At the railroad track crossing near Oma Wienke's, Helen stopped. A boy behind her was looking at the ground, and he walk squarely into her back. Helen stumbled forward. Her foot came down on the track and she jumped back to Mamie's side.

"What's wrong?" the boy asked. "Why'd you stop?"

"Nothing's wrong," said Helen. "We're just listening for a train."

The boy half-smiled and pushed past them. "Chicken."

"Donkey," Helen said, and she grabbed Mamie's hand and pulled her across the tracks.

They walked on. Two blocks to the school.

"Now, when we get there," Helen said, looking around, "don't expect me to be right beside you all the time. I'm in third grade and you are in first, so you will be with the first graders and I will be with the big kids."

"Big kids?" Mamie imagined large children too big for the desks.

"That's just what we call them. This year, I'm a big kid."

Mamie looked her over. "You aren't so big."

Helen looked down at the walk, shook her head and sighed. "It doesn't mean you are big in size, just big in knowing."

"Oh." Mamie was worried that this was going to be a lot harder than she had expected.

"Okay, here we are." Helen dropped Mamie's hand and looked around to see if any of her friends had seen her disgrace. No one seemed bothered. "We are going in now, so you stay behind me, and I'll take you up to the teacher. We call her 'Teacher.'"

"Okay." They moved into the line of children going through the doorway. They emerged into a less restricted hallway where big kids and little kids mingled about.

Mamie was glad that Helen had explained things to her. Even though Helen was being a bit odd about Mamie's presence there, Mamie didn't care. What did matter was that she, Mamie Marion Wienke, was there. In first grade! She stretched out her arms to either side. She was about to fly, and nothing could stop her now.

***

Baby Drowned in Jar

The farm neighbors of Mr. and Mrs. Reimer, living six miles west of Denison, were thrown into excitement Friday noon by news over the phone that their 2-year-old girl was dead. Inquiry found that the little one had fallen headfirst into a sixteen-gallon jar of rainwater and there drowned. The mother was busy at work when she missed the child. Coming in sight of the jar and seeing water plentiful on the ground she saw at once what must have happened. Her worst fears were realized on pulling her babe from the jar dead.

Those witnessing the grief of the mother reported the scene disheartening beyond description.

Crawford County Courier, September 19, 1910.

***

ALL THINGS DENISON
by Clara Daring
Big German Celebration

The Germans of this county, who form an important tier of the population of Crawford County, celebrated German Day in an enthusiastic manner. A large procession was formed, headed by the organization of former German soldiers honored with carrying the flag sent to them by Emperor William. The exercises were held in Denison at the German Brotherhood Hall in the park at the north of the city. Addresses were made in German and English, eulogizing the German people and what they have done for the history of Crawford County, Iowa, the United States, and the world.

The day is celebrated as the anniversary of the founding of the first German settlement in 1683 called Germantown, Pennsylvania. German immigrants found fertile ground in America for their skills. They are known today for their fine artisanship, thrift, hard work, excellent farming, and dedication to a healthy and good life. Happy Anniversary to our German countrymen.

Crawford County Courier, October 7, 1910.

***

Personal Items

Mr. and Mrs. Charles Wienke and son Royal from Beloit, Wis., spent last week with Mr. Wienke's brother of this city.

Emil Wienke of Beloit has accepted a position in the Emerson factory and is moving here with his family. Mr. Wienke has been employed as a pattern maker by the Warner company in Beloit.

H. C. Doering entertained a few friends at cards on Tuesday evening in honor of Mrs. Doering's birthday. A two-course luncheon was served. Those present were Messrs. And Mesdames V. S. Lumley, Lynn Stone, H.H. Bosshard, Wallace Woodburn, Lynn Richards and George W. Lemmers.

Woodstock Sentinel, October 13, 1910.

***

365 Lincoln Ave.
Woodstock, Illinois
October 15, 1910

Dear Clara,

I've enclosed a clipping so you can see that I was NOT being 'crazy' in my last letter. We were not invited to Bessie Doering's birthday party. This shunning began about the time John gave up the store and has only gotten worse in the last few months. Has Herman said anything to you? Mama says he has not, nor Emma. John says not to worry about it. Our children still play together occasionally either here or there. Bessie has always been just a little bit high-bred for us commoners, and now that they have gained such stature here in Woodstock, I think it has gone to her head. On the other hand, the girls and Willie are very well behaved and have impeccable manners, so she is doing a respectable job with them. John says it's just because they are Presbyterians and thus Democrats and so we have two strikes against us being Lutheran and Republican.

I stopped at his store a while back and the girl there didn't even know who I was when I asked to see him. We spent his lunch time together talking about Mama and whether we should be doing something more for her. He was not especially enthusiastic on that front. But Mama is doing fine, I guess. Emma checks on her regularly and she has even called me a few times just to chat. So maybe he's right. Maybe I just need to be humble and invite them over and have a birthday cake for Bessie. Clean slate and all that. You will tell me if you hear anything, right?

I wanted to say that your description of the German Day was so interesting. I will talk to John about starting something like that here in Woodstock. Just think of all the German people here in Woodstock who would embrace having a celebration like that. How proud you must feel that you can translate what is happening so all the people of Denison will know the story.

The article about the baby drowned in the jar was heart wrenching. Can you imagine the mother's anguish! Of course, you can. You were there. Did you see the drowned child? I would never be able to wipe that from my memory. I worry all the time about my children getting one thing or another like tuberculosis and now polio. They don't know where it's coming from. Children, especially ones like Mamie, are so vulnerable. But I never thought about them falling in a cistern.

Speaking of Mamie, she loves school. She and Helen argue over who likes it more. Isn't that marvelous? Dodi and I have a fun time baking and cooking...we are both getting to be "die Dicke" as Mama called Dodi when we were visiting. Isn't that cute? I've been using it every day. She doesn't know what it means, but she likes it because Oma said it.

I must run. I just wanted to write and see if you've any explanation for your brother's actions. I wonder if he and John had a falling out. John, of course, wouldn't mention such a thing and would downplay it now if it did happen. I'm just at my wits end about this. Please write.

Our love to you both,

Ida

***

ALL THINGS DENISON
by Clara Daring
Probably Mastodon's Tooth

The jawbone and a molar of a prehistoric animal has been found in the Denison sandpit. Diggers in the sandpit adjoining the town plat to the south found this week the tooth of a mastodon or similar large and long extinct animal. The tooth is well-preserved and still encased in a part of the mammoth jawbone, which is soft and decaying, but the tooth seems hard as flint. The grinding surface of the tooth is ten inches long by five inches wide and is of oval shape. From the bottom surface of the tooth to the top is ten inches. Huge bones have been found before in the pit where the tooth is now taken from, and it is evident that the remains of a prehistoric animal are resting there. Representatives of the state university have already made inquiries for the specimen.

Is this discovery upsetting to our local religious authorities? Seemingly not. Very few people seem too excited about such an amazing discovery. It would seem that finding these bones would push back the idea that the earth has existed for only 4000 years as indicated in the good book to millions of years. But then, who knows what a year is to God.

Crawford County Courier, October 18, 1910.

***

Brookins and his Aeroplane

Some of our Woodstock citizens were in Springfield attending the State Fair and witnessed the arrival of Walter Brookins, in his Wright aeroplane, from Chicago.

When first seen the aeroplane was a mere speck in the sky and they watched him until he reached the fair grounds and then circled the grounds several times before landing. The noise made by the machinery of the aeroplane could be heard plainly while the circle of the grounds was being made.

Mr. Brookins made the flight from Chicago to Springfield in seven hours. Including stops. The distance from the straight point in the park at Chicago, was 192 miles and he made only two stops for fuel, oil and water.

Woodstock Sentinel, October 20, 1910.

***

Tuberculosis and Heart Disease Head Mortality

Washington, D. C. – Special from the *Moline Express*. Census statistics show that consumption causes 14.8 Percent of deaths among men and 21 among women. Tuberculosis of the lungs, heart disease, and accidental violence caused more than 37 percent of the deaths from all causes in 1900 among certain classes, according to the census bureau. These classes are those "gainfully employed or occupied males." The same causes led to 39 percent of the deaths from all causes among the "occupied females."

Woodstock Sentinel, October 25, 1910.

Lowden's Children are Stricken by Paralysis

Oregon, Ill.– Special from the Moline Express. – An epidemic of infantile paralysis in Winnebago and Ogle counties has struck the two small children of Col. Frank O. Lowden bringing the congressman on a special train back from his

Arkansas ranch to his home, Sinissippi Farm, near here.

Florence and Harriet, 11 and 8 years old, respectively, are the little girls stricken by the disease. A Chicago specialist was summoned to the farm immediately and children are now doing fairly well, although both cases still are serious.

There have been several deaths recently from infantile paralysis in the neighborhood, for which local physicians are at a loss to find a cause.

Woodstock Sentinel, October 25, 1910.

***

November 18, 1910
Denison, Iowa

Dear Ida, John, and girls,
It's your dear old Aunt Clara from far away Denison writing to tell you that I love you and wish I could see you.

Things have been quiet here except for the normal havoc of the times. I've been busy chasing down stories and my dear Pearle has been busy climbing up poles to try to keep the lights on. It's in the winter with the cold and snow that the lines really take a beating, so we are holding our breath against the long nights of work he will suffer. He tells me he is doing a great job and may get a promotion soon. I suppose he'd still have to go out if the lines were down, but maybe not be responsible for putting them back up. Time will tell.

We had a wonderful German Day this year. I enclosed the article. Our Denison group invited the German organizations from surrounding towns to come to Denison to celebrate. They often do without invitation, but we hoped to get a larger turn out, and boy howdy, did we ever. We also gave prizes for the best float, best car decoration and the most people from an out of town organization. I was involved in the parade which started at the Square at 1:00. Before that there were stands with brats and beer and other German delicacies enjoyed by all. But the parade was the best part. Pearle didn't have to work so he and I lined up all the participants. John Fastje (you don't know him) and his business wagon that won first place was the best and funniest. He had dressed up his business wagon with kegs and flowers and streamers and beer drinking opas who kept toasting the crowd in funny ways and then swigging the beer. They were nearly falling off the wagon before the end of the route.

The parade ended at the beautiful Bruderschaft park just north of the city and there were speeches, but I noticed that this year only one of the speeches was actually in German. It was by far the favorite speech of those given.

After the speeches, Pearle and I found a nice tree to sit under and watched the others enjoy the sports and games. I encourage Pearle to participate but he said he would rather sit there and hold my hand. Isn't that sweet?

When the games ended, no one went home to eat supper. The town put on a huge Spanferkel to thank the German community. And then as if that wasn't enough, there was a grand ball and beautiful fireworks.

I tell you, I was tired when we got home, but so happy that Denison loves its German citizens including Pearle and me.

I just reread your letter, Ida, and I'm not sure what to say about our brother. I think they are probably oblivious to how their actions make you feel. If I were you, I'd work on including the little girls and Willie as often as you can. And maybe think about if you want to be included with his group of people. I'm not sure I would want to be. Good to have a brother but not too close.

I heard from Mama last week. Her letter was short and not really all that newsy. Seemed like she was struggling to find things to talk about. Have you seen her lately?

I'm also including one of my columns (that's what they call a newspaper article that happens regularly) on finding a mastodon tooth in the sand pit outside of town. Just think of that!! Mastodons roamed these plains just the way the buffalo do. I wonder what happened to all of them.

So, in the end, we are fine, bracing for winter, storing up wood and coal and provisions. If it's anything like last year, I will be trapped for months. Thank goodness for the telephone – did you ever think you'd hear me say that? Have you seen many aeroplanes around there? I have yet to see one. The Denison paper published a long well-written story about an aviator and it made me want to ride in one. I may have to come back east to see one or take a ride. Just think what it would be like if we could hop a plane in Denison and be in Woodstock in a matter of hours rather than days. I wonder if we'll ever see that. What do you think?

I better run. I've made scalloped potatoes that have been in the oven for about 45 minutes. I better go check and turn them. An easy dish to hold if Pearle is late. And delicious with a slice or two of Iowa ham.

Our best wishes for a happy Thanksgiving. I am thankful to have you as family...all of you. God bless you.

Love,
Clara and Pearle

***

For the Mere Man

When in doubt, make him a pocket stamp case.

The stamp case for carrying in the waistcoat pocket will prove an acceptable little present for a man and should be made in two pieces, the upper portion holding the stamps being slightly smaller in size than the other part of the case, into which it may be slipped.

The case can be made from any small remnants of silk, and when complete it should measure not more than two inches by one and a half. The back portion of each part should be stiffened with a piece of thin cardboard, and an ordinary visiting card cut to the size required will answer the purpose very well. A small loop of narrow ribbon is sewed in the center of the upper part of the case by which it may be pulled from the lower part when a stamp is required. The sketch so clearly shows the nature of this little article that further description is scarcely necessary.

Woodstock Sentinel, November 17, 1910.

Woodstock Sentinel, November 17, 1910.

***

Herman's ad – well, really Murphy and Doering's ad, and she couldn't but notice again that he had taken second billing – for the upcoming dollar day sale was certainly complete, thought Ida, as she scanned the many ads for bargains. She could always use ribbon for the girls' hair and doilies. She would stop in there and maybe have a word with him also.

She was still upset about being snubbed – John said it was "overlooked" not "snubbed" – at Bessie's party. Did they think that she and John did not read the paper? It was one thing to have a private party and keep it quiet but publishing it in the paper was simply rude to all who were not invited. It wasn't like she and John were Bessie and Herman's best friends, but John and Herman had been partners. That should count, shouldn't it? She was having trouble just ignoring it as Clara suggested.

Maybe they were acting this way because she had pressured him to help with Mama's care. Had he shared her visit to the store with Bessie? How had he characterized it? Badgering? Demanding? Unfair?

Ida could feel and hear her heart beating in her ears. That was strange. She got up and staggered just a bit. A bit dizzy, she thought. Maybe she was coming down with something. A cup of tea would help. She went to the kitchen and put the kettle on the stove.

She had carried the paper with her, so she sat down at the table and continued scanning the ads and tried to put Herman and Bessie out of her mind.

"Oh my!" she said out loud. 'A six-hole cast range with reservoir AND warming closet for $30.50.' She looked at her old faithful range. She knew the stove's every hotspot, and the oven was accurate when stoked properly. But a new stove with nickel trim would really dress up the kitchen. She didn't really need it. Her stove was totally adequate, but still....

Ida sighed. With the older children off to school and Dodi to follow in a year or so, she needed a hobby.

A hobby? Ridiculous! She had Ladies Aid and gardening and sewing, didn't she and...she thought for a minute...and she could do more at the school. She sighed again.

Why did she feel like this? Bored? Hungry? What? Dodi had just gone down for a nap before Ida sat to look at the paper, so she had a couple hours to relax. She made the cup of tea and started a list for John to take to the grocery tomorrow. Her head pounded and her vision blurred. She closed her eyes and rubbed them gently and then opened and focused. The pen scratches were clearer, but something just didn't feel right. She went to the phone and gave the girl Dr. Windmueller's number and made an appointment for the next day for a checkup. Better safe than sorry. Then she took her tea and returned to the parlor and her rocker. She sat and let her head lean back on the chair. She would just close her eyes for a few minutes.

"Mama? Mama?" a worried Dodi swam into Ida's vision.

"Dodi, honey, you're awake." Ida tried to get her bearings. She reached over and sipped her untouched tea. Cold. "My, I was tired, too. I took a nap."

Dodi looked at her mother. The concern had almost left her brow. "I cawed you, and you didn't come. Are we going to have a snack?"

"Certainly!" Ida sat forward worried the dizziness would return, but it did not. "Let's go see what's in the larder, shall we?"

Dodi's face burst into sunshine. "Yes!" she said with much enthusiasm. "Let's!"

***

Cure Your Blur

E. M Marsh, Eyesight Specialist will be at M. Schwabe's jewelry store from Wednesday to Saturday each week and will be pleased to meet any who are in need of glasses. Eyes tested free. All work is guaranteed. If others have failed to fit, you come and see him; he will tell you the truth. Will call at your house if desired.

Woodstock Sentinel, December 8, 1910.

***

Cheer for Poor Children

The Current Events Club, made up of the leading women of the city, has decided to arrange a Christmas tree for the children of homes where Christmas cheer will be appreciated. A fund of over $100 has been made up for the use of these women. The tree will be placed in the assembly room of the Carnegie library building.

Crawford County Courier, December 15, 1910.

***

Emerson Factory Lays Number Off

About thirty-five or forty men were laid off indefinitely at the Emerson Typewriter factory Monday night. It is very unfortunate, to say the least, that conditions should have reached such a stage of development that this course was necessary in midwinter.

While it is hard enough for the single man to be out of work, it is doubly so for the married man with a family. The chances of a Merry Christmas are rather uncertain in the families of the men who are unfortunate enough to be without work at this season of the year when fuel and living expenses are at the present high prices.

Woodstock Sentinel, December 15, 1910.

***

Standard Room Country School

Superintendent A. M. Selton has secured a room in the county courthouse which is to be fitted up as a standard one-room school. This room is an object lesson in seating, heating, and the equipment needed to do so. Country people and school directors may see what constitutes a standard one-room school. This will be done without expense to the public, the manufactures of the seats, stoves, blackboards, etc., supplying the equipment without charge for demonstration.

Woodstock Sentinel, December 22, 1910.

***

News from Ringwood
No Christmas Tree This Year

There was no public Christmas tree this year, the first time in a number of years, but on account of sickness among the children it was deemed best not to have one.

Woodstock Sentinel, December 29, 1910.

***

"What sickness among the children?" John looked up from the paper.

"What?" Ida also looked up from her crocheting with her new glasses perched primly on her nose. Dr Windmueller had checked her over and then sent her to see the optical specialist who had found that a change in eyesight was likely the cause of the dizziness and blurry vision.

"It happens, Mrs. We get older and our eyes get tired. Do you do a lot of handwork?"

Ida agreed that she did.

"Well, you see there. So now you need some help. Let's try a few pairs of these on and see if any of them makes things clearer."

Ida had waded through probably twenty pairs before landing on one that seemed to clear everything up for reading. However, they made the far away vision much worse.

The optician was unperturbed. "Just remove them when you have to look down the street," he said jovially.

So far, they were working fairly well, headaches were fewer and dizziness was almost gone. Things were quite a lot clearer on the right. But she reasoned, she could always just close her left eye when need be.

John smiled at her.

"What?" she said again.

"You look stunning in those spectacles," he said, a big grin on his face.

"Oh honestly, John." She removed the glasses. "I do not. But now I can see the spaces where I'm to put the hook."

"And read the paper," John added.

"Yes. And read the paper without eye strain and dizziness. Doctor's orders! I think they make me look old."

"No such thing!! You look very…very…um… intellectual."

"I have no problem with appearing intellectual, but I'd rather you'd say I looked, oh I don't know, spicy."

"OK, you look intellectually spicy! How's that?"

Ida giggled. 'I like it!"

"Now, back to the issue at hand, unless you had other ideas?" John gave her a lustful grin.

Ida gently slapped his leg. "Not now, Papa."

"OK then. In the paper, there is a short announcement about the public Christmas tree not being put up in Ringwood because of, let's see, 'on account of the sickness among the children.'"

"What sickness?" asked Ida.

"That's what I asked. I hoped you would know."

"I haven't heard anything about sickness out there. Well, no more than is normal. We've been surprisingly well this fall. I should touch wood when I say that." She knocked on the wooden arm of her chair. "Where is Ringwood, again?"

"About 20 miles northeast, above McHenry."

"I hope germs can't travel that far." Ida wasn't sure if germs traveled.

Ida had put the children to bed at the normal time, but she was sure that Helen was reading and trying desperately to stay awake until midnight. She would probably be able to hear and see some of the fireworks from the fairgrounds from her upstairs window as the year turned if she made it to midnight. Ida replaced her glasses and went back to her hooking.

"What are you making?" asked John.

"A vest for Helen. I promised her that as soon as we finished up with Christmas, I'd get started on it. I want to make one for each of them in their favorite color, but I'm starting with Helen."

"And that is Helen's favorite color? Brown."

"Yup. I asked her, and she considered and then said, 'Brown because it will go with most of my blouses.'"

"That doesn't sound like a favorite color, rather a utilitarian color."

"That's our girl. She has a lot of common sense about fashion and is getting a little more interested in baking, too. She made and decorated a lot of the Christmas cookies we gave out this year, with a little help, of course."

"And what is Mamie's favorite color?"

"Ah, Mamie is easy. Her favorite color is red. That one will be fun to crochet. I got some beautiful bright burgundy yarn at the dollar day sale and some hair ribbons that match. Helen's ribbons are orange to add a little color to the brown."

"And Dodi?"

"Dodi likes bue. I mean blue! I got sky blue yarn and darker blue ribbons. I'll probably make some leggings with that same blue for her also, so she can be warm when we play outside."

"Don't the other girls need leggings?" John liked this conversation.

"They have several pairs, so I will treat Dodi with them this time."

"Do you have leggings to play outside?" asked John.

"Yes, of course, I do." Ida glanced up. "Are you jealous? Do you want me to make you some leggings?"

"I'd like to see you in your leggings."

"Oh pshaw!" said Ida, but her cheeks had reddened.

John laughed. And with that they heard the first far away boom of the new year. They both rose and held each other in an embrace and had a good long kiss. John held on to her hand and turned her toward the back of the house and their bedroom.

"Wait." Ida stopped in her tracks.

"I don't want to wait," said John, his voice just a bit husky.

"I must check on Helen. I want to see if she is asleep before we go to bed."

"OK," he said. "I'll go with you to tuck everyone in and then you can tuck me in."

"John!" she punched him in the shoulder with her free hand. "The children—"

"Are sleeping…I hope. Let's go make sure."

And they mounted the stairs, hand-in-hand.

Rekindling the Flame (1911)

Ida put her feet down on the frigid floor. The fire must have gone out, she thought as she wrapped herself in a flannel housecoat and slipped on crocheted slippers. She'd have to steal flame from the range. As she passed through the kitchen, she continued to feel the chill only more so. The range was cold. Oh no! She scurried down the stairs to the basement. Was the air a bit warmer down here? She put out her hand an inch from the furnace. Nothing. She opened the door and saw not a glimmer of coals. Quickly she fanned the white dead coals with a newspaper. The white ash blew away like drifting snow. No red appeared, no smoke, nothing.

Ida stood erect and pulled her robe around her. This was the first time since they moved into the house that the fire had gone out. Had John stoked the fire before bed? She couldn't remember. Well, nothing for it. She climbed the stairs to wake John. They must decide what to do before the girls awoke. The second floor where the children slept didn't get much heat overnight, so the temperature was always cold in the morning until the furnace could be stoked, but now she could only imagine the cold up there. What to do?

She entered the bedroom and climbed back under the covers and woke John with her icy hands and feet. "John, the fire's gone out."

"Wha…What?" He was suddenly wide awake. He looked at his pocket watch which lay on the side table. Seven o'clock. "I didn't stoke the furnace before we hit the hay, did I?"

"I don't think so."

"Rats. I thought the fire would last through the night," he mumbled. But they had slept past their normal rising time of half past five because they had been up late last night and no work on New Year's Day. He turned back to Ida and pulled up the covers. "Must be cold outside. Maybe we could just stay here all day."

Ida smiled, but firmly dashed that hope, "The children will be awake soon if they aren't already. We must have a fire, or we'll freeze pipes, if we haven't already." New concern in her voice. "It's below zero this morning."

Ida jumped out of bed, stripped out of her robe and nightgown, and pulled on clothes and two pairs of socks. Her long skirt didn't give much warmth. She added a heavy crocheted shawl and shoes and then turned back to the bed. "Well?"

John groaned.

"Will you try tinder, or will you go borrow some flame?"

John groaned again.

"John?"

John threw back the covers, grabbed his long johns, and quickly ran to the bathroom in the nude.

Ida smiled and shook her head. That was no answer, but at least he was up. She bustled into the kitchen and listened at the stairs. No voices floated down to her. She was at a loss as to what to do. They should try tinder in the cook stove and maybe if that worked, they could transfer the little fire to the furnace. Starting a new fire was no easy task. They would need a lot of tinder, and of course, that was in the stable. She looked out the back door toward the stable on the other side of windblown drifts. I bet it's cold in there for old Jake, she thought. They should start stabling him with Frank's horses in the winter. 'More horses, more heat' was the sage advice. She would speak to John about it, but not this morning.

She found the tinderbox and removed a match and grit paper, but there was nothing to light. John would have to go to the stable.

John, now in his long johns, rushed through the kitchen toward the bedroom. A few minutes later, he came back into the kitchen pulling on a plaid wool shirt over flannel lined wool pants, heavy wool socks and work boots. He added his sheep-skin winter short coat, hat with ear flaps, and mittens. "Do you want me to ask the neighbors? They could give us coals."

"Let's start with tinder from the stable, and we'll get the cook stove going first. And bring any old newspapers if there are some."

"I may have to chop kindling. Why don't you go wait under the covers? If the girls wake up, they can get in with you."

"Mama?" A voice called down the stairs. Dodi.

"OK." Ida handed him the tinder box and headed for the stairs. She wrapped Dodi in a blanket and went to check on the other girls. Helen had not gone to sleep until after midnight and was still sleeping, but Mamie was huddled in a ball with the covers over her head. Putting a shawl around Mamie, she took the two girls downstairs and into the bedroom. Dodi was delighted with this turn of events. She climbed right up and under the thick down comforter. Ida lifted Mamie up and then crawled in herself. Dear God, she could see her breath; it must be near freezing in the house. Ida pulled the covers up over their heads making a little, dark cave.

John left by the back door trudging through the knee-deep snow to the stable. He pushed open the door and Jake nickered.

"Hello old boy. Feels pretty cozy in here. "Cozy" isn't the word Ida would have used if she had been there, but it was above freezing by ten degrees or more.

John took a leaf of hay and some oats and gave them to Jake. "Need to keep the fire in your belly burning, old boy."

He pulled down a blanket and threw it over Jake's back and buckled the cinch and front buckle.

Jake smelled the hay and snorted his thanks.

John went to the inside wood pile and selected a few of the smaller pieces. He took the axe in his hand and choked up on the handle so it operated more like a hatchet. He sliced down through the wood, peeling off thin strips to make kindling. After about 10 minutes he had filled the kindling box. Now, do I go next door or try to start this myself?

Opting for the easy route he went out and pushed through the snow to the Carlyle's who had built between his house and Al's a few years before.

Mounting the steps to the back door, John knocked.

"Just a minute," came the call from within.

Mrs. Carlyle swung open the door. Her hair was tied in clumps with strips of cloth to make it curly and her head was wrapped with a kerchief to protect the ties while sleeping. She had a housecoat, untied but pulled tightly across her chest. "Mr. Wienke! Oh no, what has happened?"

"Good morning, Mrs. Carlyle. Our fire has gone out and I was wondering if you would have a few coals to spare."

"Oh dear. Please come in." She held the door open wider. "Please forgive my appearance. We have just woken up and I—"

"Do not trouble yourself about it. I believe that my wife is hiding under the covers with the children hoping I can get the fire going again."

Mrs. Carlyle went to the cook stove and opened the door. "I believe I can give you these. We'll get more from the basement to replace them."

"Thank you so much, Mrs. Carlyle."

"Well, we can't have our neighbors freezing." She straightened up again looking worried. "Have you set your faucets to dripping?"

"My faucets?"

"Yes. Harold always has me set the faucets to drip if it is going to be very cold. I believe it somehow keeps them from freezing up."

"Hm. No, I haven't heard about that trick."

"Well, I hope they haven't frozen because you will begin to heat up the house and then the pipes will thaw and begin spraying under the sinks and in the walls and in the basement. I know. It happened to us once when we were gone and didn't think of asking someone to get the fires going. In the other house. It was such a mess. The wall plaster melted and ran. Whole sections had to be replaced, and I don't think the walls were ever the same. All the pipes had to be replaced which meant demolishing other walls." While she was speaking, Mrs. Carlyle had grabbed coals with thongs made for that purpose and put them in with the kindling in the pan. "That's when I told him we had to move." She turned and held out the pan.

John's face had worry lines etched in his forehead. He accepted it with gloved hands. "I better get home and set those faucets running."

"Hope it's not too late."

"Me too."

In the bedroom, Ida and the girls spent the time telling their dreams of the night before. Ida couldn't remember her dreams. They faded quickly in the cold. But the girls had no trouble describing in detail and embellishing their nighttime sojourns.

After a while, John came in, removed his shoes and crawled into the other side of the bed. "It should start to warm up now. I got it going in the stove and the furnace with some coals from Carlyle's. I also checked the faucets and toilets, even upstairs. All of them ran, but I left them dripping, a cold-weather advice Mrs. Carlyle gave me along with the coals. What are my girls doing?"

"My hero." Ida pecked him on the cheek.

"We're telling our dreams." Mamie volunteered.

"And what were your dreams, Mamie?" John inquired.

"I dreamed I lived on a farm with lots of fruit trees and berry bushes and a huge garden instead of a lawn. And I could just walk around and pull an apple or an orange off a tree to eat whenever I wanted to."

"Where was this farm?" John expected her to say Greenwood or Chemung.

"Beloit. And we had a red barn and a goat pen."

"A goat pen?" Ida wondered where Mamie had heard about goats.

"Yes, but no goats. Yet." The final word.

"Let me tell mine!" interjected Dodi.

"OK, what were your dreams, Dodi?" John pulled the coverlet up tighter around his youngest daughter.

"I deamed that I was a Deutscher princess and lived in a castle in England."

"In England?" Ida again was curious about the source of the setting. Maybe fairy tales?

"Yes! And I had butiful bue gowns and pates."

"Plates?" asked John.

"Yes, to eat chocolate, cocoa and corn ears on. And birds flew all around."

"Why birds, do you think?" Mamie wondered.

"I like birds. Bue birds." Dodi said as a matter-of-fact. "Lots of bue birds."

"Papa, did you dream?" Mamie looked at him with concern.

"Hm, I don't think so. I was dead to the world." John glanced over at Ida.

"Noooo," Dodi practically screamed. "Not dead!"

Ida quickly broke in. "Oh no, honey, Papa doesn't mean he was really dead, but just very, very sound asleep all night. Satisfied with his bed, bedmate, covers, everything. He means he slept soundly."

Mamie shook her head. "We don't like 'dead to the world.'"

I Will Fly to Woodstock

"OK, I'll not use that anymore. I'll just say, I slept well!" John looked over at Ida with a slight smile and winked. Ida smiled but could not hold his gaze. She blushed, and John's smile grew larger.

***

Chicken Chat

Some thoughtful hen man has hit on the idea of putting a light of glass in chicken coops to make them more cheerful when the chicks have to be shut up on rainy days.

It is little short of cruel to give poultry that is confined no outdoor shelter from the heat of the summer sun. If there are no trees in the yard this shade may be had by sowing sunflowers, giving the young plants protection during the period when the poultry would be likely to destroy them.

Woodstock Sentinel, January 8, 1911

***

Fire at Detroit (sic)

Denison. – The town of Deloit, six miles north of here on the Illinois Central, was visited by fire Sunday morning. The loud screaming of the whistle of the engine on a passing train aroused the sleeping town at 6. Town people and farmers rushed to near the depot to find the city hotel, butcher shop and barber shop in flames. Loss to John Dobson, hotel, $1,200 with $800 insurance; N. H. Brogden meat market $600, with no insurance; M. Meyers barber shop $200 with no insurance. It is believed that fire started in the meat market from a cigar stub thrown in a box of dust.

Crawford County Courier, January 11, 1911.

***

Antis to Speak
Representatives of the Anti-Saloon league of Illinois will speak next Sunday morning in several of the Protestant churches of this city. They are men of recognized ability and cannot fail to interest you.
Woodstock Sentinel, January 19, 1911.

500 Entries to Poultry Show
Five hundred entries marked the opening of the first annual poultry exhibition of the newly organized association. [T]he birds of all kinds and colors came in from all parts of the county to compete for the prizes offered.

On Saturday, Jan. 21, 1911, all the school children of McHenry County under fifteen years of age will be admitted free to the first annual exhibit of the McHenry County Poultry Association.
Woodstock Sentinel, January 19, 1911.

***

"Thank you so much, Mrs. Wienke, for coming with us today. Are you a connoisseur of poultry?"

"Well, no, not really, Miss Ives. I just thought coming would be a nice outing with the girls, and when Helen told me the class was going, I thought I might be of service."

"Of course, we needed a few mothers to come with us to answer questions and herd the children."

Ida gave the comely teacher a big smile. "My pleasure. I'm rather good at herding. We haven't had chickens for years, so I've never thought much about them. They come and go and seem very self-sustaining. I do know a bit about their feeding and candling eggs and such, but I'm afraid I will probably be just as amazed as the children."

Their conversation had brought them to the entry of the Poultry Barn.

"Wait, children," Miss Ives called out. "Pick a partner to stick with while we are inside. No one is to leave the barn without permission. If you have questions or a problem, talk to one of the adults. Okay?"

"Yes, Teacher," the children responded almost in unison.

Dodi pulled at Ida's sleeve, "I pick you, Mama."

Ida smiled at her chubby youngest daughter, "And I pick you, Dodi."

Dodi smiled back and took her hand. "Will dar be bue birds?"

"I don't know. We'll have to wait and see."

"Otay. Let's go see 'em!" Dodi lost Ida's hand and ran ahead. Ida hurried after her. So much excitement to see chickens. How fancy can they be? Ida hoped against hope that there were blue ones.

***

"Papa, dar weren't any bue birds, but dar were red an' orange an' white an' bwak an' yewo 'an...." Dodi trailed off looking to Mama for help.

"Which was your favorite, Dodi?" asked John.

"I liked da one dat looks like spun candy."

"Spun candy? Like at the fair?"

"Yes! White 'n fluffy wid big feets." Dodi squatted down, tucked her hands in her armpits, and did a surprisingly good imitation of a chicken walking, clucking, and fluffing her feathers.

Mama and Papa laughed, and so did Mamie and Helen.

"Dodi, that's really good!" Helen had a rare burst of enthusiasm. "Do it again."

And so, she did.

***

Judge Ramsey's Recent Ruling

In hearing a case in which charges of assault and battery were brought against a city superintendent by two boys in eighth grade, the following sound views were expressed by Circuit Judge Frank D. Ramsey.

"It must be admitted that a schoolteacher or superintendent of schools, having other teachers under his direction, stands in the relation of parent, under law, and he has a right to administer reasonable punishment on a pupil who breaks the rules of school and refuses to recognize the authority of the teacher. In my judgment that is the first thing a pupil has to know; that is, that the teacher has authority, and the second thing for him to know is that he has got to recognize the order of a father in the household.

"There is no question in my mind that a teacher not only has control over a student during school hours, but he has parental control over that child on the school grounds and in a measure going to and from school. I do not think a schoolboy has a right to insult a schoolteacher on the grounds and be liable to punishment and continue to insult from across the street, just across the line from the grounds and be free from punishment. It would be a mockery in my judgment, to say that a squad of boys could stand on the school grounds and insult a schoolteacher within the walls of the school building and the moment they see the teacher approaching them, seek to avoid liability by skipping away, one five feet, another ten, another twelve just out of reach of the teacher's arm. If a teacher's authority can be disputed by a lot of boys

standing on the school grounds and on the streets in a manner, we might as well turn the key in the schoolhouse doors. It is not the law; it is not right, and that is why it is not the law."
Woodstock Sentinel. January 12, 1911.

***

Poor House Plans

Denison – The board of supervisors of Crawford County has adopted the plans and specifications of Barber & Gleen for constructing a home for the worthy poor. A quarter section of land not needed will be sold March 1 and a contract let for the building of the new home. The total cost must not exceed $25,000.
Crawford County Courier, January 25, 1910.

***

Personal Items

The Woman's Home Missionary society of the Methodist church held another of their pleasant meetings at the home of Mrs. A. D. Osborn, on Jackson Street, last Wednesday afternoon. The meeting was in the nature of a dime social, and a most interesting program was enjoyed by the forty ladies present. Mrs. G. A. Hunt gave a map talk on Cuba that was very instructive. The rest of the program was as follows:

    Vocal solo – Mrs. Harry Kendall.
    Piano solo – Mrs. Emil Wienke.
    Vocal solo – Miss Leita Brooks.
    Reading – Miss Esther Young.
    Recitation – Gladys Coonrad.
Woodstock Sentinel, January 26, 1911.

***

Sickness and Death at Denison

Much sickness is prevailing here, and many cases are terminating fatally. Mrs. McClellan, wife of the city watchman, died Wednesday after a long illness. Transfusion of blood was tried in her case, but to no avail. She leaves thirteen children, one less than 1 year old. Her husband being prominent in Redmen circles, this order took a special part in providing nurses and attending the funeral exercises.

Saturday came the death of Mrs. C. Green, one of the oldest settlers of Denison. She was the wife of the pioneer brick maker of the county who survives her. The funeral was held Sunday afternoon in the M.E. church, of which she had been a member for fifty years.

Crawford County Courier, January 30, 1911.

***

Carbolic Acid

One of the most frequent irritant poisons used for suicidal purposes is carbolic acid, and a more agonizing death could not be selected. Why anyone should select this poison is hard to understand unless on account of the fact that it is cheap and easily obtainable. This form of poisoning can usually be easily recognized by the odor, which is well known and by the white burns or marks on the lips and mouth, which are typical of carbolic acid poisoning.

Send for the nearest physician, and in the meantime, as carbolic acid kills quickly, the first aid treatment must be prompt in order to get results. If possible, cause the patient to vomit by giving an emetic, such as Ipecac or salt and water, a tablespoonful to a pint of warm water. This, however, frequently fails to work on account of the irritated condition of the mucous membrane of the stomach. One of the best chemical antidotes is Epsom salt in solution. Another good chemical antidote is alcohol, the only trouble with this remedy being that it cannot be given in pure form. It has to be diluted with water and for that reason loses its efficacy.

Just exactly why alcohol counteracts the effect of carbolic acid is not known, but if, for instance, carbolic acid is splashed on the hands, and they are at once immersed in absolute alcohol there will be no resulting burn. – Dr. H. H. Hartung in National Magazine.

Woodstock Sentinel, February 9, 1911.

Don't Worry

Whatever you do, don't worry.
If you fret, the wrinkles will grow.
A bright, cheerful smile will trouble beguile
And dispel even mountains of woe.
There's nothing so catching as laughter.
It drives death oft back to its lair.
It acts on the nerves. It good health preserves
And annihilates loads of despair.
Then let it come out when you feel it.
Don't check it but give it full play.
It would drive away grief if there's any around
And illumine like sunshine your day.
'Tis like silvery moonlight at evening.
It lights up life's dark, stormy way
Does good honest laughter.
'Tis that we are after.
Then let us give it full play.

Frank Marion
Woodstock Sentinel, February 9, 1911.

Valentine's Day Next Tuesday.

Next Tuesday, Feb. 14, will be Valentine's Day and the local stores have been making a feature of this particular line of attractive merchandise for some days past. The pretty valentines of 1911 are about on the same order as they have always been and as they probably always will be.

The last few years people have not been so enthusiastic over the fussy creations of celluloid and ribbon which are of no earthly use even as an ornament. The dainty book done up in an attractive manner, a beautiful picture or some pretty gift which can be worn are often substituted, of late, for the pretty valentine. Books by our American artists are proving very popular for this purpose and flowers are also a favorite substitute for this old-time valentine.

The merchants recognize the fact that this change has come and accordingly are catering to the improved sentiment by presenting a fine line of books and pictures for the season's trade.

The old-time comic valentine is no longer a popular feature at this season of the year. Two postcards have been assigned the cause for the downfall of this ancient favorite. Comic valentines were formerly used as a means to get even with the enemy but today conditions are different.

It isn't necessary to wait until Valentine's Day to send our enemies a thoughtful remembrance. We can find the very thing, any day, wherever postcards are on sale. When we want to get even with somebody, we don't like to wait until Valentine's Day arrives anyway, so the reason for the decrease in the demand for the once popular comic valentine is easily understood.

Woodstock Sentinel, February 9, 1911.

***

Legal
State of Illinois
County of McHenry
Office of County Clerk
This is to certify that the ballots for the primary of February 25th, 1911, for the respective parties shall be printed on paper of the following colors:
Republican – White.
Democratic – Green.
Prohibition – Blue.
In witness whereof I subscribe my name, and affix the seal of the county court this, the 7th day of February, A. D. 1911.
G. E. Still., County Clerk.
Woodstock Sentinel, February 9, 1911.

***

Ida and Dodi were elbow deep in dough. They had already put three loaves of bread in the oven and the smell of baking bread filled the house with the warmth of home. Now they were making rolls, which were Dodi's favorite. She carefully shaped small round balls of dough and laid them out on a sheet pan where they would rise for a bit and then join the bread. Today was Monday, baking day. They would make enough bread to last a week and maybe some cookies, too, another of Dodi's favorites. As she made balls, Dodi sang a little song to herself.

"Go to sweep my lil, pickleninny.
Rainy fox git cha if ya don't.
Sumber on da bosom of old mama ginny.
Mama's lil abama—"

"Dodi, you are such a good helper." Ida patted the little girl on the back.

"I'm a big girl now."

Her small chubby hands picked up the dough expertly and rolled the handful softly into a ball which she lined up with the others on the pan.

"What shall we do with our day today?" asked Ida.

"Pway dollies." Dodi continued to roll balls as they talked.

"Paper dollies or real dollies?"

"Paper dollies."

"Or we could go for a walk up to the Square and see Papa."

Dodi looked up with shining eyes. "Let's go see Papa!"

"OK, let's finish up here and get these baked. The bread is about to come out. Then we'll get cleaned up and go see—"

A loud door knock resounded in the hall. The front door. Ida and Dodi looked at each other.

"Who on earth could that be this time of morning?"

"Dis time of mornin'?" Dodi parroted.

Ida dusted off her hands and wiped them on her apron. Dodi dusted off her hands and slid from the chair leaving white handprints on its back.

"I get it!" Dodi called out as she ran around to the foyer.

When Ida got to the door, Dodi was working at pushing down the lever on the handle and pulling, but the latch didn't give. Ida reached over, pushed the lever with more force, and helped Dodi swing it open. A young man in a blue uniform stood there, hat in hand. Ida focused on his hat. The cap wasn't that of the police or military, but rather of the train personnel.

"Yes?" Ida worked at a smile.

"Mrs. Ida Wiki?"

"Yes?"

"Telegram, ma'am! Sign here," was his crisp response.

Ida did as he asked, and he handed her an envelope. "G'day!" he declared cheerfully. "I hope it's good news."

Me too, she thought. But is a telegram ever good news? Oh no, Mama! She ripped open the envelope and looked to see what the sending address was...Denison?

WU N004 DL PD
WUX DENISON IOWA FEB 13 325P=

MRS IDA WIENKE WOODSTOCK ILL
PEARLE ELECTRIFIED FELL FROM POLE [STOP]
BACK BROKEN MIGHT DIE [STOP]
COME QUICKLY NEED YOU [STOP]
                                           CLARA
I=810A..

***

Another Electricity Victim

Lineman Supervisor P. F. Dye had a fall from a city pole that came near putting him out of business entirely. With Lineman Buchart, he was working at the top of the ladder just beneath the wires on a pole at least 20-feet long. As the pole was slightly unsteady due to the recent wet snow fall pulling down on the wires, the second man was at the bottom holding the ladder. As Dye worked on the broken connection, his arm brushed a live wire, and a jolt of current went through him, freezing him to the wire in his hand and shocking the Mr. Butchart on the ground so he was thrown some feet away, unconscious.

Another man, Mr. David Lionel passing by, saw the dilemma that Mr. Dye was experiencing and with a long wooden pole knocked the ladder down which pulled Mr. Dye away from the live wire, but plummeted him to the cobblestones. He was unconscious when carried to the hospital with multiple injuries. His friends wish him a speedy recovery.

Crawford County Courier, February 14, 1911.

***

Carried Too Far

On Saturday, the Northwestern train brought here an Italian emigrant woman who came direct from New York. Her baggage was marked Denison, O., but she was ticketed to Denison, Iowa. As there are no Italians at present here there was much trouble in getting from her any information. The authorities at Ellis Island were telegraphed to, as well as the chief of police at Denison, O. Citizens took much interest in the case and stood ready to help her financially. Her friends were located at Denison, O., and she was sent there yesterday.

Crawford County Courier, February 22, 1911.

***

Two weeks later, in Clara's parlor, Ida laughed right out loud at the news article. Both Clara and Dodi looked up from their paper dolls.

"What, Mama?" asked Dodi.

Ida was still chuckling. "Says here in the paper that an Italian lady came to Iowa instead of going to Ohio, and that folks here had to track down who she was and send her back to Ohio because she didn't speak English. I'm surely glad that didn't happen to us on the way out."

"Let me see. They sent her back because she didn't speak English?" Clara sounded confused.

"No, they had to go all the way to Ellis Island to track her down because she didn't speak English. I was only glad—"

Clara slapped the paper down on the table. "I didn't hear a thing about this."

"Well, my dear, you have been plenty busy with your job of getting Pearle well again. I don't think people are going to call you with news scoops, knowing the situation." Ida picked up the paper again to continue reading.

"But they must!" Clara stood now with a face red with anger. "This is our livelihood for the foreseeable future. They must call me, or we won't make it...they just must." She slumped back into her chair and covered her face with her hands.

"Here, An Clawa. You have Lettie to play with." Dodi had collected a full set of Lettie Lane paper dolls, cut carefully from Ladies' Home Journal by Mamie. Lettie was the most desired of the dolls, but her whole family and even servants were part of Dodi's collection. She had even memorized some of the stories published in the magazine, so she could tell them while acting out the parts with the various two-dimensional dolls.

"So, you've decided to stay here?" Ida could hardly believe they would stay.

Clara took the Lettie doll from Dodi and undressed her. "Pearley wants to."

Pearle had spent the time since the accident in 'traction' – basically tied to the headboard with a chin strap and to the footboard with tethers to each foot – which did not allow him to move when awake or asleep. In addition to the lower back injury which threatened paralysis, he had broken his right arm and left leg and ankle, but luckily, he had no internal injuries. And he had, thank God, not landed on his head. So far, feeling had returned to his feet and calves and the doctor was very positive in his prognosis.

"How long did the doctor say he would be in those casts?"

"Months." Clara looked despondent as her hands began to dress the paper doll.

"And tied to the bed?"

"He doesn't know. What am I going to do?"

"No! An Clawa, not wedding. Lettie already did wedding. Now Lettie is a mama."

Clara sat for a moment staring at the paper doll and then she put it down and rushed from the room, her face crumbling as she went. "I must check on Pearle," she said into her hands.

"An Clawa, come back," Dodi called after her. "I show you what a mama wears."

"That's okay, Dodi. Aunt Clara will be back in a little while. Why don't you show me what a mama wears."

"Okay." But they both looked worriedly after Clara, before beginning the lesson.

***

Denison, Iowa
March 1, 1911

Dear John,

How are you and the girls managing? Is your mother driving you nuts yet? Do you miss me?

Looks like another week, and we'll be on our way back to you. Clara and Pearle have decided to ride out the storm here. The alternative would have been to go back to Akron, but for some reason Pearle is hesitant to do that. He is fairly confident that he can find work here even if the county won't have him back. He has a reputation as a fine electrician. And Clara feels that her journalism and their savings can carry them through to the time when he is employed again.

He is really a genuinely nice man. He's polite and thankful for the help. Having these many days to get to know him better – as I didn't know him at all – has reinforced my opinion that Clara did the right thing by marrying him. And Dodi likes him so that's a good endorsement. Clara desperately wants children and spends every moment she can with Dodi.

Dodi is still talking about the train ride out here and the many animals we saw from our seats. Flocks of cranes and herds of elk and I swear at one point the train came to a standstill and I worried that we were being robbed, but it was a Bison, a Bison standing on the tracks. The man sitting next to us was also amazed. He said that they rarely saw buffalo anymore. They've all moved west. Dodi is so looking forward to the train ride home. She does miss her Papa, but I'm quite sure we have planted the wanderlust in her. She also talks a lot about Mamie - and Helen, too, - and what she and Mamie will do when she gets home. Tell them that and that I miss them, please. I think you'll find that she has grown up a lot in only the few weeks away.

  I do miss you and especially I miss having someone to sleep with who doesn't kick me all night. I didn't know what a restless sleeper our littlest one is. She has also started to tell me her dream every morning. She is getting to be a good storyteller.

  I must close now and check on Pearle. Clara is out "chasing" a story. Pearle is almost able to do everything for himself except get out of bed, but he grows stronger every day.

I love you and will see you soon,
Ida

***

Personal Items

  Mr. and Mrs. Albert Wienke of Beloit, Wis., were Woodstock visitors Tuesday and Wednesday.

  The Dorcas Society held their usual pleasant meeting at the home of Mrs. Emil Wienke on Tuesday afternoon, Mrs. Kendall was the assistant hostess. After the program, guessing contests were enjoyed and refreshments served.

Woodstock Sentinel, March 2, 1911.

***

Republic Township Caucus

  The Republican voters of the town of Dorr are requested to meet at the courtroom in the court house, in the city of Woodstock, Ill., on Saturday, March 18, 1911, at 2 o'clock p. m. sharp, for the purpose of placing in nomination candidates for the office of supervisor, one commissioner of highways, (Second district), one trustee of schools, to be voted for at the coming township election, also the selection of a town committee and the transaction of such other business as may be properly brought before the caucus.

ROBERT McLEAN,
JOHN WIENKE,
A.J. MULLEN.

Woodstock Sentinel, March 9, 1911.

***

***

Lone Man Robs Train

Denison – A masked man, who climbed aboard the rear end of train No. 8 on the Northwestern eastbound last night, forced the flagman at the point of a revolver to go ahead into the sleeper. The stranger held up A. C. Hanson, of Olympia, Wash., for $14 and a diamond ring, valued at $40, and relieved J. W. Hendell, of Wichita, Kan., of $35 and a gold watch. He then jumped from the train and escaped, four or five miles east of Denison.

The man is described as being about five feet eight inches in height and weighing about 160 pounds. He was thought to be about 40 years old.

Crawford County Courier, March 25, 1911.

***

"Ida!" John came into the kitchen. "I've made a decision!"

Ida's breath caught. She looked over at him, and he gazed back at her.

"Yes, John?"

"I'm running for county clerk!" He slapped the newspaper down on his thigh for emphasis.

Ida had just finished up the dishes from supper and the girls were off to their beds or at least bedrooms upstairs. All was quiet in the house. She and Dodi had returned to Woodstock by train from Dennison ten days before. Pearle was able to get up and around now with crutches so they bid the couple ado and returned just in time for the Spring elections.

"But what about Prudential? Will you quit?" Ida's concerned look made John wince slightly.

"Quit Prudential? Oh no. County Clerk isn't a full-time job. But clerk is a better paid job than the town committee. I would have to quit the committee position if I run, but certainly not a great loss."

"Couldn't you keep the committee job just in case you lose the election?" Ida was being pragmatic. Since he had quit the grocery, politics had been taking a larger part of his time.

"No, the nominees for both positions will be selected at the caucus, and I can't run for both. What if I won both? Then we'd have to have a special election for the one and that would cost extra money, so they don't let a person run for two positions."

"What if I ran for the committee?" Ida looked at him. "Just in case."

John laughed. "Really? Don't you have your hands full enough? You are just upset that the state legislature didn't vote on suffrage during the last session."

"Don't laugh. Yes, I'm upset by their lack of courage. They won't even let the legislature vote on suffrage for women. Too afraid the cause will win. If the men can't or won't allow women to vote, we may just have to take the matter into our own hands. I am a citizen of this state and this country, and all citizens have the right to vote. Has a woman ever served in any city, town or county office?"

John's face reddened. "Not that I can remember – maybe a woman clerk way back, but not in recent history."

"And why not?" Ida now was fully engaged in the idea.

John was nonplussed. "Well, I…um…I'm not really sure…um…maybe because women are…um…too busy …with homes and church and all. You know."

"No John, I don't know. I want to put my name in."

John looked at her and was quiet for a moment.

"What?" Ida did not flinch at his gaze.

John considered his next move carefully. If he said, no, she'd run for sure. If he said, yes, she'd run for sure.

"How about we think more about your possible candidacy. Just so you know, it takes me probably an hour a day to keep up with all the politics from city to state, reading the papers, kibitzing with the other office holders at places not welcoming to women, especially women alone."

"So, you shall come with me for the first time." She was insistent.

"And then the city and county council meetings constitute another three or four or more hours a month. Then spring and fall, I meet with the others on the committee to prepare for the caucus and then run them. About six extra hours over that two-week period. Think about if you can spare that much time."

"I believe so. I've been thinking that I need a hobby." Ida's eyes slid away. Maybe not as sure as she was a few minutes ago.

"Just think about your decision for a few days, please. And then we'll talk again. Who will be with the children while you are at these meetings? Don't answer now. How will you manage supper and attendance? What if we both have to be at a meeting? How will the city and town look at two people from the same household holding office? Just pause for a day or two and consider. Okay?"

Ida dropped her eyes. "Okay." She looked back up with fierce determination in her eyes. "But I am serious about this."

"I know." John took her hand and said a little silent prayer that she would change her mind in the next few days. What an embarrassment it would be if she ran. Other men's wives don't do such things. John was trying to be supportive, but not pushing her one way or the other. She would come to her senses.

Ida squeezed his hand. "And John?"

"Yes?"

"Run for County Clerk. They really, really need a man like you."

***

"Ida, I have a joke to tell you." John had just come in and hung his coat and hat and made his way to the parlor. Cigar smoke wafted around him as it always did when he had been at one of the political meetings. He leaned and kissed her cheek and then sat down in his chair.

"A joke?" Ida looked up from her handwork. "Okay, if you must."

"Frank Wienke was walking downtown and saw a hearse starting away from a house and a long funeral procession following behind it."

"Frank really saw this?"

"No, I just used his name to make the story seem more...um...accurate."

"But it's less accurate if it didn't really happen to Frank, isn't it?"

"OK. Not our Frank, but Francis Welky – we'll call him Frank - was walking downtown…"

"Who is Francis Welky? I don't think I know him," said Ida.

"It doesn't matter who he is. He's nobody. Okay, just listen. An inquisitive man saw a hearse starting away from a house with a long funeral procession following behind it.

"'Who's dead?' he asked the corner grocer—"

"Ah, a grocery joke!"

"No, not really. Just listen. Don't try to figure it out. 'Who's dead?' he asked another man who was also standing and watching. 'Jon Schmidt!' answered the other man.

"'John Smith!' said the man. 'You don't mean to say John Smith is dead?'"

"Do we know John Smith?"

John looked at her. "No. It's just a name so I don't have to say a third man different from the first two."

"Okay, go on." Ida went back to her crocheting.

"'You don't mean to say John Smith is dead?' asked Frank. 'Vell py golly,' replied the grocer—"

"Ah the grocer is back," Ida was still looking down at her hands with a slight smile playing on her lips.

"Yes, the grocer is the second guy."

"Okay, go on."

A long silence. Ida looked up to see John staring at her. She smiled.

"I'm sorry." A laugh threatened to break from Ida's throat. "I read the joke in the paper already. 'Vell py golly, vat you dink dey doink mit him – practicing?'"

John shook his head and sighed deeply. "You are such a little tease. I'm going to bed. Coming?"

"In a bit. Just about done with this vest. Dodi's. Last one." She held the garment up for him to admire.

"Nice. Oh, by the way, I've been nominated for City Clerk."

"Is this another joke?"

"Nope! On Donovan's ticket."

Ida stood and embraced John, giving him a kiss on both cheeks. "Well, congratulations!" She held him at arm's length. "Are you going to win?"

"Maybe. If I don't, I'm done with it."

"What?" Ida couldn't believe her ears.

"I'm done with it all - not worth the money and time."

"OK, we'll see what happens, but don't throw the baby out with the bath water. This might be a chance for them to see you as more than just a committeeman."

"Maybe." He seemed a little down in the dumps. Maybe she shouldn't have teased him about the joke.

"Let's hit the hay." Ida wrapping up her yarn. "Go stoke the fire, and I'll meet you there."

John smiled. "Deal."

***

WARM CONTEST NOW ON 'TWIXT CITY CANDIDATES

Two sets of candidates are in the field for election as mayor, alderman and city clerk of Woodstock, to be decided at the city election on Tuesday, April 18.

One of these sets of candidates is led by former Sheriff George Eckert, who together with the candidates for city clerk, attorney and treasurer, was named at a mass meeting and nominating caucus at the Opera House last Friday evening, which was participated in by four or five hundred voters of the city.

Candidates for alderman were placed in the field Saturday and a full list of candidates is now in the field under the title, 'Citizens' Ticket, as follows:

Mayor – George Eckert.
City Clerk – Henry G. Fisher.
City Attorney – E. H. Waite
Treasurer – Chas. L. Quinlan.
Alderman:
    First Ward – S. A. Greenleaf.
    Second Ward – Frank J. Green.
    Third Ward – James Hecht.
    Fourth Ward – G. W. Frame.

On Saturday evening another meeting was held at city hall to name city candidates. This meeting, called a caucus, was held in the council rooms and was participated in by the political friends of Senator Olson.

George W. Lemmers presided as chairman and a full slate of candidates was named. Editor C. A. Lemmers, in an earnest and ardent appeal to the voters, nominated Mayor J. D. Donovan for re-election, which nomination received the unanimous endorsement of the voters present.

John F. Wienke was named for the city clerk, V. S. Lumley for city attorney and C. L. Quinlan for treasurer.

On the previous evening candidates for alderman in several wards had been named as follows: First ward, A. J. Olson; Second Ward, F. G. Schuett; Third ward, V. E. Jones; Fourth ward, J. S. Andrews.

It was later announced that Attorney Lumley has withdrawn his name as a candidate for city attorney.

Woodstock Sentinel, April 6, 1911.

***

ALL THINGS DENISON
by Clara Daring
Menagh's Enters Lemon Trade

George Menagh Company, Denison's downright delectable department store, has decided to enter the wholesale lemon trade. The senior member of the firm has been in California for six weeks where he has bought lemons off the trees and superintended the picking and packing. Ten carloads will be shipped to Denison and put in cold storage.

This being April and still in the cool of the Spring, one can appreciate the taste of a lemon or a glass of lemonade. But when the heat of the summer lies heavy holding us all to the toil of the long sunlit days, a glass of fresh lemonade will be an elixir not just to refresh, but to revive us from the sure death of the purgatory of summer.

Therefore, we are indebted to the Menagh brothers, for saving us from a fate worse than death - a hot-weather thirst that has often led us to insanity or worse.

Crawford County Courier, April 7, 1911.

***

Denison, Iowa
April 15, 1911

Dear Ida, John, Dodi, Mamie and Helen,
How are you all? We have had our first flash of heat, but now it is cool again and threatening snow if I read the clouds right. Such a world we live in.
We are making do. I've been making a good amount working for the paper and the county has been paying one half

of Pearle's pay until he recovers and returns to work. Isn't that generous? We had to sign papers saying that we wouldn't sue, but this seems like the better deal than a suit anyway. Plus, what is there to sue over? He brushed a wire he shouldn't have and got zapped. It's not something that can be easily prevented from the county's obligations.

I do appreciate the money sent with the last letter so much, but I must warn you that mail is oftentimes stolen when it looks like there is money in the envelope with the letter, so be careful.

Pearle is healing. It's been just over two months and they are letting him get up and walk to a chair now with crutches. He was so glad to move again. He still has the cast on his left leg and so doesn't get too far. His mood seems quite subdued or maybe resigned. He doesn't talk about going back to work at all. I've been trying to get him to talk about what he wants to do next, but he avoids answering questions about Akron. The doctor says that once the casts are off, he is going to have to learn to walk again and build up strength before he can work. So, there you are. I'm not sure if I should be encouraging him to return or not. What do you think?

Other than that, we are glad that Spring has come and would even tolerate a little late-season snow. What choice do we have? Ha! Hope all is good in Woodstock and that the new county clerk has assumed his position by now.

Love to all, Clara

***

DONOVAN WINS BY MAJORITY OF 19 OVER ECKERT

Mayor J. D. Donovan has secured re-election to the office he now holds by the narrow margin of nineteen votes over George Eckert, who was the candidate opposed to him and supported by the voters of this city who believe that the condition of the city's finances today and other conditions in Woodstock argue for a change in the management of affairs.

The total vote cast was over thirteen hundred, the largest vote ever cast in the city of Woodstock.

Henry G. Fisher, the Citizen's candidate for city clerk, proved to be the leader among the candidates as a vote getter. He ran far ahead of his ticket in almost every ward, defeating his opponent, John F. Wienke, by a majority of 236 votes.

Woodstock Sentinel, April 20, 1911.

***

John sat in his basement workshop fiddling with what would, hopefully, be his first invention to patent. He was attempting to place a small metal seesaw-like lever on the side of a can of shoe polish, which, in theory, could be turned to easily pry off the lid so one didn't have to use a knife. He needed to get the prototype to work, and the plans sent in to patent it. If he could just get a rivet for the pivot, it would allow the lever to move but also maintain the freshness of the product.

He had tried melting lead between the can and the lever and again on the outside of the lever. The lever had worked exactly as planned – as he turned it the edge of the can was pushed up allowing easy removal, but the melted bond was easily broken, sometimes on the first twist. He had squeezed a tiny tube of metal from each side allowing the lever to pivot on this fulcrum but could not figure out how to fill the center of the tube to eliminate the tiny hole at the center of the pivot. A drop of lead in the hole had just fallen out after a few uses. A solid tube would be difficult to crimp from each side into a rivet but was his best bet. In attempting the crimp, he bent the can which again disallowed the airtight seal.

He set aside the task at hand and sat down in his wooden rocker. He came to this basement retreat when the women of the household needed him to be "out of the way" or when he had an idea for a new product to try or when the noise of three little girls playing or fighting became too loud to afford a man peace to just read the paper. His mind again sifted through the options. Maybe a softer metal...make the rivet out of tin instead of lead or steel? He would have to try that...tomorrow.

He did have a lot of time on his hands now that the election was over. Turns out, he thought cynically, he was a lousy speaker. Ah well, at least Donovan won again. John could, for the time being, focus on job and family. And thank goodness, Ida had decided not to run. She seemed more upset by his loss than he was.

He listened and heard no banging or chatter from upstairs. Today had been spring cleaning day with Ida and the older girls pitching in to beat the rugs and round up the cobwebs and dust bunnies. He had helped with moving some furniture and the picking up of rugs, the hanging of them over the clothes lines in the backyard but then had escaped to the basement. He had better go see if they needed help bringing the rugs in.

He slapped his thigh. Dagnabit! He had really been looking forward to that City Clerk job! But he must accept the results. He rose and headed for the stairs. He'd pick up a new can and some tin rivets, if such a thing existed at the hardware and give the can another try tomorrow. The stairs were steep. He thought about Ida pulling herself and a basket of wet clothes up them. He had time on his hands, he should rebuild them to be an easier climb.

I'll stop at the lumber yard tomorrow, too, he thought as his hands felt the roughness of the handrail. I'll get wood and make a modern stairway into the basement...for Ida.

***

Grace Lutheran Graced
With Large Crowd

A large audience filled Grace English Lutheran church on Sunday morning, very many young people being present. The congregation listened very attentively to the sermon "Seeking the Risen Christ." After the sermon, the communion service followed, and sixty-three persons partook of the Holy Sacrament. This was the largest attendance in the four years' history of this congregation.

In addition to the fourteen catechumens, three other persons were received into membership. The congregation has now an active membership roll of 104. Some more new members will be received next Sunday. It was indeed a very happy day for the members of Grace English Lutheran Church.

Woodstock Sentinel, April 20, 1911.

Champ Clark's Wife Possesses
Many Talents

MRS. CHAMP CLARK is declared by those who know her best to be a feminine counterpart of her distinguished husband. She has been popular in Washington, and now that her husband has been advanced to [Speaker of the House] she has become a commanding figure in the society of the national capital.

While she is essentially feminine, she has a grasp of affairs that might be properly described as masculine, and she has an appreciation of humor that enables her to see fun from many angles. She knows human nature and she is tremendously interested in humankind.

Outspoken to a degree which many less keen in their convictions would consider dangerous, Mrs. Clark says pretty much what she pleases, the sting being drawn from these traits as generally expressed by an inherent and unaffected kindliness and a friendliness that is not limited to place or position, to a person or a circumstance.

Mrs. Clark is pre-eminently unafraid. Armed with the best of intentions and gifted with a giant fund of common sense, she approaches every turn in life with a poise and balance that are not to be shaken by a jostle with hidebound conventions which beset the pathway of the average resident of Washington. The codes of caste and the rules of precedence which Washington worships as a fetish Mrs. Clark usually passes by with a nonchalance that shows she places personality above rank or position.

Mrs. Clark has never taken up women's suffrage, although she is a firm believer in the advisability of enfranchising the women of the country and thoroughly out of patience with those who form anti-women's suffrage leagues to work against the propaganda.

Mrs. Clark is tall and slender. She has an erect, graceful carriage and a swinging gait, the grace owing nothing to the corset which the average woman considers a necessary adjunct to a good appearance. Although not a dress reformer, Mrs. Clark has never worn stays. Still, Mrs. Clark dresses well and in the mode, choosing her colors discreetly and having a proper observance of the becoming in fit and fashion. She has a keen, intelligent face, her chief points of beauty being large, expressive, dark gray eyes and a fine head of silky black hair, which on either side is showing a very becoming strand of silver locks.

Woodstock Sentinel, April 20, 1911.

***

Ida put down the paper, chuckling. Certainly, this reporter had a lot to say about Mrs. Clark! She was not surprised, however, that the writer had come back to her looks, dress, and decorum, as always happened when a woman was being discussed. A woman can't be only intelligent, but she must also have dark, soulful, gray eyes and silky hair. And obviously this woman is not German. I couldn't go out in public without my stays, Ida thought. She shook her head. How did that poem go?

> Dimpled cheeks mit eyes of blue,
> Lips like dey vas moist mit dew,
> Two leetl teeth just comin' through.
> Dat's little Elza.
>
> Tow-headed boy mit eyes of glee,
> Drousers all out at der knee.
> He vas playing horse you see.
> Dat's little Otto.
>
> Von hundred fifty in der shader,
> Next time she's vas veighed.
> She beats me soon I am afraid.
> Dat's mine frau
>
> Barefooted head and puddy stout,
> Fond of his beer unt sauerkraut,
> Afeared his belt will soon give out,
> Dat's me himself.
>
> One baby girl full of fun,
> One roguish, bright-eyed little son,
> One frau to meet when verk is done,
> Dat's mine family.

The old poem flowed into her head without a hitch. Did she get all the words right? Probably not. She'd have to look the poem up again. She hated it when she couldn't remember all the words. But she, herself, was certainly that Frau, the wife in the poem, ten stone if she was an ounce, and John was certainly the Mann, the husband, in the poem. All they were missing was the roguish son. She sighed. She was afeared she and Clara both might be wishing for something that would never come.

***

ALL THINGS DENISON
by Clara Daring
Invalid's Narrow Escape

Mrs. Muir, mother of the custodian of the courthouse, had a terrible experience with an oil heating stove. She is a helpless invalid and has not walked for ten years. To heat her bedroom on a cold morning, a 2-oil stove was lit, and then the family left the house to pursue the daily avocations. Soon the stove began to smoke violently, filling the small room with soot, and as Mrs. Muir expected, would set the house on fire. She was helpless to save herself. She called loud and long with no response. Finally, she was able to make such a noise on a window near her bed so as to attract attention. When found she was nearly suffocated, and her face was inky black with soot.

Crawford County Courier, April 24, 1911.

***

OPEN NEW STORE AT GREENWOOD

About two weeks ago Murphy & Doering started a store in the village of Greenwood, in the Daily building, and The Sentinel has learned that the store is proving very popular in the community. Arthur Rupert, formerly of Woodstock, is the business manager and is pleasing the public in that capacity.

This is the second store for Greenwood, the one conducted in the Westerman building is owned by Frank Rawson. This thriving little village and prosperous community ought to support two stores in good shape.

Woodstock Sentinel, May 11, 1911.

***

Their Nationality

The number of native Americans who enlisted in the Union army during the war of the Rebellion was 1,846,672. The remainder of the army was divided as follows:

```
Germans................153,500
Irish .....................144,200
British-Americans........53,500
English .................. 45,500
         Total ............396,700
```

The above figures show that there were over 80 percent of the union soldiers who were native-born Americans.

Woodstock Sentinel, May 25, 1911.

***

Local News and Personal Items

Friday was the record-breaking day of the season for heat, the thermometer registering 98 degrees in the shade the greater part of the day, and little relief was afforded at night.

Wednesday, June 14, was Flag Day and only a small number of Woodstockites displayed "Old Glory" from their homes or places of business.

Report of Woodstock public library for the week ending June 11, 1911: Number of visitors, 440; number of books loaned, 265. Mrs. C. M. Curtis, lib.

A card received by The Sentinel editor from our former esteemed townsman, C. V. Sherman, at Tia Juana, Mex., states that the city is still in the hands of federal troops.

The latest victim of the deadly automobile, barring a few chickens, is the beautiful collie belonging to Mr. and Mrs. William Flanders, who was killed last Tuesday. The neighbors sympathize and could the offering have been optional would have gladly recommended a number of substitutes. We are thankful that the majority of automobile drivers are careful people, but a few go as if they had just received a summons from his satanic majesty and were "getting there" as fast as possible.

Woodstock Sentinel, June 15, 1911.

***

Farm, Orchard and Garden
by F. E. Trigg
Center Point, Rogue River Valley, Oregon

There is no more sly or brutal enemy of the birds than the spry and graceful small red squirrels that frequent the lawns and parks of almost every town and city. It may be tough treatment, but the writer favors shooting these wretches on sight, for they perform no service that in any way compensates for their ruthless destruction of eggs and young birds.

There is many a supposedly refined and cultured woman who would not knowingly crush a worm or insect or needlessly inflict pain on cat or dog who at the same time will, with much pride, wear on her hat portions of the bodies of mother birds that have fallen easy prey to the greed of the pot-hunter because of their instinctive love for their young. In one sense such a woman is as savage at heart as the heathen female that wears sticks in her nose and weights on her lips and even more responsible, for she has had more light and should know better.

Woodstock Sentinel, June 15, 1911.

***

Photo Post Cards

George C. Bell will be in Woodstock until June 21 and will be glad to make photo postcards for you of anything you may wish a photo of. Price 75 cents per dozen or two dozen for $1.25. Call at 314 Railroad Street.

Woodstock Sentinel, June 15, 1911.

Lineman Severely Shocked

A. E. Wolf, an employee of the local telephone company, came near being killed while on duty. He was climbing a pole on Broadway carrying the end of a coil of telephone wire. When well up he put his foot on a metal step which was also supporting a loose wire of the electric lighting company. The insolation had scraped off and a voltage of 1,200 volts shot through Wolf and to the wire he carried. The shock froze him to the pole, and he hung there in agony until his helper ran and cut the telephone wire. Wolf still had sense not to loosen his grip on the pole but came near falling when the current ceased. He is now back about his work. This was the second lineman accident in the last few months.

Crawford County Courier, May 29, 1911.

***

I Will Fly to Woodstock

They sat around Sophia's table on Decoration Day evening. Sophia took the head position with her children and their spouses spread along the sides and William at the foot of the table. The children were in the parlor with a floor picnic on a blanket. Sophia looked around the table: John and Ida, Ed and Kate, Frank and Anna, William and Lizzie, Emil and Etta, and Lillian. She had a fine-looking family.

That afternoon, the Woodstock Wienkes had gone en masse to the cemetery to lay flowers on the graves of Carl, the patriarch, now gone twenty-six years, and of Bob, the little brother they had lost five years ago. Each couple and Lillian and Sophia had brought a bouquet and so the graves were now blanketed with color. It was a remarkable sight.

Frank pushed back his chair a few inches. "Ma, that was the best turkey I've ever tasted." The others made sounds of agreement.

"Pshaw. Vas simple. Gut stove. Gut turkey. Everything vas gut."

The women murmured their thanks.

"I agree. This family can really cook!" Ed chimed in.

"And bake." John smiled at Ida who had furnished three pies.

William changed the subject. "John, how is the insurance business? Making money or losing it?"

John cleared his throat. "Well…both, I guess. We had a strange claim just recently that we denied."

The table made sounds of concern.

"Why?" asked Lilly.

"A man took out a policy to insure a box of fine cigars that he was importing from Cuba. They came by boat and then overland to Chicago where he claimed them, so he insured them from storm, fire, pestilence, accident, the whole bailiwick."

"Cuban cigars are expensive. Sounds like he was justified in his worry," said Frank, his hand covering a smirk."

I Will Fly to Woodstock

John glanced at him and nodded. The storyteller continued, "The cigars left Cuba and there was a great storm on the sea. For a while, the crew thought all was lost including the cigars. But they were kept safe by a seaman who slept with them in his berth to keep them from harm. He saw them safely to the Miami train station and bid them adieu. The train started northward, but a faulty track caused a derailment and half the train plunged into a lake."

"Oh no," said Ida. "And Prudential wouldn't cover an accident like that. Shameful."

"The cigars were not destroyed in the accident. They found the wooden box floating among the debris, undamaged. The conductor saw to it that the box was put on the next train for Chicago."

Around the table, all were looking at John, eyebrows raised with expectation.

"The owner went to Chicago when he heard that the box had arrived, but the station master cannot find it. He's told that the box was either stolen or misplaced. The owner came back to Woodstock ready to place a claim, but then he got a phone call telling him that the box was found and was in good condition. He returned to Chicago and brought them home to Woodstock to enjoy."

The congregation nodded.

Ed interjected, "Imagine having the money to insure a box of cigars." The others laughed and some took drinks of after-dinner coffee.

"But what claim did you deny? Did he come in and pretend he didn't get them?"

"Oh no. He actually stopped in and told us that they had arrived and thanked us for the security our insurance had added for their purchase," said John.

The audience nodded and murmured their approval of good manners.

"Den what happens?" Sophia liked this story.

His audience brought their attention back to John. "That was last fall, and so we thought, thank goodness, the cigars are secured. It was a good policy. But..."

The word hung in the air for a moment. "Last week, the gentleman came in and asked for a claim form. We were surprised and said, 'But you said they arrived unharmed' He agreed wholeheartedly and asked, 'Their arrival didn't end the policy, right.' We said, 'Well, that's right. What happened?' His response?"

Those at the table seemed to hold their breath. "He said, 'They have been destroyed in a series of small fires over the last six months, and I am here to make a claim.'"

For a moment, it seemed that no one had caught the joke, but then William began to laugh. "A series of small fires, eh? One at a time." And the others getting the humor, burst into laughter and some applauded a story well told.

"Did that really happen?" Anna asked.

"On my honor!" John crossed his heart.

"And you denied the claim." Lizzie asserted.

"Yes, we did. On the grounds that they were destroyed in the normal use of the product. He didn't read the fine print."

Again, some laughter broke out.

"Dat gut story, John." Sophia rose from her chair. "Ida, vill du help mit da pies?"

Just as Ida rose, a gaggle of children broke into the kitchen: Ed and Kate's Edwin at ten years, Frank and Anna's Clayton and Helen at eight years, Mamie at seven years, Lillian's Linette and Dodi at five years, Emil and Etta's Harvey the youngest at four years. These were only half of Sophia's grandchildren.

Helen, the assigned spokesperson, asked, "Why were you laughing?"

Ida reached out and hugged her. "Your father told a funny story."

"Tell us."

"Yes, tell us." The children were eager to laugh.

"That's up to your father." Ida moved to the counter where Sophia had unwrapped the pies.

"Du put him on da spot." Sophia retrieved a butcher knife from a drawer.

"He's up to it."

John looked at the expectant children. "I believe I heard this one from your Opa Wienke. Back in the old country of Germany, the land of Hessen, where Oma grew up, was surrounded by forests which were home to many wolves. The goats from Switzerland had often tried to come to Hessen only to be chased off by the wolves or even worse eaten by them.

"One day a little kid goat was making his way to Hessen. He had just entered the woods when a wolf confronted him. 'I've got you now! I'm going to eat you for dinner.'

"The little goat was very afraid, but he said with as much confidence as he could muster, 'B-b-but my mother is coming, soon.'

"The wolf thought, I must not spoil my appetite with this little one. The mother will make a better meal because I am very hungry. So, he let the little goat pass in peace.

"Soon after, the mother goat appeared. The wolf was about to pounce, when she said, 'My husband is coming, soon.'

"Ah, thought the wolf. The husband will be larger and will make even a better meal. I will wait. The mother goat followed the path the little goat had taken.

"Soon enough, here came the ram goat, strutting down the path as rams are wont to do." John made movements side to side like a proud male.

The adults around the table chuckled.

John continued, "The wolf was very happy that he had waited and was about to spring when he noticed that the ram had spikes coming from his head and two huge bags...um...hanging down between his legs."

The adults chuckled again. John's face flushed for a moment, but he went back to the story.

"Tell me, ram. What are those big spikes on your head and what is in the bags between your legs?"

William lowered his eyes and covered his laugh with a palm.

"'Oh, these spikes....'" John put his index fingers atop his bald head, looking much like a ram. "'These spikes are my guns and the bags carry my powder and lead to use if there is trouble.'"

John turned in a circle lowering the 'spikes' on his head as if to lunge at the children. They squealed with delight. He bent double and twisted so he brought the 'horns' to rub on his left knee and continued the story.

"The ram rubbed his left horn against his flank and the wolf thought the ram was loading his pistol. The wolf was so afraid that he forgot all about his hunger and he ran away as quickly as he could." The children cheered their approval.

John stood erect and lowered his hands to his sides. "And thus, it was so that the first family of goats arrived happily in the land of Hessen."

John's audience broke out in applause. The children bounced around with the boys butting their heads against the girls as they screamed back into the parlor.

Sophia leaned close to Ida and whispered, "A good story mus' have somethin' for everyone."

***

ALL THINGS DENISON
by Clara Daring
Punish the Rowdies

It is greatly to be regretted that a bunch of drunken rowdies should have, to some extent, spoiled the German Kinderfest, held last Monday. The Kinderfest is a distinctively German celebration and is intended primarily as an outing and a play time for the little folks. The old folks and the youths and maidens naturally gather to the festivities and in the evening a dance is given for their benefit. Americans, who behave themselves, are cordially invited and uniformly receive good treatment, but it is unfortunate that too frequently American youths, emboldened by bad whiskey, abuse the German hospitality and a "rough house" ensues.

Since the writer was a little girl, she has known and read of these German dances, and she cannot recall a single instance of any rowdyism where the Germans were left to carry out their own festivities in their own way.

While our German fellow citizens are of such character that if confined to themselves their merry making might extend "until daylight does appear" without unpleasantness of any kind, conditions are such that we do not believe any public dance should be allowed to continue until the wee small hours unless police supervision is strict and continuous. The rowdy Americans who attend these dances and who are responsible for these disturbances should receive such punishment as will make them hesitate to repeat the offense.

Crawford County Courier, June 14, 1911.

***

Body Food for Hogs

The German settlement between this city and Schleswig was thrown into high excitement yesterday by news that John Macentum, the 19-year-old son of a prominent farmer, had committed suicide.

John had harnessed his team and gone supposedly to the field. His mother hearing a commotion in the hog lot went down to determine its cause, and found the hogs eating her boy, as he lay with his throat cut from ear to ear.

The family gives out no known cause for the conduct of the son. This makes the fourth death from suicide in that locality in the last fifteen years.

Crawford County Courier, June 18, 1911.

***

Tornado Brings Heavy Losses

The residents of Chemung were visited by a tornado Saturday afternoon, June 10. The storm struck the village about five o'clock and was accompanied by a heavy rainfall.

A timber lot owned by R. J. Beck at the outskirts of the village was visited by the storm and trees, some of them two feet in diameter, were uprooted and carried quite a distance. Smaller ones were carried into distant fields....

Ed Rohloff, a salesman for Wilson Bros., drove his team and medicine wagon into the O'Brien barn for shelter and left when the first heavy storm passed over, fifteen minutes before the tornado struck the barn. A silo across from the barn was wrecked by the same storm.

Woodstock Sentinel, June 22, 1911.

***

June 29, 1911
Denison, Iowa

Dear Ida and John and children,

Am enclosing three recent articles that either you'll enjoy or that will scare you. You decide. We certainly live in a livelier place here in Denison than I at first suspected.

How are all of you? Have you been well? You should be done with school for the season. What are your plans for summer? You should all come out and see us in beautiful Iowa.

Pearle is doing well. He still gets the shakes when he thinks about going up a pole, but his bones are healing well. He is supposed to go back to work at the end of June, but we'll see. He's been making noise about changing careers or moving back to Akron or both. I really don't want to go having established myself as a reporter here. But ultimately, he will have the decision.

I'm curious what you think about the story about the boy who killed himself in the pig pen. The whole thing sounds fishy to me. I know of a lot of ways to kill oneself but slitting the throat from ear to ear seems like an awfully tricky thing to do on oneself. And why would you commit suicide in a pig pen? If you are a pig farmer's son, you'd know the pigs would eat you. Do you think he was trying to cover up what he had done? Not a good plan, I'd say. But if someone sneaked up behind you and slit your throat from behind while you were leaning over the pig pen fence, feeding them perhaps, and then just flipped you into the pen? Well, that seems more logical than slicing your own throat yourself and then having the sense to pitch forward into the pen. I questioned the sheriff on this issue, but he was not interested in challenging the coroner's report. I'm not sure what I should do. They reported that three other suicides have happened out that way over the last several years. I might just ride out there to see if I can find out more about it. Since I can speak German, I might be able to find out more than the sheriff could. The whole thing just keeps niggling at me. Let me know if you agree that it seems suspicious.

Well, I better run. Have to make supper and then make a 7:30 City Council meeting. By the way, thanks for the books you sent, Helen. Uncle Pearle devoured them in a week. Glad we have a library, small as it is. He goes over there at least once a week to stock up on reading material.

Love to you and the little ones,
Clara

***

"Was ist das?" A middle-aged man with disheveled salt and pepper hair peered out the partially opened door of his modest white clapboard farmhouse.

"Guten Tag, Herr Macentum. Wie Geht es?" Clara greeted him. "Mein Name ist Clara Dye unt ich bin ein Zeitungreporter."

"Ja damit?" So?

"So, I was hoping we could talk a bit…about John."

"Johannes?"

"Ja, Johannes. Darf ich rein kommen?"

The man considered the request for entrance a bit and then stepped back allowing the door to swing fully open. "Komm herein."

Clara stepped into the frugal and somber scene. The curtains were pulled closed to let in as little light as possible. A few rays managed to slant their way in to add just enough light to save the electricity. The walls were gray plaster, unpainted, but clean. The floor was covered with worn linoleum in Dutch blue. As Clara's eyes adjusted to the lack of light, she saw a woman sitting at the kitchen table in the center of the room. The woman cradled a cup of coffee in her hands on the off-white oil cloth covering. Two places had been set, and now the dishes of a finished meal, most likely breakfast, were scattered about.

"Guten Tag, Frau Macentum." Clara greeted her.

"Guten Tag, Frau Dye. Kommen and setzen sie dich." John's mother motioned to an empty chair at the table. "Mochtest zie einen Kaffee?" Would you like some coffee?

"Das ware sehr net. Vielen dank." That would be nice. Many thanks.

Mr. Macentum came and sat at his place, while Mrs. Macentum rose and cleared the dishes and poured a cup of coffee for Clara and refilled their cups. "Mochtest zie Sahne oder Zucker?"

"Ja, milk would be fine," answered Clara. She added the milk offered to her coffee and laid her pencil and pad on the table before her.

"Frau Dye." Mr. Macentum's face was laced with concern. "Was Konnen wir fur Sie tun?" What can we do for you?

"Wäre es in Ordnung, wenn ich Englisch sprechen würde? My mother speaks German, but I haven't seen her in quite a while. I understand better than I speak."

"Ja, dot voud be fine." Mrs. Macentum smiled just a little.

"Gut. As I said to Mr. Macentum on the porch, I am a newspaper reporter, and I am researching the deaths of German young people who have died in strange circumstances. If you don't mind, I'd like you to tell me a bit about John."

"Johannes war ein guter junge. Immer glucklich." A good boy. Always happy. John's mother was clearly bereaved. Tears filled her eyes, and she reached for the cloth napkin on the table.

Clara swallowed hard. "Yes. I only knew him a little from the Deutsche Gesellschaft. He did seem to be a happy, sociable man. Was that true around the time of his death? Or did he seem sad about something?" The part about knowing him was a fib, but Clara thought it might open the channels of communication.

"No!" Mr. Macentum spoke up brusquely. "He vas goink to hog market dat next day. He vas aufgeregt…," he looked to Mrs. Macentum for translation.

Clara broke in, "He was 'excited' to be going to the hog market?"

"Ja, sehr aufgeregt. He vorked on da new road for money and hatte Geld spezielles Schwein kaufen."

"He was going to buy a special pig? Why was the pig special?" Clara couldn't imagine a 'special' pig.

"Was ein Deutsche pig. Ein Deutsche Swabian Hall pig. All black pig. Dat pig taste gut."

Clara smiled. "I need to ask the next question, but I'm not sure how, so please forgive me if this is painful. Do you think he killed himself?"

"Nein!" They answered quickly and in unison.

"What do you think happened?"

"Er wurde ermordet!" exclaimed Mrs. Macentum. "He vas murtered!"

"Ja, he vas!" Mr. Macentum immediately agreed. "Else how he get in pig sty?"

"How do you think he got in the pig pen?"

"He vas pushed." John's father was certain. "Only way."

"Who would have wanted him dead? Did he have enemies? Had he had any fights?"

"Nein. Jeder liebte Johannes." Everyone loved John, his mother quickly volunteered, but Clara noticed his father didn't answer. He looked at his wife and then back at Clara.

"Dare vas one." His voice was hushed.

"One? One enemy?" Clara lowered her voice also.

"Ja. One enemy."

Mrs. Macentum put her hand on her husband's arm. "Wer?"

"Yes, who?" Clara repeated the inquiry.

He hesitated. "At der Kinderfest, merken Mama? Die englischen Jungen und der Kampf." He turned his attention back to Clara. "Ein tow-head English boy and Johanne fistacuff over ein Madchen. Johanne's girl, Hedwig. Sie haben seit der Schule umborben."

"Johanne and this girl had been courting since school?" Clara wanted to make sure she was understanding correctly. "But that would be several years, right?"

"Ja, Funf Jahre. Five. I tink he would marry her." Mrs. Macentum looked down at the table. "So traurig."

"Ja, very sad." Clara turned her attention back to Mr. Macentum. "Do you know the name of this blond boy?"

"Nein. Hedwig knows or Hans, Johanne's freund. He vas dare."

"Please, may I have their last names, and I won't keep you any longer from your work."

***

As Clara climbed into the surrey, she kissed Pearle lightly on the cheek. He had forbidden her from coming out into the country alone, but she was sure he just wanted to get out and about. She welcomed the company.

"Get what you need?" Pearle took up the reins.

"Maybe. I got a couple leads and the more I hear the less logical a suicide sounds or even a simple pitching forward into the pen." Clara tied a scarf over her hair.

"Giddyap, Donny." Pearle put their steed into a smooth trot.

As they made the trip back to Denison, Clara thought about the way the world worked. Love, jealousy, revenge, death. This tragic tale had all the makings of a remarkable story. An accident was possible, she supposed. But something still seemed suspicious to Clara. She would talk to John's friends and then decide what to do.

"I've got work to do," Clara said to no one in particular. Pearle just smiled at his ambitious wife.

***

Real Estate Tax

August Wienke 108 p 619 pt lt 7/8	$500
Wm. Wienke, lt. 12 Spring City Add bk 6	$67
J. Wienke lt 8 Spring City Add Block 16	$17
F. J. Wienke, lt 1 Dacy Addition Block 2	$600
John Wienke, lt 4 Bellevue Block 1	$833
Sophia Wienke, pt lt 42	$750

Personal Property Taxes

Wienke, August	$60
Wienke, Emil	$92
Wienke, Frank J.	$86
Wienke, John	$54

Woodstock Sentinel, July 6, 1911.

***

Clara held out her hand. "Hi, Hedwig. I'm Clara." The girl looked at her, confusion framing her face. She tentatively took Clara's hand. "How do you do? Please call me Hedy. Hedwig is so old country, don't cha think?"

"I'm doing very well. Hedy it is. How are you today?"

"I'm fine." Hedy still sounded tentative.

"I was wondering if you'd have some time to talk. I'm a reporter, and I would like to ask you about John Macentum."

"What about John?" Hedy's voice was strained with skepticism.

"May I sit?" Hedy was on her lunch break from the bank and on this beautiful day had made her way to a bench outside the grocery on Main Street. Clara knew that she didn't have a long break but hoped that Hedy would answer a couple questions as she ate.

"Sure." Hedy moved over slightly.

"I was talking with John's parents, and they mentioned that you were his girl."

Hedy sniffed, not from tears, but with incredulity. "Not really. Maybe his pretend girlfriend."

"Pretend? Why do you say that?" asked Clara.

"Because we had been going together for five years, and he had yet to kiss me." Hedy took a bite of her sandwich.

"When did you start going out? Maybe he was just very shy?"

"We started going out while we were still in high school. Both our families thought we were going to marry and settle down, but...." Hedy swallowed hard and then laughed. "Shy? No, not really. He was...," she paused. "He was obsessed with pigs."

Clara couldn't help but chuckle. "You saw him earlier the week he died at the Kinderfest, didn't you?"

"M'huh," Hedy answered, her mouth full. She swallowed and took a sip from the straw in a bottle of Dr. Pepper. "We went together...sort of."

"Sort of? What do you mean?"

"We were almost always a threesome, me, John, and John's friend, Hans."

"Not your friend?"

Hedy shrugged her shoulders. "Not always."

Clara considered this strange answer. Sometimes she was Hans' friend and sometimes not. John took her to the dance, but Hans tagged along.

"There was a fight that night. A blond boy and John."

"Yes, the fight was stupid. John and Hans were being party poopers and not dancing, so when this handsome blond boy asked me to dance, I jumped at the chance. I was telling him while we were dancing that they wouldn't dance with me, and I was sick of always being a threesome and some other stuff and so when we got done, he said, 'Let's go somewhere quiet where we can talk more easily. I have some hooch if you want some.'"

Hedy's sandwich lay drying on her lap. "I thought that was a great idea, so we went back to the table, so I could get my shawl, and John stood up and said, like he owned me, 'Where are you going?' I said, 'None of your business.' And he said, 'It is my business because you came with me.' And I said, 'Ha, some date' and looked at Hans. Hans turned red, got up and walked away. Then John stepped in between me and the boy and told him to leave me alone. I told him that I could take care of myself, and the boy...he pushed John and reached around to take my hand so we could leave. Then they started hitting each other. And Hans came back and some of the boy's friends came in, and they were all ready to hurt John and Hans, but then the grownups pushed in, stopped it, and told the American boys to leave and not come again. And that's about it." She picked up her sandwich and took a big bite.

"That's a little different than the story I heard. I thought it was just American young men getting drunk on German beer and then being disruptive. This sounds a lot more personal."

Hedy shrugged.

"Just one more question. After John died, did anyone ask you about this? Did the sheriff ask you to tell him what happened that night at the Kinderfest?"

"No. The sheriff never said a word to me. Why would he? I don't know if he talked to Hans."

"OK, thank you so much for telling me your story." Clara stood up ready to leave.

"I don't think John killed himself." Hedy's eyes filled with tears. She reached for a pocket hankie.

"Do you think the pigs killed him?"

"Maybe, but he really knew pigs. He wouldn't just take a chance with them like that." She dabbed at her eyes. "He must have been unconscious or dead when he fell into the pen, or he would never have stayed down. And for the pigs to bite his neck instead of his hands or face...there must have been blood. That's just my opinion, but he knew pigs."

"Thank you, Hedy." Clara touched the young woman's shoulder and then turned away.

Did humiliation over being ejected from an event seem enough to cause a revenge killing? This story had more to it than that, Clara was sure.

***

MURPHY & DOERING

10-DAY PRE-INVENTORY SALE

Beginning Saturday, July 8th, to Tuesday, July 18th

THE BIGGEST SALE OF THE SEASON. Slashing and cutting prices in every department. We must reduce our stock before Inventory. No goods will be reserved. Everything in the store will be sold at cut prices from 10% to 50% discount. This is an unusual opportunity and will be a big saving to you for present and future wants. Don't miss this big sale, but come and bring your friends.

SHOES

[illegible] regular price, sale 98c
[illegible] Oxfords, sale $1.45
[illegible] $1.65
[illegible] Tan Oxfords, sale $1.85
[illegible] $1.98
Misses' Black and Tan [illegible] Pumps [illegible] regular, sale 98c
$1.50 Misses' White Duck Pumps, sale 98c
[illegible] sale price $1.10
[illegible] Children's [illegible] Sandals, sale 65c

Silks and Dress Goods

[illegible] Silk Taffeta and Messaline in small figures, stripes and checks, sale 35c
[illegible] Black Taffeta Silk [illegible] wide, sale 89c
[illegible] Pongee Silks for 55c
[illegible] Messaline, all the latest styles 79c
All other silk reduced [illegible] Dress Goods stock at cut prices. Staples and Fancies to go at [illegible]

Suits, Coats and Skirts

[illegible] Coats [illegible] during sale $1.98
Long Serge, Covert, Satin and Fancy [illegible] Coats, all greatly reduced
[illegible] Ladies' Skirts [illegible] sale $1.50
[illegible] Skirts $3.50
[illegible] Black Ladies' Dress Skirts $3.95
[illegible] black Ladies' Dress Skirts $4.95
[illegible] black Ladies' Dress Skirts $6.95
[illegible] Wash Skirts 98c

Ladies' Fancy and House Dresses

68c [illegible] Percale Wrappers [illegible] in dark colors, regular [illegible] values.
95c [illegible] one piece and two piece House Dresses, all sizes, regular [illegible] values
[illegible] White Lawn Dresses, nicely trimmed with lace and embroidery, sale $1.75
[illegible] White Dresses for $2.95
[illegible] White Dresses for $3.75
[illegible] two piece House Dresses, sale $1.35
[illegible] two piece House Dresses, sale $2.25
[illegible] Messaline and Taffeta Silk Dresses, sale $7.75
[illegible] Silk Dresses $8.75
[illegible] $11.75
[illegible] $13.75

MILLINERY DEPARTMENT

All trimmed and untrimmed Hats 35 and 50 discount

Children's Wash Dresses

[illegible] Wash Dresses 39c
[illegible] 55c
[illegible] 79c
[illegible] 98c
[illegible] $1.65
[illegible] Ladies' White Waists [illegible] sale 69c

Men's Furnishings

[illegible] Underwear, sale 38c
Men's [illegible] Underwear 29c
Men's [illegible] Suits, sale 42c
[illegible] Men's black Sox, sale 6c
[illegible] 4 [illegible] for 25c
[illegible] Men's Working Shirts [illegible] 35c
[illegible] Men's Dress Shirts, sale 35c
[illegible] Men's Dress Shirts 68c

Table Linen and Napkins

[illegible] extra heavy [illegible] Linen Damask, [illegible] sale 42c
[illegible] full bleached, full width Double Damask, sale 96c
[illegible] Table Linen, sale 79c
[illegible] Table Linen, sale 63c
[illegible] Fancy Towels 56c
[illegible] 39c
[illegible] 23c
$1.00 [illegible] Napkins, sale 85c
[illegible] all linen Napkins $1.65
[illegible] Napkins for $2.19
[illegible] Napkins for $2.95
[illegible] all linen Bleached Toweling, sale [illegible]
[illegible] brown Crash, sale 4½c
Fancy Linen Prices greatly reduced.

Lace Curtains and Portieres

Special [illegible] value Lace Curtain, pair 72c
[illegible] Curtains, regular price [illegible] sale 29c to 65c
Other Lace Curtains marked down in proportion
[illegible] Portieres, pair, sale $1.50
[illegible] $2.95
[illegible] $3.50
[illegible] $4.25

Embroideries and Laces

[illegible] discount on all Embroideries and Laces
[illegible] Flouncing 98c
[illegible] Flouncing 69c
[illegible] Flouncing $1.19
[illegible] Flouncing 21c

Odd Lots of Men's and Boys' Suits at Half Price

Carpets and Rugs

A good [illegible] Brussels Rug usually sold at [illegible] to 15.00, sale $9.50
$15.00 Velvet Rug [illegible] sale $11.50
[illegible] Axminster Rugs [illegible] sale $16.95
[illegible] Velvet Carpet, sale 75c
[illegible] Brussels Carpet, sale 65c
[illegible] 59c
[illegible] heavy Axminster Carpets, sale 79c

Blankets & Comforters

75c Cotton Blankets, sale 59c
85c [illegible] 69c
[illegible] extra large Blankets $1.39
2.35 [illegible] $1.65
[illegible] $1.98
All Comforters at cut prices

Wash Goods

[illegible] Percales, dark colors 6½c
Challies, choice patterns 4c
[illegible] French and Scotch Ginghams, sale 18c
[illegible] White and black Shirtings, sale 7½c
[illegible] Outing Flannels 8c
All fancy Lawns and Dimities at cut prices
[illegible] Sheeting [illegible] grade, sale 24c
[illegible] Muslin [illegible] for 8c
All other Wash Goods, Muslins and Cotton Suiting to go at cut prices

Suit Cases and Trunks

Special [illegible] all leather Suit Case, sale $2.98
[illegible] Fiber Suit Cases, sale $1.78
All Trunks at special prices
[illegible] Hammock, sale $2.28

Ladies' and Children's Underwear at [illegible] prices

Ladies' and Children's Hosiery

15c Children's Hose, sale 9c
15c Ladies' Hose, sale 9c
All other Hose at sale prices

Ladies' Muslin Undergarments

This is one of the best departments in our store and as we lack space to give prices [illegible] to get your supplies at this sale

BASEMENT GROCERIES AND NOTION BARGAINS

Duluth Imperial Flour, sk $1.25
1 lb of our [illegible] coffee free with every six.
Best full Cream Cheese 16c
[illegible] Japan Tea, sale 3 for $1.00

5 bars Snowbury Soap, it floats, 10c
Best Navy Beans 8c
5 bars Galvanic and Palm Olive Soap 25c

Pint jar French Prepared Mustard 9c
Swift's Pride Cleanser 7c
[illegible] Prunes 10c
Large size can Pie Peaches 10c
Hall's Toilet Paper 25c

[illegible] bottle Graves' Tooth Powder 10c
25c fancy China Cup and Saucer 10c
[illegible] Enamel Ware 10c
Water Glasses 8c

ALL THINGS DENISON
by Clara Daring
Transcontinental Road Gains Speed

The meeting of the transcontinental route held at Marshalltown last week was a decided success although many towns were unrepresented. The organization was perfected and made better by the addition of a number of strong men. It was difficult indeed when the organization was first made to tell who would be effective workers. There are many men who are loud in their protestations, and who are sincerely enthusiastic for the moment, but who cannot be counted on for substantial effort. "The first year has been needed to discover the real workers and to separate the chaff from the wheat," said one of the leaders. "With this year we expect real work will be done, there are tremendous possibilities in the establishment of such a route. It is but a question of a few years before the government will take hold of the matter. A permanent highway will be built from ocean to ocean. It is an economic as well as a military necessity."

There is a great deal of satisfaction in talking and working for good roads. They conflict with no man's ambitions. They increase the wealth and happiness of all without working injury to any. There is no politics about them, no factionalism, no religious differences. There is no question but that good roads increase land values. Thus, primarily every landowner is benefited, market possibilities are widened, pleasure and convenience of farm life increased, and people are brought closer together.

A few years ago, an automobile trip to Omaha was an all-day affair. Now it is but a matter of a few hours. A few years ago, township correspondents made note of every automobile that passed, now they create little or no comment.

So, to the transcontinental associations, this correspondent says "Hurrah!"

Crawford County Courier, July 19, 1911.

***

June 25, 1911
365 Lincoln Ave.
Woodstock, Ill.

Dear Clara,

How are you and Pearley dear? Your letter sounded like he was all but cured. Bones don't heal that fast. Make sure you encourage him to take it slowly so he mends well.

We have had some sniffles, but all are back to normal except Mamie. Things always hit her harder. But I believe she, too, is on the mend. I hate summer colds, don't you?

Guess what. Your brother is now selling groceries out of his dry goods shop. I sure wish John would explain what happened. Bessie has had her sister down from Racine, but the only way I know is that the news was in the paper. I'm tempted to just go over and ask what is going on, but then I would probably just make things worse, so I won't.

And come to find out, Emil's wife, Etta is quite an accomplished musician. I knew she played for their church in Beloit, but here she has become quite the star at the Women's Missionary dime lunches. I'm so glad that she found her niche so quickly in Woodstock.

Helen is reading every book in the library, just like Pearle. We are so lucky to have such a good selection of books, but she is reading above her grade level, mostly because she has read all of the children's books already. What a bright young lady we have. Her Aunt Clara should be proud.

Dodi, ah, what can I say about my little Dodi. She talks about her An Carwa a lot and wishes we could go see her and play dollies. She is more interested in cooking than either of the other girls and I do love the company. I will miss her when she goes off to school, but I have a while until then to enjoy her.

How is your sleuthing going? Have you discovered who done it? Are you going to write a book? Please keep me posted and be safe in your interviewing. It's nice that Pearle is up and about and can go with you to protect you from yourself.

My garden is beautiful right now. Mamie has shown an interest in working in the garden which I am encouraging. She especially likes to plant the seeds and see them sprout. I'm not sure how excited she will be about harvesting and canning, we'll see.

John is doing fine. He was at loose ends for a while after losing the election, but while we liked having him home more, he went and ran for town committee again and won, well really, they just kept his position open and gave the job back to him when the county clerk campaign was over. He spends quite a lot of time in the basement inventing things. I don't ask him, but he tells me once they are perfected. Did I tell you that he completely rebuilt the rickety steps to the basement 'for me'? Ha! I only go down there once a week for laundry.

I better close and get this down to the station, so it heads out to you on the overnight. I need a brisk walk and Helen was saying that she needed to go to the library again.

Our love to you and Pearle. Be safe on your adventures.
Ida

***

Clara knocked on Gruenwald's door. Theirs was one of the finest houses in town with fresh paint and a nice cobblestone walk. Flowers bloomed in beds and in window boxes and she could smell the aroma of meat cooking through the screen door. A woman scurried up to the door from the back of the house. She was wiping her hands on her apron. Clara smiled. She looked very much like her own mother, Louisa.

"Ja. We's not buying anytink and we's got religion." The woman started to turn away.

"Mrs. Gruenwald?"

She turned back. "Ja, who you?"

"I'm Clara Dye. Is Hans at home? I heard that he was working away for the summer, but someone saw him downtown last night and—"

"Ja, ja. Kommen sie hier." She swung the screen door open. "Hans! Du haben Gesellschaft kommen. Hans!!" she called up the stairs.

A slight young man appeared at the top of the stairs. He looked down on Clara and his mother but did not descend the stairs, as if he needed further invitation.

Clara stepped forward and in a louder voice said, "Hans, I'm Clara Dye. I would like to talk to you about John Macentum."

"I don't want to talk about John." The dark-haired, fine-featured young man turned away from the stairs.

"Hans, kommen sie hier! Nun!" His mother's voice was commanding. Come here! Now!

Very reluctantly, he made his way down the stairs.

"Hoflich sein. Bring diese Frau in den Salon und ich bringe Limonade mit." Be polite! Take this woman to the parlor and I will bring some Lemonade.

"Aber Mama, ich mochte nicht uber John reden." Hans again reiterated that he did not want to talk about John.

They didn't realize that Clara could speak German. She decided not to let on. She would have to be careful not to spook this boy.

Hans lost a stare down with his mother. "Come on," He moved into the sitting room, and he motioned to a chair. "Mama is getting lemonade."

"How nice." Clara followed him into the parlor looking around. "This is a lovely house." She realized after she made the compliment that it probably was to the wrong person. She was sure that Hans didn't care about the house.

"Ja, it's a good strong house. The style is called half-timbered, a German style that dates to medieval times. So, all these beams that you see in here are the structure of the house. We then fill in the spaces with first brick and then what's called waddle and daub to make a smooth surface. It's very cool in summer and warm in winter."

Clara was staring at him practically wide eyed. "You are an architect?"

"Will be. I'm going to university in Chicago in the fall, but I've wanted to be a builder my whole life, and I helped a little with building this house...when I was younger, you know."

"Hier sind wir. Some Limonade for der Gast. I am at da cookink. Hans, tell me if needs be."

"OK, Mama. We'll be fine. Danke."

What a polite young man. Clara sipped her lemonade and then nodded her approval. "Thank you, Mrs. Gruenwald. It's very good." The woman quickly left to go back to her cooking.

"Hans, I don't want to upset you by talking about your friend, but I'm investigating his death, and one specific evening may hold the answer. I'd like to talk to you about it."

"Evening? Are you with the police? I never saw a lady policeman before." Hans looked puzzled.

"No. I'm with the newspaper."

"Then I really don't want to talk to you." He put down his glass and started to rise.

Oops. "I'm interested in the evening of the Kinderfest and the fight that ensued between the blond boy and John over Hedy's hand."

"You're kidding, right?" Hans settled back in the chair. "You think that fight was over Hedy's hand?"

"That's what she said."

"It's just like her to skew the story to being about her."

"If Hedy wasn't the catalyst, what was?"

"That is no one's business and surely not a story for the newspaper."

"Hm. I suppose there are others who were at the party I could ask. Was your mother—"

"No!"

Clara waited. Sometimes silence was more powerful than words.

"What exactly did Hedy tell you?"

Clara reiterated the story that she had heard from Hedy. Trying not to leave anything out. When she was done, Hans sipped from his glass and then laughed softly.

Clara went on, "To be honest, I am trying to figure out what happened to John. Did he slash his own throat and then throw himself into the pig pen in a fit of angst? Did he swoon and fall unconscious, fall in and then the pigs did the rest? Or was he," she paused, "slashed and then pushed in with the pigs?"

Hans stared into his glass. "Does it really matter?"

"Well, yes, if justice will be served." Clara sipped her lemonade and placed the glass on the tatted doily.

"Justice? Justice does not exist. Life is not just. Love is not just. And certainly, for almost all of us, death is not just." He spoke in a monotone, looking not at Clara but rather at the perspiring glass in his hand.

"When did you last see John?"

"The night before he died."

"Really. Why was that?"

Hans' head snapped up and his eyes riveted Clara to her seat. "Why should that matter. I saw him. We met. That's all you need to know."

"Did the police know you met? Did they talk to you after he died?"

"No, they did not. And I didn't volunteer to be questioned."

"Why in the world not? If you were not involved, why would you be afraid to tell them what you know."

Hans' eyes dropped back to his glass. "You think I have something to tell them? You think I would hurt him?" His eyes came to hers and bore into her. "Are you crazy?"

Clara's mouth went dry. She reached for her glass, almost lost purchase on it, but brought it to her mouth for a long sip. She placed the glass back down on the end table and turned her eyes on him, "Did you?"

Hans held her gaze, but then his angry face crumpled, and he put his face to his hands, "God no! I didn't kill him. I loved him."

Clara sat very still and let him cry. What exactly did he mean? Of course, he loved his friend John, no surprise there.

"Of course, you did. And because of that you would want to see his death examined and explained, right?"

"NO! I loved him and he loved me and we were…we were…in love." His face turned scarlet.

He didn't just love John as a friend. They were 'in love.' But what exactly did that mean? How did it work? Clara's friend Clancy's face floated into her mind. Clancy who never dated other women but ferried her around when she needed a man with her. Clancy who had impeccable manners and was a snappy dresser. Clancy who always had a word to say about the handsome men in the saloons under the guise of discovering a mate for Clara. He always played his cards close to his chest. Clara thought about the night when Clancy wouldn't give the police detective his real name. At the time she thought he was just being goofy, but maybe he was in love with men too. Clara looked at the broken man before her. Poor boy.

When the sobs lessened, Clara said as gently as possible, "Tell me what happened that night at the party."

Hans wiped his face with his hands and looked up. He shrugged. "We three went to Kinderfest together. As always, everyone was drinking a lot at the dance. When the children have gone to bed, the adults get to play. The oompa band played a lot of polkas and waltzes. So, we sat with Hedy, and we were drinking German beer. Hedy kept wanting John to dance, so I was teasing him to go on. He would just look at me with those big blue eyes, so handsome." Hans was lost for a moment in reverie. He shook himself back to the present. "When an American boy came and swept up Hedy to dance, I think we were both glad. I remember thinking that maybe she would go sit with him for a while so we could enjoy at least part of the evening in peace. They danced a few dances, and while she was gone, John and I had our heads together planning our vacation to St. Louis which was coming up. Off to the big city where no one knows anything about us." He took a long shuddering breath and cleared his throat.

"When they came back to the table, Hedy grabbed up her shawl and said she and the American boy were leaving, that 'Harry' was walking her home. The boy had his arm around her. John got up. He asked her if she was going right home. She replied, quite snidely something like, 'Who are you my big brother?' He answered, 'Since your parents think you will be with us all evening, yes, think of me as the big brother.' Being protective; just like him." A tiny smile crossed Hans' face, but quickly faded.

He continued the story. "While they were talking, the blond boy leaned down toward me and whispered, 'Sodomite.'"

"Sodomite?" Clara wasn't sure she knew what that was.

"Yes, you know the Biblical story of Sodom and Gomorrah, right?"

"Yes." She drew out the word thinking as quickly as she could how that story went. "Was that when Lot's wife is turned into a pillar of salt for looking back?"

"I don't know. I mean, maybe, but that isn't what sodomite means. The people of Sodom were…um…the men liked men and the women liked women."

Clara thought about that. She liked both men and women. She looked at Hans who seemed to be waiting while she thought. She nodded.

He continued. "I didn't know what to do. I tried to get John's attention with my eyes, but he was in an intense conversation with Hedy. I got up and walked away from the table on the pretense of getting another growler of beer. I didn't want trouble. And I didn't want this guy, Harry, to be yelling 'Sodomite' for the whole party to hear. All of our parents and our whole community were in attendance." Hans wiped his tears and looked off through the large sitting room window as he talked.

"The boy sneered at me as I walked away and again whispered, 'Sodomite.' I couldn't hear him, but I read his lips. Then he walked over, pushed John aside, grabbed Hedy by the arm, and attempted to pull her away. I was watching and immediately turned back, expecting trouble. He was saying to her, 'Let's get out of this place where such abomination is allowed.' John looked at him, confused I think, and then back at me, maybe hoping for my help, and said something like, 'She's not going with you.' John is…um…was strong - stronger than me, but then I saw other American boys coming up behind Harry and Hedy, so I signaled to some of our friends, who put down their glasses and came over to see what was going on. Some of the older folks came over, too, and we were in a stand-off." Hans sighed and took a large gulp of lemonade.

"Hans, if this is too painful—" Clara began.

"No, I need to tell you now. Harry again said that he was taking her away from this abomination. And then John stepped right up to him and said, 'No! You are not!'" Hans nearly shouted the words. "Then the boy pushed John hard, but he didn't fall, and John came back with a mean punch that broke the boy's nose, I think, and made him let go of Hedy who was hustled off by one of the opas...um...grandfathers. I was afraid that everyone was going to pile into a fight, make a real brawl of it, but they didn't. Everyone just stared at each other, and then the bloodied kid said, 'Sodomites!' again, loud enough for everyone to hear. At that point, the main grandpa told the American boys to leave, and they did. I was surprised that they gave in so easily, but when I turned around, we were fifty strong facing down their dozen. I was proud," Hans again smiled a little at the memory.

"The band took up a polka again, couples swung out onto the floor, and things went back to normal, and John whispered to me that he was leaving and reached for his coat. I said, 'Not alone, you're not. Stay and have another beer and we'll leave in a group.' We looked around, afraid we might be the center of attention, but the music was playing loudly, and the beer was flowing. No one seemed the least bit interested in us or in what had happened. But we knew the cat had escaped the bag and behind their hands they were whispering. John stayed; we drank and went home with our parents." Hans drained his lemonade and put the glass down with a thump.

"No one said a word to us about the fight or the slur. Not my parents, not his parents. Hedy was really, really mad at him that night, but some of the ladies took her aside and calmed her down and a couple of the grandpas walked her home later. I'm not sure if she and John talked to each other again before...."

Hans had run out of steam and sat staring at his empty glass. "I guess the situation was a little about Hedy, wasn't it?"

"It was. But about a lot more, too. Do you think those American boys might have gone after John later at his home?"

Hans shook his head miserably. "I don't know. It's possible, I suppose. I don't think we'll ever know. John was such a kind soul. I had never seen him fight back like that. I was so proud of him and then...." He lowered his face to his hands again and his shoulders shuddered with a sob.

Clara rose and crossed the room, putting her hand on his shoulder. "Maybe the telling will ease the pain a bit," she soothed. "I do understand why you didn't step forward with this motive for murder. The police would have question those American boys and their parents and your parents and friends. It could have gotten a bit sticky."

Hans was suddenly alert practically leaping from his chair. "You aren't going to put this in the paper, are you? Are you going to tell the sheriff? Please don't. I could be arrested or thrown out of town. I will be going to university in the fall, away from here. Please don't."

"Arrested? But you had nothing to do with John's death."

"No, I mean arrested for sodomy." That word again.

"They wouldn't do that. Denison is very progressive."

"Not that progressive. You have to promise that you won't tell anyone."

Clara considered. She slid a hand behind her back and crossed her fingers. "OK, I won't tell anyone. I had a good friend in Racine who I believe was like you, I think. We had great times together. Friends thought maybe we might marry, but he didn't...didn't...seem interested in marriage."

She saw Hans visibly relax. "A lot of us do marry, most do, in fact. I am marrying architecture. No time for romance." His voice lacked conviction.

"Oh Hans, don't give up on romance. The right gi...person will come along. Love will find you even if you aren't looking. Thank you for trusting me with your story."

He smiled and on impulse stepped forward and gallantly kissed her on each cheek. "Thank you for listening....and understanding."

***

Later, at home, Clara sat down across from Pearle. "Well, I got my story."

"Good."

"But I don't know if I can tell it."

"Why not? You spent a lot of time interviewing people. Couldn't you figure the story out?"

"Nope, could be a suicide... reasons existed...or could have been murder...reasons existed...or it might have just been an accident. No one knows except John and the pigs."

Pearle laughed and then covered his mouth, "Oh sorry, didn't mean to laugh at death. But why can't you write the story up as a mystery never to be solved."

"I suppose I could try it, but I'm not sure it would be much of a story without a conclusion, and I promised my last interviewee that I would tell no one!"

"OK, now you have me hooked. Tell me the story."

Clara outlined the people in the story and the situation and the fight at the party, and the pain of Hans and the parents.

Pearle nodded. "You are right that this story should probably not be told and certainly not in the county."

"Why not. I could change the names or use party of the first part and party of the second part or something to disguise who I'm talking about."

"That won't work. People will quickly put two and two together and know who you interviewed. And if the police are mean-spirited, they might get into the act and charge either Hans or the blond boy – Harry, was it? – with the murder. At the very least, Hans would be run out of town on a rail."

"But why? I don't understand why that would happen. What would the charge be?"

"Sodomy."

"But what is sodomy? Looking back when the Lord says don't look back?"

Pearle laughed. "No, it doesn't have to do with Lot's wife. It has to do with the wicked people of Sodom who asked Lot to turn over the men he had put up for the night – actually angels – so that they could...so the men could have sex with them."

Clara considered. "Oh. But that has nothing to do with love."

"No, my dear, it doesn't. And neither does the law which says sodomy is punishable by imprisonment."

"I could write the story with names changed, but I don't really know who would publish it. Maybe in Chicago or New York."

Pearle took her by the shoulders. "I love you, Clara. I love you because you always try to do the right thing."

"Like running away with you?"

"Exactly."

***

Thompson's Condition Favorable

Jacob Thompson, who had his feet crushed near Smith's crossing east of Union, is reported to be in a favorable condition at St. Joseph's hospital at Belvidere, having rallied well from the effects of the operation, in which both of his feet were amputated.

He has made no explanation as to how he came to be lying with his feet on the rail. He was a farmhand, and this accident will leave him a pitiful object the rest of his life and unable to care for himself.

Woodstock Sentinel, July 13, 1911.

Remarkable Growth of Corn

George W. Brodwell of Harvard took the measure of a stalk of corn, and it was 42 inches from the ground to the top of the leaf. Seven days later he measured again, and it was 73-1/2 inches

I Will Fly to Woodstock

in height and twenty-four hours later he affirms it had grown 9 inches more.

Woodstock Sentinel, July 13, 1911.

***

Add Wednesday to Closing Nights

Beginning next week, Wednesday will be included in the Tuesday and Friday early closing scheme of the Woodstock merchants.

This arrangement was perfected this week among the following merchants: Woodstock Dry Goods Co., Weaver & Hayden, Belcher Bros., H. A. Stone & Son, M.N. Wien, Murphy & Doering, J. P. Alt Clothing Co., A. W. Wagner, C. F. Thorne & Son, and A. D. Osborn. The grocers are not included.

Under this agreement the Woodstock stores referred to will close at 6:30 p.m. on Tuesday, Wednesday and Friday evening of each week.

This leaves Monday, Thursday and Saturday evenings for trading by those persons who find it inconvenient to do their trading during the forenoon or afternoon.

The Sentinel heartily commends the merchants for making this new move in early closing. It is a step in the right direction, which should be shorter hours for both employer and employee.

The new law which forbids the employment of women during more than ten hours a day was also an influence in bringing about the arrangement. With three evenings of each week for the public to shop in and three evenings early closing for the benefit of the clerks it would seem that all should be pleased with the agreement.

Woodstock Sentinel, August 3, 1911.

***

Lutherans Enjoy a Day in the Grove

The English Lutheran Sunday school held its annual picnic last Saturday in A. J. Olson's grove. Two large hay racks filled with picnickers left, for the crowd was greatly enlarged by late comers. The entire day was given to amuse the children. By evening they were a tired but happy crowd. It was by far the most largely attended and most enjoyable picnic held by this Sunday school, and this was largely due to the conveniences in the grove and the kindness of Mr. Olson.

Woodstock Sentinel, August 3, 1911.

***

Puts Blame on Elders

Dr. C. Stanley Hall has collected facts regarding the fears of children. These fears are generally created by their elders. He found that 1,701 children had 6,456 fears, the leading ones being the fear of lightning and thunder, reptiles, strangers, dark, death, domestic animals, disease, wild animals, mice, rats, robbers, high wind, etc. A few of these fears are rational. In one place children were found who dreaded the end of the world – a fear created by adult teaching.

Woodstock Sentinel, August 3, 1911.

***

"What are you doing, Mama?" Mamie climbed up next to her mother at the dining room table.

"I'm going to start putting my favorite poems in this book. See how it has no writing on the pages. I will cut them out of magazines or the newspaper and paste them in here, so I won't forget the words or can look them up if I do."

"Oh. I like poems, too. Miss Ives just read us 'The Children's Hour' by a long fellow."

Ida laughed, "By Longfellow."

"That's what I said."

"The poet's name is Henry Wadsworth Longfellow. Longfellow is his last name like your last name is Wienke."

"Oh. I like 'a long fellow' better. It's funny."

"Did she read 'Paul Revere's Ride' to you? Or 'The Song of Hiawatha'?"

"No. Can you do that?"

"I can. Those are a little long to put in a poem book. Here's the one I found that I'm putting in first. It's call 'Misspent Time'." And she began reading...

Misspent Time

There is no remedy for time misspent,
No healing for the waste of idleness,
Whose very languor is a punishment
Heavier than active souls can feel or guess.
O hours of indolence and discontent,
Not now to redeemed, ye sting not less
Because I know the span of life was lent
For lofty duties, not for selfishness.
Not to be whiled away in endless dreams,
But to improve ourselves and serve mankind,
Life and its choicest faculties were given.
Man should be ever better than he seems
And shape his acts and discipline his mind
To walk adoring earth with hope of heaven.
Sir Arthur de Verv Harvey

Mamie considered this poem. "What does 'whiled away in endless dreams' mean?"

"Well, that means that when you should be working and instead you gaze out the window daydreaming and then the work doesn't get done."

"Oh." Mamie liked to gaze out the window and daydream. "What if while I was gazing out the window, I was thinking about something important, like memorizing a poem."

"I suppose that wouldn't be daydreaming then, would it?"

"Okay, I won't daydream anymore, but just memorize poems."

Ida laughed. "Little girls should daydream a little because they are making plans for the future."

"Oh, so it's okay if I gaze out the window?" Now she was confused. "Is the poem wrong?"

Ida reached over and hugged her child and then looked her square in the face. "Mamie, you don't need to worry about doing everything a poem means. Poems usually say different things to different people." Ida withdrew to her own chair and Mamie thought about this for a few minutes.

"I liked 'The Children's Hour' better because it reminded me of Papa. I will memorize that one, but not this one." She pointed at the one Ida had just secured in her book. "Can I do a book too?"

"Of course, you can. We'll get one next time we are at the Square."

"Okay." The little girl slid off the chair. "I'm going to go play dollies with Dodi when she wakes up. Can we bring them down to this table?"

"Of course. We will eat supper in the kitchen. Run up and see if she is awake and bring the dolls down here."

Mamie started toward the stairs, but then she tripped on something that was nothing, she stumbled forward, and fell.

Ida started to rise, but Mamie jumped back up and continued toward the stairs. Ida went back to looking through the newspaper for good poetry clippings. Then she looked up again with a furrowed brow at the place where the stumble had occurred.

***

Taft Receives Tea

President Taft's wife receives many presents from those who are seeking social position in Washington. Her latest present consists of several sacred tea plants from the Garden of the Buddhist priests in Ceylon from a social climber who is traveling abroad. These plants will be cared for on the tea farms of the Carolinas, which are under government supervision.

Woodstock Sentinel, August 10, 1911.

***

The Happiest Heart

Who drives the horses of the sun
Shall lord it but a day.
Better the lowly deed were done
And kept the humble way.
The rust will find the sword of fame.
The dust will hide the crown.
Aye, none shall hail so high his name.
Time will not tear it down.
The happiest heart that ever beat
Was in some quiet breast
That found the common daylight sweet
And let to heaven the rest.
-- John Vance Cheney
Woodstock Sentinel, August 17, 1911.

***

"Oh, how lovely." Ida clipped the poem from the page and tucked it in her scrapbook. Mamie would enjoy hearing this later. She set the paper aside. Enough lollygagging. She had taken far too long over breakfast. The children were already off on their activities for the day. Helen had gone to a friend's house for an outing. Mamie had banged the screen door on her way to the garden. And Dodi was…where was Dodi? Then she heard the lullaby coming from the front room in a sweet little girl voice:

"Go to sweep my litto pickle-ninny.
Rainer fox will GIT you if you don't.
Slumber on the bue some of old Mama Ginny
Mama's litto Alabama Coo ooo ooo.
Undaneat da sliver shutted moon.
Hushabye, rockabye, hushabye my baby.
Mama's litto Awabama Coooooo."

Ida peeked into the parlor and saw Dodi sitting in the rocking chair with her doll cradled in her arms, rocking and singing. How had she learned the words to that lullaby? Did they really sing it that much? Maybe so. Clara had taught that song to her years ago, and it had become one of the girls' favorites. The tune was one of the first songs plunked out when they had gotten the piano. She smiled as her youngest started the song over for the fourth time.

Ida turned to go back to the kitchen. She had work to do. Suddenly the room spun and she grabbed for a chair to steady herself. Whoa. She must have turned too suddenly. Oh no, she was going to vomit, she rushed into the bathroom, not even closing the door, and threw up her breakfast into the commode.

"Mama?" Dodi stood in the doorway.

Ida was kneeling in front of the commode trying to get her control back. "Yes, Dodi."

"Mama, can I eat nutter egg...the hard ones, I like to peal dem and dey are so cute in da middle wid jiggly white and the yellow ball like..."

Ida's hand reached over and closed the door right in Dodi's face.

"Maaammaa...." Dodi whined through the door.

"Yes, you may have another hard egg. But please go outside to peel it. Mamie is out there."

Ida took some deep breaths and began to feel better. That was strange. She rarely threw up. Maybe she was coming down with something. She stood up, pulled the chain to flush the commode, washed her face and hands and pinned her hair back away from her face. That's better.

By the end of the week, Ida was fairly sure she knew what she was 'coming down with.' When she crawled into bed with John, she spooned with him and then whispered in his ear. "I'm going to go see the doctor on Monday."

He turned toward her so he could see her face. "Why? What's wrong? You or Mamie?"

"Well." Ida kissed him once on the lips. "I think we have one more chance for a boy."

"Oh my!" He turned fully toward her and took her in his arms, holding her close. One more chance. Thank you, God.

"But...," Ida whispered.

"But, what?" John pushed back to look at her.

"But since tomorrow is Saturday, could you make breakfast for the girls? The smell of eggs and sausage makes me want to throw up."

"I can do that, and you can sleep in for a while. We'll know on Monday?"

"Maybe. I'll go on Monday, and the doctor will have an opinion. But I have all the signs, so I'm pretty certain."

"Wonderful! Are you happy?"

"Since you asked me now, I can say an unequivocal Yes! Ask me in the morning and the answer could be quite different."

"Then let's not think about morning right now."

Ida turned over and John spooned up behind her and held her in an embrace that lasted all night.

***

Household Tip

When the tomatoes have attained their size and two-thirds colored, the ripening process can be hastened considerably if they are carefully picked and put stem side up in the bright sunshine, where one's own or the neighbor's chickens cannot get at them.

Woodstock Sentinel. August 24, 1911.

Half a Million Acres Open to Settlement

President Taft has proclaimed the opening of the Rosebud Reservation in Mellette County, and the Pine Ridge Reservation in Bennett County, So. Dakota. Registration points, Gregory, Dallas, and Rapid City, S. D., October 2 to 21, 1911. Drawing at Gregory Oct. 24. Direct Route, the Northwestern Line – convenient train service. For rates and descriptive literature concerning the opening apply Ticket agents, Chicago & Northwestern Ry., or address A. C. Johnson, T. M., 226 W. Jackson Blvd., Chicago.

Woodstock Sentinel. August 24, 1911.

***

My Aeroplane Adventures
By J. Armstrong Drexel

Man has invented nothing that looks so graceful and so easy as an aeroplane in flight. Skimming overhead with broad, outstretched wings and with no effort apparent in any part, so far as the beholders can see, the aviator sitting calmly in his seat seemingly doing nothing but enjoying himself, this modern aircraft looks to be the very acme of comfort, of ease, of exhilaration.

Yet a few hours in the air in an aeroplane is the hardest day's work that any man can do. What is hard about it? There are three kinds of strain in flying.

Roughly, the strain of flying can be divided up into three kinds – the physical, the mental, and the nervous. With the man who attempts to break any of the records established today these three become in a great measure interdependent and inseparable. I mean by that when a man's brain becomes tired his body becomes tired with it, and that when his nerves are shattered, his body and brain give way too. ....

Woodstock Sentinel, August 31, 1911.

***

Miscellaneous Assortment of News Items in Condensed Form for Busy People

The town of Florence, Wis., is said to be overrun by skunks and it is a question whether the skunks or the people will move out.

President William H. Taft will be in Waukegan Oct. 28 to preside at the dedication exercises of the United States Naval Training station.

From Lake Geneva Herald: Mrs. William Quin, corner of Williams and Marshall streets, has a hen which certainly can claim to be the oldest in the county if not in the state, for it is reported to be seventeen years old and still laying her regular quota of eggs.

As time goes on the campaign against saloons in Waukegan is becoming more and more vigorous. Father Gavin stated last Sunday in his sermon that there were five saloon keepers in his congregation, but regardless of this, he condemned every saloon in Waukegan for selling liquor to the recruits of the naval training station.

McHenry Plaindealer, August 31, 1911.

***

New Stable Opened

John Dennis has opened a livery, feed, tie and sale stable in the barn known as the Ladd Austin barn and will give the best care and attention to all business entrusted to him. Mr. Dennis is well known and will doubtless secure a generous portion of patronage from the people of this community.

Woodstock Sentinel, September 14, 1911.

***

September 14, 1911
Denison, Iowa

Dear Sister Ida,

I have news! Pearle has accepted a job with a company called J. R. Watkins. The Watkins Company is a door-to-door sales company of health and home care products. He will have his own medicine wagon and will travel around the district, which is quite large – from Des Moines to Omaha and south to the Missouri border. They've been in business for 50 years. Isn't that wonderful? No more poles. I will miss him, but it's gotten easier and easier to keep in touch, so I'm not worried. He'll still have his home base here in Denison which is just about at the center of his territory.

And I've decided, since I'll have so much time while Pearley is gone, I'm going to write a book about the German community in Denison. I don't know right now if the book will be fact or fiction or both, but the story of the boy and the pigs is just too juicy to give up on. I will never know the real story, but I can use the situation in the book, changing the names, of course. I'll see what other stories I can glean from the community. I have some new friends there because of my interviewing.

Must stop. I have deadlines to meet, don't cha know? Just wanted to get this on the train so you'd hear the good news sooner than later.

Love,
Clara

***

Crystal Lake Lineman Dead

The death of Charles Schultz, the Crystal Lake lineman who was burned by an electric wire at Langehelm, occurred Wednesday, Sept. 8, in a Chicago hospital after intense suffering. Lockjaw was the direct cause of his death.

Woodstock Sentinel, September 14, 1911.

Rain Cuts Fair Crowd

Heavy rains Wednesday night and threatening clouds until nearly noon Thursday kept the crowds away from the Fairgrounds yesterday, so that instead of 20,000 people on the grounds there was only a small fraction of the usual attendance of the big day of the Fair.

Woodstock Sentinel, September 14, 1911.

LOST – Wednesday evening, Sept. 13, between 843 Seminary Avenue and Vaudette, string Niagara Spar white beads. Easily distinguished, are the only ones in the city. Return to Carrie Lawson, 843 Seminary Avenue, and receive award.

Woodstock Sentinel, September 14, 1911.

***

Steam Laundry Needs Help

The entire working force at the Woodstock steam laundry walked out last Saturday because they were unable to make the proprietor admit that they ought to receive more wages. Those who went out were W. E. Stearnes, Misses Bertha Trebes, Emma Sahs and Lizzie Davis. Surely Woodstock is putting on metropolitan ways with a vengeance. Manager Chaboudy has been trying to replace the striking help since their walk out.

Woodstock Republican, September 21, 1911.

***

"John, your cousin Emma Sahs is in the paper." Ida and John were reading the *Woodstock Republican* and the *Woodstock Sentinel*, respectfully, and sharing tidbits.

"Now what?"

"She and other workers at the laundry walked out on strike."

"Really? Did that rag you are reading have an opinion about it?"

"It says Woodstock is getting too 'metropolitan'."

"What does that mean?" John sipped his coffee.

"I was just going to ask you the same thing." Ida turned to the next page and folded the paper in half.

"Maybe 'metropolitan' is a codeword for Socialist?"

"Mmmm...maybe." Ida didn't think so but wasn't about to argue this early in the morning. "Is going on strike for a living wage socialist thinking?"

John looked at her. "Well, I don't know. Myself, I can't imagine going on strike because the owner of a company isn't willing to do my beck and call. I didn't know you cared about such things."

She looked back at him and smiled. "Well, John, I need to know about such things to vote, don't I?"

John laughed, and his eyes perused his paper. "And when are you going to do that?"

"Or to run for office." Now Ida sounded a bit perturbed, but her eyes stayed riveted on the paper.

He stopped laughing. Oh no. "And are you going to run for office?"

"Maybe."

"What office?"

"Maybe I'll run for mayor and oust your precious Donovan." Ida still did not look up.

John laughed. "Good luck doing that. You want my town committee position?"

"Maybe." Serious as a judge.

John smiled and went back to his paper. New elections weren't until next spring. He could see Ida now: Out on the stump and eight months pregnant. "Maybe you should have this baby first and think about politics second." Just a friendly suggestion.

"Oh, I don't know. A pregnant woman might get the sympathy vote."

"Not from men she won't. And the sympathetic women can't vote." John was not laughing now either.

"Oh my, how could I forget that women are treated like second-class citizens." Ida put on a mock southern accent. "Even the darkies get to vote.'" She dropped the accent, "And what do the Republicans think about that situation, pray tell? I'll tell you what they think. The Republicans agree unanimously that the women shouldn't get the vote. Now don't lie to me, John. Have you not joked with your pals about how much trouble the women's vote would cause?"

John knew he had joked about that, but now he said, "Ida, I think women would be excellent voters. But the truth is, as of now, they can't vote."

"Do you not think I am aware of that. I am not stupid. I'm just a woman who cooks a man's meals, cleans his house and clothes, bears his children, keeps the whole family going to church, makes sure his children are doing well in school and are healthy, and is, of course, available to the man anytime he chooses. Who has time to vote?"

"Don't get all worked up now. It's not good for the baby."

"John Wienke, don't you dare patronize me! I know what is good or bad for the child I am carrying."

"I didn't mean—" John stammered.

"Of course, you did! You meant that my emotional outrage might harm this child. Well, let me tell you something! Women

I Will Fly to Woodstock

NOT voting is more damaging to children than a little emotion while pregnant. If women could vote, more opportunities would exist for the care of orphans and more help for working mothers and less chance of a man putting a woman in an insane asylum, ripping her away from her children, simply because she expresses opinions he doesn't want to hear or is depressed by her lot in life!"

"Ida, I don't—"

Her eyes were blazing, and the fire was directed straight at him. "Don't you ever accuse me of doing something to harm my children! Do you understand?"

"Yes, but I didn't—"

"No buts! It's time men gave women more respect and responsibility for having a voice in this world." She looked down at the table. "The very idea that we have to ask men's permission to vote galls me. The very idea that men have kept the vote from us for over a hundred years of 'democracy,'" Ida's hands made the quote marks around the word democracy, "is so against what I believe this country stands for that…well…I just don't have words to describe the feeling."

"You, my dear, have plenty of words to describe—"

"You are right, I have many words, but the question is, are you listening to them or just thinking about how to defend yourself and the Republicans? What is the main thing the Republican's want?"

John thought about the question. Some might say that they wanted control, but that answer probably wouldn't help this situation. "They want prosperity," he answered.

"To what end?"

"So that everyone can live a happy life without fear of becoming destitute."

"OK. What do you really mean by EVERYONE?"

"All the people. Everyone has the same opportunities to get rich. That is equality."

"What about those already destitute?"

"They have made their own lot in life."

"Really? Have they had the same chance at jobs that you have had?"

John thought about the several years that he had spent picking up odd jobs. "Yes," he said firmly. "When my family needed money, we were poor, and I was working all the time at whatever I could find."

"I'm not talking about you. I'm talking about negroes and the Italians and the Irish people. Do you think today that this crowded village has enough jobs for everyone? Do you think those poor people would have the same chance to find jobs? Do employers sometimes turn away people who they don't want as employees based on things other than talent or experience? Let me be more specific. Can a negro get the same job as a white man? Can a woman get any job that a man can?"

"Well, no...I mean, yes, those things do happen. Besides there are no negroes in Woodstock."

"And are there no women? Are there no Italians? Are there no Irish? All of them get the same treatment as a Negro would."

"Okay. But what can I do about it?"

"You can vote!" Ida's voice had a triumphant tone and she slapped the paper on the table. "Voting is the way we make change in America. Voting is the only way that a person can tell the machine what they want or maybe even overthrow the machine. But first we ALL need to have a voice!"

John shook his head, smiling just a little. In different circumstances, she would make a good mayor, he thought. He looked at her, rosy in the cheeks and firm in her jaw. He would vote for her...in different circumstances.

I Will Fly to Woodstock

"Pearley dear," Clara cooed. "I was wondering if I could send some Watkins samples to Ida. She cooks a lot and I think she'd really like the spices for Thanksgiving, and John would probably enjoy some of the liniments."

"Maybe." Pearle reached over from chair to chair to hold Clara's hand. "Do you think it would lead to sales? I don't really want to get into taking away another Watkins man's livelihood in Woodstock."

"Ida's not mentioned that they have Watkins in Woodstock."

"Oh, surely, they must. Watkins is all over the midwestern states."

"If I ask her and she says they don't, can I please have some samples to send?"

Pearle didn't answer immediately.

"Pwease. Whose widdle ducky?" Clara stroked his hand using the baby talk they had loved when first together.

"Ize your little ducky," Pearle responded.

"I can guarantee that she will make an order once she has tried the products."

"Okay, I'll pick out some things I can spare. Those come out of my pocket, you know."

"I know, but Ida's our sister, and she came all the way out here when you were hurt on her own dime."

"That's true. I should think of it as a thank you."

"Yes. Exactly."

"I'll give you some samples in the morning. Are you about ready for bed?"

"Mmm. Let's let the fire burn down a little more. It's so cozy in our little house. And it's so good to have you home."

"It is good to be home. I think there will be one more outing before the snow flies, and then I'll be home in harsh weather at least, when the roads are impassable."

"Do you ever think they'll find a way to plow the snow so the roads are always passable?"

"I do. The improvement to the roads just this year has been amazing. I actually have signs to guide my way instead of asking for directions or spending most of my time lost on the prairie."

"I don't like to think of you lost on the prairie." Clara stuck out her bottom lip in a pout.

"Well, sweetheart, you don't have to worry about that with all the advancement in motoring."

Clara got up and came over to sit on Pearle's lap. "I do miss you so when you are off on your rounds." She kissed him softly on the lips and lingered there.

Pearle's hand began to explore Clara's back and her rounded buttocks. Clara's hands went to the back of Pearle's neck where she played with his hair.

"You need a haircut," she said lazily.

"I do?"

"Yes, but not tonight." Her hands worked their way down his torso. "It's hot in here. You have too many clothes on."

Pearle laughed. "I do? What about you? It will take twenty minutes to untie you."

Clara laughed. "Or longer. We better get started."

He kissed her passionately. As they kissed, he reached around to her back and started loosening the ties his hands found – her apron and then her blouse.

Clara broke off the kiss and said in a sultry voice, "Why Mr. Dye. You do realize that we are in the parlor."

Pearle reached down and took her foot in his hand. He undid the shoe lacing, slowly hook by hook while looking her directly in the eyes. Without looking, he pulled off her shoe, his hand grasping her small foot, his thumb rubbing its sole. He moved on to the second shoe removing it more quickly. His hands encompassed her waist, and he stood her up on her stocking feet and rose to face her. He looked deep into her eyes; a little smile played across his full lips. His hands untied the bow holding up her skirt, and the garment drop to the floor.

Clara could feel how exciting the undressing had been for both of them. Her fingers began their own unbuttoning beginning with his collar which she dropped to the floor. She continued unbuttoning his shirt and trousers.

The heat of the fire had eased, but the room was still warm enough as she melted into his embrace.

***

Lights Back On

The electric light company is congratulating itself that the break, which occurred some ten days ago, has been fully repaired and the lights are again in commission. The company was considerably embarrassed, not because of the loss of income, but because of the failure to furnish streetlight during the dark nights while the revival services were being held, and because of the unjust criticisms indulged in by a few on account of the absence of the lights. People generally, however, were charitable enough not to find fault, because they knew it was not the fault of the company that the delay in restoration of the lights occurred.

Denison Review, November 29, 1911.

***

John and Ida lingered at the dining table after Sunday supper. The girls had asked to be excused and had gone – the two younger ones into the parlor to play and Helen upstairs to read.

"What did you think of the sermon today?" asked John.

"It was good. I always enjoy a sermon on the 'peace that passes all understanding.'" Ida sipped her tea.

"Yes, I thought this sermon was a fine one also."

"Did you see the bulletin about the up-coming sermon series for the Spring?"

John smiled. "Yes. Are you excited about them?"

"He's taking a chance, don't you think?"

"I trust he's got the situation under control."

Ida pulled the bulletin out of her apron pocket. She had forgotten to take it off before she sat down, and now she was glad. She read aloud:

> A series of sermons about women will take place in the Spring. The sermon titles will be as follows:
> Sunday, January 28
> "Three Remarkable Conversions Among Women of the Bible."
> Sunday, February 25
> "The Woman Who Had Five Husbands."
> Sunday, March 31
> "The Woman Who Lived with Her Mother-in-Law."
> Sunday, April 28
> "The Woman Who Had a Mind of Her Own."

Ida looked up and met John's eyes. "The titles are very intriguing, aren't they?"

"Yes, I'm looking forward to them. To change the subject. Are you planning to go to Racine on Monday or Tuesday?"

"Monday. Christmas Day on the noon train? Emma is bringing Mama back to Racine that day, I believe."

"Good. We'll go up on Christmas Day, and I will come back to gather you home on New Year's Eve Day, right?"

"Yes." Ida reached over and took his hand. "Thank you."

John smiled. "For what?"

"For facilitating the girls and me seeing Mama whenever I want. For going with us. For…oh I don't know…for being a good husband."

"You got me a hat for Christmas." John rubbed his head.

"What does that have to do with it?" Ida squinted at him.

"As long as I get a hat every Christmas, I know I'm still in your good graces."

"That is a lot of hats!" Ida chuckled.

"What's that you always say? A bald man can't have too many hats. If ever I don't get a hat, I'll know I'm in trouble."

"Oh, you! We might just run out of styles."

"Then at least a homemade stocking hat."

"That I can do. And so will the children be able to do it. Did I tell you? I've got Helen started with knitting needles."

"Well, good luck. I'm not sure how she will knit and read at the same time."

Ida chuckled again. "Yes, that small conflict does exist. But she must know how to do handwork."

"Must she?"

"Yes, to be a proper wife and mother."

"What if she is a businesswoman or like your sister a reporter or even a teacher, does she have to have those skills then?"

Ida considered. "Yes, I believe she does. Or at least knowing how to knit won't hurt her."

John considered. "Let's see what the last of Rev. Kauffman's sermons tells us."

Ida looked at the bulletin. "'The Woman Who Had a Mind of Her Own?'"

"Don't you think that fits Helen to a T?"
"I do."
"And you."
"And me?" Ida blushed. "Oh, go on with you." Then, after a pause, she said, "Now I'm even more anxious to hear these sermons."

John patted her hand. "Me too. Time for a Sunday nap? I can clean up here."

"Oh, would you? See I said you were a good husband."

"You and Junior deserve it." John rose and reached for the dirty dishes. "Do I have to wash them also?"

Ida swatted him on the hinder. "What do you think 'clean up' means?"

John sighed, but he was smiling.

***

Personals

Mr. Dye, the medicine man, is in Jackson township supplying his customers for the winter. Mr. Dye has turned out to be one of the fast agents of the company.

Denison Review, December 6, 1911.

***

Concerning the Churches
Grace English Lutheran

Choir practice on Friday evening 7:30. Catechetical class on Saturday at 2:30 p.m. Service at 10:45 a.m. on Sunday. Sunday school at 9:30 a.m. The Christmas festival will be held on Sunday evening at 7:30. Everybody is welcome. All those willing to give money or eatables for those who are in need, will please take it to the home of Mrs. John Schroeder on Washington Street.

Woodstock Sentinel, December 20, 1911.

A Protest

Editor Republican: -- the writer has been informed that on last Monday night the city council at the request of certain members of the fire department, passed a resolution that the city employ a man and a team of horses to sleep in the fire apparatus rooms and be in readiness to haul out the apparatus in case of fire. It hardly seems possible that the city council intends to convert the city hall into a horse stable and spoil it for any other purpose. They must surely know that the horse stable odor will make the whole building undesirable for anything else. There seems to be no crying necessity for a team and man to be ready at all times to haul out the fire apparatus, anyhow. Will someone kindly furnish information as to any fire losses that have occurred that would not have occurred had a team and a man being in readiness to haul out the apparatus? All the citizens of Woodstock who are proud of our city hall, should rise up and protest against this proposed misuse of it. It isn't too late yet for the city council to reconsider.

FIREMAN.

Woodstock Republican, December 22, 1911.

Judge Donnelly is Not in Good Health

Word comes that Judge Charles Donnelly is in very poor health. Judge Donnelly has enjoyed rather poor health for some time and his friends are genuinely worried.

Woodstock Sentinel, December 22, 1911.

***

Weather Report

During the early cold weather in the fall the weather prognosticators were howling about a severe cold winter already set in. Since we have had several days of mild weather these same fellows observe many signs of a very mild winter before us.

Clark Haeger pulled out eighteen snakes one day last week. Another man saw the striped snakes and others corroborate these facts. Angle worms are coming up thru the ground, and the hair on the caterpillars is said to be a little shorter than usual. At the high price of coal and other fuel, we poor mortals would enjoy a very warm winter.

Marengo Republican News, December 22, 1911.

***

John and Ida Wienke sat watching their girls play with their Christmas gifts. Christmas Eve was when they traditionally opened their gifts from each other. In the morning, each girl would have one gift under the tree from 'Santa' although Helen, who already knew that her parents were Santa, had been sworn to secrecy for the sake of her younger siblings. Helen had received a book from each member of the family – four books...to-keep books not library books. She was already sitting against the front wall, legs pulled up under her, reading. She paid little attention to the play and games of her younger sisters anymore. Something Ida regretted seeing happen. She tried to remember when Helen had stopped playing with her sisters but couldn't remember.

After Santa and church in the morning, the five of them would board a train for Racine and spend Christmas night with Oma Louisa. She assumed that Emma and her family would be there, too. John would come back on the 26th but she and the girls would stay for the week. John would retrieve them on New Year's Eve.

"Mama, lookie." Dodi held up her naked doll.

"No, Dodi." Mamie seemed appalled. "Put clothes on her. She will be cold. It's winter." She tried to take the doll from Dodi to dress it.

"No! My dolly!" Dodi grabbed the doll back, but Mamie was undeterred.

"I'm just going to put clothes on her." Mamie grabbed the doll's arm and pulled.

Ida intervened. "Wait, wait, wait! You are going to hurt the doll if you fight over her like that." Mamie dropped the arm, and Dodi pulled the doll into a protective embrace. "It's okay if she doesn't have clothes right now, isn't it, Mamie? We're in the house, not out in the cold." Ida's voice was gentle.

Mamie pouted for a bit. "Alright, I don't care about your old doll anyway." She opened the wooden box in front of her and drew out a sheet of paper and three pastel sticks in bold colors. "I'm going to draw a dolly for you, Dodi."

Dodi looked at what Mamie was doing and dropped her naked doll. "I wanna draw it, too!" She scooted over to where Mamie had set up her lap box.

"No, these are mine. They are too old for little girls!" Now Mamie held the sticks close to her chest. Dodi started to cry.

John looked at Ida and shook his head. "How do you stay so calm?"

Ida smiled, reached down, and picked up Dodi. "I think die dicke ist müde!"

John clucked Dodi under the chin. "Papa is tired too, Dodi. Maybe it's time for bed?"

"Nooooo," wailed the older girls.

"OK, then Papa has a story for you, and I want you to listen, even you Helen." John's eyes stayed focused on her. Helen let out an exaggerated sigh and put down the book.

"It's a story about Mama and Papa Bear and their three little bears."

"I already heard this one." Helen reached for her book.

"No, you haven't. I promise." Ida's eyes fixed on Helen, who sighed again and left the book where she'd dropped it.

John began. "This story takes place in a large forest we'll call The Woods. The place was called The Woods because it was, after all, a woods. In the center of The Woods was a small town with a square, and in the middle of the Square was a huge cuckoo clock that counted minutes, tick, tock, tick, tock. The clock didn't cookoo every hour like the regular cuckoo clocks, but rather only at midnight on New Year's Eve. People often came from miles around to see it. The name of the town was Tock."

"Woodstock!" Mamie chortled and threw her arms up in victory.

"No. Just Tock. Tock of the Woods, the people called it." Mamie smiled, as if she were in on the secret. He was talking about them.

"Because of the clock, Mama and Papa Bear knew exactly how many years it had been since their children had been born: Heloise had been born eight years ago, Margie had been born seven years ago, and Edwina had been born 5 years ago. He knew because that's what the clock said."

Helen shook her head and looked at her abandoned book.

Mamie giggled, "Edwina." John smiled at her.

"Mama Bear and Papa Bear worked hard every day to keep the little bears healthy and happy. Because Papa Bear worked hard, they had food and a wonderful cave to live in." Helen rolled her eyes. "You think that's funny, young lady, but providing a good cave is not an easy task."

"Yes, we went through four caves just since you were born, Heloise." Ida's eyes urged attention and politeness from Helen.

"Keep going, Papa Bear." Mamie gave a side-long look at Helen.

"Because Mama Bear worked hard, the little bears had clothes to wear and pork sandwiches with sauerkraut."

I Will Fly to Woodstock

Mamie clapped her hands. "Pork and sauerkraut sandwiches are my favorite."

"My favorite." Dodi fingered her new doll's hair.

"But one thing that Mama and Papa Bear always hoped for, every single year as the clock struck...can you guess what it is?"

The children were silent, and then Helen answered, "An automobile?"

"That would be nice." John winked at Ida. "I would like an automobile, but that wasn't what both Mama and Papa wished for."

"A dog?" Mamie guessed.

"Well, that would also be nice, but not a dog."

Mamie's face fell. "I would like a dog."

Papa looked at Dodi for an answer. "A dog called Freckles."

"Nope."

Dodi looked up at her mother, "What do you want most, Mama?"

John continued "What Mama and Papa Bear had always wanted every year was another little bear to call their own. A little baby bear that they could all hold and play with and love. Mama and Papa had hoped and prayed and wished for a little bear for years...for five years...and then they found out that their wish had been granted and that they were going to get a new baby bear."

"Yay," clapped Mamie with glee. "We're going to get a baby bear!" She looked at Dodi. "That's better than a dog. We can name it Freckles if you want."

Dodi sat up. "Yes, a baby bear named Freckles!"

"Really?" Helen's eyes were wide with wonder. "But you are so...so...old."

Ida and John looked at their oldest daughter and burst out laughing. Ida looked at her husband. "Can't get anything past this one." And then switched her gaze to her daughter. "We are, my dear Heloise, not too old to have a baby. And we will be doing so next April if all goes well."

"A baby person or a baby bear." Mamie seemed a little less enthusiastic.

"A baby bear," Dodi quickly reinforced, "Named Freckles."

John looked at Ida. "I've lost control."

"Just a baby person, right?" Mamie's eyes shifted slightly to Helen. "I think we have enough girls. So, can this one be a baby boy?"

"We won't know if it will be a boy or girl until it comes into the world. A boy would be nice, but another girl would be just fine, too." Ida patted John's hand.

"Will he be named Freckles?" Dodi's face had fallen.

"Probably not." Mamie shook her head going back to her pastels.

"And then, will you have another one and another one?" Helen looked ready to find a new home at the very thought of it.

"Helen, one doesn't know if they are going to have or not have. That is up to God. All we know is, knock wood, we will be blessed with a tiny life just as we were blessed with you all those years ago."

"And me," said Mamie.

"And you," said John.

"And Dodi," said Mamie.

"And Dodi," said Ida.

Helen picked up her book and buried her face in it. "I suppose it will cry all the time."

"Yes, babies do cry." Ida glanced at John.

"And I suppose, I'll have to take care of it." She looked up defiantly. "I'm NOT going to take care of it all the time."

"Okay, Helen, that's enough. It's time for bed. We need to be up in the morning to go to church and then catch the train. We can talk more about this tomorrow."

John got up and took Dodi from Ida's arms and headed for the stairs.

Ida was still looking at her eldest daughter. "Helen, are you listening?"

Helen lowered her book, "Yes, Mama bear."

Ida paused and drew breath. "If there's anything you want to take along, I've put bags on each of your beds. You'll need to pack those tonight, so they are already to go first thing tomorrow."

"Yes, Mama," said both girls, and they obediently rose and also headed toward the stairs.

Mamie turned and ran back to her mother and hugged her tight. "Good night, Mama. Thank you for getting us a baby brother!"

Ida hugged her back and thought, oh, I do hope so!

***

Dog Gone Home

A large black shepherd dog answering to the name of "Will" and belonging to Thomas Anderson, who moved November 1 last from what is known as the old Cal Pease farm in Bonus to one near St. Peters, Minnesota, and which was taken along with some horses, came back alone overland and was discovered Wednesday morning by a boy named Dewayne lying on the front porch of the old home in Bonus, where he arrived sometime in the night before. The distance by rail from Belvidere to St. Peters is 367 miles and as the road follows pretty nearly a straight line for the average between the two points, this will approximately represent the distance traveled by the intelligent animal in making his way back to the farm here. When Mr. Anderson shipped his horses to St. Peters the dog was given a berth in the box car they occupied, and that it

should be able to take the back track and the route over the country roads and fields and land at the destination aimed at is a wonderful and mystifying occurrence. The dog disappeared three days after arriving at the farm near St. Peters.
Belvidere Republican Northwestern, December 26, 1911.

***

Thank You Sheriff

To the Sheriff of McHenry County: The persons in the charge of the said sheriff take this way in expressing their many thanks for the favors extended by this big, kind-hearted man. Thanksgiving, Christmas and all preceding holidays have been the same – just one continued round of pleasure and good things to eat. Therefore, we one and all wish the sheriff and his household a very, very happy New Year and many of them.

THE PRISONERS.
Woodstock Sentinel, December 30, 1911.

Work Progressing Now

So great is the need for more of a city water supply that the city authorities are even now drilling for another well, and over two miles of pipe is being laid to reach those heretofore deprived of a city supply. In the face of these facts, can you consistently, as a progressive, loyal, broad-minded citizen, oppose the issuance of city bonds at the election next Tuesday, that these improvements may be carried out?
Woodstock Sentinel, December 30, 1911.

***

"Wave to Oma," said Ida as they reached the corner. The little girls turned and waved back up the street where Louisa stood on her porch in the cold.

"Oh, Mama, go back in. It's too cold to stand out on the porch." Her mother was too far away to hear Ida's words. Beside her stood Emma, her efficient big sister. Ida raised a hand of farewell, and John took her arm to help her down the slippery curb.

Emma would be staying with Louisa. The decision had been made that Louisa would move to Jefferson with the Fishers. The Fishers were moving to Jefferson to open a bakery, and they could not make the weekly trip back and forth to Racine and run a business, so Louisa had been convinced to move with them.

Emma had told Ida in private that their mother was not remembering things well. "She's going slightly crazy. We don't know why, but she needs day-to-day care now, and we have room. Don't worry. We won't leave her here alone even if she insists."

And insist she had. Eventually, she relented. "Alles klar, ich werde gehen." I will go! And Ida and Emma breathed a sigh of relief.

Ida and the girls had spent their week in Wisconsin, packing boxes and sorting through things. Ida would get Louisa's desk that had come on that long voyage from Germany. It would be shipped to Woodstock along with other things she'd claimed from the house.

"I wish Clara could have been here for this week," Ida told John now as they walked to the station. The girls skipped on ahead, excited by the possibility of getting home in time for the fireworks. "Helen, please keep track of Dodi, so she doesn't dart off," Ida called out.

"Yes, Mama." Helen corralled Dodi away from the street.

"She's in a better mood." John's nod indicated Helen.

"Yes, I think she's come to the realization that her lot in life will be to have younger siblings to watch over."

"A good thing." John had had many younger siblings to worry about.

"Yes, a very good thing. I think her Aunt Emma had a talk with her about the responsibility of being the oldest."

"Your mother seems…um…not totally with it."

"Yes, it's very sad. Several times she called me Clara, and at one point, she said I was lazy and needed to get back to work."

John laughed. "Is Clara lazy?"

"Clara was young and not interested in sewing. She and Mama were always at odds about how much work was being accomplished. I think things were better once they were here alone after Herman and I left. Then Clara took the reins and didn't let Mama boss her quite as much. But Clara always used to complain to me about Mama's discipline and work ethic. She said Mama's ethic was all work and no play."

"Here we are. Right on time." John released Ida's hand, but then noticed the girls leaning over and looking down the track to see if the train was coming.

"Stand back girls away from the tracks." His deep voice commanded, and all three quickly backed up several steps. "Come over here. Your mother can sit and rest, and you can keep her company." They perched like little birds on the bench, and soon, they could hear the far away whistle of the approaching train.

Dodi stood and jumped up and down. "Here it comes! Here it comes! Mama? Come on, Mama! We have to get on."

"Yes, Dodi."

"Can we live on a train when I get bigger?"

Ida thought about the possibilities before answering. "I guess anything is possible, but probably not. It would get tiresome."

"No, it wouldn't. We lived on the train when we went to see An Clara."

The train's approach drowned out Ida's response.

"Here we go." John picked up the bags and herded his family toward one of the gaps between the cars as the train pulled to a stop. The conductor opened the gate and stepped off onto the platform offering assistance.

John helped Ida aboard and then handed up the two little girls beginning with Dodi. He let Helen just take his hand as she climbed aboard. He then handed up the luggage and pulled himself up onto the train.

The Conductor looked around for other patrons, and finding none, called out, "All aboard." He signaled the engineer, climbed up, closed the gate, and helped the Wienke's to their compartment. Once they were all inside, he punched their tickets and closed the door on his way out. John and Ida took the bench riding forward, and the three girls sat across from them riding backward. John put a protective arm around Ida and asked, "Was your Mama excited about the baby?"

"Emma was happy for us. And Mama kept asking when the baby was due for some reason. I thought she was just experiencing failing memory, but at one point she counted not just the months, but the days. Very odd."

"Hm. Is she planning to come down for the birth?"

"I think not. Emma might bring her, but not to stay as she has in the past. She is really not well enough."

"Are you alright with no live-in help during your confinement?"

"Well, I must be, mustn't I? I have many other people to help. I can count on Ma Wienke to help with the girls. And I'm fairly sure Bessie would take them for a few days also." Dodi got down and came over to stand beside John, looking out the window at the darkness outside the glass. The wheels clicked along the track. The engine gave occasional blasts on hits whistle.

"John, what happened with Herman?"

"Nothing. Honestly. He came to me and said that he was ready to have his own store. We had agreed to split as soon as we each could stand on our own, and I was also glad to get my own store where I could do what I wanted."

"That's it?"

"I think he may have been a bit miffed when I didn't sell him my inventory when I closed, but his store didn't sell groceries. I suppose, if I'm honest, I was a bit embarrassed to ask for his help again, so I didn't ask if he was interested. But I think the problem is that Herman and Bessie run in different circles than we do."

"We run in circles?"

"You know what I mean. They are Presbyterians, and we are Lutherans. He is a shop owner, and I am a working man. She is a social climber and you are..." uh-oh, be careful, he thought. "You are...."

"A social misfit?"

"No, you are a dedicated mother and wife."

"And Bessie isn't?"

"I suppose in a way she is, but she doesn't keep a home like you do."

"Really, how do you know that?"

"I remember discussions with Herman. She wants a maid and a cook and so forth, so she can have more time to pursue other pastimes."

"And that's fine with my brother?" Ida took a deep breath. "Their children are very well behaved and polite. I never worry when they and our three are together, but...."

"But what?"

"I didn't tell you at the time, but last month I went to talk to Herman about Mama. Herman surprised me when he said that he had done enough for his family. It hurt my feelings just a little as I thought he was happy about his start in Woodstock. It was like he had made a great sacrifice to start the store with you."

"Hm. I can't say that I noticed he felt that way at the split up. I know he was anxious to give it a go on his own...and look at him now in the department store business with Murphy...an old name in Woodstock. He's proved himself."

"To hear him tell it, he's had all kinds of challenges."

"Herman's a good businessman, and he was always one to want the big profits first and foremost. He told me once I was less interested in profit than I was in making my customers happy. I tended at the time to agree with that analysis."

Ida looked at John. It was the most she had gotten out of him about the split up since it happened. "So, you left him on a friendly note?"

"I guess. Certainly not an unfriendly note. So, he doesn't want to help you and Emma with Mama?"

Ida returned her gaze to the gloved hands in her lap. "Herman doesn't see how the problem is growing. He did volunteer to travel to Racine and back to Woodstock with Mama if he was free and had the time. But we aren't even to entertain the notion that she would come live with them even for a brief time. At this point, I don't want to ask him for any help no matter how small. He's done enough for his family, afterall."

John put his arm around Ida and she looked up to see that Helen and Mamie were looking at her, attracted by the tension in her voice. She smiled and the girls relaxed back in their seats.

John leaned close and whispered, "This is why I just say, 'we don't run in the same circles.'"

"I understand." Ida kept her voice low. "I want to be friendly with them, not live in each other's side pockets. But I do want to be friendly and family. Things seem even more strained since I talked to him."

John squeezed her slightly.

They rode in silence, until Dodi exclaimed, "Ooooooh."

All of them looked out the window. Beyond the dark glass, fireworks exploded like tiny bright chrysanthemums over a passing town.

"Oh, how beautiful!" Ida slid forward in the seat so she could see better, and Mamie and Helen went to stand next to Dodi at the window.

"And look! More." Helen pointed off in another direction at the colorful bursts in the sky. As the children pressed their noses to the glass to watch the display, Ida sat back on the bench, and John took her hand.

Ida was overwhelmed with emotion. "What a wonderful New Year's Eve. All of us here together. The new year right around the corner. Our wishes and dreams still before us. I love all of you so much!!"

Dodi, forsaking the firework show, crawled up to sit between John and Ida. "We love you, Mama."

"Yes, we love you, Mama and Papa." Mamie climbed up to sit on Papa's lap where she could still see out.

Helen, who had been watching this public display of affection in the reflection in the dark glass, decided she was not to be left out. She crossed the compartment and squeezed in beside Ida. "Me too."

"Go, train, go!" Dodi urged.

"Yes." Mamie's eyes shone with excitement. "Go, train, go. Take us home to Woodstock."

And they sat all piled on one bench seat, watching the flashes come and go as the towns passed, all the way home to Woodstock.

***

Cold crisp air greeted John and Ida as they climbed down from the train to the platform in Woodstock. John looked about for the horse and sled that was to meet them and carry them home. The train was several minutes early, but still, it was too cold to wait long. Then he heard the jingle of far-away bells approaching — and a robust jolly elf drove his trusty steed off the roadway coming forward for their pickup. The driver had a ruddy face and a winter beard frosted white with his breath. He wore a red stocking cap and scarf over a heavy sheepskin coat. Roger Kauffman gave a hearty, "Whoa Gertie!" as he pulled on the reins bringing the sleigh to a skidding stop on the ice-covered surface.

"Guten Abend!" he shouted to those assembled on the platform.

"Guten Abend," John, Ida, and Helen answered in unison.

"Wie geht es?" Roger asked. His voice echoed in the cold air. Then noticing the two sleeping little ones slung over shoulders, he shushed himself laying a finger to his lips.

He sprung from the sleigh and took Dodi out of Ida's arms.

"Here, my dear. Let me take this burden from you," he said, lowering his voice. "Better that you have just yourself to worry about on an icy night, especially—"

"In my condition," Ida finished his thought, placing her free hand self-consciously on the swelling at her waist. "She's not such a burden, although I'd like it if she would stop growing quite so round." As she transferred the child to him, she noted the transport. "I see you brought the sleigh. We feel like royalty."

"Oh, I've been up to Queen Anne's Parish for service this evening. The station was on my way home," he demurred.

Roger cradled the sleeping five-year-old on his shoulder and gave the other hand to Ida to step down off the wooden planks onto the icy ground. "Here you go then," he said. "Be careful, the footing is less than perfect, and we wouldn't want you to fall."

Ida took his hand and stepped gingerly down. She felt her foot slip, but then it caught on gravel poking through the ice. Roger guided her over to the sleigh and allowed her to pull herself up into the rear seat without assistance and handed Dodi up. He turned his attention to John who had one-handedly gathered the luggage to the near side of the platform. Roger loaded the luggage beside Ida, and Helen climbed up to the middle position in the front. John made his way to the sleigh and climbed up, sheltering Mamie's face from the cold blast with his gloved hand. All they needed was for her to get sick again.

Roger jumped up and took the reins. "I'll have you home in a jiffy. Wintry night, aina?"

"Sure is," said John. "The train was warm by comparison even without heat."

"Great way to travel, but certainly not perfected," agreed Roger. "Come on, Gertie. Let's go. Hold tight to your precious cargo!"

As the roan began to pull, the sleigh slid sideways rather than forward, and Gertie had to put her back into it to get the sleigh out onto the street. The village of Woodstock lay quiet on this night of transition. Tomorrow would begin a new year with its promise of prosperity, but they heard no revelry as was common for such a night. Not a sleigh or sled in sight. As they left the station and headed toward the Square, the quick clop of Gertie's feet was the only sound and the moon above the only light.

"Where are all the people?" asked Helen.

"Hunkered down at home in front of the fire, I would guess," answered Roger.

But then they rounded the corner onto the Square. The Park was lit with hundreds of electric bulbs in all the colors of the rainbow. People, their faces muffled in gayly-colored scarves, bustled here and there. Muffled, but lively, music issued from the speakers at the hardware store, and people were happily coming and going from several of the saloons on the Square. It was a scene they would long remember.

"Oh." Helen stood up to get a better view. "How beautiful. Do you think there will be fireworks tonight, Papa?"

"Maybe. But, I hope, we will all be sound asleep by then." John kept one hand on Helen's back as the sleigh swayed side to side.

Bang! Bang! Rata-tat-tat! Firecrackers broke the crystalline air. Gertie was taken by surprise and shied away from the sound, sending the heavily loaded sleigh into a skid. They spun, and Gertie lost the ability to control the momentum. Bags flew from the rear seat as Ida clung to Dodi with one hand and the front seat with the other. John lost purchase on the front seat and slipped one foot out to stand on the right runner, hanging on tightly to Mamie and the front rail. Roger pulled Helen to him as he too clung to the rail. The world slowed – the sleigh turned, dragging Gertie in a half-circle.

They came to a stop facing the wrong direction on the one-way street around the central park. Gertie had somehow kept her feet, and they, sleeping children and all, had stayed in the sleigh. A silent moment ticked as everyone remembered to breathe. Mamie opened her sleepy eyes and looked around. "Woodstock," she sighed and laid her cheek against her father's rough wool coat.

John smiled. "Yes, we are home in Woodstock," he whispered to the top of her head. Mamie smiled a little and slipped back into sleep.

Roger clambered down, making comforting sounds to Gertie whose breath came in frosty steam puffing from her nostrils. He retrieved the bags and was back in a flash of good humor.

"We meant to do that," he said, looking at Helen. "Gertie and I have been practicing our skating all week just for you." Helen giggled.

"It's a bit icy," said John.

Roger chuckled. "Yes. Ice storm yesterday, don't cha know? You may not have electricity at your place. The whole town was out. The electricity is certainly back on here at the Square." Roger carefully turned Gertie in a sharp circle to continue the journey. "We best just walk, Gertie. No more skating. We want to get these folks home in one piece."

The horse walked up Cass Street, past the old grocery shop, and turned right on Throop, past Ida's brother's house. They continued left on Judd, past the place where Helen had lost her mittens on the way to visit Papa at his 'tore. Gertie pulled onward, turning right on Tyron and then left on Lincoln Avenue. The way was circuitous, but it was always nice going through the Square when coming home. Halfway up Lincoln Avenue, Roger gently reined Gertie to a stop in front of 365, the house that John built.

"Here we are!" he announced. "Home Sweet Home!" Helen giggled again. She loved the way Roger talked, often a bit too loud and always cheerful.

Someone had sanded the street and the front walk which gave better footing to both the four-legged and the two-legged. The transfer of children and bags was quickly done, and Roger took his leave, responding to expressions of thanks with a hearty, "Frohes neues Jahr!"

While John checked the fire in the basement furnace, Ida unbundled the children and herself. The house had been standing empty overnight, but the fire was in good shape from an earlier stoking – Roger again.

With the children tucked into bed, John flopped down on the davenport next to Ida. Their eyes met, and he smiled. "How is Mama?"

"Mama is tired. And Papa?"

Before answering, John glanced around the room with its sturdy walls and large front window looking out onto the wintry night. The Christmas tree was still up, and the room smelled of pine and wet wool, with just a hint of leftover cooking smells from Ida's kitchen. "Well, Papa is glad we're all back safely. I'm always lonely when you and the children are in Racine."

"I'm sorry. Maybe next time you should stay for the whole week instead of just taking us to Racine and coming back to retrieve us. Oma would love to have you all week."

"Maybe," and he leaned over and kissed her, his hand resting on her rounded belly. He pulled away slightly, leaving his hand in place. "How is my boy tonight?"

"I think he rather liked the train ride."

A quick punch under his hand took John by surprise and he jumped.

Ida laughed. "I think he's telling you himself that he is fine."

"Just three more months?"

"Two and a half," Ida corrected.

Off in the distance, church bells began to play the music of the arriving year. The peals echoed from the Catholic belfry at the end of the block and bounced across the village, being joined by the two Lutheran bells, the Presbyterian bell, and the Congregational bell, all ringing the glad tidings of boundless joy that the world had made it through another year. The distant booms of fireworks added syncopation to the tune, and the rata-tat-tat of close-by firecrackers kept the beat going for long moments before fading away.

"Happy New Year," they said with one voice and pecked a kiss in celebration.

"I hope the children sleep in a bit in the morning."

"Don't count on it."

"I only count on you," said John.

Ida smiled. "And me on you."

Printed in the USA
CPSIA information can be obtained
at www.ICGtesting.com
JSHW031722160823
46613JS00002B/154

9 780578 253763